NORTH CAROLINA LITERARY REVIEW

N C L R

number 28

2019

FEATURING NORTH CAROLINA AFRICAN AMERICAN LITERATURE

IN THIS ISSUE

D1227838

■ **Art** *in this issue* ■

North Carolina Literary Review is published annually in the summer by the University of North Carolina Press. The journal is sponsored by East Carolina University with additional funding from the North Carolina Literary and Historical Association. *NCLR Online*, published in the winter, is an open access supplement to the print issue.

The 2019 issues of the *North Carolina Literary Review* are supported by the North Carolina Arts Council, a division of the North Carolina Department of Natural and Cultural Resources.

North
Carolina
Arts
Council

*Fifty years
of leadership*

NCLR is a member of the Council of Editors of Learned Journals and the Council of Literary Magazines and Presses, and it is indexed in EBSCOhost, the *Humanities International Complete*, the *MLA International Bibliography*, and the *Society for the Study of Southern Literature Newsletter*.

Address correspondence to

Dr. Margaret D. Bauer, *NCLR* Editor
ECU Mailstop 555 English
Greenville, NC 27858-4353

252.328.1537 *Telephone*
252.328.4889 *Fax*
BauerM@ecu.edu *Email*
NCLRuser@ecu.edu
NCLRsubmissions@ecu.edu (for submission information)
www.NCLR.ecu.edu *Website*

SUBSCRIPTIONS

SUBSCRIPTIONS to the print issues of *NCLR* are, for individuals, $15 (US) for one year or $25 (US) for two years or $25 (US) annually for institutions and foreign subscribers. Libraries and other institutions may purchase subscriptions through subscription agencies.

To subscribe: Go to the *NCLR* page on the University of North Carolina Press website:
www.uncpress.org/journals/north-carolina-literary-review/

Call or send your request and payment to:
Suzi Waters, Journals Manager
919.962.4201 / suzi_waters@unc.edu
Journals Department, UNC Press
116 South Boundary Street
Chapel Hill, NC 27514-3808

Individuals or institutions may also receive *NCLR* through membership in the North Carolina Literary and Historical Association. For more information go to:
www.ncdcr.gov/about/history/lit-and-hist/membership.

Individual copies of the annual print issue are available from retail outlets and from UNC Press. Back issues of our print issues are also available for purchase from *NCLR*, while supplies last. See the *NCLR* website for prices and tables of contents of back issues.

SUBMISSIONS

NCLR invites proposals for articles or essays about North Carolina literature, history, and culture. Much of each issue is thematically focused, but a portion of each issue is open for developing interesting proposals – particularly interviews and literary analyses (without academic jargon). *NCLR* also publishes high-quality poetry, fiction, drama, and creative nonfiction by North Carolina writers or set in North Carolina. We define a North Carolina writer as anyone who currently lives in North Carolina, has lived in North Carolina, or has used North Carolina as subject matter.

See our website for submission guidelines for the various sections of each issue. Submissions to each issue's special feature section are due August 31 of the preceding year, though proposals may be considered through early fall.

Issue #29 (2020) will feature
North Carolina Expatriate Writers.

Please email your suggestions for other special feature topics to the editor (BauerM@ecu.edu).

This *NCLR* issue is number 28, 2019
ISSN: 1063-0724
ISBN: 978-1-4696-5412-6

African American Writers of North Carolina, From New Sensation Stephanie Powell Watts Back to George Moses Horton

by Margaret D. Bauer, Editor

I have been thrilled by the enthusiastic reception to our 2019 special feature topic, which inspired more submissions than we've ever received, including four interviews. I knew as soon as I heard an NPR interview with Stephanie Powell Watts that I wanted an interview with her for this issue, and I thank DeLisa Hawkes and Maia Butler for taking on this assignment. Thanks too to Jennifer Larson, who accepted my invitation to interview Jason Mott. And finally, thanks to Lisa Sarasohn and George Hovis for proposing interviews with Glenis Redmond and Randall Kenan, respectively. As it turned out, while Lisa and Glenis were working on their interview, the poet had four poems selected as finalists in the 2018 James Applewhite Poetry Prize competition, including one for third place. That one and another are here; read the other two in *NCLR Online* 2019. And about the time that George was interviewing Randall, we received the news that Randall would be a 2018 inductee into the North Carolina Literary Hall of Fame (read about that too in the online issue).

I want to express special thanks to L. Teresa Church, one of the poets featured in these pages, who helped us to spread the word of our 2018 competitions through the Carolina African American Writers' Collective (read her essay on the Collective in *NCLR* 2016). I certainly hope that the writers who discovered *NCLR* through Teresa's prompting will continue to submit in years to come. I was pleased to match three of the finalist titles with Teresa's name. One appears here, the other two in *NCLR Online* 2019. We thank Amber Flora Thomas for selecting the 2018 Applewhite Prize winners and for sharing three of her North Carolina poems with us. Finally among the poetry you will read in the pages to come is another familiar name I was pleased to unveil as a finalist: Kevin Dublin, who served as an editorial assistant when he was a graduate student at ECU several years ago.

More literary scholars than usual responded to this issue's call for submissions, and the seven essays published here offer a variety of critical perspectives on African American writers. Patrick Horn takes a biographical, intertextual approach, examining George Moses Horton's relationship (it's complicated) with his writing patron, Carolina Lee Hentz, while Justin Williams reads Horton poems from a political perspective. Ashley Burge provides a feminist/gendered critical analysis of Harriet Jacobs's *Incidents in the Life of a Slave Girl*. Trudier Harris examines Charles Chesnutt's conjure stories under a contemporary cultural studies lens, while Jennifer Harding takes a more reader response approach to the writer, providing an overview of his oeuvre within her own pilgrimage to pay homage to him. Francine L. Allen applies her interest in literature and religion to introducing a little-known 1980s novel by C. Eric Lincoln. And Jessica Cory applies ecocritical theory to Stephanie Powell Watts's novel *No One Is Coming to Save Us*.

I will add that Jennifer Harding's Chesnutt essay "Looking for Charles" received second place in the 2018 Alex Albright Creative Nonfiction Prize competition. And Patrick Horn's essay on Horton and Hentz was selected for the premiere John Ehle Prize, which *NCLR* established with Press 53 to honor the writer's memory. Thanks go to Terry Roberts for serving as the judge this year, choosing from essays accepted for publication whose subjects are writers who have not been given the critical attention they deserve.

We also thank the North Carolina Arts Council, which awarded *NCLR* a grant that provided honoraria to writers featured in this issue. This funding also contributed to our ability to attend more events than usual so as to host our writers at bookstore readings, to sell subscriptions at literary festivals to make sure their writing is read, and always, to tell other writers about what it is we do in our pages: preserve the rich literary history of our talented state.

And finally, speaking of talent, thank you to all of the artists and art sources who allowed us to complement the African American literature of North Carolina with work by many of the state's African American artists. ■

FEATURING NORTH CAROLINA AFRICAN AMERICAN LITERATURE

ALSO IN THIS ISSUE

LEAVING HOME TO RETURN HOME: WRITING NORTH CAROLINA HOMEPLACE FROM THE PARTICULAR TO THE UNIVERSAL

PHOTOGRAPH BY BOB WATTS

by DeLisa D. Hawkes *and* Maia L. Butler

An Interview *with* Stephanie Powell Watts

STEPHANIE POWELL WATTS WAS BORN in Lenoir, North Carolina, a city named after William Lenoir, an American Revolutionary War general, a city where a Confederate monument still stands in the town square. Watts received her BA from the University of North Carolina in Charlotte and her PhD from the University of Missouri in Columbia, where she held a Gus T. Ridgel Fellowship. Watts is an Associate Professor of Creative Writing and Literature at Lehigh University, but she brings readers to her familiar homeplace of the North Carolina foothills in the pages of her fiction. Though we look forward to the long career ahead of her, her accolades are already numerous: she received the Ernest J. Gaines Award for Literary Excellence in 2012, the Whiting Award in 2013, the NAACP Image Award for Outstanding Literary Work in 2017, and her short fiction has been included in two volumes of the *Best New Stories from the South* anthology.[1]

---

[1] "Family Museum of the Ancient Postcards," originally published in *Oxford American*, was selected for *New Stories from the South 2007, The Year's Best,* edited by Edward P. Jones. "Unassigned Territory," first published in *New Letters*, is in the 2009 volume, edited by Madison Smartt Bell.

Watts has also been honored with a Pushcart Prize. Her 2011 collection of short stories, *We Are Taking Only What We Need*, will soon enter reprinting. Her second book, the 2017 novel *No One Is Coming to Save Us*,[2] is the inaugural Sarah Jessica Parker pick for the American Library Association's Book Club Central and was named one of the most anticipated books of 2017 by *Entertainment Weekly*, *Nylon*, *Elle*, *Redbook*, and *The Chicago Review of Books*. *The Wall Street Journal*, *The Washington Post*, *The Seattle Times*, and *O Magazine* each named *No One Is Coming to Save Us* the 2017 Best Summer Read.

Grounded firmly in a long tradition of North Carolina literature, Watts situates her works at the nexus of strong traditions in Southern literature, African American literature, and women's literature. *No One is Coming to Save Us* is a novel thick with representations of place, space, and home. Watts's African American characters long for those spaces where they can feel at home, both in their changing community – rapidly changing in some ways, slowly in others – and in their distinct North Carolina foothills region within the broader South. Talking with Watts about her experiences in North Carolina, her aims for the novel, and the questions the novel asks concerning the representation of a people in a changing time and place illuminates her approach to crafting a Southern space at once unique and also familiar. Her work reflects her position as a black Southern woman writer who feels compelled to portray a place she knows to be her home, an impulse to explore the dynamics of family tradition and memory, and a will to grapple with the changing public sentiment and economic forces that are impacting real people. Watts explores African American experiences of remaining in the South, sussing out what underpins a deep rootedness to place.

> *" I've always written fiction, even when I was a little girl. I have four younger brothers, and I was always babysitting them and trying to keep them occupied. So I told them stories, bits and pieces of stories I had read because I've always been a big reader. And I just embellished them and changed them to suit our lives. So I feel like it's always been a part of who I am and who I wanted to be. "*

Her work also examines the increasingly common experience of returning to the South after a search for something beyond the bounds of home and the familiar. Her characters face a sense of home and belonging that resides on slippery ground. Her work feels pressing when relics of a racist past and present, such as "Silent Sam" at UNC Chapel Hill, have come down in places that we love but may not be entirely comfortable. A variety of other issues face these communities as well. Industries are impacted by shifting centers of production leaving entire communities unmoored in their wake. Young people

[2] Stephanie Powell Watts, *No One Is Coming to Save Us* (HarperCollins, 2018); *We Are Taking Only What We Need* (BkMk, 2011).

RIGHT **View of the Square, Lenoir, NC, showing the Confederate Monument (dedicated in 1910) and Caldwell County Courthouse, circa 1930–45**

L-18   VIEW OF THE SQUARE, LENOIR, N. C.

SHOWING CONFEDERATE MONUMENT AND CALDWELL COUNTY HOUSE   E-0830

are faced with integrating inherited knowledge about how to be and move in a family and community that looks much different from previous generations. Watts says of her characters living, struggling, and pressing on in her rendering of a North Carolina that she knows and loves, that ultimately "they understand that there are a lot of negotiations that they're going to have to do no matter where they are. And they have home. It's not exactly what they might imagine in their wildest dreams, but it's theirs and it's home."[3]

To start, would you talk a little bit about how you got started writing fiction?

STEPHANIE POWELL WATTS: I feel like I've always written fiction, even when I was a little girl. I have four younger brothers, and I was always babysitting them and trying to keep them occupied. So I told them stories, bits and pieces of stories I had read because I've always been a big reader. And I just embellished them and changed them to suit our lives. I feel like writing fiction has always been a part of who I am and who I wanted to be. I didn't really think about being a writer until much later because I am a first-generation college student. And I'm the oldest, so I felt like I needed to do something that's stable, so that I can get a decent paying job. You know, help with the rest of the family, that kind of thing. You just feel like you have to be the one that's able to take care of herself. I thought for a long time about being an accountant. I was actually an Accounting major at North Carolina State University before I graduated from UNC Charlotte in 1997 with a degree in English. When I was a kid, the goal was to get a desk job. People who grow up like I did know that education is the only viable path to a life without constant economic struggle. I wanted to go into a stable profession where I could find immediate and somewhat lucrative employment. I hated accounting, and accounting hated me.

So, when you were first starting to write fiction, were you setting your stories in North Carolina? Have you always considered yourself a North Carolina author?

I do because I'm from North Carolina, but more importantly, that's where my subjects are, where my home is; that's the place where everything is set. And I feel like I really started writing about North Carolina when I went away for a little while, which is not uncommon. When you're in something, it's hard to see the contours of it; it's really hard to see it as an entity until you step away a little bit.

    The first story that I feel was a turning point story for me was "Unassigned Territory" – and if you're a writer you know what this feels like. You're kind of writing a certain way about a certain thing, and it's all sort of at one level, and then you write something and you feel like, this is the best thing I've ever done. You feel like you've made a turn, you've had a growth spurt. I was in Prague, and I was really missing home. I was there for several weeks with this writing

> **"***I'm from North Carolina, but more importantly, that's where my subjects are, where my home is; that's the place where everything is set.***"**

ABOVE **Stephanie Powell Watts at a reading with Marjorie Hudson, Randolph County Arts Council Gallery, 11 June 2015**

3 This quotation is from the interview with Watts, which DeLisa Hawkes conducted by telephone in July 2018, with questions she and Maia Butler prepared together. A recording was transcribed by *NCLR* intern Zak Sheppard. Hawkes and Butler then edited it for clarity and style (while being careful to remain true to the voices of the speakers).

"I STARTED WRITING THIS STORY ABOUT BEING IN NORTH CAROLINA AND BEING A JEHOVAH'S WITNESS AND BEING OUT IN YOUR ASSIGNED TERRITORY, TRYING TO REACH PEOPLE THAT ARE WAY OUT THERE IN THE BOONIES, WHERE YOU HAVE TO DRIVE DOWN LONG DIRT ROADS. I FEEL LIKE THAT'S WHERE THE HEART OF MY STORIES ARE: IN NORTH CAROLINA."

program writing nonfiction and I saw these Jehovah's Witnesses. My mother is a Jehovah's Witness, so is my brother, and I used to be a Jehovah's Witness. So I saw them in Prague, and I didn't know any Czech, and they didn't know any English. But I was talking to them, and I was trying to tell them, "I know what you're doing! I used to do that!" And I felt this connection back to home, and I started writing this story about being in North Carolina and being a Jehovah's Witness and being out in your assigned territory, trying to reach people that are way out there in the boonies, where you have to drive down long dirt roads. I feel like that's where the heart of my stories are: in North Carolina.

That is actually related to my next question. Do you feel like writing outside of North Carolina helped you to fine-tune your ideas about specific issues you write about?

I think that there are a couple of things that happened. One, I think I grew up a little bit. You know when you're a kid and you're outside playing in the grass, and it's a gorgeous summer day and you're jumping in the pool? You're not thinking, how beautiful is this? You're just in it, living it, and doing it. When I was there I was just living it, and then to pull back and say, OK, let me really think about that. In critical, constructive, and destructive ways, let me think about the place I'm from and what it really is.

Do you see yourself as a Southern writer given your ability to write about the South from these critical and constructive perspectives?

I do, yeah, I do. I do because I'm from the South and I write about the South. I'm not someone like Richard Porter from Mississippi; he doesn't always write about the South and he doesn't consider himself a Southern writer. But that's my subject matter and that's my home. I think either of those things can qualify me, but I do them both. I feel that there's this question, Is there such a thing as Southern writing – of regional writing – anymore? And what is it? When you start to define it, that's where it gets tricky. For me it's like if you're a Southern cook you might go to culinary school and learn French cuisine. You might learn lots of those sorts of things, but when you decide who you are as a chef, it's going to be infected with where you come from and what you know. Even if I write about something else that's not North Carolina, I feel that it's infected by who I am and what I know.

How would you define Southern writing in a few sentences?

I do think that there is a real sense of place in Southern writing. I think that place is concerned with issues of race. I think by definition it kind of has to be. Even if it is humor writing, I think there has to

be space, place, and race all mixed together in the narrative. You see how slippery that gets. There are novels like Daniel Woodrell's *Winter's Bone* (2006), set in the Ozarks. Is he a Southern writer? It's certainly talking about a very particular place, but it's not about race. It does get slippery. With Southern writing, and especially the Southern writing that I love, there is a special attention to the sound of language. That's important. With somebody like Charles Frazier, who is a real masterful writer, you feel like you're immersed in the language. He has such careful collections of words and paragraphs. I feel like that's part of it too.

While reading No One Is Coming to Save Us, *I noticed a lot of places in North Carolina. For instance, I picked up on the furniture industry in the Greensboro or High Point area. You mention East Carolina University, your character Henry works at ECU. I picked up on a couple references to Raleigh. This text is obviously representative of North Carolina in many ways. Would you say that this text is representative of the South in general or of African American or Southern communities throughout the United States? What makes North Carolina the perfect setting to discuss issues such as race, declining economy, immobility, or mobility?*

I think that you hit on a lot of the things that I was trying to do in the novel. I really wanted to talk about this place that is like so many places in the country. It had one or two big industries and those industries have declined or are gone. It is a place that has had many kinds of racial issues and racial questions. It's a place where people are still in family groups, not nearly as much as they used to be, but there are still pockets of family units. And it's also in a very beautiful part of the world. Not every place is beautiful, but in this case it is a very lovely part of the world. So I wanted to talk about what you do when the industry leaves. What do you do when the family you had is either scattered or non-existent? Because there are so many people who are facing those kind of issues, issues of loneliness. How do you behave? And I wanted to talk about the generation that I'm in, post-segregation, post–Jim Crow, post–Civil Rights. A non-segregated generation. I never had to live in a place with "Colored" or "White" signs, but the ghosts of that are everywhere. People still live in this part of town or that part of town. They still go to this church or that church. And so there are still those ghosts of Jim Crow all over the place. There are still those places you know that you don't go. I wanted to write about my community and this community in particular. I think that when you're writing about the particular, that's where people see the universal. You have to get it as right as you can, get the

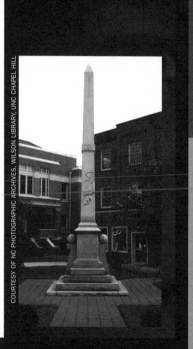

"I NEVER HAD TO LIVE IN A PLACE WITH 'COLORED' OR 'WHITE' SIGNS."

ABOVE TOP **Lenoir, NC, circa 1910**

ABOVE BOTTOM **Caldwell County Confederate Monument, Lenoir, NC, dedicated 1910** characters the best as you can, and then people can see the universal in it. People have said to me, "I saw myself in that seventy-year-old black woman from North Carolina who lived through a racist South and is now trying to negotiate, 'Well, who am I now? What do I do now? Now that I'm by myself, without a husband, without children.'" People who live very different lives than that would say, "I understand that." That's what I'm hoping that writing can do for people. Bridge that gap between those sorts of differences that make your life and that make you who you are but aren't essentially what's inside.

It definitely hit home for me. That reminds me of Simmy's restaurant in your book. Henry's father had the choice to walk into Simmy's, and the key word there is "choice." It made me think of a restaurant that I know of today, where black people obviously have the choice to eat in, but they mostly pick up their orders from the back entrance. The novel also made me think of individuals I know back home in Virginia or from North Carolina. Do you create characters and places based on real people and places that you know?

Not exactly, but I do think that every character has gotten filtered through me and my experiences, who I know, who I love, and different things that I have witnessed in my life. So in that way there are similarities. Sylvia has many similarities to my grandmother; she has this sort of vulnerability, but she is also very upfront and decisive. I wanted to mirror that in her character. No one in particular, but there are certain sorts of inflections that feel like people from real life.

We talked a little bit about how particulars in the text's communities can be reflective of the United States overall or of the South or of North Carolina specifically. What do you make of individuals in the text being tied to particular places, objects, or people?

> *I am fascinated with this question really: why some people never leave home. They might go off to college, but they'll come right back; they want to be in that space.*

I am fascinated with this question really: why some people never leave home. They might go off to college, but they'll come right back; they want to be in that space. And then others say, I want to travel the world, I want to live here, I want to live there. What is that thing that makes one person do one thing over another? I do think, even when there is this huge difference, even though some people are more adventurous, there is still this call to home. People want to be in a place where they feel safe and respected and secure. And a whole lot of people don't have that space, so they take the best they can get. I feel like my character Jay was trying to figure out "What is the best I can get?" and found his way back to Pinewood, back to family that took care of him when he needed it most. I do feel like we're all tethered to some imagining of home. There are some differences – sometimes they're subtle, some are starker than others – but there is that home-spot in our bodies.

> *It's not until she can really understand that she has to make her life, she has to fight for her life, that she can have one.*

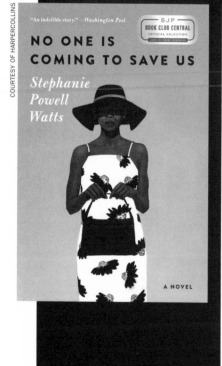

Where would you say is Ava's home, since at one point she retreats to an online community? How does that contrast with the other communities in the text?

Ava is kind of a lonely person. That is one of the things I wanted to talk about in the book because I think that there is that epidemic of loss of community and loss of closeness with other people. She has a very different attachment to home. Her home is her mother and, to a lesser extent, her aunt. Because they are there, that's home for her. And she has an imagining of a family that she feels will make a home for herself.

In Great Britain they have a Minister of Loneliness, a new position they've created, which I think is kind of great. They have an epidemic – and so do we – of people who are by themselves, people who, at holidays, have no one to see and who are really struggling with that, as would anybody. Ava is in that space, and she's trying to figure herself out. She's at a turning point age-wise. She's about to be forty; she's knocking on that door. Also, the end of her fertility is coming up. She's not happy in her marriage, and she knows it's not a good marriage. She even knows that her husband is not faithful to her. But she's going to block all that out to try to get this thing that she thinks will complete her life. It's not until she can really understand that she has to make her life, she has to fight for her life, that she can have one.

So Ava is using the online community to imagine a home. What about the idea that the novel is trying to imagine a post–Jim Crow but not post-racial society? What would your response be to the idea that the novel is trying to imagine a weird post-moment despite the continued presence of the ghosts of Jim Crow?

That is a goal: to be in that weird, funky space that we're in, for the characters to feel that and try to operate within that space. I'm sure you've heard there have been all of these incidents all over the country of the police being called because black people have been in different places, eating at Subway, walking around canvasing for a State Representative – sleeping! I'm a professor, and students sleep anywhere anytime. I think that that's one element of this tension. Some white people are like, "I know that they can be here, but I'm just not sure what their intentions are." So it's this collision of this past thinking and this thinking that you kind of know you should have. And that's where I feel like this epidemic of loneliness or of isolation has really hurt us in some incredible ways. Because virtually all of these incidents could have been resolved if one person had walked up to the other and just asked, "Hey, what's going on?" Just some kind of friendly conversation. That would have bridged the whole thing. But we're isolated, and we feel like we have these force fields around ourselves. We also have these strains of racist or backwards thinking. That's where my characters are, and they're trying to figure it out. There's one moment in the book where Jay and Ava are eating together at Simmy's and he sees the waitress looking at him. He doesn't

ABOVE **Paperback edition with cover art by Amy Sherald, painter of First Lady Michelle Obama's official portrait for the Smithsonian National Portrait Gallery**

know if she's looking at him because she needs to take care of him or if she's looking at him trying to figure out if he's going to do something sinister. Jay has to live in that space all the time. That's the kind of the thing I wanted to get through in the book.

COURTESY OF THE BATON ROUGE AREA FOUNDATION

I've read another author refer to that space as "Black Noise," a space where one always has to double think about others' actions. Would you say that characters having to deal with that type of mental space are also dealing with psychological damage? Do you feel like that comes out in the book?

It is a kind of double consciousness, having to always put yourself in two spaces. You know when you swallow something that is too much? It's this sick, full, icky feeling that makes you know that you can't ever fully belong. That's where I think my characters are. Sylvia has worked for a long, long time at her job, and she knows that she is not like the other people that work there. Certainly, they are nice to her. But she's not one of the gang, she's not invited into their space. It's not that way for her, even though she's good at her job and she does what she's supposed to. She's worked her way into a position that she's just like most everybody else, but she knows that there is a divide.

Do you feel like the characters have a sense of hope to get out or to erase that divide?

I don't think I do. I think that they are ready to accept it and then figure out what to do next. I'm hoping I can get them to a space that they can push through and figure out the rest of their lives. I think that they are sadly accepting that this is the way it is, but maybe I can maneuver around it. I think people who have been labeled "other," who are minorities, always have to do that action. Before the #MeToo movement, women did this everywhere and all the time: "Don't be alone with this person." "Don't say anything about x, y, or z." All these sorts of negotiations that you have to figure out, because there's nothing you can do except negotiate. Maybe you could move around this obstacle and then maybe you can keep going where you need to go. Laugh at the stupid jokes and just keep on going until you get to the point where you're in a different position. That's where my characters are. I'm just floored by the #MeToo movement. I'm so happy for it. It's really exciting to me. It's hard to imagine the things that so many of us went through and put up with. I think the idea that maybe some other women will not have to do that is just astonishing. It's an amazing moment. I think that's what my characters are feeling. They obviously know that the world has changed. I don't mean to suggest that the world of the United States or the world of North Carolina has not changed. And I don't mean to suggest that there are not wonderful people who want to see those

"I'M JUST FLOORED BY THE #METOO MOVEMENT. I'M SO HAPPY FOR IT. IT'S REALLY EXCITING TO ME. IT'S HARD TO IMAGINE THE THINGS THAT SO MANY OF US WENT THROUGH AND PUT UP WITH. I THINK THE IDEA THAT MAYBE SOME OTHER WOMEN WILL NOT HAVE TO DO THAT IS JUST ASTONISHING. IT'S AN AMAZING MOMENT."

ABOVE **Stephanie Powell Watts with Ernest J. Gaines on the occasion of her receipt of the Ernest J. Gaines Award for Literary Excellence from the Baton Rouge Area Foundation, Baton Rouge, LA, 2012**

changes and who are working hard for them. But there's enough that is the same that it still puts you in that space of constant negotiation.

It seems that you're suggesting that the characters are at a crossroads between immobility and mobility, they can either sit and stay in this segregated space or move out beyond that. Do you feel that any of your characters – and I'm thinking particularly of Jay – are more apt to be the first to move the community out of that space? Or do you think someone else is?

I don't think Jay is that person. I think my characters are clear-eyed about some kinds of things. It is a difficult world. It's a really difficult world if you're poor, black, and a woman. Most of my main characters understand that. They understand that there are a lot of negotiations that they're going to have to do no matter where they are. They have home. It's not exactly what they might imagine in their wildest dreams, but it's theirs and it's home. Some people, generations up through the seventies, waves of African American migrants, went to different parts of the country. They experienced many different kinds of things, different types of racism to be sure. And they had to leave their homes to do it. Half of African Americans did this, moved to other places. But that means about half stayed. I wanted to talk about the people who stayed. If you didn't go work in a factory, you didn't go to a Ford plant or go to Washington, DC, to find a job, what did you do? How did you make it? Because the world was still as it was if you stayed behind. I was really interested, especially in African American women, and people who were poor, people who did not live in ideal circumstances by any stretch. What happened to them?

I'm wondering the same because there is a moment in the novel where one character has a picture of President Obama in their house. I think that was very intentional in exploring what you were just mentioning – people who left, people who stayed. Who did the people who stayed behind have to look up to? What do we do with the picture of President Obama in this very intimate space, and what did his picture mean for the people who stayed?

When I was growing up, in every barber shop, in most beauty shops, and in many homes, there were pictures of John F. Kennedy and Martin Luther King, Jr. They were just in every public space and many private spaces. And now it's Barack Obama, especially for older folks. These people who really cared about change were really heroes for everybody. I think that African Americans all over the country felt that kind of kinship with these monumental figures in history – in the South for sure, but in different parts of the country. So many of my relatives and many waves of African Americans went North over these different waves of the Great Migration. The news that they brought back was usually good, but the reality of what they were doing was really, really

> “*I think my characters are clear-eyed about some kinds of things. It is a difficult world. It's a really difficult world if you're poor, black, and a woman.*”

COURTESY OF DURWOOD BARBOUR COLLECTION OF NC POSTCARDS, NC PHOTOGRAPHIC ARCHIVES, WILSON LIBRARY, UNC CHAPEL HILL

COURTESY OF CITY OF LENOIR, NC

ABOVE **Lenoir, NC, circa 1905–15**   LEFT **Downtown Lenoir, NC, today**

hard. They were often living in tenements, there were often vermin, they were often working terrible jobs. The stories that they brought back were about culture and they did get to partake in those sorts of things, but the reality of it was really difficult. It seems, sometimes, that the ones who were timid or weren't smart enough stayed, while the ones who were adventurous or after a better life left. That's not the story, that's not even close to the reality of the story.

The novel represents imagined communities and connections between these characters. What about the relationships between individuals? I'm thinking of Sylvia and Don, or Sylvia and Marcus, Ava and Jay. These are not imagined, but what do they offer us for this conversation?

I think that in every case there are people trying to reach out in the ways that they can. We're often talking at cross-purposes with each other. We're always trying to get something that we need, but we're often inarticulate when we're trying to do that. These characters are all desperately in need of something. Sylvia really needs a friend, and Don is probably her closest and most stable friend. And he cannot help but betray her; he cannot be the person she needs him to be. So she really needs a friend. She isn't religious, she doesn't have friends at work, casual friends, and she doesn't go anywhere so she doesn't have that kind of life. She found an outlet to have a connection with somebody, and that's really important to her. All of the characters are trying to reach out (Ava with the online community, for example). She's desperately embarrassed because she feels like she can't do the thing that anybody can do. We know that's not true, but that's how she feels. She can't talk to her mother because her mother doesn't understand it, so she feels like she needs somebody to work through these things with, and the community she finds is online. Everybody's reaching out in their own lame ways that people do, trying to find something.

Do you feel that generational differences and experiences figure in the novel? I'm thinking especially considering depictions of black womanhood, maybe a little bit with Ava and her online community. What do you think about the generational differences between Sylvia and her sister?

This is something that I find incredibly interesting. You think about the changes that have happened, especially in African American life, in the last fifty years, and they have been monumental. There are some things that have not changed; racism as we know is alive and well. It's just amazing; there are people who are alive who remember not being able to go into a restaurant – my father and mother are some of them – who remember having to go to the back of the bus. In South Carolina, my mother said, they would have to walk on a different side of the street if white people were walking on the street. They remember this, this is in their lived experience. My mother isn't very old, but my mother's life and my life are very different.

"WE'RE OFTEN TALKING AT CROSS-PURPOSES WITH EACH OTHER. WE'RE ALWAYS TRYING TO GET SOMETHING THAT WE NEED, BUT WE'RE OFTEN INARTICULATE WHEN WE'RE TRYING TO DO THAT."

> **"WATTS'S BOOK ENVISIONS A BACKWOODS AFRICAN-AMERICAN VERSION OF *THE GREAT GATSBY*. THE CIRCUMSTANCES OF HER CHARACTERS ARE VASTLY UNLIKE FITZGERALD'S, AND THOSE DIFFERENCES ARE WHAT MAKE THIS NOVEL SO MOVING."**
> **—JANET MASLIN, *NEW YORK TIMES***

I remember one time I was talking about being in the locker room with my schoolmates, and she was asking me about them. Most of them were white, and she was asking me about their habits, what they did, like it was some kind of sociological research or something. It dawned on me that she had never been to school with white people. So there are some real differences. Some of the advice that I would hear from the past generation just felt so weird. And I don't mean that it wasn't true, or it wasn't sound. It just felt weird. Like, "Don't trust white people; they will always let you down. If they had to choose between other white people and you, they will always choose other white people." Those kinds of things. Is that true with everybody? It was one hundred percent true for their generation, I can't deny that, and that is real. But then having to figure out how we talk across generations. If someone were looking at my mother or someone of her generation in a store, that person is definitely trying to find out if she's a thief. I don't know in my generation. There are all these kinds of questions that are fascinating to me. How much can you take from a previous generation, and how much do you have to reinterpret and move into another space? There was a time in human experience where you figured, I'm going to live just like my parents lived, I'm going to live just like my grandparents lived. But somewhere along the line that changed. Now you don't necessarily live in one little area. There was a time when, if you moved, you might never see these people again, or you might see them every couple of years. That sort of way of life, because of technological advances, it's just changed. Those are the things that are just rolling around in my head, that I find so interesting. I want to figure out how to get my characters to work through some of those issues.

People have compared No One Is Coming to Save Us *to* The Great Gatsby*; what are your feelings about that comparison?*

In a lot of ways, *The Great Gatsby* is about a family and someone who is coming from the outside who is trying to join that family, or at least take what he can get from that family and make his own family. In that way *No One Is Coming to Save Us* is reminiscent, at least in conversation, to *The Great Gatsby*. I don't feel like it is in other ways. I was at this ceremony and someone asked me, this is before the book was published, "What are you writing, what are you working on?" And I said, "It's just like *The Great Gatsby*, except for the people are Southern and poor and black and its set in the 2000s and they live in North Carolina." It was a joke, but I think that it kind of stuck. I was clearly meaning it as a joke. But there are some resonances with *The Great Gatsby*, which is a book that I love

ABOVE **Stephanie Powell Watts with actress Sarah Jessica Parker at the American Library Association, Chicago, 2017** (Parker selected *No One Is Coming to Save Us* as the first book for her Book Club Central.)

and that I have a lot of interesting intellectual issues with. It's a book that I go to over and over.

Do you see your work in conversation with Thomas Wolfe's attempts at drawing attention to the region since he was a contemporary of Fitzgerald and Faulkner and also brought the North Carolina landscape and people into his work?

I grew up reading and loving Thomas Wolfe. *Look Homeward Angel* was such a moving and beautifully created world that felt so much like worlds I knew myself. I just visited his home in Asheville for the first time. Most writers use the worlds they know as influences for their work. In Wolfe's novels and stories, he often didn't change the names of his characters and he rendered the landscape much as it appeared in life. I want to create a landscape and an atmosphere that readers will recognize emotionally but not that they know because they live there. I want there to be enough space in the writing that it doesn't turn into a parlor game of whether you recognize this character or know this town. I think Wolfe attempted and succeeded in highlighting what the residents of Asheville didn't know about the worlds they spent their lives in and the people they loved. Consider how difficult this task is! He knew people would recognize themselves and their time, but he knew that he had something relevant to say about both. My purpose is similar but not identical. I want to evoke a feeling but not a literal recognition.

Do you feel like some of the issues that you deal with in this novel also come up in your short story collection, We Are Taking Only What We Need? *If so, how do they tease them out differently? Does genre play into a different approach?*

I do think that there are different techniques for doing one or the other. When I think of a short story, I usually start with this image, something that I can't quite get out of my mind. And I start rolling it around and start thinking about where the story comes from, out of that image. I hope that the stories are about the people. When you really feel something, when it gets into your heart, when it's really meaningful to you, it's because you've connected to the person in the story. Whether you are sad for them or you feel like that's something that you recognize or you know or, if it's I don't understand you, I want to understand you. Maybe I don't even like you, but I want to understand you. I feel like when it gets in there with the person, then the kinds of things that we're talking about are things like what do you do in a world where racism is different than the racism that your grandma knew? What do you do in the world when the jobs and the work that your parents did is no longer available to you? What do you do if you want to come back home after you go to college and become the person that you feel like you wanted to be, but there's no place for you at home? It's like, what are you doing here?

> *I want there to be enough space in the writing that it doesn't turn into a parlor game of whether you recognize this character or know this town.*

COURTESY OF HARPERCOLLINS

THE ART OF THE STORY

We Are Taking Only What We Need

Stories

"Lorrie Moore meets Eudora Welty."
—The New Yorker

Stephanie Powell Watts
Author of No One Is Coming to Save Us

ABOVE **Paperback edition with cover art by Amy Sherald, painter of First Lady Michelle Obama's official portrait for the Smithsonian National Portrait Gallery**

> "FICTION HAS A REALLY IMPORTANT ROLE IN THE WORLD, IN UNDERSTANDING THE WORLD, AND IN CHANGING HEARTS AND MINDS."

I had somebody at a reading say to me, "Why in the world would Ava come back home? She's an educated person." It had never occurred to me that anybody would wonder about that, about why somebody who is an educated person would want to come back to their home. But he did, and he was very serious about it. Those kinds of questions, I think, you can start to take on if you care about the character. That's where fiction has a really important role in understanding the world and in changing hearts and minds. That's where we, as fiction writers, can do that work. Once you have that investment in a human being, it's hard not to see them as a fully formed person. Once you do that, then you're well on your way to not hating them, to want good for them. I'm hoping that that's the way fiction works. And I think it does. The Civil War started because of people reading things and saying, "I had no idea. There are real people in this fight. There are real people whose real lives have been stunted or collapsed because I wasn't brave enough, and now I want to be brave enough." So I hope that's the kind of work I'm doing.

What advice would you give to someone who is looking to write about their home?

I think that no matter how well you think you know a landscape, there are many, many things you don't know. There are many, many stories that you have no idea about. So I would say, go talk to some people. People will talk to you. I talked to a funeral director in a small town in North Carolina, and he was fantastic. He was helping me understand the embalming process. There was a lot more information than what probably saw its way into the book, but I feel like I had a good grounding in it and then I knew what I was talking about. So just go talk to some people, ask them some questions. For example, I had no idea that in my home town that there was a special place where black women went for their gynecological exams. I had never heard of that in my life. It ends up in the book when Sylvia has to go to a doctor who is extremely rude to her. She was a heavy woman, and he didn't want to deal with her. He said something rude to her when she had her exam, and she just vows she is never going to go back to him. She knows that she is pregnant, but she waited and waited and waited because she did not want to go through this ordeal. I found out by talking to some people in the town that that's the way it was for black women. There was either no care or generations of this substandard and rude care. I had no idea. So you might think you know your place, but you don't. There are many things that you can learn about the literal landscape, but also the psychological landscape.

Thank you so much for this wonderful interview, Stephanie. Our conversation has definitely helped me think about No One Is Coming to Save Us *and about home and Southern spaces in some new and interesting ways!* ■

COURTESY OF DELISA D. HAWKES

> "*There are many, many stories that you have no idea about. So I would say, go talk to some people. People will talk to you.*"

ABOVE **Left to right, Maia L. Butler and DeLisa D. Hawkes during the SAMLA conference, Birmingham, AL, Nov. 2018**

DELISA D. HAWKES is a PhD candidate at the University of Maryland-College Park where she studies representations of intraracial tensions in nineteenth-century African American literature.

MAIA L. BUTLER is an Assistant Professor of English at UNC Wilmington. Her research and teaching centers on representations of interracial tensions in home and migration, specifically with black communities across the diaspora.

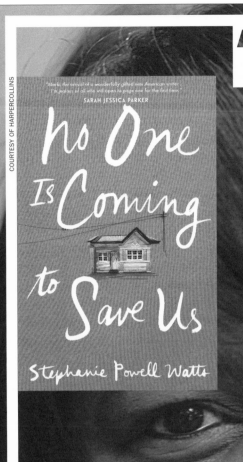

COURTESY OF HARPERCOLLINS

"Marks the arrival of a wonderfully gifted new American writer. I'm jealous of all who will open to page one for the first time."
SARAH JESSICA PARKER

No One Is Coming to Save Us

Stephanie Powell Watts

"WILDNESS WAS NOTHING TO ADMIRE":
AFRICAN AMERICAN ENVIRONMENTAL THOUGHT AND THE IMPORTANCE OF PLACE
IN STEPHANIE POWELL WATTS'S *No One Is Coming to Save Us*

by Jessica Cory

WITH ART BY

DAVID C. DRISKELL

PHOTOGRAPH BY DOUG BENEDICT

1 Paul Outka, *Race and Nature from Transcendentalism to the Harlem Renaissance* (Palgrave, 2008) 3; subsequently cited parenthetically.

WRITINGS BY AFRICAN AMERICAN AUTHORS are given very limited attention in the study of literature and the environment. Paul Outka observes, "[T]hat the intersection of nature and race – perhaps the two most perniciously reified constructions in American culture – has yet to be thoroughly examined underscores the longstanding, often normative, whiteness of ecocriticism."[1] While some facets of ecocriticism, particularly postcolonial ecocriticism and ecofeminism, can and do analyze race and ethnicity as part of the literary experience in conjunction with the work's environment, greater representation of African American authors, particularly those from the South, would provide a more inclusive understanding of the human experience. Of course, broad generalizations about how to view race and the environment are problematic. This essay does not advocate a prescriptivist approach to studying African American Southern literature through an ecocritical lens. Rather, it reveals what considerations may need to be made when studying such literature, why those considerations are important, and why, too, African American literature (and particularly African American

> **This analysis of Stephanie Powell Watts's 2017 novel *No One Is Coming to Save Us* shows how race, class, and environment comingle, particularly in the life of Sylvia, the matriarch of the family, and what we can learn from her experience and Watts's representation of the African American environmental imagination.**

Southern literature) are largely absent from the ecocritical conversation, as well as the concerns that arise from this absence. This analysis of Stephanie Powell Watts's 2017 novel *No One Is Coming to Save Us* shows how race, class, and environment comingle, particularly in the life of Sylvia, the matriarch of the family, and what we can learn from her experience and Watts's representation of the African American environmental imagination.[2]

As Carolyn Finney notes in the preface to *Black Faces, White Spaces: Reimagining the Relationship of African Americans to the Great Outdoors*, "Conceptualizations of the environment, the legitimization of certain definitions, and the shaping of debates are created and constructed by people who, in turn, are informed by their own identity, their life experience, and the context in which they live."[3] Finny's point helps us better understand why many perceive environmental issues and engagement with the great outdoors to be what a black student of hers calls "a white thing" (xiii). Finney notes that many media portrayals of African Americans have expanded public perception of black professionals, such as lawyers, doctors, and the like. However, in Finney's experience, the perceptions of African Americans and the outdoors has not kept pace, which then seems to legitimize African American invisibility in outdoor spaces.

The lack of African American representation in nature writing and ecocriticism does not simply do a disservice to the academy, it does a disservice to our students, as Latria Graham explains:

> When African American literature entered my consciousness, it was all about urban spaces, created by writers who, as a result of the Great Migration out of the South, lived in cities like Chicago and New York. I needed to give voice to my experiences, too, and their urban revelations were at odds with what I knew. Nobody cared about stories like mine, I thought, and by extension nobody cared about me. Professors could smell the desperation, the sour hint of terror-sweat on my skin. Still, my body could not endure the erasure of my ancestry, of the adventurer in me.[4]

By examining the African American environmental imagination, we are legitimizing the experiences of Graham and the many African Americans who engage in their natural environments, including those individuals who engage differently than white Americans due to a cultural history of trauma. Graham also addresses this in her essay when describing her father's apprehension at visiting a Southern national park and camping in its proximity in 2013 because in the 1950s, he had experienced the cruel reality of the Jim Crow South, which understandably haunted him.

Sylvia Mayer adds that prior to the 1980s, many African Americans held a distrust of environmental organizations and that this demographic did not feel comfortable being involved in such organizations until they "develop[ed] an additional political focus."[5] According to Mayer, once these organizations began to consider the roles of race and class in the discussion on environmentalism, then African Americans began to participate. Mayer also references Dana Alston, an African American environmentalist whose much-needed redefinition

[2] Stephanie Powell Watts, *No One Is Coming to Save Us* (HarperCollins, 2017); subsequently cited parenthetically.

[3] Carolyn Finney, *Black Faces, White Spaces: Reimagining the Relationship of African Americans to the Great Outdoors* (U of North Carolina P, 2014) xiv; subsequently cited parenthetically.

[4] Latria Graham, "We're Here. You Just Don't See Us," *Outside Online* 1 May 2018: web.

[5] Sylvia Mayer, "Introduction," *Restoring the Connection to the Natural World: Essays on the African American Environmental Imagination*, ed. Mayer, Forum for European Contributions to African American Studies (Lit Verlag, 2003) 2; subsequently cited parenthetically.

of *environment*, delivered as part of a speech in 1991 at the first national People of Color Educational Leadership Summit, better serves communities affected by racism and classism:

> The environment, for us, is where we live, where we work, where we play. The environment affords us the platform to address the critical issues of our time: questions of militarism and defense policy; religious freedom; cultural survival; energy-sustainable development; the future of our cities; transportation; housing; land and sovereignty rights; self-determination; employment – and we can go on and on.[6]

COURTESY OF DAVID DRISKELL STUDIOS

Lake and Forest (linocut, 9.5x9) by David C. Driskell

When we analyze Stephanie Powell Watts's work using this definition, the role of the environment in the novel becomes much more foregrounded and readers are able to more thoroughly appreciate the attention that Watts pays to the African American environmental imagination.

Watts wrote *No One Is Coming to Save Us* as a response to *The Great Gatsby*, sharing in an NPR interview, "I loved it when I was a kid and read it for the first time. . . . But subsequent readings, I felt like I'm seeing other things. I'm seeing all of these black characters – never thought about them before. I'm seeing the women and the tiny, tiny roles that they have in the book, and I want them to speak. I want to hear what they have to say."[7] Watts's novel revolves around Sylvia, the matriarch of her family; her daughter, Ava; Ava's unfaithful husband, Henry; and Jay, a longtime friend of the family whose recent return with plans to build his dream home complicates the lives of these other characters. Themes throughout the novel include struggles with self-acceptance in a postcolonial and patriarchal society, the complex familial and societal roles of women (particularly African American women in the South), masculinity in the African American community, and the negotiations of occupying space and natural environments while existing as African American in the American South.

Throughout the novel, characters are repeatedly shown to experience ecophobia, far preferring the safety and comfort of the indoors over the unknown threats that exist outdoors. This does not mean they are disconnected from their environments, but suggests that Watts's characters experience these environments through a slightly different lens than their non–African American counterparts, perhaps due to a cultural history of trauma that resulted in limited access and associated apprehension. Dianne Glave explains that one likely cause of this fear is that the history of many African Americans, "whose forefathers and -mothers experienced nature intertwined with fear and violence" has resulted in "these terror-filled experiences [being] passed to future generations, though only the essence of the original stories remain[s]."[8] This concept of cultural and generational trauma may certainly help us understand more about the African American environmental imagination, particularly in the South. In more concrete terms, we often inherit many ideas, fears, and values from our immediate family members, including the way we think about nature, wilderness, and the environment. If one is raised to believe that the outdoors are unsafe or to be feared, these beliefs then

6 Quoted in Robert Gottlieb, *Forcing the Spring: The Transformation of the American Environmental Movement*, rev. ed. (Island Press, 2005) 34.

7 Ari Shapiro, "Fitzgerald Didn't Satisfy This Author, So She Wrote Her Own *Gatsby*-Inspired Novel," *All Things Considered*, National Public Radio, 13 Apr. 2017: web.

8 Dianne D. Glave, *Rooted in the Earth: Reclaiming the African American Environmental Heritage* (Lawrence Hill, 2010) 4–5; subsequently cited parenthetically.

become internalized and passed on to future generations. Watts makes it clear that, as much of the literature suggests, engagement with the outdoors is often learned from one's family, and Sylvia's family didn't nurture this aspect of their lives. Despite growing up "in the woods . . . surrounded by green rolling hills, a pebbled creek [that] bubbled just out of sight, and the clearing where they burned garbage circled by rows of honey blond broom straw, none of them had thought to consider the place beautiful" (18).

Finney describes these learned biases as "discourses of heritage" that help cement families and communities (53). She adds that identity and memory are intrinsically involved in any attempts to reconcile cultural trauma, then expands on this notion of fear in a section on collective memory. Outka picks up on the connection Finney makes and explains that "trauma can be transmitted and experienced through widely disseminated forms of representation as well as individual memory" (103), demonstrating not only historical discomfort, but contemporary concerns as well, especially in the age of social media and instant news stories. We see these "discourses of heritage" embodied in Watts's novel chiefly by the female-identifying characters, beginning with Sylvia's mother, Mabel. Mabel is described as a woman who "cringed in fear from the threat of rapists, popping balloons, the shrill horror movie sound of wind chimes," and we learn that these fears were due to traumatic events from Mabel's youth, in which she was "always too accommodating, especially when it came to men" and perhaps also due to "interactions with Sylvia's father" (20). Sylvia seems to have inherited her mother's anxieties. She "thought many times that she'd spent her whole life tensed and waiting for the worst thing to happen" and wondered how she could have "ended up like her mother" (21). Sylvia perceives Ava to have avoided this fearful fate, describing her daughter as "confident" and "a professional woman, a woman with a profession" (26–27), perhaps unaware of the depths of Ava's insecurities about her body and the larger world. Later in the novel, we see Ava hole up in a dorm room for days, feeling safe in the "stale little cinder block space" and anxious about "the unknown future," though she does readily admit that she "would have to get on with it again" (305). While Ava's apprehension and concerns may not be rooted in the cultural trauma described by Finney and Outka, the fear that started it all, resulting in generations of scared and anxious women, was undoubtedly founded in the trauma experienced by African American women in the Jim Crow South.

In addition to fear, accessibility to the outdoors plays a key role in understanding the African American environmental experience as portrayed by Watts's characters in *No One Is Coming to Save Us*. Throughout the novel, readers are shown how this transition from land-based living to more modern living impacts the characters' views of the natural world, often resulting in ecophobia. As Ava and her younger brother Devon were raised in a suburban area with limited

Mother and Daughter (relief linocut print, 16x12) by David C. Driskell

> **[D]isregard for history, particularly African American and environmental history, causes younger generations to see these ways of living as 'backward' or 'other,' often resulting in viewing environmental engagement as not valued or unnecessary.**

access to outdoor recreation, they grew up more distanced from the natural world than previous generations. We can see the effects of this even in their childhoods, such as when Devon is hissed at by his grandfather's geese and his reaction is to scream and turn away from them and into his mother. The geese, however, were penned and so not a threat to Devon or Sylvia, though she admitted that "she'd wanted to scream too" (12). However, exposure to outdoor recreation doesn't just affect Sylvia's children; Jay is affected as well, as we see in his negative reaction to the reservoir, a place utilized by "families [who] would line the shore with sand toys and buckets of Kentucky Fried Chicken" and "small boats [that] would float or buzz through the muddy water" (301). Despite these positive, fun images, Jay dislikes the place, though he is unsure if it is "the brownish murky water" or "the drive through the woods that always felt menacing to him" that unnerves him the most (306). Glave discusses how, historically, nature study was an integral part of the curriculum at rural African American teacher-training schools and like institutions (106). Similarly, there is certainly a rich history of African American farming, preservation, conservation, and communion with the land. This is especially true in North Carolina, as many African American families raised hogs and tobacco. However, as bell hooks discusses in *Belonging: A Culture of Place,* many African Americans have become disconnected from their environmental roots as they physically move outside of regions that don't value these connections "in modern society, without a sense of history, [where] it has been easy for folks to forget that black people were first and foremost a people of the land, farmers. It is easy for folks to forget that at the first part of the 20th century, the vast majority of black folks lived in the agrarian south."[9] This disregard for history, particularly African American and environmental history, causes younger generations to see these ways of living as "backward" or "other," often resulting in viewing environmental engagement as not valued or unnecessary, furthering anti-environmentalist stereotypes which are, in many cases, not accurate.

While we know that African Americans indeed engage with the environment, part of the difficulty in dispelling harmful stereotypes to the contrary is that the written history of African American environmental experience is quite limited in quantity. One of the contributing factors, according to Glave, is that many of the collections that have been donated to universities and libraries have been curated by white people who may feel "the papers too insignificant to save and collect" (10). Glave also cites illiteracy as a major cause for the absence of this type of work, as many slave masters disallowed education to their chattel. Related to slavery, Kimberly Ruffin explains that "omitting work from America's ecological narratives" is largely to blame for these misperceptions and adds that "this omission has left African Americans with a limited acknowledgement of the realities of enslaved life and the misperception that the enslaved were ecologically mute and moot."[10] Glave also notes that "racism and segregation resulted in inequitable access to quality land, including agricultural and environmental amenities like parks for leisure or play" (9) and goes on to clarify that this legacy still endures today, with wealthier, and

[9] bell hooks, *Belonging: A Culture of Place* (Routledge, 2009) 36.

[10] Kimberly N. Ruffin, *Black on Earth: African American Ecoliterary Traditions* (U of Georgia P, 2010) 53; subsequently cited parenthetically.

often white, people having more access to land and outdoor recreation opportunities. This idea of ownership and accessibility is quite prominent in Watts's novel, particularly in Sylvia's understanding of *home*. Early in the novel, Sylvia recalls her own childhood ideas of home, living in poverty in one of "the poorest crannies of the county" in a neighborhood of "dirt roads and clusters of men on front lawns playing cards, fighting again" (19). She makes clear that her parents "moved to escape it all," in hopes of overcoming the poverty that had oppressed them and defined their neighborhood. The upward mobility of Sylvia's parents inspired Sylvia to continue their legacy and she felt that raising her children to never know poverty so intimately imbued "a feeling of triumph . . . like nothing else she had ever known" (20). However, despite providing their children with a stable home in a neighborhood unlike the one from Sylvia's youth, Sylvia and Don are not able to access home ownership in the exclusively white and wealthy area of Pinewood in which Jay plans to build his home.

The neighborhoods described in Watts's novel intimately examine the inequalities and intersections of class, race, and environment. Early in the novel, Sylvia shares an observation from her youth about Brushy Creek, the area in which Jay is constructing his home: "What a relief that in our hearts we knew that no coloreds, no negroes, no blacks, were welcome, even if they could afford to buy there. At least we didn't have to believe that we'd done everything wrong and were not the ones that God has chosen" (3–4). This idea of inferiority follows Sylvia throughout the novel, and she tries to boost her self-esteem by believing herself to be better than other African Americans in her town, as we see in her explanation for why she and Don purchased their home on Development Drive two decades prior. The street is described as containing "small houses owned by black families" and "one of the nicer places for blacks to live in town." While certainly there is nothing wrong with wanting to better oneself, part of Sylvia's rationale was that a "few black people would slowly move up in the world and would want homes without junk cars. A development for them would do the trick and keep them all on their own streets" (19). This notion of "development" seems to be rooted in the old ideas of "civilization" and links Sylvia's desires with performing whiteness and establishing her own value based on what white residents of the town think of her. This desire for acceptance in a racist system that upholds whiteness while oppressing people of color feeds Sylvia's actions. Utilizing an ecofeminist framework, the foundation of which espouses that the same forces that oppress nature also oppress women, people of color, and animals, the connection between Sylvia's self-worth and her apprehension toward communion with the natural world and her environment becomes clearer.

When returning to the home she shares with Don after a drive through the wealthy neighborhood, Sylvia feels the gap between the classes broaden: "Returning . . . means returning from those mountain drives to their sagging furniture that was old when they got it twenty years before and to a yard that looked even smaller than they remembered. That beautiful house is just a street away, but as out of reach as the moon" (3). The relevance that the wealthy folks resided

> **This idea of inferiority follows Sylvia throughout the novel, and she tries to boost her self-esteem by believing herself to be better than other African Americans in her town.**

on top of the mountain brings about images of rulers overseeing their peasantry or perhaps biblical images of prophets and holy men who ascend mountains to hear more intimately from God, and only return to the valley to disperse their revelations to the common man. In a more realistic and classist approach, in many mountainous areas, those with fewer means live in valleys because the housing and land are less expensive, often due to the increased risk of flooding and smaller lot sizes, as valleys are more easily cleared for building. This is obviously the case for Sylvia, who notes that "the black people in town [lived] in dog trots and shotgun houses at the bottom of the mountain, houses stuck in the sides of hills scattered like chicken feed" (3), something she desperately tries to avoid.

Lady Day (linocut, 8x6) by David C. Driskell

Having separated from Don, Sylvia describes her apartment as "a one bedroom apartment with builder-white walls and the stink of industrial carpet she couldn't rid the place of even after five years." She fantasizes about the materials that would make her apartment feel like a home: "drawings of nudes and Persian rugs, books that lined built-in shelves, weavings made in countries where the brown people were not the usual black folk variety of dirt road North Carolina" (24). Two things are clear from this passage. One is that Sylvia's ideal self, "worldly and sophisticated," can only be realized through personal possessions and the spirit they imbue her with, as well as having those possessions viewed by others, who by valuing the items in her possession, value this version of Sylvia as avant-garde and worthy of their attention. The second observation is that there is an element of internalized racism in Sylvia that causes her to create this ideal self to feel some measure of self-worth. The fact that she speaks pointedly of the "black folk" in North Carolina shows that she considers these other "brown people" to be superior to herself. While it is not clearly stated in the previous passage that the audience her ideal self would entertain is white, it is certainly suggested: "In her imagination she was *That Black Girl*" (24; Watts's italics). This phrasing suggests tokenization, which leads one to believe that Sylvia sees herself as not only a sophisticated black woman, but one who has earned value and respect by a white majority through performing the tokenized role.

This intersection of race, class, and environment is reiterated earlier in the novel during a conversation between Marcus, a young incarcerated man who initially contacted Sylvia by mistake, but whom she's become fond of, and Sylvia. Sylvia perceives Marcus as trying to convince her that

he was a nice man from good people who kept their houses clean, didn't set cars on blocks in their yards, didn't hang their oversize panties and BVDs on the clothesline for just anyone to see. He wanted her to believe that they were the kind of black people that whites saw some good in. They were a better, more acceptable subset of the race that spoke well and presented well, more and better than a cut above the great mass of regular black folks that they (whites and the special blacks) all looked down on, tolerated, and pitied. (17)

COURTESY OF DAVID DRISKELL STUDIOS

Brown Venus (woodcut/serigraph, 13.5x11) by David C. Driskell

This concern about how others indentify them (both Marcus and Sylvia) speaks to DuBois's idea of "double consciousness," though in an expansion on how others might perceive them based solely on skin color. They are also aware that the materials that compose their environments affect others' judgments. It is also notable that their desire to be superior to "regular black folks" and "the kind of black people whites saw some good in" speaks to their own internalized racism. This inferiority, undoubtedly due to cultural and historical trauma as well as systemic racism, affects not only their self-worth, but how they interact with the world around them, specifically in the places they feel able to move freely, which does not include the natural environment.

Sylvia holds many fears of the natural world, which she likely inherited from her mother: "The list of fears was long: spiders, snakes, and death were all reasonable and easily understood, but like her long-dead mother Mabel . . . she was afraid of everything else too" (21). However, this does not stop Sylvia from engaging with a restricted version of nature, her garden: "Of all the spaces in her home the yard was the only area she worked on and primped like it was a loved child. What she'd inherited by scrabble ground, a few pokeberries, choking weeds, and honeysuckle rooted in among the high weeds, skinny sticks of maple trees sprouted up around the perimeter of a half-acre lot" (18). Her gardening may seem at first glance contradictory to Sylvia's nature. However, her desire for control makes this hobby a perfect task for her. Being able to physically manipulate a swath of ground from unseemly to something more "appropriate" plays right into Sylvia's concern for keeping up appearances. Don even notes her "industry" and claims that while "Sylvia never kept a neat house . . . her yard was another story altogether" (127). Watts's inclusion of this aspect of African American environmental engagement is representative of the gardening and agricultural traditions of African American women. Gardening allowed, according to Ruffin, "the enslaved to experience ecological beauty in the midst of incredible burdens," even though the gardening often had to be completed "by moonlight not only after a full day of labor but also on a holiday" (32–33). After slavery, accordingi to Glave, "African American women developed [gardening] expertise from community knowledge, from their own interpretations of agricultural reform, and from the training they received in horticulture in the Cooperation Extension Service, African American schools, and other places."[11]

This tradition does seem to be decidedly female, which Watts pays homage to in her novel; for example, when Jay begins constructing his home. In order to access his property, a road must first be built.

[11] Dianne D. Glave, "Rural African American Women, Gardening, and Progressive Reform in the South," _"To Love the Wind and the Rain": African Americans and Environmental History_, ed. Glave and Mark Stoll (U of Pittsburgh P, 2006) 37–38.

12 Luisah Teish, "Women's Spirituality: A Household Act," *Home Girls: A Black Feminist Anthology*, ed. Barbara Smith, 1983 (Rutgers UP, 2000) 325.

13 Jennifer C. James, "Ecomelancholia: Slavery, War, and Black Ecological Imaginings," *Environmental Criticism for the Twenty-First Century*, ed. Stephanie LeMenager, Teresa Shewry, and Ken Hiltner (Routledge, 2011) 163–78; subsequently cited parenthetically.

Watts notes that the men in town are particularly interested in the road. However, the women are uninterested in this aspect because "they knew from their own yards how difficult it was to make a way to get from there to here. They'd dug their own paths, moved their own dirt and rocks in the stubborn Carolina soil" (5). Watts also states, referring to Sylvia and Don's home on Development Drive, that the developers "slung a handful of grass seed, spit with a go from God, and hoped it would take root on the red clay hills. The seed promptly got carried by wind or washed down the sides of the yard into ditches" (19). The careless nature in which these seeds are scattered contradicts the meticulous gardening engaged in by African American women, described by Ruffin and suggested by Watts. Because of this contradiction, readers may perceive the developers flinging this seed to be male, as the suggestion is that women would be more mindful of sowing the seed. This implicit distinction is significant because it again highlights the difference in gender roles throughout the novel.

When discussing culture, gender, and environment, it is frequently necessary to include the religious or spiritual beliefs of a person, group, or culture. In her essay, "Women's Spirituality: A Household Act," Luisah Teish discusses origins of African American spirituality including Black Christianity, the Pan-African Culturalist School, and the Voodoo traditions that she believes to be the closest representations of what her foremothers practiced. Teith notes that many West Africans, and surmises that perhaps all Africans, "shared a belief in Nature worship" including the idea of animism: "in an animated universe . . . all things are alive on varying levels of existence."[12] One aspect of animism that has survived is the importance of and communication with ancestors and others who have passed on. Jennifer C. James expands upon the African American belief in animism by providing several examples, including a WPA slave narrative in which "an elderly man in Mississippi insisted that even a bucket had a spirit,"[13] reflecting that such beliefs were present in the South, as we see in several of Watts's characters. One example can be seen in the construction of Jay's home, as it is described as "walls rising up like raptured dead" (5). Later in the novel, Ava makes the observation that she and Jay "were surrounded by ghosts they nudged out of the way just to get up in the morning" (308), suggesting that those who had passed away were still able to influence the living. The idea of reincarnation in the natural world also speaks to the concept of animism. Ava shares with Henry an insight her daughter conceived: "I told May about perennials, you know the flowers? You know what she said? . . . She said, 'Mama if I die, I'll come back, but maybe not in the same way'" (343). While these may be more straightforward examples of animism in the novel, other characters exhibit their connections to the natural world, particularly through their connections with animals, even if those animals are food.

Sylvia's use of animal imagery can be seen throughout the novel including when she describes the "young slick skinned black men" she recalls from her youth, how they "moved like robots in the factories, restaurants, and yards" with their "lizard-dead-eyed faces," although a few, she notes, "would take their places among the secure

"

This analysis of Stephanie Powell Watts's 2017 novel *No One Is Coming to Save Us* shows how race, class, and environment comingle, particularly in the life of Sylvia, the matriarch of the family, and what we can learn from her experience and Watts's representation of the African American environmental imagination.

"

. . . ruled the room, sailed into clubs and parties, like beautiful ships, dressed to the hilt in their high glossed gator shoes" (27). From an animal studies perspective, it is noteworthy that both references to animals involves creatures who are deceased, in the "lizard-dead" faces and "gator shoes." We see a similar morbidity associated with the natural world in Sylvia's dietary choices:

> The cleaned-out shell of her sweet potato, vacant like an abandoned snakeskin. The Y-shaped bone from her pork chop was gray and left over on her plate like the remains of a dinosaur. She'd even chewed the gross spongy fat of the meat for punishment. She should never eat anything recognizable from an animal's body. (298)

While the representation of the pork chop may be unsurprising from an animal welfare standpoint, Sylvia's description of the sweet potato, using terms like "vacant" and "abandoned," implies that she feels disconnected, almost betrayed, from this vegetable that simply sprung from the earth and traveled to her plate. Further, the use of a snake skin, something rooted in regeneration but understood from a religious and superstitious stance to be a bad omen, displays Sylvia's fearful view of not only the natural world as wilderness, but also the life that springs from its earth.

Interestingly, Sylvia's views of eating animal flesh seem to originate out of her perceived superiority to animals rather than the ethical dilemma of taking a life from a creature who values its life as much as she values hers. It is as though by eating the deceased animal that she is somehow lowering herself to its level. In this scene, as she consumes the meal, Sylvia focuses on her transgressions and past mistakes, both "the nasty ones she knew about, and the sad ones she hadn't understood at the time" (298). Because of this inner awareness, the consumption of the meal is portrayed as a penance, or a rite, as one may take communion, consuming the body and blood to feel cleansed from unrighteousness. Her view of unprocessed food (the pork chop and sweet potato) when compared to her view of processed food displays her predilection for things altered by human hands: "Very soon, she despised the realness of foods and ached for the sweet, just sweet. She even liked the strange, exotic sounding word, *sugar*" and had "almost given up eating at all" (33–34).

This same superiority over nonhuman animals while still understanding their animism can also be seen in Henry. Later in the novel, as Henry drives to visit his nephew, he takes notice of some turtles crossing the road. Not wanting to run over them, he "stopped his car to watch them plod their way past. Henry didn't like turtles especially, but it made him hopeful to think that nature still interested him, moved him enough to make him stand still and look." However, this interest and hope in the natural world is not biocentric, but instead anthropocentric: "Just maybe he wasn't as unreachable as he feared." This interaction centers Henry's existence and needs rather than the turtles' or the natural world. While he does act out of kindness toward the turtles, he avoids "popping them under his tires" not for their sake, but because "he [can't] stand the idea" of doing so (340). This superiority of human needs over nonhuman animal concerns, particularly among African Americans, Outka suggests, may be in response to "whites frequently conflat[ing] African Americans with domesticated animals," comparable to how Native Americans have been associated with the "precapitalist 'untouched' savage wilderness."

Outka points out that these notions exist in stark contrast to the "central intersection between white supremacy and environmental practice" (7), likely explaining why white environmentalists put the planet first, but oppressed peoples may be less inclined to follow their lead. Ruffin supports Outka's statements, noting that "children were met with the message that nonhuman animals and African Americans shared the same status" and that this equation was "a direct impediment to developing a healthy sense of ecological citizenship [that] continued through adulthood" (33).

Part of the discomfort or ecophobia experienced by Watts's characters appears to be due to unpleasant memories experienced in nature. James speaks to this "return of memory through nature" by linking it with the notion of animism discussed earlier, claiming that "'natural memory' represents a belief in organic proximity and reciprocity; the lines separating humans from nature, the living from the dead, are scarcely determinable" (163). This connection between the living and dead existing in the natural world is evident repeatedly in *No One Is Coming to Save Us*, especially if we extend the living/dead binary to the forgotten dreams of the characters, as is the case for Jay and Ava.

Near the novel's conclusion, as Jay and Ava reminiscence about their youthful fantasies while looking out over the landscape, the following exchange occurs:

COURTESY OF DAVID DRISKELL STUDIOS

The Guardian (woodcut/serigraph, 11x15) by David C. Driskell

"We used to think about having a house up here. Remember that? We were going to live on the water," Jay said.

"Yours is better than all the ones we picked. Isn't that amazing?

"I never really liked it here," he said and looked around at the landscape as if confirming his original idea.

Ava stared at Jay, not sure what to think, "Why didn't you tell me that?"

"I knew you liked it. It's pretty, baby. I just never got it like you do. I want to take you to a desert. Have you been?" (302)

Their recollection of adolescent dreams is certainly no happy topic. Add to that Jay's admission that he would have agreed to live in that landscape (and, indeed, he did) as a sacrifice to Ava, which Ava would not have wanted, and complications become messier. It should also be pointed out that the landscape in the above scene, both physical and metaphorical, form a wedge between Jay and Ava. While Jay clearly dislikes this North Carolina landscape, he assumes (perhaps

erroneously) that Ava enjoys it. However, Jay's preference for the desert is also at odds with Ava's desires. The desert's barren "moonscape" is what draws Jay to it; however, Ava has been struggling to escape – before she eventually accepts – the barren landscape that is her own body. While she has kept it mostly to herself (and her online support group), Ava is desperate to have a baby, a goal seemingly intensified by her discovery that another woman was able to procreate with her husband. Ava even later refers to her body as "a graveyard" (309). Seeing one's body as a type of environment that cradles only death seems clearly at odds with the infinite possibilities alive in the desert skies for which Jay yearns.

This thin line separating their worlds is also evident immediately following the above excerpt when it becomes clear that Jay's love of the nighttime sky and desert landscape is short-lived and filled with disappointment: "Years ago he'd gone there [the Mojave Desert] to get a message from his mother. He knew it couldn't be true, he was not insane, but he couldn't shake the idea that with the arrival of Hale-Bopp he would see her too . . . but the message from his mother did not come" (302–303). Jay's yearning for solace, comfort, and perhaps a message from beyond is echoed by Ava and Jay returning to the spot where Devon was stuck by a car and killed. Upon their arrival, Ava immediately remarks, "It feels like a horror movie out here," noticing as "dust swirled in the light, like in a dream, the light a living thing pushing back the dark, a losing battle anyone could predict" (279). Ava's perception of the animism imbued by the dust and light speaks to spiritual notions explored by James, that thinning of the veil that allows connection between the physical world and the spiritual one. As Ava and Jay exit the car, they notice flowers "dyed improbable colors" that someone, likely Devon's recent love interest, left at the scene of the crime to honor his memory. It's significant that the flowers are dyed unnatural colors not only because this provides a stark contrast to what one might expect to find in a more natural environment, but also because the altered flowers' manmade status is supposed to provide comfort and remembrance, quite a difference from the concept of "dust to dust." As they stand there longer, Jay readies himself to leave. "'Not yet,' Ava said as they watched the dust swirl in the headlights. Moths were coming already into the white beam. 'We might feel him here. Do you think that's possible?'" to which Jay replies, "'No, Ava. That's the last thing that

COURTESY OF DAVID DRISKELL STUDIOS

The Hibiscus (linocut/serigraph, 7x5) by David C. Driskell

will happen'" (280). While Ava desperately tries to believe that the natural world, and more precisely the place of her brother's death, might allow him to reach out to her, Jay refuses this belief, hanging on to the idea of human superiority over the spiritual realm.

This struggle between a biocentric worldview and an anthropocentric worldview throughout *No One Is Coming to Save Us* speaks to African American history, cultural trauma, and the current concerns within the American environmental movement, and by association, ecocriticism. By educating ourselves on North Carolina's African American history and better understanding the intersections of race, class, gender, and the environment in the state, we can more thoroughly critique and comprehend the ways that these intersections function today, as well as how they are represented in the area's African American literature. Stephanie Powell Watts, and certainly many other African American authors, are furthering readers' knowledge of these important issues, if only we will open up and listen. ∎

> " By educating ourselves on North Carolina's African American history and better understanding the intersections of race, class, gender, and the environment in the state, we can more thoroughly critique and comprehend the ways that these intersections function today. "

ABOVE *NCLR*-organized panel for the South Atlantic Modern Language Association, featuring papers on African American writers of North Carolina; left to right former intern Ebony Bailey, who chaired the panel; Wendy Miller; Jill Goad; Jessica Cory, author of this essay; and Maia Butler (see preceding interview with Watts)

JESSICA CORY earned a BA in English from Ohio University and an MA in English with a concentration in creative writing and a certificate in Multicultural and Transnational Literatures from East Carolina University, and she is currently pursuing a PhD in English at UNC Greensboro. She teaches composition courses at Western Carolina University in Cullowee, NC. Her work had been published in such journals as *A Poetry Congeries*, *Menacing Hedge*, and *…ellipsis*.

DAVID C. DRISKELL grew up in Forest City, NC. He studied at Skowhegan School of Painting and Sculpture in Maine and has a BA from Harvard University and an MFA from Catholic University. He is currently Distinguished Professor Emeritus at the University of Maryland, where the David C. Driskell Center for the Study of Visual Arts and Culture of African Americans and the African Diaspora was established in his honor in 2001. His paintings can be found in such major museums as the National Gallery of Art and in private collections around the world. His scholarship in the history of art includes numerous books and over forty catalogs for curated exhibitions, including, in 1976, "Two Centuries of Black American Art: 1750–1950," a seminal exhibit that laid the foundation for the field of the African American Art History. In addition to many other awards and honors, he is cultural advisor and curator of the Cosby collection of Fine Arts. in 2000, he was awarded the National Humanities Medal by President Bill Clinton. In 2007, he was elected as a National Academician by the National Academy. See more of the artist's work in *NCLR* 2012 and in *NCLR Online* 2018.

BY AMBER FLORA THOMAS

Fable in the Storm

I slept with a pillow pressed against my hips, as though a lover were
meeting me in the dunes   and my wake could be   an unfolding.

I fell asleep in a dream   about a son I'd adopted.   I sat on the edge of his bed
and told him, "Go to sleep now. Know I love you."   My joy simmered
at his smooth brown edges and   in the curl of his eyelashes.

If I could have slept through the storm,   not been at the window   checking the water,
I would have made him breakfast
and sent him to school.

> *You should leave now.*
> *You should leave before it's too late.*

To be sand,   some part of me knew   how to give out,
weary and changed,   blown across by wind   and deposited elsewhere.

> *You should leave now.*
> *You should leave before it's too late.*

The aluminum roof on the barn bubbled with gusts.   Water filled the street.
I went back to my lover and turned   like a dune in winter   flattening into a moon
       between the road and sea.

In the morning, I brought my child to the window and pointed at a table
floating in flood waters,   a bleach bottle twisting its dented boat at a branch.
The surge was below,   licking at houses,
wiping itself on brick and siding.

It's too late to leave now.

*

AMBER FLORA THOMAS is the winner of the 2004 Cave Canem Poetry Prize, the Ann Stanford Poetry Prize, and the Rella Lossy Poetry Award. She has an MFA in poetry writing from Washington University in St. Louis, and is now an Associate Professor at East Carolina University. She has published three collections of poetry: *Eye of Water* (University of Pittsburgh Press, 2005), *The Rabbits Could Sing* (University of Alaska Press, 2012), and *Red Channel in the Rupture* (Red Hen Press, 2018; reviewed in *NCLR Online* 2019).

When my son found me,
he was hungry enough   to come to my door   and ask
if I needed him to do yardwork.   I fed him

and sent him away with food.   He came back the next day
and I fed him again,   showing him his room.   "This is your room, if you want it."
And, he did want it.   I draped string-lights along the wall

and bought him new clothes.   We collected a few things
from the apartment where his mother abandoned him
and we went home.

Was I supposed to leave him?
                         I could not leave him.

Debris & Dangled Dreams Resurrected for Sleeping Trees #062818 (walnut ink, sumi ink, silver leaf, pigments, minerals, gofun on torinoko paper, 8x8) by Krystal Hart

North Carolina native and resident **KRYSTAL HART** received her BFA from the New York Institute of Technology. Her honors and residencies include a 2009 and 2012 Limner Society Residency, a 2011 and 2017 North Carolina Regional Artist Grant, and the 2018 Mass MoCA Masters of Abstraction Workshop in Residency. Read more about the artst and see more in this series and others on her website at krystalhart.com.

COURTESY OF THE ARTIST

Surface (mixed media collage on canvas, 36x48) by Monique Luck

BY AMBER FLORA THOMAS

To the Island

Passing through the channel, we
roar across a dolphin pod. Cameras come out.
A woman leans beside the signs: *Keep your hands
inside the boat. No swimming.*
Their diving follows a krill run

until there are fewer gray circles
in the waves. I make   the first movement
toward memory,   drawing loss.
The engine starts up again, the boat
cruising a curved route we follow
to the island.

*

I remember being poured
into the sky afterwards because
this was where our eyes ended up,
gazing out the window. Separate selves
preparing to leave.

Look how we met through branches, like
enveloped camellias pressing the same
space into fray. You and I, young still,
bumping and slick, our
infinite   conceptual   petal bombs.
Ask me about magenta:
nowhere other than inside you.

*

We bank alongside a kid emptying
a bucket of fish guts into the sea
and gulls drop to riot over the meal.

I couldn't admit to being a lesbian
        until I'd loved you
                all these years. Your absence:
                wish-filled and absolute.

*

Again, I draw my finger through sweat along your spine
and stash it in my mouth.

I'll return a call from my mother
so she can wish me a happy birthday.
You'll go off to make dinner.
And work tomorrow.

*

It tears me up to think of you.

MONIQUE LUCK is from Charlotte, NC. Her numerous honors include the Judges' Choice award and Best in Show at Festival in the Park and Best Bearden-Inspired Collage at the Mint Museum, both in Charlotte. Her art has been exhibited in many galleries and museums across the US, including the African American Museum of Dallas, the South Carolina State Museum, the Heinz History Center Museum in Pittsburgh, and the Harvey B. Gantt Center Museum in Charlotte. See more of her art on her website at moniqueluck.com.

BY AMBER FLORA THOMAS

To Home

The third mile, and by then
the mountain flattens in the river's green trench.
I am looking west.

Horses corralled beside banking shadow
slouch in the heat. Deep breath
flares in a muzzle marbled by dust. Velvet

wrinkles as she takes the grass,
a single water-bead running from her nasal
cup. She crushes the grass into its last rain,

quieting as a cloud's brief journey cools.
Her eyelids lower. She wakes again,
pawing the earth. I give her handfuls

from the ditch along the road, breath
rattles through her belly. Sleeping
while eating: habitual. The jaw's slow

evolutions work in her eyes. Sweat starts
inside my elbow where her head rests.
I slip back into forms I recognize,

shapes I can take up again. Thick
through the flank, rough coat shivering
about a horsefly. Everywhere else is gone.

Quadra II (pencil, gouache, and watercolor on wood panel, 25.5cmx25.5cm)
by Pamela Phatsimo Sunstrum

PAMELA PHATSIMO SUNSTRUM, born in Mochudi, Botswana, is a figurative artist and designer. She received her BA with Highest Honors from UNC Chapel Hill in International Studies with a concentration in Transnational Cultures in 2004 and her MFA from the Mount Royal School of Art at the Maryland Institute College of Art in 2007. In 2013, her work "ab initio" was featured at Davidson College in Davidson, NC, while she was artist-in-residence. Her recent exhibitions and performances include FRAC Pays de Loire in France in 2013, Brundyn Gallery in Johannesburg in 2014, MoCADA in New York in 2011, and the 2012 Havana Biennial. She currently lives and works between Johannesburg, South Africa, and Ontario, Canada.

"seeing the opportunity in tomorrow":

An Interview with Jason Mott

by Jennifer Larson

With his critically acclaimed and wildly popular debut novel, *The Returned* (2013), Jason Mott quickly became one of North Carolina's brightest literary stars. *The Returned* centers around Harold and Lucille, an elderly couple, and Jacob, their eight-year-old son. Jacob died in 1966, but suddenly reappears, along with countless others around the world. The family's small hometown of Arcadia, North Carolina, becomes a microcosm of the world's disorientation and prejudice when the government establishes a military installation there to detain "The Returned," who come to represent both the past's most painful wounds and the future's potential for healing those wounds.

Mott's popularity grew with the adaptation of *The Returned* into the ABC drama *Resurrection* and with the success of his second novel, *The Wonder of All Things* (2014), which is slated to become a Lionsgate film adaption by acclaimed director Cheryl Dunye. Again, set in North Carolina, *The Wonder of All Things* tells the story of a young girl with miraculous healing powers that harm her as she helps others. Mott has also published two volumes of poetry, *We Call this Thing Between Us Love* (2009) and *. . . hide behind me . . .* (2011), and he was nominated for a 2009 Pushcart Prize.[1]

Mott's most recent novel, *The Crossing*, was released in 2018.[2] The novel follows two runaway orphaned twins, Virginia and Tommy, as they journey to Cape Canaveral to watch the launch of a probe that will explore Jupiter's moon Europa. The mission represents the last glimmer of hope in a world devastated by plague and war.

Amidst all this success, Mott still remains firmly connected and committed to his home state. He hails from Bolton, a small town in Eastern North Carolina. He earned a BA in fiction and an MFA in poetry from UNC Wilmington, where he is currently a Writer-in-Residence.

This interview was conducted in early August 2018, and was minimally edited to streamline questions and consolidate answers.

JENNIFER LARSON: *How do you think your work has changed – or perhaps evolved is a better word – between* The Returned *and* The Crossing*?*

JASON MOTT: That's actually a pretty tough question. My work has definitely changed, but it's a little tricky defining exactly how it's changed. In the time between *The Returned* and *The Crossing*, I've had a lot of personal changes. I've gone from working a job I hated to doing my life's passion for a living. I've also had a lot of changes in my personal life. So combine all of that with my natural progression as a writer, and it's a recipe for a lot of change. To nail it down though, I guess I'd say that I've become a little more aware of my voice as a writer. We spend years trying to figure out what we're trying to say as writers, and while I still think there's more for me to learn, I like to believe that in the last five years I've come to understand my own voice a bit better. I hope that I've learned to be myself as a writer, which is one of the hardest things to do, in my opinion.

You have said in other interviews that you see yourself reflected in Agent Bellamy of The Returned. *Do you see similar reflections in any of the characters from your more recent works?*

I'm always hiding behind characters. I feel like I always have been, and I always will be. So I'm most definitely in my more recent works. In my second novel, *The Wonder of All Things*, I took up residence inside the father of the main character, Ava. Bellamy was a man trying to do the best that he could for his family and, sometimes, failing at it. That's a very common fear for me, and so I used that character to explore some of those things within myself. And, for *The Crossing*, I split myself between the two main characters, Tommy and Virginia. Virginia, with her perfect memory, represents the things I can never forget. And her brother, Tommy, with his inability to remember anything, represents the things that have gone and can never come back. They were a pair of characters inspired by mythology, and, in the same way that mythology represents cultures, they stood in for me.

Any specific mythology?

There isn't any specific one, actually. Twins are features in multiple mythologies, especially twin brothers and sisters: in Egyptian mythology, there were Nut and Geb; in Greek mythology, Apollo and Artemis; and many, many others. Twins in mythology are almost always used to represent related opposites. Opposite sides of the same coin, if you will. So with Tommy and Virginia, I used that same type of inseparable connection in trying to create them and tell their story.

Another fascinating element in The Crossing *is "The Memory Gospel," the vast collection of memories Virginia keeps because she can't forget anything she sees, hears, or experiences. What was your inspiration for this?*

That came from my inability to let certain things go in my life. At least, that's where it first came from. There are certain life events that I've never been able to let go of and forget, no matter how much I may want to. And, naturally, they can be burdensome at times. So I tried to imagine what it might be like if you were always carrying around every moment of your life that way. I tried to think about how that might manifest itself, what it would be like to truly never be able

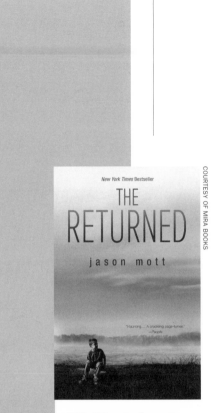

New York Times Bestseller

THE
RETURNED

j a s o n   m o t t

"Haunting... A crackling page-turner."
—People

COURTESY OF MIRA BOOKS

"Writing's tough.
. . . you have to
commit to it in
a way that most
people don't
expect."

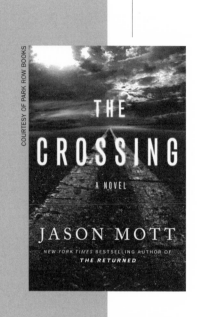

to let go of anything. And the more I thought about it, the more I realized just how terrible it would be. Forgetting is a healthy thing, even if they are the things we don't want to ever forget. The brain needs to let go of certain things in order to move forward. I wanted to have a conversation about that, and Virginia and Tommy became the medium for that conversation.

"The Memory Gospel" also allows Virginia to tell much of the novel's story since she can report others' reminiscences as well as her own. The result is an engaging first person/third person semi-omniscient hybrid narration. Was this challenging to write? Fun? Or something in between?

It was extremely challenging to write. My editor and I wrestled with a lot of that in the revision process. There were constant questions of how characters would know certain things and how we could convey that to the reader. It took a lot of nuance and careful rereading. But, if I'm honest, I'll have to say that it was also pretty fun at times as well.

I also see this nuance in the father's letters. They are so beautiful and inspiring. One of my favorite lines in the novel is actually from one of these letters. He writes, "the future was always meant to be a promise, not a threat" (41). Do you agree? The alternate present/future that The Crossing *offers is pretty scary at times.*

I definitely agree with that. I have to remind myself of it some days. It's so easy to get caught up in how terrible everything seems. Social media, in particular, is good for fear mongering. Everything seems terrible, and we're perpetually afraid of what tomorrow will bring. But I don't believe that's the way it's supposed to be. I think we could all benefit from seeing the opportunity in tomorrow and not the threat.

And how do you think we can do that? The father is a writer. So is writing, perhaps, a kind of vehicle for this?

I wish I had the answer for that. But it's different for everyone. For me, writing is definitely the vehicle for that. It's the way through which I understand myself, others, the world, and life itself. But that's not true of everyone. We all have to find the vehicle that allows us to find some degree of optimism about what tomorrow will bring. And we have to hold on to that thing and, at the same time, share it with others.

Another line I kept coming back to was Virginia's claim that, "We build oceans of life under the surface of ourselves. And those around us only get to see what they choose to see, never what we are" (317). This is a very challenging idea, and I found myself really thinking about what it is I choose to see in others. Is this a kind of call to action?

I think it's hard to show ourselves to others. I'm as guilty of it as anyone else. Honestly, I'd probably say I'm more guilty. And the blade cuts the other way as well. It's hard to see people for who they are. We adorn others with our own expectations of them without ever really allowing them time to show us who they are independent from our expectations. From the moment we meet someone, we expect certain types of things from them – manners, eye contact, civility, whatever – and they do the same toward us. So with that recipe, it's difficult to strip away that veneer of social programming to really be ourselves. So we all skip across the surface of one another like stones that never sink. But how wonderful it would be to really dive into another person, to really see them for who they are, wholly and complete. And how wonderful it would be to be truly "seen" by someone else.

Meanwhile, the foster father, Gannon, who I found to be a very enigmatic character, tells Tommy that "the world can only be one way" (241). This assertion almost seems to be the antithesis to the rest of the novel; yet, it's a tempting philosophy. What were you hoping readers would take from Gannon?

Gannon was a very complex character for me. In fact, I'd argue that he might have been the most layered and complicated character in the novel. He's someone who exists with a well-defined version of what the world is, of what life is, and he refuses to deviate from that path. That creates a powerful type of character with a powerful world view. With Gannon, my hope was that characters would see him as someone who, just like Tommy and Virginia, was trying to do his best. He's not an evil man; he's just committed to his belief of how the world is. Whether or not that belief is wrong is up for debate, and that debate is what I wanted readers to walk away with.

Speaking of debates, much of the novel feels like an intense philosophical debate over the nature of – and relationships among – memory, history, trauma, and healing. Did you feel your ideas about any or all of these changing as you were writing the novel?

Yes and no. I spent a lot of time researching memory and trauma as I worked on this novel. I wanted to be able to cite real-world things and use them as lighthouses as I drifted out into the sea of fiction. So I went into the writing with a fairly open mind in regard to what memory, history, etc., meant to me. And, over the course of the writing, I let my characters create the conversation all on their own. I learned about myself as my characters learned about themselves. What I came away with was a belief that we each have to decide how much sway the past holds over us. Memory can imprison or liberate; the choice is ours.

Virginia even goes so far as to say that "life without memory" would be "freedom" (215). Yet, Tommy doesn't always seem to see it this way. Is this disagreement part of the debate?

Exactly. Those two characters are opposites for that exact reason. The fact that they're twins adds a bit of the mythological element I talked about earlier. In olden days, a brother and sister – one who always

> **"Reduced by time and distance to little more than a pinprick of noiseless light. That's how memory was supposed to work. A narrowing down. A softening that made it possible to let go of unwanted or painful memories."**
> —*The Crossing* (20)

forgets and one who never forgets – would have been right at home in any mythological pantheon. I grew up with a love of mythology and folklore almost from the moment that I could read, and so it was very rewarding to create these two semi-mythological characters.

Folklore can also sometimes be very tied to a specific location. What is the role of "place" in The Crossing*? The Returned is very much situated in a specific place, even to the point that rural North Carolina feels like a character in itself. In* The Crossing*, though, the focus is on the journey. What inspired this change?*

Honestly, that mostly came about as a way of pushing myself as a writer. I tend to gravitate toward stories that are confined to a single place. It's where I'm comfortable as a writer. But I'm always looking to evolve and grow as a writer, and so I wanted to do something different for this novel by having it be an odyssey of sorts. So I put the two of them on the road and waited to see what awaited them.

It's kind of a "space" odyssey, I suppose. In fact, the novel seems very focused on the science of some of the novel's key events. Are you a science buff? Or did you have to do significant research?

I'm such a nerd! You have no idea. Even though I'm a fiction writer, about three-quarters of my reading is nonfiction. Maybe more. Science and philosophy are my favorites. I subscribe to science magazines. I spend hours drinking in the decadence of philosophy theories. In *The Crossing*, Jupiter's moon Europa is the focal point of Tommy and Virginia's journey. And that's because Europa is my favorite moon. – Yes, I'm the type of nerd who has a favorite moon.

I love that. And it's awesome to see this reflected in the novel. You also mentioned trauma studies and mythology, but, thinking more generally, what kind of and how much research do you usually do for your writing?

It depends. I'm always researching something or other. Sometimes that research features prominently in my stories, and other times it doesn't. For *The Crossing*, I went down to Cape Canaveral to watch a rocket launch. Sadly, the launch was scrubbed two minutes before launch, but I still had the great enjoyment of walking around the Kennedy Space Center and seeing the decommissioned rockets first hand. My inner eight-year-old was giddy the entire time.

Sometimes when I was reading The Crossing, *I could almost see the movie version in my head. Do you think about this possibility as you craft a text? And since* The Wonder of All Things *is also headed for the screen, what lessons learned from* Resurrection *do you hope to apply to working on the next adaptation?*

I watch a lot of movies and my writing style has been called "cinematic" before. I guess that one influences the other sometimes. But I don't think about whether or not something will be made into a

"My goal is always just to give the readers a world to live within and to let them take from it what they choose to."

ABOVE **Jason Mott speaking at the North**

movie when I'm writing it. I just focus on telling the story and letting it unfold however it best needs to unfold. My goal is always just to give the readers a world to live within and to let them take from it what they choose to. I try to create as many conversations as I can within the world of a story.

Your work is also a bit critical of media, TV and movies included. How do you hope that critique comes through in the adaptations?

I hope that it simply comes through as one of the many "conversations" I try to have in my work. Yes, I can be critical of media in my writings, but I try to be critical of a lot of other things as well. It's important for all of us to think critically about the world around us. None of it is meant to be disparaging about the media, simply to say that we all need to examine them rather than, as we so often do, sit idly by and let them wash over us.

So how did working on Resurrection *shape your feelings about writing for the screen?*

I feel like *Resurrection* was faithful to the heart and spirit of my novel, and I think that's the most anyone can ask for. The fact of the matter is that television and film are dramatically different mediums. So it's impossible to expect adaptations to be exactly the same. Personally, I really enjoyed *Resurrection*. Aaron Zelman and the cast worked really hard and made something to be proud of. I've always been a television and movie fan, and I've long toyed with the idea of writing within those mediums. And so when I got to see the inner working of *Resurrection* and how things happened there, I actually had a conversation with the showrunner, Aaron Zelman, and mentioned to him that I was thinking about writing for TV and film. He was surprisingly supportive and even began to act as a type of mentor for me. And, since then, I've entered into the screenwriting world and have been thoroughly enjoying it. Having said that, however, I try not to let it color my novel writing. Novels are very special things for me. They're the reason I love writing the most. And so, when I work on a project, I try to do it in a vacuum. I don't think about whether or not it will be adapted. I just try to make it the best project I can.

Do you think your literary influences show in your writing as well? As I read your work, I feel like I hear and see allusions to a diverse group of writers, including Faulkner, Morrison, Yates, and Mosley, just to name a few. What writers or artists do you see as influencing you most significantly or profoundly?

My two biggest influences are John Gardner and William Golding. They're the writers I most admire. John Gardner's *Grendel* is the book that made me want to be a writer. And William Golding's *Lord of the Flies* is the book that I most admire as a writer. I could talk for hours about their influence on me.

PHOTOGRAPH BY DAVID LEONE; COURTESY OF THE NORTH CAROLINA WRITERS' NETWORK

"The South is in a state of flux right now. It has been for a while. It's a region that's struggling to both define and understand itself."

More immediately, what are you reading now or what have you read lately that's really moving you?

As I mentioned it's mostly nonfiction for me these days. Lots of science books. But, for fiction, I've become a big fan of Taylor Brown and Wiley Cash. Now, I'm biased because they're both local writers that I know personally, but they're both doing great work apart from our friendship. They're both writers who are committed to talking about the Southern experience. They talk about its past, present, and future, and those are things that don't get discussed enough. So I really enjoy their work. Plus, they're just a couple of really cool guys.

Speaking of literary traditions, where do you see yourself fitting in to North Carolina's literary traditions?

Honestly, I have no idea. I don't think I get to decide that, and I wouldn't even know how to speculate. I'm just happy to have the opportunity to contribute to the tradition.

That's fair. So how about this: What do you see as the future of North Carolina literature?

I think the future of North Carolina literature is one of change. The South is in a state of flux right now. It has been for a while. It's a region that's struggling to both define and understand itself. In the midst of those changes, I think some blistering new voices will emerge and stand as touchstones of a Southern writing tradition that is different than what we may know right now. And I think that's vitally important.

More tangibly, as you guide the next generation of North Carolina writers – your students at UNC Wilmington – what advice do you give them?

I mainly just offer practical advice about the reality of writing. Writing's tough. Really tough. And you have to commit to it in a way that most people don't expect. So I talk to my students mostly just about understanding why they want to be writers and what that dream might look like as reality.

Finally, the quintessential end-of-interview question: What's next? Another novel? More poetry? A totally new adventure?

I love your enthusiasm. As for what's next, I've got a couple of novel projects in the works. I'm always working on something. But I'm really hoping to get my legs underneath me in the world of screenwriting. I've had some small successes there, nothing I can talk about right now though. And, hopefully, that will continue to progress, and I'll be able to talk about a lot of cool new things on the horizon. ■

FINALIST, 2018 JAMES APPLEWHITE POETRY PRIZE

BY KEVIN DUBLIN

Divorce

He caches good judgement in the same bag
as love for his enemy.
Reach for one and grab the other.

Disorder is a source of many mistakes.
The last of which was simply loving.
The warped reflection of face
in the doorknob covered by hand.

Closing a room emptied of its dark corners,
full moon glow washes through windows, the whole floor,
with no furniture and only memory of shadow:

Bars of a crib against far wall,
crawl of static through monitor,
scrapbook pages cricut and turned over –
now just freeway woosh scratching screen mesh.

His first step frictions into the long hallway –
walls closer than when he entered. Ears pierced
by the needle of silence – a heavy ring.

Fault divined in a crow's caw –
or maybe it's less.
When he empties his bags,
he'll place each item with more care.

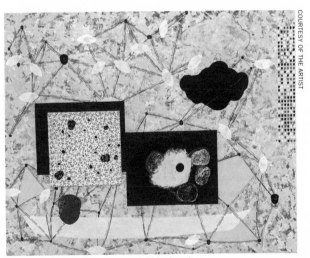

COURTESY OF THE ARTIST

Elegy X, 2017 (acrylic on canvas, 4x5) by Juan Logan

KEVIN DUBLIN is the author of the chapbook *How to Fall in Love in San Diego* (Finishing Line Press, 2017) and editor of Etched Press. He holds an MFA from San Diego State University, an MA from East Carolina University (where he served as an *NCLR* editorial assistant and was selected the department's Most Outstanding Graduate Student when he graduated), and a BFA from UNC Wilmington. His poetry has appeared in *Rogue Agent, Menacing Hedge, Poetry International*, and more. He also makes video adaptations of poetry and works with emerging artists and writers in the community. He has taught at Duke Young Writers' Camp and North Carolina State's Teen Writing Workshop and currently teaches as a part of LitQuake's Elder Writing Project and The Writing Salon in San Francisco.

Born in Nashville, TN, **JUAN LOGAN** received his MFA from the Maryland Institute College of Art. He now lives in Belmont, NC, and is the Conservation Manager at the Vollis Simpson Whirligig Project for the City of Wilson. He has received fellowships from the John Michael Kohler Arts Center, the North Carolina Arts Council, and the Mid Atlantic Arts Foundation, a Carolina Postdoctoral Scholars Fellowship, and a Pollination Project grant for *The Waiting Project*. His work has been exhibited nationally and internationally. His pieces can be found in private, corporate, and public collections, including the Whitney Museum of American Art, the Philadelphia Museum of Art, and the Baltimore Museum of Art. Recently, his piece *Some Clouds are Darker* became part of the Smithsonian's National Museum of African American History and Culture. See more of his work in *NCLR* 2018 and on his website at www.juanlogan.com.

Glenis Redmond:
Poet,
Teaching Artist,
Griot

an interview by Lisa Sarasohn

PHOTOGRAPH BY WILL CROOKS

Glenis Redmond entering a room is an event. Glenis entered my home in Asheville on a Saturday afternoon in June. She arrives wearing a black t-shirt, with white letters spelling out "'We the people' means everyone." The sentence circles an upraised fist.

Glenis is rooted in family. She is Jeanette Redmond's devoted daughter, mother to twins Amber and Celeste, and Gaga to grandson Julian. As a friend and colleague, I've witnessed her Afro-Carolinian profession of poetry for more than twenty years. Her accolades and achievements as poet and teacher of poetry are many. Just a sampling: MFA in Poetry from Warren Wilson College in Swannanoa, North Carolina; a Cave Canem Fellow; co-creator of the Writer-in-Residence program at the Carl Sandburg Home National Historic Site in Flat Rock, North Carolina. Mentor Poet for the National Student Poets Program; Artist-in-Residence at the State Theatre in New Brunswick, New Jersey; and Poet-in-Residence at the Peace Center for the Performing Arts in Greenville, South Carolina.

In her post at the Peace Center, Glenis has created and continues to curate Peace Voices, the program through which she conducts school and community poetry-writing workshops and mentors teens as Poetry Ambassadors. She also organizes and moderates Poetic Conversations, a series of free community events that feature acclaimed poets in readings, dialogues, and audience talkbacks on topics reflecting the diversity of Greenville's population.

> "When I put pen to paper, a fire started within me."

Her publications include poems published in the *North Carolina Literary Review*, *When Women Waken*, *Obsidian: Black Literature in Review*, *Red Rock Review*, *The Cortland Review*, *The Tidal Basin Review*, and *EMRYS*. She has also published poetry collections: *What My Hand Say*, *Under The Sun*, and *Backbone*.[1]

COURTESY OF PRESS 53

What My Hand Say

Poems
Glenis Redmond

---

[1] Glenis Redmond, *What My Hand Say* (Press 53, 2016; reviewed in *NCLR Online* 2018), *Under The Sun* (Main Street Rag, 2008), and *Backbone* (Underground Epics Poetry, 2000).

Seven of her poems have been finalists in *NCLR*'s James Applewhite Poetry Prize competition since 2011; her essay "Poetry as a Mirror" was selected by Tayari Jones as runner-up for the Teachers & Writers Collaborative's 2018 Bechtel Prize; her workshop on place-based poetry, "Writing to Right Place," was selected for presentation at the 2018 International Teaching Artist Conference on artists' roles and impact in global communities; *Women of Consequence*, the multi-media production animating her poems on three influential African American women, "The Three Harriets," was selected for presentation at the 2018 Dance and the Child International/World Dance Alliance Congress.

As a poet and teaching artist, first with Asheville-based Poetry Alive! and Loyd Artists and then with the John F. Kennedy Center for the Performing Arts, Glenis has toured statewide, nationwide, across the border to Canada, and to points around the globe for more than twenty-five years. She's consistently logged more than thirty-five thousand miles of touring a year. Even with her Peace Center and State Theatre New Jersey residencies, Glenis still takes poetry on the road. In the last two years, for example, touring has taken her from Asheville to Adelaide, Australia; from Hendersonville to Hawaii; and to many places in between.

Wherever she presents poetry, Glenis begins by "charging the atmosphere." Being present, being mindful, being intentional – Glenis inhabits these attributes as she launches poems into presence. She speaks poems out, yes. And she sets the stage for listeners to take them in. She engenders listening, shaping a space in which her audience becomes available, receptive to poems in their essence. The atmosphere she charges becomes the medium through which people connect to poetry. In her poetry and her presence, Glenis enlists word and image to speak truth and stand in dignity. Moment by moment, she lives the poet's life. Even so, she expands "poet" to mean imagination activist, social justice warrior, and – in alignment with her West African lineage – *griot*.

In this conversation, Glenis reflects on poetry as sustainer, healer, and refuge in her life as a black woman confronting racism in North Carolina and the nation.[2] Glenis arrives as an emissary of unity, and love, in the struggle for justice. Receive her words as you would an all-encompassing embrace.

LISA SARASOHN: *How has North Carolina figured in your writing life?*

GLENIS REDMOND: I always say that South Carolina planted the seed of poetry and North Carolina made me come full bloom.

I was living in South Carolina when I started writing poetry in middle school. When I came back to poetry, after graduate school in Texas and Virginia, I was living in Simpsonville, South Carolina. I moved back to South Carolina in 1990. Two years later, I was diagnosed with fibromyalgia. I was twenty-nine. I knew that I needed to connect to my heart and my spirit again, and so that's where poetry came in. I heard Lucille Clifton's line: " . . . everyday / something has tried to kill me / and has failed."[3] I asked myself, "What is it

"North Carolina made me come full bloom."

ABOVE **The dancing Harriets of** *The Three Harriets*, **a Peace Passport Field Trip Series production of the Greenville, SC, Peace Center; front to back, Amber Rance as Harriet Jacobs, Ikira Peace as Harriet Tubman, April Singleton as Harriet E. Wilson**

2 Lisa Sarasohn interviewed Glenis Redmond on 2 June 2018 (with follow-up questions via email). *NCLR* interns Alyssa Coleman, Jordan Crawford, and Dylan Newitt Allen transcribed the recorded interview. The interviewer then edited the transcription for ~~~th clarity and flow while preserving the voices and intentions of the speakers.

3 Lucille Clifton, "won't you celebrate with me." *The Collected Poems of Lucille Clifton 1965–2010*. ed. Kevin Young and Michael S. Glaser (BOA Editions) 2012. 427.

PHOTOGRAPH BY HERBERT RESPESS, IV

that can help me celebrate life and not feel like I am dying?" and I remembered poetry. I was a clinical counselor for the State of South Carolina, and that was killing me; I was giving away too much. I was not tapped into my spirit.

Two things happened simultaneously. A flyer from the North Carolina Writers' Network came to my mailbox – I don't know how – announcing a poetry slam. I got on the phone and called the number: "What is a poetry slam?" I went up to Asheville and found the Green Door on Carolina Lane, and found out what a slam was. Right around that time, in 1994, I was leaving the counseling world. I was at my last conference as a counselor. I was buying all these books, and I told my friend, "Don't let me buy one more book!" Of course, there was one more book; it was *The Artist's Way* by Julia Cameron, and I picked it up.[4] I was buying my books from Malaprop's Bookstore, and that was my first encounter with Asheville's independent bookstore. I started traveling up to Malaprop's, and every time I'd go up and spend time there, it seemed like a book would just fall off the shelf into my palm. Those two things simultaneously, the slam and Malaprop's Bookstore, were guiding me.

Even before that, I'd come up to Asheville on a weekend with my then-husband, Blane Sherer. I'd been very sick; it was fibromyalgia, but I didn't know that at the time. I was really sick, and I wanted to get away from Simpsonville. We stayed on the outskirts of Asheville. I picked up a newspaper, the *Mountain Xpress*, and I opened it. Asheville Poetry Festival was happening that weekend. I was like, "Oh my God! A poetry festival!" and that blew my mind. I was too sick to go, so I put it in the back of my mind and said, "I'm going to come back to that; one day I'll get back to that."

So those were the entry points to North Carolina for me. When I got up to the poetry festival the next year and had such a great time, I told Blane, "I want to live here." I needed to get out of South Carolina. With the conservatism of South Carolina, I just couldn't be my full self. I couldn't flare; I couldn't be full-fledged. I gained my poetry wings in North Carolina. That sixty miles up the mountain to Asheville allowed me to have another perspective, to breathe.

I felt like I was being driven by my ancestors in the Cherokee mountains. There is a connection moving through those sixty miles. My father later told me that his mother would walk from South Carolina to North Carolina. She would walk on the weekends to Asheville to visit family. I feel like that's what I'm always doing with my poetry, tracing the migration of my ancestors.

I've never defined myself as a slam poet. But the slam was a great venue for me because it's open to call and response, my Afro-Carolinian style. I don't mind being called a "performance poet," but I really don't think that what I'm doing is performance. I like the word *griot*, I like the singing tradition of West Africa – that is what suits me best. But I am grateful to slam because it was a doorway in.

> "I feel like that's what I'm always doing with my poetry, tracing the migration of my ancestors."

Poetry Alive! was another doorway in.[5] The very first time I came up to the slam in Asheville, there was Bob Falls, co-founder of Poetry Alive!, sitting in the audience. I was doing "Hats"; that was one of my earliest poems. He came up to me and said, "I really like your style. Would you want to go on the road and do poetry?" I said, "Sure, sign me up!"

I was immersed in poetry. Working with Poetry Alive! I was memorizing contemporary and classic poetry, going into the schools nine a.m. to three p.m., putting on three shows a day, five days a week. I was slamming at night. I was going to churches, I was going to Girl Scouts; anywhere somebody would have me, that's where I went. I wanted to express myself fully, creatively.

I put myself on the accelerated path, and I did it intentionally. I read the *Poet's Market* and it said, "Poet, don't be content with writing a book. Go out and create your audience." And that's what I did. Nonstop. I was going out and creating an audience. I appreciated the call-and-response aspect of poetry, creating spaces with live poetry, having a conversation with the audience. It was circular to me, and it was healing. That's what got me here.

The first house I lived in when I moved to Asheville in 1995, I say it chose me. I had already seen that yellow house on Forest Hill Drive. Before I even knew it was for rent I said, "This is the house I want to live in." So when Hedy Fischer told me that she had a house to rent, I was blown away when it was that yellow house. I was determined to buy that house. But after my divorce from Blane in 1997, my daughters and I had been living below the poverty line. I mean, I was indigent. The prospect of buying that house seemed to be out of the question. Then, when I went national as a solo artist, that changed my finances. I was able to purchase that house when it came on the market in 1999. A lot happened when I was living there, and I believe I was supposed to be there.

When I moved to Asheville, people were saying there had been no slaves in Western North Carolina. Not true. Living in that yellow house, I lived three blocks from a slave cemetery. I learned that Forest Hill Drive follows the track of a major Native American trail. I knew I had a couple of drops of Native American blood. I don't profess to be Native American, but I have some drops, and I knew that ancestry guided me. And right behind that yellow house was a Confederate cemetery. So, imagine the confluence of where I lived – Native American trail, slave cemetery, Confederate cemetery. My house was a spiritual weigh station. I blew open. I started to ground myself and become more aware of my ancestry, what the ethers are trying to tell me.

In *A Poetry Handbook*, Mary Oliver says that there are two documents in poetry. There's the craft document, which everybody studies. That's the devices, how to work yourself around a page. And then there is the mystical document, which no one talks about. Those are

> "I appreciated the call-and-response aspect of poetry . . . having a conversation with the audience."

COURTESY OF MOUNTAIN XPRESS

the ethers; the inspiration, for lack of a better terminology.[6] Asheville spoke to me mystically as a poet. It helped me to open up.

Eastern Carolina has been a powerful space for me, too. I came across Harriet Jacobs when I was doing my travels in Edenton. She hid in an attic for seven years to escape her slave owner, who had

raped her. She escaped, went north, and became an abolitionist and published her autobiography. I wrote "House: Another Kind of Field" for her.[7] Being in Edenton also got me connected to my ancestors. I was surrounded by cotton fields, no television, hardly any internet or cell phone service. There were three plantations; I went to two of them. I wrote the poem for my great-grandfather, "What My Hand Say," in Edenton. A lot has opened for me there.

Opening began for me in 1989 with the birth of my daughters – my twins, Amber and Celeste. As soon as I was carrying them, that is when I became a different being. In *Under the Sun*, there's a poem called "Birthdays." When I talk about multiples in that poem, I'm including myself because there was a part of me being birthed along with them. When I became a mama, I became more in tune with the world and the universe. That was a creative opening. I landed with a force: I am here now. It was like I was waiting on these two beings to come into my world. It was more imperative than ever to create when my children came into the world. I shifted.

How did the Ku Klux Klan help launch your career?

> *"Living a life artistically and creatively, that's rebellion, and it's the way I encounter social justice."*

Just a few years ago, you could say "KKK" and everyone would be shocked and go "Huh?!" But now people say, "Well, there's been a resurgence." In 1997, it was that "Huh?! Really? They're marching here? In our town?" But here's the thing about Western North Carolina, and about living in Asheville for me as a black woman and poet: it doesn't take you but a mile or two to get out of the city limits and face that hate. And believe me, I have been in those sundown towns where if you're black, by sundown you need to be gone. I knew that existed, but we live in a little bit of a bubble in Asheville. Then these KKK people were going to march through downtown, they're penetrating our bubble. Kali Alaia Brewer called me and said, "We've got the KKK; we're doing a unity rally, and we want you there." And I said, "Of course I want to be there!" At the Reid Recreation Center, at a distance from downtown, people were going to be singing and dancing.

That has always been my way to protest: artistically. Living a life artistically and creatively, that's rebellion, and it's the way I encounter social justice. Maya Angelou says that you come as one, but you "stand as ten thousand."[8] At this Stand & Sing rally, there were probably twenty, thirty thousand ancestors with me. I was doing a poem called "If I Ain't African." It was one of those poems that just came in, and I didn't edit it – it is the way it is. It's one of those singing poems, I would call them, from West Africa.

With my poems – this is why I don't call them a performance – when the ancestors show up, it's an experience, even for me. They showed up that day in 1997. I guess they knew we were doing battle and they were like, "these people need us." And so they were there with me. I was empowered; I was emboldened. It wasn't me; a force was moving through me. When I got finished with "If I Ain't African," swinging my braids around, dancing, and doing whatever I was doing, everybody got up on their feet, and it was this moment. John Loyd and Peggy Baldwin, co-owners of the Loyd Artists booking agency, were at the rally. They came up to me and said, "If that's what you do, I think you might work on our roster." I signed the very next day with Loyd Artists. What I find heartening about that intersection – this is the key to my work, social justice. The thread is social justice, pushing back. For me to gain national recognition through that act talks about who I am.

Where in North Carolina have you worked as a poet and teaching artist?

In my early days, I worked a lot with non-profits in Western North Carolina: the YWCA, homeless shelters, half-way houses, the rape crisis center Our Voice, the domestic violence agency Helpmate. I became the poster child for every non-profit in Asheville. There was an after-school program in Asheville called Project STEAM. Christopher Tunstall created it. He said, "I'd like you to come over and talk to my kids." These were kids from disadvantaged homes, but they weren't disadvantaged students. They were talented. I would work with them every Monday from three to five p.m. for eight weeks. That was my first residency in my town, Project STEAM. There was another after-school program in Brevard, called Rise & Shine.[9] Fay Walker got ahold of me and she convinced me to travel to Brevard every Friday. This was 1997; I was in my old rickety Suzuki Sidekick that I could hardly drive; it was a stick. I would go to Brevard every Friday and do after-care there.

Those are examples of me working in the community, working with young people. Even though I was traveling, I would come and be invested in young people in my area. It taught me a lot of how to be in the community. I toured as a poet and teaching artist with

> "When the ancestors show up, it's an experience, even for me."

PHOTOGRAPH BY AMY RANDALL

Poetry Alive! in 1994, and then with Loyd Artists in 1998. In 2004, the Kennedy Center for the Performing Arts put me in their national directory. As a Kennedy Center Teaching Artist, I started working with even more schools and colleges all over the country. That catapulted me out of North Carolina. But then I was at a conference, having a conversation with somebody from the North Carolina Arts Council and I said, "You know, I really don't work in the state much." And the Arts Council person was like, "What's wrong with this picture?" So I did a showcase for the Arts Council, and I started traveling all over the state. You name it, I've been there. In the last twelve years, I'd have to say the eastern part of the state really adopted me – Wilmington, Kinston, Burgaw.

What happens in your classrooms and workshops?

I'm very intentional. I hold an intention that something powerful is going to happen here, and that I'll let it be what it's supposed to be. I don't know what it's going to be; I'm just opening the space to that. When I come in, then, I'm creating a circle. I think about my arms, long arms, wrapping around the whole space, like I have my arm around everybody that's in the room. That's how I think of Harriet Tubman. That's not to say that I know what each person needs; the universe knows that. What I'm doing is creating a safe space for us to create.

You come as one, but you "stand as ten thousand." I know that I have this legion of folks in the spirit world behind me. They're not all Africans; they're my literary ancestors; they are my bloodline. They're folks who are behind me because they've chosen me, and I'm honored. I feel like everyone has a lineage. When I walk into a room, I'm conscious that the room is full of all of these folks. You have twenty-five students; just think of the legions you have in that room. It's crowded!

When I come into a room, I am acting as a catalyst, I am lighting a fire. I consider myself a supplement, like I'm a vitamin. I am infusing nutrients of the imagination. I charge the environment just by walking into the room. I am walking into the room with my poet self, a storyteller, with ten thousand ancestors. Boom! I am a black woman with natural hair. A lot of kids have not seen the likes of me, ever. A lot of times I come in and I don't have a book in my hand. I am just saying the poems and they're like, "What?" There's something about words in the air that charges the air. I make myself a little magical. I envision myself in a patchwork dress, words all over my dress, this magical creature with poems in my pocket, poems in my heart. And then when I walk in, I am just giving away poems to people. That's all

> "I consider myself a supplement, like I'm a vitamin. I am infusing nutrients of the imagination."

ABOVE Glenis Redmond as Harriet Tubman for *The Three Harriets*, a Peace Passport Field Trip Series event, Gunter Theatre, Greenville, SC, Feb. 2019

PHOTOGRAPH BY WILL CROOKS

I'm doing, just giving away poems. Yes, there are lesson plans, there's craft. The biggest thing I do – I come with my backpack or my pockets full of poems and my heart full of poems. They're poems that are charged. They're charged for me.

How do you enlist poetry to charge the atmosphere?

I come into a space and ask myself, "What do I want to do for these people?" I don't know ahead of time; I usually figure it out when I get there. One of my favorite poems to open with right now is the poem "I'm Fly," for "Peg Leg" Bates, the one-legged tap dancer. At one time it was "Sing Your Song, Girl," an anthem to women to be yourself.

I did the commencement speech last week at the Fine Arts Center, and I did two poems for them. One poem is called "How I Write." It's an *ars poetica* poem. It talks about me going into the kitchen and cracking my whole self against the island counter. With one hand folding the yolk of myself into the container of a poem and stirring in the salt of my tears and the cayenne of my rage with my foremothers at my back. Only when they say "ready" do I serve. That is the recipe. That's how I write. The other poem I opened with was "Poetry Lesson 101," which is about me going into prisons for young people. It ends:

> I with nine-year-old heart
> on bended knee.
> I teach them poetry,
> they teach me
> how to Love.[10]

At the Fine Arts Center, I borrowed a page in my mama's book and talked to them about love. That was the way I chose to charge the atmosphere.

I don't have all my poems memorized, but there are certain poems where I'll go, "Oh! This will open it up." If I start in a performance way it can shock, in a positive way. Because they're like, "I'm not ready for this." It doesn't always have to be an energetic poem. I try to be true to myself. I might be sad. Then I'm either going to read a sorrowful poem, because this is the place I'm in, or I might read something to lift my spirits. Charging can happen in very different ways. Sometimes a quiet poem allows for us to go deeper in the writing process than a high-gear poem. I trust my intuition on that. I might start with a quiet poem, like the poem that I wrote for my middle school teacher who was a lifeline. She didn't know she was saving my life. I get back to the original place of creating the poem; that's the moment I want to give away.

---

[10] An early version of this poem appears in Redmond's collection *Backbone* (84–86). The Fine Arts Center in Greenville, SC, provides advanced instruction to high school students in theatre, dance, visual arts, music, creative writing, and filmmaking.

> *"I see pencils as magic wands. I tell them to tap the pencil to their heart and then write."*

COURTESY OF STATE THEATRE NEW JERSEY

What happens next?

Then I question them. What I'm doing as a poet is asking questions, intentional questions. I'm asking people to go on a quest. You go there, and there might be tears. There might be sadness. There might be sorrow. There might be laughter. I don't know what you're going to find. I do it very intentionally, and I do it very methodically. Then I say, "Write!" I see pencils as magic wands. I tell them to tap the pencil to their heart and then write. You are only limited by your imagination. I don't know what they're going to say. I can only create a rich environment. They get ten, twelve minutes. That's all they get, and magic happens. I am not doing therapy. The process may be therapeutic; it may be cathartic; it may be a catalyst, yes. We're in a pressure cooker because we're doing things quickly.

You call yourself an "imagination activist." What do you mean by that?

When I walk into a classroom, sometimes I see that kids have a failure of imagination. One time, I gave this superhero prompt: What are your superpowers? What do you wear? What would you do? And these kids were staring in the air. They couldn't even get into the land of imaginary play. I try to excite the imagination. I am trying to infuse that, expand that. I had a little middle schooler this past week. His name is David. He's a little kid who had been bullied. But I was in the classroom, and he just started talking. The teacher was embarrassed because he wouldn't stop talking. I said, "Let David talk." And David said, "Poems are so important. I was writing a poem to you. Do you want to hear it?" He read his poem on the spot and he said, "I always say that with my pen, I can do anything. My mind is like a pencil with unlimited lead." Everybody in the room went "Huh." And I said, "David, I am not worried about you. I am not worried." The land of metaphor is powerful. Kids learning to be fluent in metaphor is powerful.

You mentioned you think of yourself as a griot. *What is a* griot?

It's a West African tradition. It comes from a lineage where there's no written language, so to keep the lineage alive they had to tell the stories. They had to have a person who would sing the lineage into being, or recite it into being – history, songs, and poems. This person, the *griot*, would go village to village, making sure that people had memory of who they were. Keeping the lineage alive. Telling stories and connecting the community. Keeping the heart-fire alive.

I don't think women were technically *griots*, but it's a new world, so I consider myself one of those new world *griots*. I'm a woman who is a road warrior. I tell stories; I write poems. I try to connect people – especially connect with their heart, understand through the heart, navigate through the heart. I'm creating spaces.

I do like circles. I believe that what I'm creating is a sacred circle. I love to be in a circle with people. Not so much about hierarchy. I don't consider what I'm doing workshopping. I consider myself more of a facilitator or a guide.

I've taken a deep plunge as a poet. When I come back to the surface, I have something to give. I see my work as doing that deep-diving, coming back, and showing the treasures I've found. Here's this shell; this is what it's done for me, how I've rescued this part of myself. It's a part that belongs to me; I didn't know it belonged to me, but I need it for my journey. That's what I help people do – collect tokens and memories that they need for their journey. Or unburden things that they need to let go. That's some of the work that I do as a poet.

What have you discovered about your African ancestry?

In 2005, when I was pursuing my MFA in Poetry at Warren Wilson College, I decided to trace my genealogy. I found out that I am Cameroonian on my mother's side and Nigerian on my father's side. I learned the percentages of my ethnicity. I am 91.4 percent West African. When I was reading Judith Gleason's *Leaf and Bone: African Praise-Poems*, preparing to teach a workshop at Warren Wilson, I read that Nigerians were the chief praise poets of Africa.[11] This connection felt uncanny; previously unknown pieces of my lineage were connecting. I believe that, as a teenager, I had been guided by my ancestry to write praise poems. I did not consciously know the form or the history then, but my creative, mystical self knew.

My writing journey, and my dedication to writing praise poems, began at age thirteen. Ms. Sergeant had commanded, "Class, you are going to write in your journals for fifteen minutes every morning." I had protested loudly. But the last laugh was on me: when I put pen to paper, a fire started within me. My friends would stand in line and wait for me to take their poetic inventory. I'd go home and return in a few days with a poem that honored them. There in middle school, I was busy doing what Alex Haley, author of *Roots*, had commanded: find the good and praise it. Simultaneously, members of my church family at Bethlehem Baptist Church were calling upon me when someone died to deliver elegiac poems. It did not matter that at four feet, nine inches I could barely see over the pulpit. With my poet's

> "I see my work as doing that deep-diving, coming back, and showing the treasures I've found."

> "The bloodline and spiritual lines are strong and have long been at work to make me a griot."

voice I was armed with purpose and praise. When I was in middle school I thought that I was just writing poems for my friends. Years later, I discovered that I am part of that West African line of praise poets. Although the Middle Passage and slavery severed the rites and traditions, the bloodline and spiritual lines are strong and have long been at work to make me a *griot*.

What is a praise poem?

In West Africa it's verse that, line by line, declares and celebrates a person's place in nature, their ancestral line, and the community in which they live. Fàsa, the word for "praise" in Bambara, a West African tongue, literally means "tendon." Therefore, the instruction for writing a praise poem is to connect. Find connections with yourself and the rest of the world. Praise poems are conversations that help us understand ourselves and the world more intimately. Writing praise poems requires the deep reflection that leads to making literal and metaphorical connections.

I am mindful that praise poems can seem simple. But it can be quite difficult when the command is to find the good. For some students, this instruction rides against how they were raised. They were told not to boast. Some find difficulty in affirming themselves. I tell my students to lift up and take a bird's-eye view of where they are in their lineage, to look beyond the present and imagine both the past and the future. The form is a great tool of discovery. It enables students to strengthen their voice and gain a stronger sense of agency. They speak up and out for themselves.

Many of my poems can be categorized as praise poems. Writing praise poems has literally and metaphorically rooted me. It has grounded me as a poet to connect with a form so profoundly. Praise poems emphasize the circular nature of life. That's especially true for me, learning of my West African lineage. Praise poems have become my lens through which to look at the world.

What projects are in the works?

Presently, I am working on David Drake. He was an enslaved South Carolina potter poet. I'm working with University of Delaware professors Dr. Lynette Overby, who's a choreographer, and Dr. Gabrielle Foreman, a specialist in African American literature.[12] We have people dancing. I am writing Dave. There's music to Dave. And there's

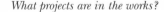

PHOTOGRAPH BY AMY RANDALL

PHOTOGRAPH BY AMY RANDALL

Jonathan Green, a Gullah landscape and portrait artist, who already painted Dave back in the '90s. We are envisioning a beautiful book which combines my twenty-eight poems with Jonathan Green's paintings and essays from each of us about our process.

Our collaboration started with another project, *The Three Harriets*. We combine history, poetry, and dance to tell the stories of Harriet Jacobs, from Edenton, whom I've mentioned; Harriet E. Wilson, the first African American novelist; and Harriet Tubman, the famous conductor of the underground railroad.[13] There is a fourth Harriet, who no one talks about. That's Harriet Powers, who was a quilter. I haven't written for her yet, but I know she's been talking to me. Also, Jason Miller, a professor at NC State, is working on a film, *Origin of the Dream*, on the connection between Langston Hughes and Martin Luther King. He discovered an unpublished poem Langston Hughes wrote for a tribute King organized for A. Philip Randolph. Ruby Dee spoke the poem at the event. Jason asked me to do it for the film.[14] I went into Raleigh and shot that. That was powerful. I don't know where the project is; they are probably fundraising to complete it. But I'm really, really excited to be connected with those two men. And to know another element, another layer of King. He was looking to the poet, of course, to speak to the people, to use metaphor. "I have a dream" is solidified; it will never go away.

And – ?

Next up is a poetry manuscript titled *The Listening Skin*. It chronicles how I use dance and poetry to address lineage, fibromyalgia, racism, and ultimately the satisfactions of being a black woman. A memoir, *Poetry Road*, is about the life I have lived for the last twenty-five years, in and out of classrooms, conferences, and festivals. Capturing the highlights, recording the special moments. What I have done that has worked, what hasn't worked, the beauty in the work. I've been moving over so much territory, covering America and some of the world, going, "Yes, yes, yes!" to every invitation. Now I am trying to slow down and deepen the work. That's my intention with *Poetry Road*, to talk about poetry in a deeper way. Another book, *Poetry Circles*, is craft-related, answering questions like: What are the prompts I use? Why is place-based poetry important? How do I teach teachers, students, and non-poets to write? How I am doing it in circles, creating spaces.

What do you see for yourself in the future?

My dream is to have a cottage somewhere, very remote. I would see people maybe twice a week, and on this cottage the sign would be "Poetry Healer." People would come and they would just talk to me. I would prescribe poems to them: "Here are the poems you need to read. Here are the poems you need to sit with. You need to work with this poem and let it work with you." It's not a workshop; it's a healing. They tell me stories, I tell them stories. I would sit with them to get to know them. Then I would pull the books off the shelf and write them the prescription, and they have to do it. Then they come back and tell me their reflection. That's all it is. There's no third-party payer. There's no insurance. I would just be the Poetry Lady. I do think poetry heals. I believe it saves lives, because it saved mine.

Poems have saved me! When I read Rumi, it's medicine. Poems are powerful, they're packed. And they just keep working. I might know how a poem works, but it still works even when I know how it works. It's like when a young person says, "Tell me that story again" because they want to have that experience again. It's like lyrics to a favorite song. I don't get tired of hearing them. I want to hear them over and over. They mean different things at different times in my life. Hearing something over again is powerful. Learning poems by heart, we don't do that enough. I'm not saying do rote recitals; I'm saying memorize by heart. I am such a geek for poetry. There are poems I have memorized by heart and said for twelve, thirteen, fourteen, fifteen years. Then I'll say the poem one more time, and it opens. A poem is like a dream. You can investigate that poem, you can dissect it. That's why you come back to poems. If you come back to the poem, it speaks to you. I revel at the depth of what a poem can do. That's why I'm on this path, because it takes you down to so many layers of your self and it never gets old.

How does social justice thread through your work?

I've been following this social justice thread from the time, basically, since I was born. I was born August 27, 1963, the day before Martin Luther King, Jr., gave his "I Have a Dream" speech in Washington, DC. I am a King baby. Then when I'm in fifth grade, I hear my first poem, a socio-political poem, Jackie Earley's "One Thousand Nine-Hundred & Sixty-Eight Winters . . ."[15] I hear this social justice poem about black people not feeling welcome in a white world. It woke me up. I think the pathway has already been marked for me, and I've been waking up along the trail. My soul wakes up, I wake up and go, "Oh! This! This is where I'm supposed to be!" I always knew I was different. I always knew I was an "other." Even in a family of artistic people, I always felt "other" in my family.

PHOTOGRAPH BY HERBERT RESPESS, IV

LISA SARASOHN is an award-winning poet, essayist, and fiction writer. Focusing on women's health and spirituality, her books include *The Woman's Belly Book: Finding Your True Center for More Energy,*

ABOVE **Lisa Sarasohn talking about interviewing Glenis Redmond for *NCLR* 2019, at Malaprop's Bookstore, Asheville, NC, 3 Feb. 2019**

[15] Jackie Earley, "One Thousand Nine-Hundred & Sixty-Eight Winters . . .," *Black Culture Weekly* Dec. 1968; rpt. in *My Black Me: A Beginning Book of Black Poetry*, ed.

> "Poetry has allowed
> me to navigate the
> minefields of hate."

PHOTOGRAPH BY WILL CROOKS

> "Poetry is mirrors.
> Poetry allows me
> to reflect; it allows
> me to give other
> people mirrors to
> look at as well."

I read deeply; I have always been a voracious reader. I begged my mom at age four to get me a library card. How did I know about the library? I do not think my three siblings had a library card at the time. My mom walked me to the library several blocks from our house on McChord Air Force Base in Tacoma, Washington. The librarian told me that I could not get a library card until I could sign my name. I went home and practiced and practiced. Unfortunately, I used the inside of my chest of drawers to sign my name with a large green marker. I got my butt beat for that. I spelled Glenis with the e turned backwards. I was slightly dyslexic. However, by the time I was five I could sign my name.

School was mostly going through the motions. I didn't find much that I gravitated to, except for the arts and reading and dance. Those were the things that brought me alive. That's how I've survived, because I came from a very impoverished – physically, not culturally – world. My parents were children of sharecroppers, from the South, and black. Poetry and social justice are personal. I had to save myself first. Then, when I had something to give, I could give it away. Poetry became that vehicle.

I knew that Jackie Earley's poem "1,968 Winters" was huge when I was in the fifth grade. I didn't know until this last year how huge it was. I've been unpacking that poem and unpacking that poem. I remember one of my professors at Warren Wilson saying, "You can't study this poem. I don't think it's craft-worthy." I was offended. I was mystified by that statement, and I said, "Who is to say what's worthy?" There are things that we are discounting that need attention. That's why I'm writing these books. I feel there's something I have to say about poetry that hasn't been said before. I know it in every fiber of my self: Glenis Redmond, poetry *griot*, has something to deliver to the world. Because there's a lot of misconceptions about what poetry is.

To me, the world is upside-down right now. I'm not saying I'm the end-all, be-all. But helping to heal the world – we all have a piece of that mission. I feel like we all have these things that we must do, that we must give, and that's what makes us valid. We're valid just by being, don't get me wrong. But we each have a piece to give the world and that's what I know I have to do. A lot comes back to race, unfortunately, and we see this erupting in America right now. Poetry has allowed me to navigate the minefields of hate. Poetry has helped me more than anything navigate being a black woman in this world. Poetry has been the way that I buffer myself and alchemize. So I still go in, even feeling all beat up and cut up, talking about social justice, feeling like I have something to give and something to offer, not turning hardened and mean and angry. I do have rage, but I am determined not to give in to rage. I want to be like my grandmother and mother, who have continued to love. I'm learning to love myself, learning to love others, learning to create a space of love. At the end of the day, that's what I'm giving away. Poetry is mirrors. Poetry allows me to reflect; it allows me to give other people mirrors to look at as well. ■

KAREN BALTIMORE designed this interview, the essay on C. Eric Lincoln, and the poetry in this issue. Find other samples of her work and contact information for your design needs on her website at www.skypeak.com.

THIRD PLACE, 2018 JAMES APPLEWHITE POETRY PRIZE
BY GLENIS REDMOND

Dreams Speak: My Father's Words

For Harriet E. Wilson

I had to coax my heart open to see
what my bones already know. Follow

how the blood road travels back
to understand – how the tree root shoots

from solid ground. If I stand still
long enough, I can feel how the earth turns

by my father's dark hand. How he lifts
the veil, so I can stare into the worlds

between the worlds. The branched bottles
hold his clear voice as he dream speaks

in my ear. Shows me how destiny's wheel turns.
How trouble will hound me many of my days.

How grief will rob me of my son,
my beloved held at my breast. How work

will do its best to beat my body down.
He says trouble will stand next to me

Read about **GLENIS REDMOND** in the interview in this issue. Final
judge Amber Flora Thomas said of her third-place selection, "In this
poem, the father's voice is grounded in the earth and offers an honest
message about the pain that is cyclic, especially relevant now as more
Americans become aware of the way African American people are
brutalized by police and racism plagues our society. Yet, the message
in this poem is one of hope, a turning, as all change is inevitable."

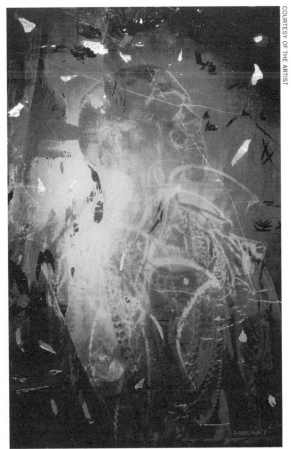

like kin. Bedridden, I will beg to die.
But he chants, fair daughter, you will rise.

You will rise and follow the leaves.
The call of my dream voice will guide you

to trace your palms. Close your eyes.
Feel the pulse. See how the future connects

to your strong life line. Your legacy
blown on bottles, etched in books.

Gifts held by others. You will be known:
The Earnest Eloquent Clairvoyant.

On this dirt path paved, you will conjure
what the world hands you. Navigate the heart.

Palm smooth jagged rocks into fortune.
Divine daughter dance between the worlds

Curtains drawn open. Peer. Gain inner sight.
See how at the core all turns and turns.

Parts of My Soul in the Dark I Pray with All My Light (mixed media on stretched canvas, coated in epoxy resin finish, 24x36) by Darryl Hurts

DARRYL HURTS was born in Alexandria, LA, and now lives in Charlotte, NC. His work appeared in the *Black on Black* exhibit at the Visual Art Exchange in Raleigh, NC in 2016 and was featured in the *Fashion After Dark* exhibition in Charlotte, NC. In 2017, Hurts created a mural at Andaz 5th Avenue in New York City, which was featured in *The Fourhundred Magazine*. See more of his work on his website at www.darrylhurts.com.

FINALIST, 2018 JAMES APPLEWHITE POETRY PRIZE
BY GLENIS REDMOND

Every One of My Names

For Harriet Tubman

Every one of my names, I earned.
'Cept de first: Araminta Ross.
Given to me at birth.
Didn't take too much to it.
Sounds like a flower standing in a field.
Araminta. Araminta.
Got God's covering.
I keep de prayer and music from it.
For short dey say *Minty*.
I like how dat sing.
Got more of my sting.
I stood up to massa no matter
who was wronged
he head-butted me
into dreams and visions.

Took Tubman from my man.
My husband left me,
cause I wouldn't stay put.
He wanted me rooted
to his need and de cabin
Lawd knows I loved him,
but I was meant for more.
I belong to de many.

Dey calls me: Harriet.
I took Harriet from my mama.
Her love circle around me
like my wrap around my head
like my shawl hug my shoulders.
Dey call me brave, 'cause I wrap
my long arms around my peoples.

Dis how I stand: rooted and ready for battle.
Dis is how I love – fitted for fight.
My face is not fixed on pleasing –
what good is a smile in war?
I busy in battle.

Called me Conductor too
'cause I head dis foot train
with hounds at my bloody feet.
I still runs.
I runs and I runs.
I told Fredrick once
I ain't never lost a passenger.
I know which way is North
with my ear to God's mouth.

General too dey call me,
'cause I at de head,
where no woman suppose to be,
but I out smart every slaver's hunt.
Fear for what?
Once I break chains.
De minds be next.
No matter what dey call me –
my mind is fixed a mission.
If dey even thinkin about turnin back,
I point pistol to head.
Say, *A dead negroes tells no tale*.
Dis de way my spirit rise up.
My fire be both a curse and a blessin.
Dis fire burns – never snuffed out.

Dey call me Moses –
"Mah people mus' go free."
Dey whisper me Spy too,
when dey speak of me
'cause I got my hand
in so many plots.

Dey give me names so many mannish –
but by God's grace I go
– able – all woman
wid dese hands
to answer every call.

Forward (tempera on masonite panel, 23⅞x35¹⁵⁄₁₆) by Jacob Lawrence

Originally from Atlantic City, NJ, **JACOB LAWRENCE** (1917–2000) studied under Harlem Renaissance sculptor Augusta Savage and taught painting at Black Mountain College in 1946. Known best for his *Migration Series*, which starkly showcased the African American Experience in America, Lawrence has had his works displayed all around the world, including *Forward* (shown above) in the North Carolina Museum of Art in Raleigh, NC. He has received numerous awards for his outstanding achievment in art, including the U.S. National Medal of Arts and the NAACP's Spingarn Medal.

A *Visitation* with RANDALL KENAN

an interview by George Hovis

with art by Antoine Williams

COURTESY OF NORTH CAROLINA LITERARY HALL OF FAME

Randall Kenan's debut novel, *A Visitation of Spirits* (1989), established him as a major voice in contemporary American fiction; the tragic story tells of a young gay black man's failed attempt to accept his emerging sexuality and follows the efforts of family members to understand their own complicity in Horace's death by suicide. Like *Visitation*, Kenan's second book, a collection of stories, *Let the Dead Bury Their Dead* (1992), was set in the fictional community of Tims Creek, based on Kenan's hometown of Chinquapin in Duplin County, North Carolina. *Let the Dead Bury Their Dead* was nominated for the Los Angeles *Times* Book Award for Fiction, was a finalist for the National Book Critics Circle Award, and was among *The New York Times* Notable Books of 1992. Kenan is also the author of a young adult biography of James Baldwin (1994), and he wrote the text for Norman Mauskoff's book of photographs *A Time Not Here: The Mississippi Delta* (1997). His travelogue and "spiritual autobiography," *Walking on Water: Black American Lives at the Turn of the Twenty-First Century* (1999), was nominated for the Southern Book Award. *Walking on Water* chronicles Kenan's six years of travel across the American Continent visiting diverse communities of black Americans in search of an answer to the question "What does it mean to be black in America today?" His collection of essays *The Fire this Time* (2007) provides further meditation on this question. Kenan also edited *The Cross of Redemption: Uncollected Writings of James Baldwin* (2010) and *The Carolina Table: North Carolina Writers on Food* (2016).[1]

Kenan is a professor in the Department of English and Comparative Literature at the University of North Carolina at Chapel Hill. During the summers he regularly serves on the faculties of Sewanee Writers' Conference and Bread Loaf Writers' Conference. Previously, he has taught at Sarah Lawrence College, Vassar College, Columbia University, and the University of Memphis. He was the first William Blackburn Visiting Professor of Creative Writing at Duke University in the fall of 1994. He served as the 1997–98 John and Renee Grisham Writer-in-Residence at the University of Mississippi, Oxford, and he held the 2003–04 Lehman Brady Professorship at the

ABOVE **The portrait of Randall Kenan hanging in the North Carolina Literary Hall of Fame in Southern Pines, NC, 2018**

---

[1] Randall Kenan, *A Visitation of Spirits* (Grove Press, 1989), *Let the Dead Bury Their Dead and Other Stories* (Harcourt, 1992); *James Baldwin* (Chelsea House, 1994); Norman Mauskopf and Kenan, *A Time Not Here: The Mississippi Delta* (Twin Palms, 1996); Kenan, *Walking on Water: Black American Lives at the Turn of the Twenty-First Century* (Knopf, 1999); *The Fire This Time* (Melville House, 2007); Kenan, ed. *The Cross of Redemption: Uncollected Writings of James Baldwin* (Pantheon, 2010); *The Carolina Table: North Carolina Writers on Food* (Eno, 2016; reviewed in *NCLR Online* 2018). Quotations from these books will be cited parenthetically.

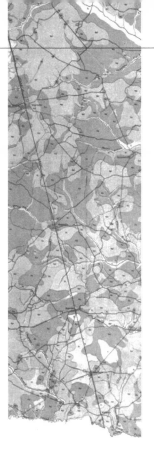

Center for Documentary Studies at Duke University. Kenan is the recipient of a Guggenheim Fellowship, a Whiting Writers Award, the Sherwood Anderson Award, the John Dos Passos Award, and the 1997 Rome Prize from the American Academy of Arts and Letters. He was awarded the North Carolina Award for Literature in 2005 and in 2018 was inducted into the North Carolina Literary Hall of Fame.

In the following interview, Kenan discusses his life and work, both the fiction and the nonfiction, as well as his literary roots and his family's roots in North Carolina. He also talks about his experiences with editing and what he has learned from others' works. We began this conversation in March 2004, en route from Murray, Kentucky, to Nashville, Tennessee. We picked it up again by email in July 2018.[2]

GEORGE HOVIS: *In the novella "Let the Dead Bury Their Dead," we learn that the town of Tims Creek, the heart of your fictional universe, was formed as a maroon society. Is there a similar legend about your hometown of Chinquapin? Is the character of Ezra Cross, who reportedly amassed one hundred acres by 1875, based on one of your ancestors?*

RANDALL KENAN: That was completely made up about the origins of Tims Creek, based on the various things I'd read about maroon societies. Actually, only recently are they discovering maroons in the Dismal Swamp that parallel what I made up, which makes me very happy. But the Dismal is much denser than Angola, the swamp closest to where we grew up. As for the parallels between Ezra Cross and my great-great-grandfather Richard Caesar Kenan, who was the manumitted ancestor, I didn't do any actual research. It was only based on received family lore, and the documents are probably there in Liberty Hall, but I figured I'd save that for a later date, for something done in nonfiction. I think he went farther southeast in the county than any of the former Kenan slaves. And his original holdings covered what could have been like ten miles. I don't think that was continuous. Again, this is all very anecdotal; my grandfather would say, "Well, granddaddy owned land."

Within the radius of ten square miles, he owned plots here and there. He didn't own ten square miles. But, again, to the white Kenans, I don't think that was diddly. I don't know how much of that was actually given, how much he worked to pay for. I found out a few years ago, and I haven't pieced this together, but there was a period where he went to Alabama. And I don't know what that was about. Apparently, he went there because there was some sort of big paying job. He moved to Alabama for a while, came back, and bought more land. But he had six children, and a lot of that land was sold and divvied up and dissipated by the time my father was born.

[2] This interview has been edited for style, clarity, and flow, while being careful to remain true to the voices and intentions of the speakers.

COURTESY OF THE ARTIST

Cause You are the Son of Slaves, Your Daddy was a Bastard, 2014 (transfer on found paper on wood, 89x60) by Antoine Williams

Ezra Cross reminds me of William Faulkner's Thomas Sutpen from Absalom, Absalom!, *especially the legends regarding his acquisition of Sutpen's Hundred and how he wrested a plantation from the jungle.*[3]

Mmmm, well, you know I can't deny that there was probably influence, from The Dixie Limited. But it's interesting: my colleague Jim Seay, the poet, is from the Delta – he's from a town right near to Oxford – and Jim is full of all these stories from his grandfather about clearing the Delta. This went on into the late nineteenth and early twentieth centuries. Some of these people were alive in the seventies, and Jim actually went back and interviewed them. So hearing some of the stories Faulkner tells, even though the geography is a little different, it's not that different from some of the stories I've heard about clearing land in eastern North Carolina.

[3] William Faulkner, *Absalom, Absalom!*
(Random House, 1931).

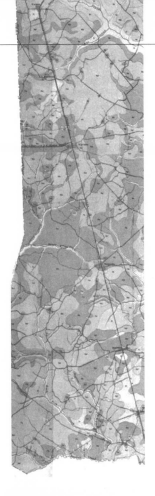

In the book of photographs you worked on with Norman Mauskoff – A Time Not Here: The Mississippi Delta *– did you feel a similar recognition of familiar landscape and culture?*

Yes, the more time I've spent in Mississippi and learned about it, the greater the similarities abound to me and excite my imagination. Originally I was assuming a lot, basing things largely on what I had read and the music, blues especially. But the similarities are real. The differences can be subtle, like how tamales is a Mississippi thing. The North Carolina blues tradition is so very different from the famous Mississippi Delta structure.

In A Visitation of Spirits, *Horace Cross participates in the Crosstown The-atre's production of an outdoor drama entitled* Riding the Freedom Star, *which celebrates the white Cross family's warped vision of its own history. Growing up near Kenansville, were you aware of that history of the white Kenans? (Of course, when you got to Chapel Hill, you encountered the name everywhere.) To what extent did your family retain memories of a history shared with the Kenans on the other side of the county? Of slavery?*

They weren't that impressed. It was not something we talked about that much. Yes, I was in *The Liberty Cart*, which was the basis for *Riding the Freedom Star*. *The Liberty Cart* is the outdoor drama about the Kenan family, in Kenansville, set in the Revolutionary War and the Civil War. And the weird thing is that I lived in this house my senior year at UNC Chapel Hill, a place called "the castle." It was this room-ing house on Friendly Lane. All four roommates were gay. I moved in when I was twenty-one. And one of the founders of the place was Ran-dolph Umberger. He taught music at North Carolina Central. And he wrote *The Liberty Cart*, a coincidence I always found very creepy. It's a horrible play. No, my family never really embraced it.

The last living child of my great-great-grandfather Richard Kenan – her name was Erie Catherine Kenan Sharpless – lived into her nine-ties, and people would come to interview her, but she really didn't have much to say about that. She had no real memories of that earlier era, so anything she would have said about living on the plantation would have been secondhand. Richard would have been the last one to have any actual contact with them, and we were so remote in those days. I mean, it wasn't that far, but we had no contact. And also by that time, the Kenans had moved pretty much to Wilmington or Louisville or New York, so they were pretty absent. I'm writing about it now, because the history is just too juicy to leave alone, but, no, there was no real awareness or handed-down knowledge.

A Visitation of Spirits *begins with a haunting scene in which the teenaged Horace Cross casts a demonic spell hoping to transform himself into a red-tailed hawk and thus escape his own flesh and the homosexual desire that plagues him with unremitting guilt. For me the scene echoes a similar passage in* Narrative of the Life of Frederick Douglass, *the famous scene in which*

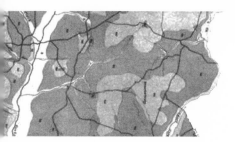

"... he could not see transforming himself into anything that would not fit the swampy woodlands of Southeastern North Carolina. He had to stay here.

No, truth to tell, what he wanted more than anything, he now realized, was to fly. A bird. He had known before, but he felt the need to sit down and ponder the possibilities. A ritual of choice, to make it real. A bird."

—*A Visitation of Spirits* (11)

Douglass observes the freedom of sailing craft on the Chesapeake Bay. Like Horace, who contrasts his own hopeless situation to the freedom of the hawk, Douglass's vision of white sails leads to a contemplation of how all of creation excepting enslaved mankind is born free: "Could I but swim!" Douglass cries out. "If I could fly! O, why was I born a man, of whom to make a brute!" [4] *There is broad consensus that slave narratives are the single-most important wellspring of the African American literary tradition. Is it an important influence on your work? If so, what have you borrowed? What have you chosen to revise?*

That influence might have been there, specifically in terms of Douglass, but I was certainly not conscious of it. And even though I'm fascinated by the slave narratives as a form, I probably am more drawn to them in terms of history and the facts of the slaves' lives and what it was like, especially for the runaway slaves, and also what it was like living on plantations. I have borrowed helter-skelter from them. To be an egghead about it, the most direct influence probably comes from the wish-fulfillment folk tradition that once-upon-a-time Africans could fly. Read Toni Morrison's *Song of Solomon* or Paule Marshall's *Praisesong for the Widow*.[5] Beyond that, I think of the representative "I," which has always been this resonant piece of African American literature. It's hard to get away from that, especially from its legacy among the post-Harlem Renaissance writers, whether it's Richard Wright or James Baldwin. It's hard to get away from the representation of that central protagonist as witness because it's such a huge influence. And I think black writers are only now, in the main, sort of moving away from the notion that the central character must be representative in the same way that the runaway slave is representative of the black experience. In a way, Horace is the anti-hero in that he doesn't escape, even though his desire is to escape. If anything, it's an inversion. I was very nihilistic in spirit when I wrote that book.

Visitation offers a very balanced portrait of the culture. The novel celebrates your home, especially in the elegiac frame for lost agricultural practices of harvesting hogs and tobacco. And yet, in light of Horace's tragic failure to accept his sexual orientation, it's highly critical of Tims Creek and its culture. I'm wondering about the book's reception back home.

You know, I'll never forget the day I was standing on the subway platform at 3rd and 53rd with a friend of mine, and I'd just sold the book, and I was talking to him about it, and it struck me that, Oh my God, people are actually going to read this thing. And I had a panic attack.

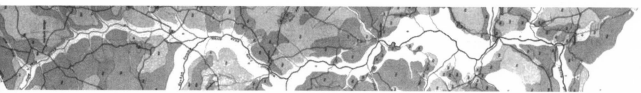

4   *Narrative of the Life of Frederick Douglass, an American Slave* (1845, Documenting the American South, UNC Libraries, 1998) 64.

5   Toni Morrison, *Song of Solomon* (Knopf, 1977); Paule Marshall, *Praisesong for the Widow* (Putnam, 1983).

The Knife and the Wound V, 2016 (acrylic, collage, ink, graphite on canvas, 48x24) by Antoine Williams

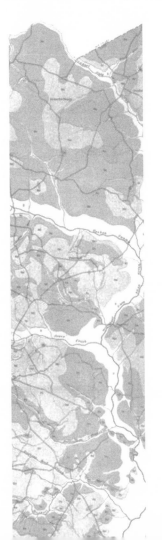

But, you know, I think in Thomas Wolfe's day, people read more than they do now. I swear I would be shocked if more people than I can name on my fingers have read that book in Chinquapin, which is fine with me. I think my third-grade teacher – who is also my cousin – has read it. (That's the other thing: everybody is related to you there.) Yeah, I really think they know that I have published stuff, and somebody might even own the book, but I don't know if they've actually read it. If it were a movie or a video, that might be a different thing entirely, but a good way to keep a secret in Chinquapin, North Carolina, is to publish it in a book.

Once – I believe it was at the Tennessee Williams/New Orleans Literary Festival in 1996 – I recall you expressing a special fondness for Faulkner's character Quentin Compson. After reading Visitation, *I was forced to read Faulkner completely differently. Following T.S. Eliot's instructions regarding the canon and the new work of art, I see Quentin in Horace and Jimmy, but I also see Horace and Jimmy in Quentin. As a reader of Faulkner, how do you view the sexual component of Quentin's suicide?*

I must say, I read Quentin that way when I first read Faulkner's novel, but I think a lot of that may well have been projections. It's been a while, but there were things I interpreted as clearly evidence of his queerness or what not. And my reading of *The Sound and the Fury* may have been affected – you're not going to take me seriously after this – by one of the first films I ever saw: *Ode to Billy Joe,* based on the song by Bobbie Gentry. Max Baer made a movie out of it starring Robby Benson and Glynnis O'Connor. I know subconsciously that movie and song affected me. And, of course, the gay subtext is not in the song at all, so it's the movie that brings it out. And that had a huge impact on me. So anytime a young man commits suicide in literature, I'm, "Ah ha! Billy Joe McAllister!"

"Of course it's a way of life that has evaporated. You'd be hardpressed to find a hogpen these days, let alone a hog. . . . But the ghosts of those times are stubborn; and though hog stalls are empty, a herd can be heard, trampling the grasses and flowers and fancy bushes, trampling the foreign trees of the new families, living in their new homes. A ghostly herd waiting to be butchered."

—*A Visitation of Spirits* (9–10)

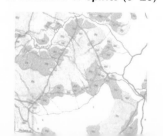

It's a commonplace for Southern writers that you have to leave home in order to write about the South. What effect on your creative vision have you noticed after moving back to North Carolina and spending more time in Chinquapin with family?

As I'm in the middle of it, I don't think I can evaluate it properly. The only thing I do is look to a role model like Eudora Welty and say, well, if it worked for her, by God, I have no excuse. And I also think working on nonfiction is helping ease that transition. It forces you to be an outsider regardless. And so when I'm interviewing these hog farmers and finding out about the history of Wendell Murphy and how he revolutionized hog farming, it's making me look at Duplin County objectively. So even if I'm going home and helping my mama hoe the collard greens or pick the beans, I'm still on the outside, in a way.

Could you talk a little more about this hog farming book and your inspiration to write it?

Swine Dreams is what I'm tentatively calling it. North Carolina has become one of the nation's largest pork producers. I want to talk about how we've gone from individual hog farmers raising hogs on their farms to this Orwellian centralized industry, which is a science. There are more hogs than people in North Carolina. The man who started it is from Duplin County, Wendell Murphy. He became a billionaire, briefly, and his company is destroying the environment, but I'm not convinced that he realizes the enormity of what he's done, which makes it poignant to me. He's not merely a villain. It's going to be a mixture of memoir, reportage, and natural history. It's fascinating, our relationship to pork.

In Walking on Water, *rural communities and small cities appear to be healthier environments than cities such as Chicago and Los Angeles. For example, one of the men you interview, Darryl, a graduate student who has left New York to study history at the University of Wisconsin, argues, "Cities really do break spirits. . . . We have to get out of the cities" (147–48). Darryl and his friends argue that "land linkages" in the South help maintain cultural continuity for blacks and that the commercialism one finds more prevalent in urban America serves to deplete and deracinate black culture (149). Do you share these views?*

I don't think I have an overt bias against cities. But perhaps it does lurk there subconsciously, because I think that I love cities in the way that Joseph Mitchell loved them. North Carolina boys are obsessed with cities. You know, Joseph Mitchell, David Brinkley, Charles Kuralt – I'm not trying to compare myself to them in that Thomas Wolfe way

ABOVE **Soil survey of Duplin County, NC, 1905**

Because They Believe in Unicorns, 2016 (surplus WWII military tents, wood, thread, marker collage and acrylic on sheet-rock, 120x48x120) by Antoine Williams

– but, as I said in that last chapter, small town boys are fascinated with cities in the way that small town boys are fascinated with pretty much anything outside of their small towns. But, there's something in there – and this is pretty much Calvinist – that you believe at some point the big city is the Whore of Babylon and that you need to get back home to your mama's cooking. So there is an approach/avoidance thing with the cities. And then when you think of African American culture, there's that cycle, that thing in Jean Toomer's *Cane*.[6] I don't think it's true only for black folk. It's true for everybody: you're in the South, or you're in the rural areas, I should say, and you move to the cities, and then you go back. For African Americans, you think of the cauldron of places like Harlem and Chicago, and belatedly I think we'll recognize Los Angeles and smaller cities as magnets and places where people have gone to learn and be apprentices, and then that cycle continues. Maybe we're on the other end of that. It's going to be interesting to see with Atlanta, because Atlanta is now sort of the Mecca of the black world. It seems as if that's going to be a terminus (ironically, that was its original name). Where do people go from there? Is that going to be a new part of the legend? Returning to Atlanta? Then it becomes something else. But I don't think I hate cities. I think I'm fascinated with them. But I mistrust them.

---

[6] Jean Toomer, *Cane* (Liveright, 1923).

COURTESY OF THE ARTIST

Crown Vic, 2017 (acrylic, ink, screen print, collage and transfer on canvas, 28.5x 23) by Antoine Williams

What you're saying now about cities and rural spaces reminds me of that line from Walt Whitman, which you quote in Walking on Water: *"Do I contradict myself? So I contradict myself. I contain multitudes" (639). This quote seems the perfect language to describe the book's project – your Whitmanesque effort to encompass the rich diversity of the black experience in America while nevertheless seeking some underlying, unifying experience of blackness. Were there moments during your journey when the achievement of this balance felt untenable?*

First let me say, *thank you.* Often there were moments of doubting the entire project. And that would maybe come out when I was interviewing somebody and they'd question the project. I would momentarily be agreeing with them, and I would say, "You're absolutely right, it's silly," and then they would turn around. One of the people who did that was Ida Leggett. She was a lawyer, the first black federal judge in that part of Idaho. And, in first talking to me, she was saying, "Ah, being black, what are you talking about? I'm here, I'm having a good time, da da da da." And then she starts telling all these horrendous things, of discrimination, of being not only black but a woman in a position of power in Idaho. She took me on this mental ride from making me doubt the original premise of my visit to confirming so much of what I suspected and teaching me so much.

In Walking on Water, *many of the folks you interview assert that one of the unfortunate effects of desegregation was to facilitate the flight of the "Talented*

> "Yes, when I call another black man 'brother,' or a black woman 'sister,' I mean it. But being able to hold conflicting, complex views in my head does not cause me to short-circuit; rather, it leaves me with a rich concotion to look toward, with pride, with wonder, with awe. To paraphrase Whitman: Do I contradict myself? I contain multitudes."
> —*Walking on Water* (639)

Tenth" away from black communities into white ones.[7] Do you agree with that assessment? And, if so, what can be done about it?

If you think of black folks as the ur-Americans, as I think they are, everything that happens in America happens to black folk before, and they mirror or magnify the American experience. It seems odd that we condemn black people when they "make it," for moving to the nicer neighborhoods, for "moving on up," to quote a pop cultural reference, *The Jeffersons*. Of course people want to do that. And then the question becomes, how important is physical proximity in a community? And this leads to questions like, do these communities really exist anymore? Has this thing broken down? Case in point, again, *The Jeffersons* as an archetype. And, even more importantly, are there infrastructures? Are there ways of being involved, for people who care? And we're also proceeding from a false assumption that all middle-class black people cared about the welfare of the black community, because some of them didn't give a hoot about the race. So, for people who care, are there ways that they can participate, contribute to the infrastructure, and build up the race – if you want to be essentialist about it – in ways that are just as, if not more, influential? And I point to the interview I did with the judge in St. Simons Island, Georgia, "a hundred black men of Glynn."[8] Physically, they all didn't live in the same community, but they adopted young black guys. And that's happening all over the country. It's not touted a lot. It's not in the news all the time, because if it's not bleeding it's not leading and that sort of thing. But I think that's a way for people who care to be involved. And, again, there's this perpetuation of the myth that when the black folk lived "in the neighborhood," they actually contributed. It's a really complicated question.

If you were to undertake the writing of Walking on Water *today, if you were to set off on that journey now, two decades later, during the era of Trump, of Black Lives Matter, of increased mass incarceration (what Michelle Alexander has come to identify as "the New Jim Crow"[9]), do you think you would find radically different answers to the question "What does it mean to be black in America today?"*

I plead the interwebs. I think, due to the internet explosion, not only would the approach and methodology be significantly different, but the substance would be altered as well. And if you think about the penultimate chapter in the book, which is set in Cyberspace, USA, I was already thinking about how the rising phenomenon was going to change the idea of "blackness." And I think it has.

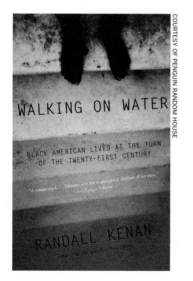

COURTESY OF PENGUIN RANDOM HOUSE

WALKING ON WATER

BLACK AMERICAN LIVES AT THE TURN OF THE TWENTY-FIRST CENTURY

RANDALL KENAN

---

[7] W.E.B. Du Bois coined this term that is used to describe the likelihood that, with formal education, one in ten black men would become leaders in the African American community.

[8] In the chapter "Walking On Water," from his book by the same name, Kenan interviews the elder descendants of one of the oldest African American communities in the US; it was formed by freed slaves in St. Simons, a location that marks the culmination of the Middle Passage.

[9] In her book by the same name, Alexander studies the current scourge of mass incarceration, which disproportionately afflicts black men. She posits that the 700% increase in the U.S. prison population since 1970 resulted from the war on drugs, which was deliberately waged as a form of social control to replace the Jim Crow state and local laws that had been dismantled during the civil rights era of the 1960s.

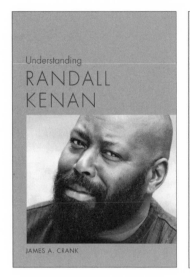
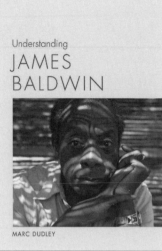

"Already most Americans live most of their lives virtually: through television, or through a screen, or at a terminal, or over the phone. This way of living is not new news, it is self-evident; moreover, these modes and manners are reshaping what it means to be American, and, in some ways, what it means to be human, and yes, what it means to be black."

—*Walking on Water* (619)

You've contributed substantially to the legacy of James Baldwin, authoring a young readers' biography as well as editing a collection of his uncollected writings. And, of course, your reflections on race in The Fire This Time *respond to and update Baldwin's famous collection from the 1960s* The Fire Next Time.[10] *With the uncollected writings, what were you most surprised to find? More broadly, what observation of Baldwin's about America still rings most unfortunately true?*

Baldwin, I firmly believe, never really had much hope of White Americans changing or, more precisely, I think he was cynical about their willingness to change. He had a very sophisticated understanding of power for a man without a college degree, and he saw America very clearly: who was in charge, what motivated people. I think Barack Obama would have moved him, but not surprised him, nor would the backlash that came as soon as he was elected. Baldwin would have had great fun writing about Trump, and I suspect he would be coming up with tropes and language about the First Real Estate Family that would be making headlines.

[10] James Baldwin, *The Fire Next Time* (Dial, 1963).

You recently edited a collection of essays entitled The Carolina Table: North Carolina Writers on Food. *What does food tell us about ourselves as North Carolinians?*

Food is central to the American experience, the specific experience, as is true of every country or culture. That is what fascinates me about it as a topic. For the Tar Heel, we are talking about very specific foods often borne out of our landscape and our specific histories. Whether you're talking about shad and trout from our rivers or pigs grown on our lands – or in our factories – or okra toted here from Africa three hundred years ago, it defines us in ways we take for granted.

In your fiction, some of your most interesting characters are ministers: Reverend Barden, The Atomic Reverend Spike, and, of course, a character who might be read as your alter ego, the Right Reverend Jimmy Greene. Did you ever consider the ministry? Did your mama consider it for you?

I did. She did, though I think she would have been even prouder if I'd become a mortician. I was quite pious for a period of my teenage years, until my hormones caught up with me. And I still am interested in theology. It was interesting that my best friends in college all wound up becoming ministers. The late Richard Wimberley, whom the book is dedicated to, went to Duke Theological Seminary. My closest friend right now, Randy Page, went to Union Seminary. Another friend went to Wake Forest. And another friend, Larry Manning, became a lay minister in Oakland. And they were all sort of hell raisers, too. They were bigger hell raisers than I was, actually. We would sit around and talk about theology and the Bible into the wee hours of the morning. And so we had that sort of thirst in common. But I learned fairly early that the ministry was not going to be something for me. Christendom itself frightens and repulses me in a way, which makes it a wonderful thing to write about. I've only scratched the surface.

In his article "Toward a Black Gay Aesthetic," Charles Nero offers a critique of the contemporary black church. Despite its historical importance to the liberation of black people, Nero points out that the church is often used as a vehicle for upward mobility within the black community and thereby acquires the intolerances of the mainstream society. "The church is eager to oppress gay people," he notes, "to prove its worth to the middle class." Numerous other scholars have acknowledged the role of the rise of a black middle class during the twentieth century as a cause for increasing homophobia in black communities. Cheryl Clarke argues that black communities prior to the 1950s and '60s tended to be more tolerant of sexual variance.[11] Do you find such critiques

---

[11] Charles Nero, "Toward a Black Gay Aesthetic: Signifying in Contemporary Black Gay Literature," *Brother to Brother: Collected Writings by Black Gay Men* (Alyson, 1991); rpt. in *African American Literary Theory: A Reader* (New York UP, 2000); Cheryl Clarke, "The Failure to Transform: Homophobia in the Black Community," *Home Girls: A Black Feminist Anthology* (Rutgers UP, 1983).

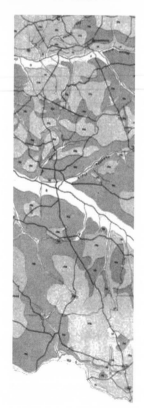

linking homophobia to the rise of a black middle class convincing? Or do you feel otherwise?

That is a complicated question. Boy, I like Cheryl Clarke. I know Cheryl Clarke. I'm not familiar with that theory. I don't know any evidence to agree with her or not. But I want to look into that, because I just don't know. But the Nero is more convincing to me. And it seems that it's a great stew of different reasons, one being that the black middle class is inherently conservative, for whatever reason. Anthropologists will tell you this is syncretism, that Africans are pretty conservative in terms of cultural values. It's sort of a mystery to me, the conservativism of the black middle class. And that goes back to E. Franklin Frazier's *Black Bourgeoisie* on up to now.[12] That view is still fundamentally true. Conservative with a small "c" in terms of family values. And I don't mean in the Republican sense of the word. In how they think about the family unit, in terms of what they think about the role of women and so forth and so on. And it comes out in talks about gay rights. The black community, at large, has still not accepted gay and lesbian folk into their bosom. A lot of it has to do with how people construe identity. And often people are asked to choose: "Are you gay, or are you black? Because you sho' can't be both." It becomes really problematic when people see identity in a very essentialist way. And it becomes too complicated to talk about identities overlapping or merging and so confusing the issue. And so it just becomes politically expedient for people to say, "Okay, you make a choice, because we don't have time to be splitting hairs and making exceptions." And again, at one level, it speaks to the inherent conservatism of the black middle class and their simplified and overly streamlined political agenda.

Maybe my favorite novella ever is the title story of your collection Let the Dead Bury Their Dead. *You once explained to me that you originally intended it to be the culminating sequence of the novel* A Visitation of Spirits, *but your publisher found the structure too experimental. (I still teach the novel and story together.) "Let the Dead Bury Their Dead" purports to be an oral history of the origins of Tims Creek, recorded by the Reverend Jimmy Greene, with his extensive annotation in the form of elaborate footnotes. After Jimmy's untimely death, his editor, Reginald Gregory Kain, collects and publishes the manuscript. Could you talk a little bit about Randall Garrett Kenan's relationship to Reginald Gregory Kain and to your alter ego, Jimmy Greene?*

Oh boy. I was having all sorts of postmodern glee when I did that. I don't know how much Jimmy is based on any part of me. I think he's much sweeter and controlled and dutiful and heterosexual.

[12] E. Franklin Frazier, *Black Bourgeoisie*
(Free Press, 1957).

Really? You think he's heterosexual?

Rob McRuer has written a lot about that, and I really don't get it.[13] It was not my intention if he came off otherwise. Yeah, Jimmy is much more tame than I am. As a stand-in, I feel that he became his own person. I created him as a straight man. In those first-person passages in *Visitation*, I felt he was moving into becoming his own person. His sexuality felt defined by his relationship with his late wife, but I was more interested in him theologically than sexually. In truth, now that I look back at it, Jimmy was fairly asexual at that stage of his life.

Yesterday, you told a priceless anecdote about returning to Chinquapin on the date of Jimmy's death.

I had written that he dies on the trip back home to Tims Creek from Atlanta, and I had the temerity to actually give his death a date (277). After it was published, I began to say, Oh Lord, I better not be travelling anywhere near that date. After the fact, I realized that either a few days before or a few days after, I was actually going home into Chinquapin around that date, because I had completely forgotten about my prediction of Jimmy's demise. So I hope that's a good thing, which means at that point he became a character and not a surrogate. In Stephen King's universe, he'll be calling me up soon, wanting royalties.

I'm fascinated by the various botanists in your fiction, especially Horace Cross, who is studying tropism, the growth of an organism toward an external stimulus. What an interesting metaphor for his emerging sexuality. How did you come upon this interest in plants?

I love plants. What else can I say? I love growing them, watching them grow, eating them. There was a period, when I was in about the fifth or sixth grade, I wanted to be a botanist. Don't ask me how I came upon this inspired career choice. After that, it was Egyptology. But I was most vocal about wanting to be a botanist. Growing up in Chinquapin, on the farm, my mother was horticulturally obsessed. Even years later, she would say, There's this fern I want, and she'd send me on these wild goose chases, looking for this plant that no nursery in North Carolina, or certainly not in the Triangle, had. So I've always been acutely aware of flora and taking care of it. And I had terrariums. I went through a period when I would have those microcosms in terrariums all through high school. So it was something I've always

---

[13] See Robert McRuer, "'But What If I Can't Change?': Desire, Denial, and Melancholia in Randall Kenan's *A Visitation of Spirits*," *Southern Literary Journal* 40.2 (2008): 259. See also McRuer's discussions of this story in "A Visitation of Difference: Randall Kenan and Black Queer Theory," *Journal of Homosexuality* 26.2-3 (1993): 221–32, and in "Queer Locations, Queer Transformations: Randall Kenan's *A Visitation of Spirits*," *South to a New Place: Region Literature, Culture* (Louisiana State UP, 2002) 184–95.

ABOVE **Talmadge Ragan and Randall Kenan** after his induction into the NC Literary Hall of Fame, Southern Pines, 7 Oct. 2018

PHOTOGRAPH BY DAVID POTORTI

been interested in. But I don't know its true origins. I know scientists hate it when you do that, but it's wonderful in terms of metaphors, to mine plant life.

I'm still trying to work out the gender dynamics of Tims Creek. According to its own stories, the town was established by founding "fathers." The positions of authority in the church seem reserved for men, and yet characters like Johnnie Mae and Ruth are by turns both propping up and challenging the patriarchy. Do you see the place you came from as a matriarchal community or patriarchal?

COURTESY OF THE ARTIST

Portrait of a Super Predator Who was Made to Believe She was Cute to Be Dark, 2018 (acrylic on acrylic skin, 36x72) by Antoine Williams

It's that wonderful tension in real life. It's not easily resolved. On the one hand, you have this narrative that we live by, which has real world consequences: the myth of matriarchy, and the figure of the mother or the grandmother or a woman of honor, as opposed to what we've created in terms of the single mother or the way women are actually treated in the world. I think of Zora Neale Hurston's comment that the black woman is the mule of the world. And I think that segues into a certain patriarchal power, which is tempered by the matriarchy, which gets its power by the matriarchy, which is sometimes cruel toward the matriarchy and tries to section it off, but it's like a war of powers. I think of James Goldman, who wrote *The Lion in Winter*; Henry II and Eleanor of Aquitaine are a perfect example of how the two work. You can't discount black patriarchy. And I think that's one of the things that novelist Ishmael Reed is up to when he attacks black women writers in *Reckless Eyeballing* for overdoing the role of black matriarchy and denigrating black men, because they're still a power to be reckoned with.[14] And I'm not sure if that's not true of all cultures at the end of the day.

Speaking of patriarchs, I want to pick your brain about Booker T. Washington. In recent decades, he has been largely rehabilitated by Houston A. Baker, Jr., among others. In your story "This Far,"[15] Washington is depicted ambivalently, but most of the references to him in Walking on Water *seem positive. I take it from your fiction*

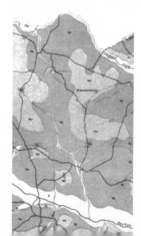

[14] Ishmael Reed, *Reckless Eyeballing* (St. Martin's, 1986).

[15] "This Far" is included in *Let the Dead Bury Their Dead and Other Stories*.

that Washington was an important voice for earlier generations of your family. What value, if any, does he hold for a contemporary audience?

PHOTOGRAPH BY MARGARET BAUER

Yeah, he was held up in high regard. I think for people of my grandfather's generation, in particular, he was seen as this unmitigated, larger-than-life, wholly positive figure. So when I come to something like Louis Harlan's double-volume biography, and all these revelations about what a S.O.B. he was, it makes for a much richer character. I never meant that story to portray him solely in a negative light. I was thinking about what is it like to be such a political wizard and run an actual network, to have achieved so much. Objectively, to go from such lows to become that high, even when he was being lauded, people didn't realize how successful, how influential, he really was. Outside the country, even, he was treated like a potentate. How much money, even though he didn't have a huge personal fortune, how much money he controlled, it was really astounding. He had an actual machine, in the sense of the American political machines, like Tammany Hall or Daley in Chicago, or Honey Fitz in Boston.[16] And it covered a much broader geographical area. He was a pretty astounding character. So dealing with him in the sense of dealing with a Caesar, that's what I wanted that story to do, to deal with the psychological underpinnings.

And now, especially, as you're reading people like Sun Tzu, all those pop psychology writers, people like Jack Welch, the former Chief Executive Officer of General Electric, there are so many lessons to be learned from Washington, in terms of management and understanding power, especially from a minority point of view, and that's what's astonishing about him. This reality wasn't minority in our sense of minority, that you come from a disadvantage, you have dark skin, but you can still become president of American Express. No! In his day, that was undreamt of. Not taking anything away from Ken Chenault, or the head of Time Warner, Richard Parsons. They've had their great odds. But such current-day realities were so far out of the realm of thinking in Washington's day that to do what he did is extraordinary. And did he bust some heads in doing it? Did he bend, break, totally defy laws? Of course he did. There's no way he could have gotten that sort of power without doing it.

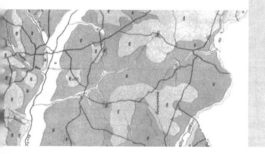

ABOVE **Randall Kenan and Nancy Werking Poling, whose essay he selected for** *NCLR's* **2018 Albright Prize (in this issue's North Carolina Miscellany section), North Carolina Writers' Network Fall Conference, Charlotte, 2 Nov. 2018**

[16] Tammany Hall was a Democratic Party political group formed in 1789 that influenced New York City politics and immigrant mobility; Richard J. Daley was from the Irish Catholic community and served as Mayor of Chicago beginning in 1955; John F. Fitzgerald was a Democratic congressman and the Mayor of Boston in the early 1900s.

You have a novel in progress set in Tims Creek. What's the story about? When will we get to read it?

There's a Man Going Round Taking Names. The protagonist is Elihu McElwaine. It starts in the seventies when he kidnaps two children – one black, one white – initially as a political statement, but things get out of hand. The kids get away free, but the group of kidnappers, who call themselves the Army of the Perambulating Prestidigitators, sort of vanish and are presumed dead, along with the money. And twenty years later the two boys are in New York. The white guy is a theology student at Union Theological Seminary. The black kid is a lawyer at a white-shoe law firm. And Elihu McElwaine comes back into their lives, much changed and besotted with his ill-gotten gains. Sort of like a Mephisto, he comes back into their lives with this request of them. And it sends them both into soul-searching.

What other projects are on your plate these days?

The next immediate thing will be a collection of short stories, *If I Had Two Wings.* I still have some nonfiction writing ideas I'd like to explore about black cowboys, and I do need to finish this novel. Even my desk has started to complain to me.

I'm looking so forward to all of that! Thank you, Randall, for talking with me, and thank you so very much for sharing the gift of your words, your wisdom, and your stories!

Thank you! ■

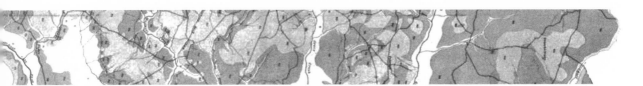

STEPHANIE WHITLOCK-DICKEN designed this interview and the interview with Jason Motts in this issue. She has been designing for *NCLR* since 2001 and served as Art Director 2002–2008. Contact her at stephaniewdicken@gmail.com for freelance graphic design work.

A Professor at SUNY Oneonta, **GEORGE HOVIS** earned his PhD in English from UNC Chapel Hill. He teaches creative writing and American literature and is the author of numerous essays on and interviews with Southern writers, including many from North Carolina. Read his interviews with Clyde Edgerton in *NCLR* 2017 and Wiley Cash in 2013 and his essay on movies that should be made from North Carolina literature in *NCLR* 2012. His essays have also appeared in *Southern Cultures*, *The Thomas Wolfe Review*, and *Mississippi Quarterly*. He is the author of a novel, *The Skin Artist* (SFK Press, 2019), and a scholarly book, *Vale of Humility: Plain Folk in Contemporary North Carolina Fiction* (University of South Carolina Press, 2007). His most recent short stories have been published by *Carolina Quarterly*, *New Madrid*, and *The Fourth River*. Currently, he is at work on a novel about a North Carolina mill town adjusting to desegregation in the mid-1970s.

ANTOINE WILLIAMS earned a BFA in Art with a concentration in Illustration from UNC Charlotte and an MFA in studio art at UNC Chapel Hill. He is on the faculty at Guilford College and has completed residencies at Golden Belt Galleries in Durham, the Indie Grits Film Festival in Columbia, SC, and Elsewhere's Southern Constellations Fellowship in Greensboro. He received the Ella Fountain Pratt Emerging Artist Grant for 2014–2015. He has published in *nineteen sixty-nine: an ethnic studies journal* at UC Berkeley and in *NCLR* 2018, and his work has been shown in solo exhibitions, including the Sumter County Gallery of Art in South Carolina and the Alcott Gallery in Chapel Hill, as well as in numerous group exhibitions such as the Ackland Art Museum in Chapel Hill and the Harvey B. Gantt Center in Charlotte. See more of his art on his website at antoinewilliamsart.com.

FINALIST, 2018 JAMES APPLEWHITE POETRY PRIZE
BY L. TERESA CHURCH

Bombingham, 1963

When the blast blew Jesus'
face from the stained glass
window otherwise left intact,
He just stood there

speechless, blood-splattered.
Aggrieved in dusted robe,
He could not bear look
at what dynamite had done.

Addie Mae Collins,
Cynthia Wesley,
Carole Robertson,
Carol Denise McNair,

we shouted your names,
figured – prayed really,
maybe you couldn't hear
us over the commotion

& that's why you didn't
answer as our hands
shoveled through
God's splintered house.

Mothers & fathers we
fingered shards
from Jesus' face,
asked Him why?

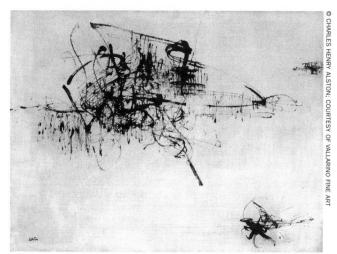

Untitled (Civil Rights), circa 1960 (oil on board, 18x24) by Charles Henry Alston

L. TERESA CHURCH has been a member of the Carolina African American Writers' Collective since 1995 and serves as archivist and membership chair for the organization. Read her essay about the Collective in *NCLR* 2016. She is an independent scholar/archival consultant and sole proprietor of LTC Consulting in Durham, NC. Her poetry has previously appeared in *NCLR* 2004, 2016, and 2018, and *NCLR Online* 2016. Read two more of her poems that were finalists in the 2018 Applewhite competition in *NCLR Online* 2019. Her writing has also appeared in venues such as *Simply Haiku*, *The Heron's Nest*, *Obsidian*, *Solo Café*, *Nocturnes: (Re)view of the Literary Arts*, *African American Review*, and *One Window's Light: A Collection of Haiku* (reviewed in *NCLR Online* 2019), and she published a chapbook, *Beyond the Water Dance* (LTC Publications, 2002).

North Carolina native **CHARLES HENRY ALSTON** (1907–1977) earned a BA from Columbia University and an MFA from Columbia's Teachers College. After he moved to New York, he became an influential painter and prominent figure during the Harlem Renaissance: the first African American supervisor for the Works Progress Administration and founder of the Harlem Artists Guild. Alston also worked as a sculptor, and his cartoons and illustrations were published in popular magazines like *The New Yorker* and *Fortune* during the 1930s and '40s. His work is in the permanent collections of the Metropolitan Museum of Art, the Whitney Museum of American Art, and the Detroit Institute of Arts.

"let them be black and beautiful":

A Black Southerner's Grasp at Self-Respect in

C. Eric Lincoln's *The Avenue, Clayton City*

by Francine L. Allen

with art by Ivey Hayes

The Avenue, Clayton City

a novel by
C. Eric Lincoln

"C. Eric, my Brother, you can write your head off! The only thing wrong is that you wrote this book instead of me!" ~ALEX HALEY

In the 1920s, Alain Locke spoke of a new generation of African Americans who were moving to Northern cities and acquiring a perspective about themselves that dispensed with past notions of inferiority and dependency, notions that had been strapped upon them during slavery and the Reconstruction era. Locke argues that this new perspective was emerging as African Americans, especially those who were artists and intellectuals, celebrated their unique culture here in the United States and as they learned of their motherland in Africa.[1] Yet this new perspective that Locke associated with the movement of African Americans from the South to the North during the Harlem Renaissance, between 1919 and 1940, leaves unaddressed how black Southerners, those who stayed in the South during this period, devised ways of clinging to self-respect in an environment bent, since slavery, on forcing them to believe in their innate inferiority, an environment that challenged African Americans of all ages, including children.

Former Duke University Professor of Religion and Culture C. Eric Lincoln recalled being nine years old growing up in Athens, Alabama, and going one day to the county courthouse for immunization shots. Though not fully cognizant of the racial dynamics of the time, he did notice in the courthouse the presence of two lines: one line for black children waiting for their shots and another shorter line for white children who were ushered in much more quickly to get theirs. Lincoln said that when he stepped up with a group of newly arrived white children, raising his arm for a shot, a nurse grabbed his arm and pushed him back into the wall, telling him, "All you niggers have to wait!" Lincoln said that the nurse's physical contact with him in that instance produced a pain that went beyond the physical: "As I stood against the wall rubbing my arm, I soon came to realize that it was not my arm that was hurting, it was my soul. There was a sort

Sandra, 1999 (archival quality ink on water-resistant canvas, 9x12) by Ivey Hayes

COURTESY OF IVEYHAYESARTWORKS.COM

of numbness, a *dead* feeling. The pain was *inside* me and I would never be able to rub it away."[2] Lincoln's feeling that he might never be relieved of his discomfort reflects, perhaps, a youthfulness new to racial humiliation. But in the South of the 1920s and '30s when Lincoln was encountering the county courthouse nurse, there were adults who had been fighting against such attitudes all their lives, living out what it meant to be a "New Negro" just as Locke was introducing the term to the black intelligentsia of the North.

Lincoln would model his character Mama Lucy upon such elders in his novel, *The Avenue, Clayton City*, which is set in a Southern town during the period of the Harlem Renaissance in the 1920s and '30s.[3] In a community and society that denigrates blackness, one of the novel's principal characters, Lucy Lunceford, better known as Mama Lucy, is able to cling to self-respect through home ownership and through a moral perspective grounded in faith. The former allows for agency while the latter provides physical and psychological shielding from the unrelenting humiliation faced by her and by all black Southerners as they are confronted daily with a racial status quo that deems them inferior. Unlike Mama Lucy, though, some of the characters in *The Avenue* lose their dignity and also their lives as they are devoured by their personal flaws and by their inability to wrestle with the social indignities imposed upon them.

Though living in a town in which a racist power structure rules almost all social institutions and controls the daily operations of the town, Mama Lucy resists the inferiority that such a situation seeks to impose upon its African American citizens by clinging to the agency that home ownership provides, an agency about which she teaches her children, discussing with them the value of the six-acre homeplace on which they live that was built by her parents: "the land was theirs, and the house was theirs, and the right to be proud and independent on account of it was all theirs, too" (219). Mama Lucy is fierce when it comes to protecting her family's possessions. Sweet Feet, a young man whom she and her husband, Lucius, raised from infancy after he was left on their doorstep, recalls the day a white man came to the Lunceford household selling a load of slabs. Since Mama Lucy has no money, she agrees to trade with the man, taking some slabs from him and giving him, in return, the family's planter. After the man unloads and delivers the slabs, he takes, in return, not only the planter but the singletree that Lucius had made. This enrages

"In a community and society that denigrates blackness, one of the novel's principal characters, Lucy Lunceford, better known as Mama Lucy, is able to cling to self-respect through home ownership and through a moral perspective grounded in faith."

---

[2] C. Eric Lincoln, "'All Niggers Have to Wait': A Child's First Lesson in Jim Crow," *Journal of Blacks in Higher Education* 11 (1996): 60.

[3] C. Eric Lincoln, *The Avenue, Clayton City* (Morrow, 1988); subsequently cited parenthetically.

Loretta, 1990 (archival quality ink on water-resistant canvas, 9x12) by Ivey Hayes

Mama Lucy, and she hollers at the man to return the singletree, an invaluable tool for helping Lucius guide and balance his workhorse.

After Mama Lucy runs the man off her land, she explains to Sweet Feet that the man's attempt to take the singletree was so disturbing because the singletree represented the work and hard labor of her husband: "Lucius *made* that singletree. He *made* it!" (242). Thus, it represents triple ownership – that is, ownership and control many times over: it resides on the land that Mama Lucy and her family own, it sits in the barn that they own, and it was created by the very hands of Lucius. The singletree belongs to the Lunceford family in every way. Contrary to the man's assessment that it "Ain't worth nothing" (241), it stands as one of the most valuable pieces of property on their land, in Mama Lucy's eyes.

> "[W]hen I'm standing on my own property, my name is Lucy Lunceford to everybody unless I say different! I ain't never let no po' white trash A'ntie me, an' I ain't about to start with him."—*The Avenue* (242)

Ownership also enables Mama Lucy to maintain her dignity by controlling her identity. Sweet Feet remembers, too, how he had questioned Mama Lucy about her anger at being addressed as "A'ntie" by the man since the white people for whom she worked downtown called her by that title. She explains that the man "ain't from downtown, and I don't *work* for him. And when I'm standing on my own property, my name is Lucy Lunceford to everybody unless I say different! I ain't never let no po' white trash A'ntie me, an' I ain't about to start with him" (242). When Mama Lucy is in the workplace – that is, in spaces and places in which she holds no ownership – she cannot control how she is identified. People who bear no biological connection to her can call her "A'ntie," and she must accept this moniker. However, in her own home and on her own land, strangers must call her by her name; they must acknowledge her as a unique individual and not, as the title "A'ntie" implies, an unnamed inferior to the white family for whom she works.

In rejecting the label "A'ntie" and demanding that the man get off her land, not only is Mama Lucy exercising agency and protecting her dignity and identity, she is also engaging in politics. As a working-class woman living in the Jim Crow South, her political life is lived out, not in the voting booth or in social activity but in her resistance against the status quo that upheld white supremacy. This type of rural politicking was common for rural working-class black Southerners of this time, according to D.G. Kelley:

> Too often politics is defined by *how* people participate rather than *why*; by traditional definition the question of what is political hinges on whether or not groups are involved in elections, political parties, grass-roots social movements. Yet, the how seems far less important than the *why* since many of the so-called real political institutions have not proved effective for, or even accessible to, oppressed people. By shifting our focus to what motivated disenfranchised black working people to struggle and what strategies they developed, we may discover that their participation in "mainstream" politics – including their battle for the franchise – grew out of the very circumstances, experiences, and memories that impelled many to steal from an employer, to join a mutual benefit association, or to spit in a bus driver's face. In other words, those actions all reflect, to varying degrees, larger political struggles. For southern blacks in the age of Jim Crow, politics was not separate from lived experience or the imagined world of what is possible. It was the many battles to roll back constraints, to exercise power over, or create space within, the institutions and social relationships that dominated their lives.[4]

Mama Lucy fights a political battle on her own turf – on the land and in the home she owns. She aims to halt the ways in which white supremacist ideology seeks to control and minimize her and the black community generally. While she may not be able the stop the influence that this ideology has upon the institutions and the daily operations of the town, she can most certainly stop its oppressive presence in the life she lives on her own property.

Negotiating this community in a way that allows Mama Lucy to maintain her self-respect is possible also because of her faith, revealed, to some degree, in her religious practices, but most evident in a lifestyle in which her role as a mother becomes divine-like and in which her faith-based worldview protects her from the predatory nature of racism. While Mama Lucy teaches her children that the black community claims its self-respect and agency through land and home ownership, she stresses also that possessions are not enough. She tells her children that they must also have faith. She emphasizes this point to them after affirming their personal worth, telling them that they are as good as anyone: "And by *anybody*, she meant white and colored, on or off The Avenue. Having your own land, and owning your own house, and being in good relations with the Lord went a long way toward self-respect" (219). Mama Lucy's faith is evident in her religious activities and in her worldview that places God as the center, which she passes down to her children. Unlike her husband, Mama Lucy

"Lincoln was anxious to address a character he believes has been neglected – the extraordinary black person." —*Durham Morning Herald* 8 Jan. 1988

COURTESY OF IVEYHAYESARTWORKS.COM

Maybe Someday, 1981 (archival quality ink on water-resistant canvas, 9x12) by Ivey Hayes

[4] D.G. Kelley, "'We Are Not What We Seem': Rethinking Black Working-Class Opposition in the Jim Crow South," *Journal of American History* 80.1 (1993): 78.

> "Now, Lord, these is your chillum. You made 'em and you made 'em black. So, Lord Jesus, in your name let them be black and beautiful. Let them stand the test. Amen!"
> —*The Avenue* (223)

and her children attend church regularly. At home, Mama Lucy prays over her children, asking, "Now, Lord, these is your chillum. You made 'em and you made 'em black. So, Lord Jesus, in your name let them be black and beautiful. Let them stand the test. Amen!" (223). Her prayers here suggest that while she views the destiny of children as being the eventual manifestation of their God-given abilities, she is not naïve about the challenges they will face as African Americans.

The value Mama Lucy places upon prayer and land and home ownership also point to Mama Lucy connecting to a larger cultural and ancient tradition established by marginalized communities. For these communities, land and home ownership and faith all constitute a strong tradition, a triple threat against the indignities of racism and oppression, and they reveal to newly liberated people how they are to live out their liberation. For Mama Lucy, land and home owner-ship stand as elements of tradition because both were passed down to her from her parents, and she will pass them down to her children. Beyond the particulars of Mama Lucy's situation, land and home ownership and faith constitute important elements of tradition for the black Southern community in its struggle for freedom. The own-ership of land and a home reminds the community of how a group once owned has been lifted from that bondage and transformed into owners. This community's practice of religious faith or, as Mama Lucy describes it, of having "good relations with the Lord" (219), explains this change in status. Change did not occur merely by the community pulling itself up by its bootstraps, as the popular American sentiment identifies as the reason for success and advancement. Rather, for the black Southern community, God changed its status, freeing it from slave bondage. Thus, land, a home, and faith serve as symbols of a living tradition that, accord-ing to Douglas F. Ottati, "shape present life by furnishing a common memory or heritage that, in turn, yields a guiding orientation."[5]

Ownership of land and a home and the embrace of faith allow members of the black Southern community to remember its enslavement and God's transformation of that situation. Also, these elements enable the black Southern community to connect with an even older, larger tradition as expressed in the Old Testament concerning the Israelites. In this tradition, as James H. Cone notes,

COURTESY OF IVEYHAYESARTWORKS.COM

Church Dinner, 2004 (archival quality ink on water-resistant canvas, 9x12) by Ivey Hayes

God liberates the Israelites, a people enslaved and oppressed, and invites them into relationship with him. This liberation and relationship are accompanied by God granting the Israelites land and home ownership in the Promised Land. Yet living as free people came with stipulations, requiring the Israelites to help other oppressed people to acquire freedom. As Cone says, God's invitation to the Israelites "is an invitation to Israel to enter into a responsible relationship with the God of Exodus wherein he will be her God and she his 'special possession.' The covenant not only places upon Israel the responsibility of accepting the absolute sovereignty of Yahweh, it also requires Israel to treat the weak in her midst as Yahweh has treated her."[6]

Mama Lucy takes on this responsibility given divinely to her ancient forefathers. As such, in her role as a mother she becomes messianic. It is a role nurtured, ironically, by the religious hypocrisy of her father, Omar, who abandoned his family. Omar's departure resulted in Lucy taking on a much larger parental role:

> At nineteen, with one child of her own, she inherited the care of four younger brothers and sisters passed on to her when [her mother] Big Lucy died in childbirth and Omar decided he had a call to go on to Kansas after all to preach to the black pilgrims from the South. Nobody knows if Omar ever made it to Kansas after he took up preaching, for he was never heard from after he left Clayton City. But Little Lucy raised his brood along with six of her own and an undetermined number of other orphans and strays the Lord and the circumstances sent her way, and nobody remembered when she ceased to be Little Lucy and became Mama Lucy to a whole community. (220)

Fields of Prayer, 2000 (archival quality ink on water-resistant canvas, 9x12) by Ivey Hayes

Little Lucy became Mama Lucy after she chose to pick up her father's moral slack and support her abandoned siblings.

The title "Mama" is suggestive of an omnipresence that is associated with God, described in Isaiah 66:13 as maternal: "As a mother comforts her child, so I will comfort you; you shall be comforted in Jerusalem."[7] Just as God in Christ gives humanity life, Mama Lucy spends her life seeking to keep children alive, children like Sweet Feet. Mama Lucy and Lucius prioritized the care of children: their home "had more than its share of children, and anybody else's children who happened to need some place to stay. Mama Lucy treated them all alike. She took them to church, sent them to school, and fed them as best she could. She taught them how to work and then expected to see them work" (223).

" She didn't talk about what went on in the colored community either, and any effort to pry information out of her was apt to be met by the blunt declaration that since it wasn't none of her business, she had made no big effort to find out about it. Mama Lucy usually made her point, and when she had said all she wanted to say, she was apt to be let alone."
—*The Avenue* (22)

Mama Lucy's faith leads her to interact in the world rather than escape from it, but in spite of her faith, she is still cautious, acknowledging the viciousness of racism. Mama Lucy does not allow herself to become so comfortable with the white community for whom she works that she reveals private information about herself or the black community:

> The white folks found Mama Lucy to be a puzzlement, sometimes to the point of exasperation, but never enough to compromise her value as a servant. She was an excellent cook, turning out extraordinary cakes and pies or Sally Lunn or Charlotte Russe with effortless perfection. She kept an immaculate house, and she could work the arrival of unexpected guests into her routine without panicking or requiring extra supervision. But Mama Lucy never did let the white folks know what was going on inside the private recesses of her mind. She didn't talk about what went on in the colored community either, and any effort to pry information out of her was apt to be met by the blunt declaration that since it wasn't none of her business, she had made no big effort to find out about it. Mama Lucy usually made her point, and when she had said all she wanted to say, she was apt to be let alone. (222)

Mama Lucy understands that maintaining her agency in an oppressed community requires remaining, to some degree, mysterious to the oppressor. For disenfranchised people, to reveal themselves to those in power is to open themselves up to potential manipulation. This perspective is one that Zora Neale Hurston also shared with many black Southerners during the period of the Harlem Renaissance. In reflecting on her anthropological work on Eatonville, Florida, where she collected folklore, Hurston spoke of the mystery that many black Southerners maintained when even she, a black woman, sought to collect information from them:

> And the Negro, in spite of his open-faced laughter, his seeming acquiescence, is particularly evasive. . . . The Negro offers a feather-bed resistance. That is, we let the probe enter, but it never comes out. It gets smothered under a lot of laughter and pleasantries. The theory behind our tactics: The white man is always trying to know into somebody else's business. All right, I'll set something outside the door of my mind for him to play with and handle. He can read my writing but he sho' can't read my mind. I'll put this play toy in his hand, and he will seize it and go away. Then I'll say my say and sing my song.[8]

Mama Lucy's faith has helped her to understand in a spiritual sense that the more those in power know about the thoughts and interior

[8] Zora Neale Hurston, *Mules and Men* (1935, Harper Perennial Modern Classics, 1990): 2–3.

lives of those over whom they have power, the more able they are to use that information to manipulate, misuse, and malign the marginalized. She sees the ideology of racist power structures as evil; she is aware that good and evil are in the world, as is evident in how she prays, asking God, who made her children black, to enable them to "stand the test" (223), to deal with the attacks that they will face from a society that does not equate beauty with blackness. She believes that God is good and has created goodness and beauty but also that evil seeks to destroy that beauty. Her awareness of evil makes her cautious about what she says around the privileged people of her community.

The author, C. Eric Lincoln, notes that this same awareness is as necessary for surviving wolf-like social structures such as one that exists in Clayton City. Lincoln speaks of the black citizens of Clayton City living in a world that offers them no affirmation. The societal structures disparage their personhood. Thus, they live knowing, as Lincoln describes it, that "life in the black community [is] cheap. Life in the black community [is] negative. People who [are] black [are] nonentities." The key to negotiating such a world, Lincoln suggests, is awareness – that is, recognizing the existence of these structures and from there, strategizing as to how to deal with them, how to maintain one's self: "Be aware. Be aware. In other words, be aware of what is going on in this world and what is happening to you, the sources of your distress, because awareness is the only key to avoidance."[9]

Make Your Move, 1999 (archival quality ink water-resistant canvas, 9x12) by Ivey Hayes

COURTESY OF IVEYHAYESARTWORKS.COM

Mama Lucy's awareness protects her from the demoralizing racist structures that humiliate black citizens daily. Her awareness is a product of her faith, which allows her to live cautiously, caring for her children while remaining private in a community animated by a systemic and ferocious racism. In her faith, then, Mama Lucy finds grace. Such cannot be said for some of the other black citizens in Clayton City. Characters such as Coley and Dr. Walter Tait lack faith, resulting for Coley, in his activity in the world being diabolic rather than divine. He is undone by both the racist forces without and the amoral bent within his own heart. For Dr. Tait, a lack of faith leaves him vulnerable to predatory, racist forces that overwhelm him.

Coley aims only to advance his monetary and material holdings; he is completely uninterested in nurturing even the most vulnerable in his community. As a bootlegger, Coley sells moonshine out of his house, paying off white police officers to avoid legal trouble. Although he hates one of his regular customers, he accepts Roosevelt's

[9] Yvonne Ochillo, "The Universal Black Experience: An Interview with C. Eric Lincoln," *Journal of Negro History* 75.3–4 (1990): 115, 118.

business and avoids offending Roosevelt so that his secret plans to marry Roosevelt's sister, Queenie, will not be thwarted. As part of his machinations, he convinces the community's shell-shocked World War I veteran Shelly Mahaley that the goggle-wearing, motorcycle-riding Roosevelt is a German on the hunt who should be shot. With Roosevelt gone, Coley surmises that he can rush in to support Queenie in her grief, marry her quickly, and move into her house to make his moonshine business stronger and his self-worth greater. Thus, in contrast to someone like Mama Lucy, for whom marriage allowed the building of family, with her home becoming a refuge for the abandoned, Coley sees no need to concern himself with the outcasts in his community, except to use Shelly. Ironically, when Coley later tries on Roosevelt's goggles, Shelly kills him too.

The amorality that allows Coley to plot murder with no tweak of conscience is fed by social conditions that have so severely stripped him of dignity that murder seems his only means of acquiring any sort of personal worth. Coley has accepted society's view of his inferior status as a black man in the community, but he also seeks to distinguish himself among his peers:

> Coley never denied that he was a nigger – that'd be mighty hard to sell, him being both black and humble – but Coley always believed that he was a nigger in a class by himself. He knew he was smarter than the average colored man he'd ever seen, or heard about, and half the white folks who thought he was a coon were going to wake up someday and learn he was a fox. (66)

Outwitting others gives him a kind of self-respect; to him, plotting a successful murder is confirmation of his personal worth rather than a reflection of immorality. His life reveals what can happen to black citizens in a racially oppressive society who have no real means of socioeconomic advancement. Coley wants more than his socially inferior status allows him. He represents the black citizen who debunks the usual stereotypes of black people being concerned primarily with the fulfillment of base needs. In speaking of such stereotypes, Lincoln said that black people, particularly in literature, are presented often as "people who don't have enough to eat, people trying to find jobs. This is what we see when we see 'black.' I am trying to say [in *The Avenue*] to America, among other things, that black people are also human, that [they] have needs and desires that are above the visceral."[10] Coley wants more, but he is trapped in a system that expects him, because he is black, to focus only on the visceral, rather than humanistic concerns.

Dr. Tait, Clayton City's only black doctor, represents another kind of faithlessness that opens itself up to the viciousness and wolflike nature of racist forces. Dr. Tait allows racist forces to enter his private life, not realizing until too late the dire consequences. By the

" I had the idea to write about the ways in which a town shapes its people – their relationships and their destinies, sometimes even before they are born."
—C. Eric Lincoln
("Prof's Novel"))

---

10 Joan Oleck, "Lesson Along the Avenue," *Duke Perspectives* 74 (1988): 13; subsequently cited parenthetically.

end of the novel, Dr. Tait admits that Hoyt Horacio Butler (called Captain), a member of one of the most powerful families in town, has for years manipulated him into regularly providing morphine under the guise of medical care. The doctor who worked in Clayton City prior to Dr. Tait's arrival had refused to interact with Butler, but Dr. Tait submits to Butler's request "as part of the price of doing business in Clayton City" (271).

COURTESY OF DAVID M. RUBENSTEIN RARE BOOK AND MANUSCRIPT LIBRARY, DUKE UNIVERSITY

Butler's regular visits to the doctor's home lead to a degree of familiarity that allows Butler to sexually exploit Dr. Tait's wife, Ramona, whom he impregnates three times. Though Ramona gives birth to the first child, Dr. Tait gives Ramona abortions after the other two pregnancies. Then, in the showdown between Dr. Tait and Butler at the end of the novel, Dr. Tait reveals that his daughter, Makeda, is Butler's child. Even more shockingly, though, Dr. Tait hints at the fact that this daughter is pregnant and that the unborn child is, perhaps, Butler's, too.

With this revelation, the danger of having allowed Butler into his private life becomes even clearer, for he has ruined Tait as a husband and father and as an upstanding citizen. Dr. Tait had believed that respectability was all that he needed to deal with Butler and with the racist forces he represented, that if he simply caved into the will of these forces, his life would be spared the challenges facing other black citizens in the town. It was a misguided way of thinking because, as Lincoln says, racism has persisted throughout the decades in defiance of laws and the socially acceptable behavior of the oppressed: "When you consider the roots of racism, the why of racism, then you have to understand that it isn't going to go away simply by the fiat of law, or by the fiat of respectability" (Oleck 10). Despite all of his medical knowledge, Dr. Tait fails to understand in a way that is clear to Mama Lucy that the marginalized must keep their lives private if they are to maintain dignity in a racist society. In terms of Dr. Tait's family, Butler's persistent presence renders Dr. Tait an impotent opponent. Instead of standing up to Butler and, therein, protecting his wife from Butler's exploitation, Dr. Tait merely ends the pregnancies, saying, that he was seeking to avoid being "overwhelmed with the Butler presence in my house" (285). With this action Dr. Tait stands in great contrast to Mama Lucy. The beauty and strength that Mama Lucy wished for her children are absent from Dr. Tait's life. In allowing Butler to burrow into his life, Dr. Tait becomes a disfigured personality, something even he acknowledges when he finally confronts Butler:

ABOVE **C. Eric Lincoln at the Duke University Library, circa 1971**

In short, Captain, for all your titles and for all your power, you know from introspection, and I know from observation, that you and fresh chicken droppings have a lot in common. I can't claim any more for myself, but at least I know the reality of the charade. The rationale, if there is one. What you and I are involved in is the official version of fun and games for this godforsaken town. And for the same reasons: to avoid a reality that is simply too rotten to bear. (283)

COURTESY OF DAVID M. RUBENSTEIN RARE BOOK AND MANUSCRIPT LIBRARY, DUKE UNIVERSITY

Until this confrontation, Butler has had, as a representative of the white power structure, the advantage of expecting Tait's silence in the face of insult and humiliation. However, in deciding to confront Butler, Tait is finally returning the insult. Doing so means, though, he must exit the game. Because he dares finally not to remain silent, Tait knows that he can no longer live. As a black man, even though he is a doctor, he had been expected to accept his inferior status. Refusing to do so means suffering the wrath of the power structure. Therefore, Tait's only choice is, after confronting Butler and after witnessing his wife kill Butler, to commit suicide.

Unlike Tait, Mama Lucy is faithful in keeping her life private. Thus, she has no need, like Tait, for a direct confrontation to escape entrapment. Clayton City's racist forces, while at times frustrating and antagonizing her, never caught her. Her ability to cling to her dignity in the face of these forces explains why she stands as the anchor of this novel.

The Avenue does not follow the traditional structure of a novel. Rather, each chapter reads like a self-contained short story. Lincoln himself described the novel's structure as "episodic."[11] Many of the characters appear disconnected, with their only similarity being their presence as black citizens living in a small Southern town. They wrestle daily with the wolf-like presence of racism, a racism that threatens their personal sense of worth, a racism not yet disturbed by the voices of social activists that would arise in the 1960s. Thus, these characters must deal with a white supremacy that challenges their human worth. Mama Lucy responds to this threat by finding refuge in the agency that home and land ownership provide. In her own home and on her own land, she can protect her family's possessions as well as her identity from denigration, engaging in a kind of homemade political activism that seeks to shake the status quo by means other than the voting booth. The agency that home ownership provides

ABOVE **C. Eric Lincoln teaching in the Divinity School at Duke University, Durham, NC, 1981**

[11] Quoted in "Prof's Novel Drawing Critical Acclaim," *Durham Morning Herald* 24 Jan. 1988: 15A.

"The People who inhabit *The Avenue* are one's neighbors, friends and acquaintances if one is black and has lived in any small town in the South. If one is not black, this is a remarkable introduction to the other side of the coin that is seldom seen and so well portrayed by [C.] Eric Lincoln in this book."—John Hope Franklin ("Prof's Novel")

COURTESY OF DUKE UNIVERSITY PRESS

for her is undergirded by a faith that encourages her to grapple with rather than escape from the personal and social challenges she faces and to care for the most vulnerable in her town while being astutely aware of the diabolical nature of racism and protecting herself against it by keeping the interiority of her life private. Unlike Mama Lucy, Coley is void of any moral compass; he manipulates rather than serves the vulnerable in his community in order to acquire greater material success and social prominence, both of which, he believes, will reveal the dignity he deserves but that society assumes he fully lacks. Coley seems to contrast with Dr. Tait, who is endowed, because of his role as the town's only black doctor, with assumed importance. Yet Dr. Tait loses this dignity and his life when he submits to the racist powers of his community, keeping the Jim Crow status quo undisturbed. Dr. Tait, Coley, and Mama Lucy point to the diverse personalities and experiences of rural black Southerners living in the Jim Crow South. Even in their distinct differences in terms of age, gender, and profession, they all face the same struggle: finding dignity and self-respect in a world that has cast them as inferiors and that resists thinking of them in any other way. Their world – their town, Clayton City – is one in which psychological survival is as necessary as physical survival. Their souls need affirmation as much as their bodies need food. Few social structures and no civil rights organizations and legislation exist to support them psychologically. The church provides Mama Lucy some support, but Coley and Dr. Tait find no comfort there. The lives of these three characters testify to the fact that true freedom in a society is rooted in an ideology that affirms its citizens' humanity as well as in a social structure that provides equal access to opportunities and resources. ■

FRANCINE L. ALLEN is an Associate Professor of English at Morehouse College. She is currently working on her Master of Divinity at the Candler School of Theology at Emory University. Her research has focused on James Baldwin. Her broader research goals have aimed at exploring the intersection of literature, theology, and social justice, studying the ways that ancient narratives of scripture serve as archetypes for modern narratives.

C. ERIC LINCOLN (1924–2000) was a Professor of Religion and Culture at Duke University from 1976 until he retired in 1993. In his honor, Duke University created the C. Eric Lincoln Minister, a position at and the C. Eric Lincoln Fellowship. His other books include *The Black Muslims in America* (Beacon Press, 1961) and *Coming Through the Fire: Surviving Race and Place in America* (Duke University Press, 1996).

North Carolina native **IVEY HAYES** (1948–2012) earned a BA from NC Central University and and an MFA at UNC Greensboro. He spent much of his professional life in Wilmington, NC, where he was known for painting abstract figures in bold colors. He received many accolades in his career, including the North Carolina Azalea Festival Master of Arts in 2005 and the Order of the Long Leaf Pine Award in 2006. His work has been exhibited across the state and in such cities as Boston, New York, and Washington, DC (a solo exhibit at the Capitol Rotunda).

ABOVE **Duke University Press 1996 paperback edition of the novel**

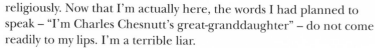

COURTESY OF JENNIFER HARDING

2018
AlexAlbright
Creative Nonfiction Prize
SECOND PLACE

LOOK ING FOR CHARLES

AN ESSAY BY JENNIFER HARDING

Lake View Cemetery

As I sit in the cemetery director's office, I doubt whether I can lie. I have made this pilgrimage to Cleveland to try bluffing my way to the gravesite of Charles Chesnutt, my favorite author, whose stories I teach religiously. Now that I'm actually here, the words I had planned to speak – "I'm Charles Chesnutt's great-granddaughter" – do not come readily to my lips. I'm a terrible liar.

I had expected to find Chesnutt in a small out-of-the way cemetery. I'm surprised by the beauty and enormity of this old cemetery where he's buried. It is "Cleveland's Outdoor Museum," a brochure jauntily informs me. I am currently being assisted by the director, who punches in "Chesnutt" on his computer and pulls up a map of the cemetery. On the director's desk are small stone rectangles that remind me of the countertop samples at Ikea. I guess I'm not his typical patron. This man must help people pick out gravesites and headstones, because, as a brochure reminds me with gothic glee, "Lake View is not full." He looks up from his screen and says, "Let's go," and we leave the office together on a quest to find the Chesnutt plot. I sense that the director doesn't know who Chesnutt was. He seems confident, but I'm worried that the Chesnutt site will elude us.

Back out in the bright hot summer day, I join my husband in our Volkswagen and follow the director's minivan on its slow drive through the hills of Lake View Cemetery, like a tiny funeral procession passing an uneven marble skyline. We drive by obelisks and mausoleums and the final resting places of John D. Rockefeller and President James Garfield, until we finally reach a peaceful section of flat headstones and dappled shadows.

JENNIFER HARDING is an Associate Professor of English at Washington & Jefferson College in Washington, PA. She has published numerous articles on Charles Chesnutt's short stories, including an essay in the MLA volume *Approaches to Teaching the Works of Charles W. Chesnutt.*

Harding also lectured on Chesnutt's stories as a Fulbright scholar in the Czech Republic in 2017.

Upon selecting this essay for second place, final judge Randall Kenan wrote, "I like this piece a lot. Very complicated. Very unexpected."

A part of me, I admit, has been hoping to recreate the recovery that Alice Walker describes in her essay "Looking for Zora."[1] At the time Walker made her own pilgrimage in 1973, Zora Neale Hurston was all but forgotten in the literary world. Not only was her work rarely read or studied, but her grave was unmarked and overrun with weeds. To convince the Florida cemetery staff to help her find the gravesite, Walker claimed to be Hurston's niece. This fib inspired my own plan to pose as Chesnutt's great-granddaughter. And by coincidence, my family tree has a gap in exactly the right spot.

My own great-grandfather, long dead now, was my progenitor only genetically. At age sixteen, my great-grandmother, Mima, became pregnant and was sent away to have her child. Mima and the baby, my grandmother, were taken in by a childless cousin. My grandmother told me she never learned anything about her biological father and didn't even know his name until she got a copy of her birth certificate when she was in her eighties. So, my thinking is this: if this man named Bernard abandoned Mima and my grandmother, then can't I abandon him back? Men used to choose not to acknowledge their children and – poof – fatherhood disappeared, as if these babies didn't have fathers at all. Can I, in response, walk away from Bernard, not only make him disappear, but replace him with Chesnutt, the African American author who sent his own daughters to Smith College and wrote my favorite stories?

My companions and I step gingerly past several rows of low headstones and spot the modest graves of the Chesnutt family among Birks, Carlsons, and Monteleones. A sign nearby identifies Chesnutt as "Lawyer, author of short stories and novels." I'm happy for this trace of his fame, but sheepish that I thought, or maybe even hoped, that finding an obscure grave would demonstrate my loyalty.

"Are you a descendant?" the director asks me.

"Still working on that," I answer.

> "A PART OF ME, I ADMIT, HAS BEEN HOPING TO RECREATE THE RECOVERY THAT ALICE WALKER DESCRIBES IN HER ESSAY 'LOOKING FOR ZORA.'"

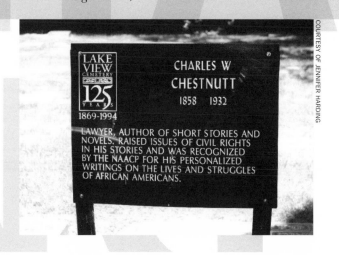

COURTESY OF JENNIFER HARDING

OPPOSITE TOP **Essay author Jennifer Harding at the headstone of Charles Waddell Chesnutt**

RIGHT **Lake View Cemetery, Cleveland, OH**

[1] "Looking for Zora" is included as an afterword in Alice Walker's *I Love Myself When I Am Laughing and Then Again When I Am Looking Mean and Impressive* (Feminist Press, 1979) 297–313.

> "HE WROTE
> THAT HE WOULD
> 'CRUSH OUT'
> THE PREJUDICE
> OF HIS ERA,
> PRIMARILY
> THROUGH HIS
> DEDICATION TO
> BECOMING AN
> ESTABLISHED
> AUTHOR AND
> DEPICTING
> THE BLACK
> EXPERIENCE
> IN AMERICA."

ABOVE **North Carolina Historical Highway Marker for Chesnutt, placed in 1950, located on Gillespie St. in Fayetteville (The text was updated in 2016 by East Carolina University Honors students.)**

On Legitimacy

Chesnutt and I don't exactly look like great-grandfather and great-granddaughter, but neither do we look as different as you might think. Descended from German and British immigrants, I've got blue eyes, blondish hair, and the kind of pale white skin that never tans. Descended from white and black North Carolinians, Chesnutt was an African American who appeared nearly white. He was a handsome, elegant man with a slight build. In a photograph taken when he was young, he has an angular face, earnest eyes, and a trimmed moustache.

In an early journal, Chesnutt reports strangers mistaking him for a white man and of repeatedly having to correct this mistaken assumption. He wrote that he would "crush out" the prejudice of his era, primarily through his dedication to becoming an established author and depicting the black experience in America. As Langston Hughes later described, Chesnutt was a "voluntary Negro," yet he not only lived his life identifying as a black man; he devoted his life to the uplift of African Americans.[2]

As a young man, Chesnutt was inspiringly determined. He kept a journal while teaching black students in rural schools in North Carolina. In it he records that at night he studied German and piano, while by day he taught former slaves to read. He copied the poems of Robert Burns into his journal alongside his own early attempts at literature. He declared that his "high, holy purpose" was to carve a place for people of his race in the literature of America (Brodhead 139). His ambitions for himself and for his race intertwined. By the time he turned forty-seven, Chesnutt would publish three novels, two collections of stories, and a biography of Frederick Douglass, not to mention numerous essays.

I am in awe of Chesnutt's courage. He charged boldly into complicated racial issues a full generation before the writers of the Harlem Renaissance would take up the same subjects. One set of stories – known as his "color line" stories – are about biracial Americans like himself.[3] He wrote candidly about the consequences of sex between the two races, historically based in the extreme power difference between white men and black women and the prevalence of rape, and he did not shy away from the issue of sexual violence and exploitation. Most notably, in his story "The Dumb Witness," Chesnutt depicts an enslaved woman named Viney who lives in a common law marriage with her master until he plans to displace her for a white wife. She tells the intended wife something – readers never learn exactly what – that ends the engagement.

[2] Richard Brodhead, ed., *The Journals of Charles W. Chesnutt* (Duke UP, 1993) 93; subsequently cited parenthetically; Langston Hughes, ed. *The Best Short Stories by Black Writers 1899–1967* (Little, Brown, 1967) x.

[3] Chesnutt's color line stories are collected in *The Wife of His Youth and Other Stories of the Color Line* (Houghton Mifflin, 1899); quotations from these stories will be cited parenthetically from the University of Michigan Press 1968 edition.

Her master then beats Viney mercilessly, destroying her power of speech. When his uncle dies, and she is the only person who knows the whereabouts of the will securing his inheritance, she continues to remain silent. For years he pleads, cajoles, and attempts to extract the information, but she remains "dumb" and only babbles incoherently. Only after his death does the narrator reveal the depth of Viney's resistance; in the conclusion, she speaks English.

In most of his "color line" stories, Chesnutt's primary focus is on the mixed-race descendants of such secret pairings, people like himself with both black and white heritage. As he put it, "all of my writings . . . have dealt with the problems of people of mixed blood, which, while in the main the same as those of the true Negro, are in some instances and in some respects much more complex and difficult of treatment, in literature as in life."[4] He depicts some biracial characters who are elitist, struggling to accept their connection to an African heritage and legacy of slavery.

Not only candid about these issues of identity, Chesnutt also exposed the exclusion of biracial children from legally-enforced notions of marriage and family. Chesnutt's stories reveal how power protected the fiction of white families in the nineteenth century, when the combined forces of white male exploitation of black women, white fathers' privilege of protected denial, and widespread legal prohibition of interracial marriage all combined to maintain the illusion that biracial children were "bastards" with no fathers.

In one of Chesnutt's stories, "The Sheriff's Children," a biracial man has the opportunity to call out his white father, a town sheriff who must now protect his son from a white mob. The young man admonishes his father for abandoning him and his enslaved mother, saying "other white men gave their colored sons freedom and money, and sent them to the free States. *You* sold *me* to the rice swamps" (85). He is about to shoot his father, but the sheriff's daughter arrives just in time to shoot her brother first, thus protecting the white construction of family by eliminating this "illegitimate" branch of the family tree. In another take on the excluded biracial child in "Her Virginia Mammy," a fair-skinned black mother reunites with her long-lost daughter, who has been living unknowingly as an orphan and white woman. The mother chooses not to identify herself, instead telling the woman a story that lets her believe the mother was actually her plantation "mammy," a story her daughter is eager to accept. By eliminating herself from the story, the mother enables her daughter to pass as a white woman and to accept a marriage proposal from a blue-blooded white suitor.

These stories dramatize the prevalence of white fatherhood and secret families outside of marriage, and especially the consequences for biracial children. Much of Chesnutt's short fiction shows readers the specific kinds of isolation and invisibility experienced by biracial people in a world of black and white.

> "NOT ONLY CANDID ABOUT THESE ISSUES OF IDENTITY, CHESNUTT ALSO EXPOSED THE EXCLUSION OF BIRACIAL CHILDREN FROM LEGALLY-ENFORCED NOTIONS OF MARRIAGE AND FAMILY."

OPPOSITE TOP **Charles Waddell Chesnutt, twenty-five years old, circa 1883**

4 SallyAnn H. Ferguson, ed., *Charles W. Chesnutt: Selected Writings* (Houghton Mifflin, 2001) 104; subsequently cited parenthetically.

COURTESY OF THE CLEVELAND PUBLIC LIBRARY FINE ARTS AND SPECIAL COLLECTIONS DEPARTMENT

Lamont Avenue

After visiting the cemetery in Cleveland, I decide to continue my pilgrimage by finding the location of the Chesnutts' former home. Their longest residence, from 1904 until the 1930s, was on Lamont Avenue, located just a short walk from my hotel near Case Western Reserve University.[5]

There are pictures of this large beautiful Victorian house at the Cleveland Public Library. The pictures show that the house was a strikingly large home with an unusual rounded porch and decorative siding, with a garage and an elaborate garden with a rose trellis. A picture of Chesnutt inside the house shows him in his library, seated at a desk, surrounded by busts and books. The house is protected on all sides by lush trees and shrubs. I want to see this evidence of Chesnutt's financial success. Also, I love old houses. I plan to visit the site of the Chesnutts's Victorian estate and hope that it's still standing.

On a muggy summer morning, I set out on foot, intent to find Chesnutt's house and another clue to his life and status in Cleveland. As I get closer to Lamont Avenue, it becomes obvious that the neighborhood where Chesnutt once lived has changed. I walk by an apartment building with its two bottom floors completely boarded up, but with curtains hanging in the windows of the upper floors, suggesting that people still live there. In the next block, former storefronts, long-deserted, are overhung with the rusted skeletons of awnings, though one has hours posted for a Sunday church service. When I turn onto a side street, I finally see the large houses I was expecting. Dilapidated old Victorian houses sit side-by-side with newer, plainer, ranch houses. As I continue walking, I notice that people driving cars and the few people I pass on the street are all African American.

I try to imagine the Chesnutts' house on this street, in this neighborhood. Old Victorian homes are the remnants of his era, but their opulence has seemingly given way to a new era of blight. Signs of attempted revitalization sit side by side with distressing evidence of poverty and decay. This neighborhood displays an obvious, painful fact: economic and geographic segregation still exists in America, and things appear worse in this neighborhood than when Chesnutt lived here over a hundred years ago and committed himself to the elevation of his race through literature.

I walk by a building labelled on my map as an African American history museum. It is closed and locked up. I wave to a middle-aged man pedaling by on a bike and ask him if he knows anything about the museum's status. "It closed, but they've been getting it cleaned up," he tells me. He yells "have a blessed day" as he rides away. I imagine what it would have been like to visit the museum and see pictures of Chesnutt, the neighborhood's own great author.

> "AS I GET CLOSER TO LAMONT AVENUE, IT BECOMES OBVIOUS THAT THE NEIGHBORHOOD WHERE CHESNUTT ONCE LIVED HAS CHANGED."

ABOVE **Chesnutt in his home library Cleveland, OH, circa 1905**

5 Description of the house at 9719 Lamont Avenue is based on pictures in the Cleveland Public Library's Special Collections. I want to thank the library for granting me access to these and other photographs.

When I arrive at the Chesnutt's former address at 9719 Lamont, I find nothing but a grassy plot where the house used to be. The evidence of Chesnutt's status and lifestyle is gone.

On the Color Line

Despite the fact that Cleveland now appears very racially segregated, Chesnutt's Cleveland was surprisingly integrated, according to sociologist Kenneth L. Kusmer in his book *A Ghetto Takes Shape*.[6] He describes the Chesnutts' era as a moment of surprising racial ease and integration in Cleveland and Chesnutt himself as a man who easily crossed racial boundaries. This ease may seem surprising considering that the end of the nineteenth century is an era when segregation, racial intimidation and terrorism were acceptable practices in many places. Yet in Ohio, interracial marriage was legal, schools were integrated, and colleges had been granting degrees to black students since before the Civil War. In late nineteenth-century Cleveland, Chesnutt and his family moved quite easily between black and white communities. His family attended a white church and socialized with white Clevelanders while also belonging to black social and charitable organizations.

Yet Chesnutt wanted more. He wanted to be a famous writer, and he wasn't afraid to take risks by being outspoken. He crossed the color line again and again in his life and in his literature. He gained fame by knowing how to interact with white publishers and audiences while writing about slavery and African Americans. He seemed comfortable in both worlds.

> "CHESNUTT WANTED MORE. HE WANTED TO BE A FAMOUS WRITER, AND HE WASN'T AFRAID TO TAKE RISKS BY BEING OUTSPOKEN. HE CROSSED THE COLOR LINE AGAIN AND AGAIN IN HIS LIFE AND IN HIS LITERATURE."

In Cleveland, Chesnutt joined The Rowfant Club, an elite white men's literary society, even though he had been blackballed when his name was first put forward for membership (when members literally placed two black marbles on a voting board). Chesnutt joined the club when an invitation was finally extended in 1910. According to a biography written by Chesnutt's daughter Helen, Saturday nights at the Rowfant Club were a highlight of his life for the next twenty-two years.[7] For their part, members of the club praised his presentations and printed special collectors' editions of his stories.

On a national stage, Chesnutt's status was evident when he was invited to attend Mark Twain's seventieth birthday party in New York City, along with Andrew Carnegie, William Dean Howells, and Mary

COURTESY OF THE CLEVELAND PUBLIC LIBRARY
FINE ARTS AND SPECIAL COLLECTIONS DEPARTMENT

ABOVE **The Chesnutt house at 9719 Lamont Avenue, Cleveland, OH**

6   Kenneth L. Kusmer, *A Ghetto Takes Shape: Black Cleveland 1870–1930* (U of Illinois P, 1976).

7   Helen M. Chesnutt, *Charles Waddell Chesnutt: Pioneer of the Color Line* (U of North Carolina P, 1952).

COURTESY OF LIBRARY OF CONGRESS

E. Wilkins Freeman, among many others. In a picture taken at the party, Chesnutt sits in his tuxedo – dignified, relaxed – at a table with white luminaries from the New England literary scene.

As these examples show, when other blacks were excluded, Chesnutt was the exception. If someone unfamiliar with Chesnutt looks at old photographs of the Rowfant Club or Mark Twain's party, though, it is not obvious that there is a black man in the picture. But Chesnutt's status as a black man was never in question. He didn't pass; he simply stepped back and forth across the color line.

Chesnutt wrote one story – my favorite story – that provides a hint about what this kind of social adaptability required. We learn about a slave named Grandison who is invited – encouraged – to run away by his master's son. The son takes him north, provides him with funds, and yet Grandison will not leave. The son eventually has him kidnapped into freedom in Canada. Why would a spoiled son of a planter do such a thing? To impress a woman, of course. As the opening line informs us, "When it is said that it was done to please a woman, there ought perhaps to be enough said to explain anything; for what a man will not do to please a woman is yet to be discovered" (168). But the story has a secret – Grandison, who performs the role of loyal slave to utmost perfection and eventually even runs away from Canada to return to the plantation – is not who he appears to be. The story ends with a twist when Grandison; his fiancée, Betty; and several other family members escape to Canada. It was done to please a woman, indeed.

The story is a satisfying depiction of a slave outwitting his buffoonish master, but what adds to the irony is that Chesnutt titled the story "The Passing of Grandison." Grandison does not pass in the traditional sense of being taken for white, but he passes as a loyal slave, he passes from slave status to freedom, and he passes across the border into Canada. The story highlights the degree to which crossing boundaries, performance, and transformations are intertwined themes in Chesnutt's stories.

Though in his lifetime he never achieved the degree of literary fame he sought, Chesnutt was presented with the Springarn Medal from the National Association for the Advancement of Colored People in 1928. He traveled to Los Angeles to accept it, saying that the NAACP was "the first successful and worthwhile organization for the protection of the rights and the promotion and advancement of . . . the American Negro." He noted, "I am proud to be numbered among them and to be found worthy of their esteem" (Ferguson 95).

In his lifetime Chesnutt crossed the color line between the worlds of black and white over and over again – every Saturday night, for example, to attend the Rowfant Club. He passed back and forth repeatedly, yet did so without passing.

> "IN HIS LIFETIME CHESNUTT CROSSED THE COLOR LINE BETWEEN THE WORLDS OF BLACK AND WHITE OVER AND OVER AGAIN."

ABOVE **Chesnutt (back center) at Mark Twain's seventieth birthday party at Delmonico's, New York, 5 Dec. 1905**

"I AM BLESSED BY THE LEGACY OF CHARLES CHESNUTT. BUT SOMETHING ABOUT CHESNUTT STILL SEEMS TO ELUDE ME."

A Tavern

Back in my hometown – Washington, Pennsylvania – I'm still not sure I have found Charles Chesnutt in Cleveland. I am a white scholar who spends a lot of time teaching and writing about African American literature, in particular Chesnutt's two major story collections known as the "color line" and "conjure" stories. Yes, I would tell the man on the bike in Cleveland, I am blessed by the legacy of Charles Chesnutt. But something about Chesnutt still seems to elude me.

I discuss these issues with a friend as we sit at a bar having a drink. This bar is unique. It is actually a tavern, situated at the back of a nineteenth-century house that is now our town's toniest restaurant. The tavern is decorated with nineteenth-century memorabilia, including a slightly-too-handsome portrait of Abraham Lincoln. The narrow room is abuzz with fancy drunk people sipping from stemmed cocktail glasses. I'm drinking a beer that smells like geraniums.

Intrigued by our surroundings, my friend and I discuss the past and present of this old home, which according to its owners housed escaping slaves 150 years ago. One of my historian friends has taught me to be skeptical of the many claims like this one linking old houses in our region to Underground Railroad activity. But in this case, it just might be true. The time period of the house is right (built in 1837), and our region *was* home to prominent abolitionists who did help escaping slaves in the nineteenth century. We want to believe it.

Overhearing snippets of our conversation, the bartender realizes that we have an interest in the house and its history. When he needs to make a trip downstairs, he invites us to follow him to the basement, where he tells us there is a hiding place used by escaped slaves. An interested restaurant hostess descends the narrow rickety staircase with us, where the bartender sorts through bottles of beer and wine stored in a room directly below the bar.

The hostess shows us the various other dank, dark rooms that constitute the house's basement. We walk gingerly from room to room; they have the irregular configuration and mysterious doors that seem typical of all old-house basements. The hostess points to a pile of coal stones and rocks in one back room and claims that this is the room where "they used to hide the slaves." We stand in contemplation and whisper about what we see. Both of us have spent a lot of time trying to find slaves.

My friend, who is African American, has told me of her own quest to find records of her ancestors who were slaves, a search that has been only moderately successful. She wants to piece together a family narrative, which has proven difficult to assemble because some people

"TONIGHT, MY FRIEND AND I BOTH TRY TO HARNESS OUR IMAGINATIVE RESOURCES TO GRANT HUMANITY TO THE SLAVES WHO MIGHT HAVE HIDDEN IN THIS HOUSE."

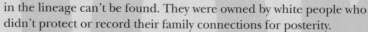

in the lineage can't be found. They were owned by white people who didn't protect or record their family connections for posterity.

My quest is different. As a professor of African American literature, I spend a lot of time thinking about what life was like for slaves and encouraging my students to empathize with them. We read Chesnutt's stories of slavery, including the clever story of a runaway slave told in "The Passing of Grandison." Tonight, my friend and I both try to harness our imaginative resources to grant humanity to the slaves who might have hidden in this house. "I wonder where they came from, and who they left behind," she says to me. "I wonder where they were going, and whether they made it," I respond.

I am white; she is black. I teach African American literature; she mentors African American students. Tonight, we are on a shared quest to understand the fear and hope of people who just might have occupied this same dark basement over 150 years ago. Trying to discover and understand the real meaning of slavery through the lived experiences of slaves was also the literary quest of Charles Chesnutt.

On Slavery

The conditions of slavery led to the existence of people like Charles Chesnutt, biracial Americans with ancestors on both sides of the color line. Yet Chesnutt was never a slave; his mixed-race mother and father were never slaves. Though Chesnutt was born in 1858, years before the end of the Civil War and passage of the Thirteenth Amendment, at that time his parents were free and living in Ohio. So, Chesnutt never suffered the direct effects of slave life, but he witnessed those effects on people of his race, especially the rural black citizens of North Carolina who were his students when he was a young man. From his other writing, it is clear that Chesnutt turned a careful ear to their dialect, their stories, and their horrors. Chesnutt published some of the most complex stories of enslaved life, his "conjure tales."[8] They have proved to be a centerpiece of Chesnutt's legacy, but also an enduring puzzle for readers.

The conjure tales are wildly fantastical accounts of slavery. They appeared in esteemed literary journals of the nineteenth century, and readers at first did not know that Chesnutt was African American. Depicting the lives of slaves, each story is framed by the narration of a smug white man, John, who has travelled from Ohio to North Carolina after the Civil War and purchased a vineyard. A former slave

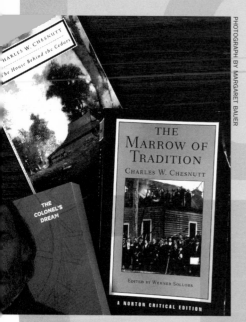

PHOTOGRAPH BY MARGARET BAUER

---

[8] Chesnutt's conjure stories were first collected in his first book, *The Conjure Woman* (Houghton Mifflin, 1899); quotations from these stories will be cited parenthetically from the 1969 University of Michigan Press edition.

"THESE STORIES, LIKE CHESNUTT'S OTHER CONJURE TALES, REPRESENT THE TRAUMAS OF SLAVERY – POWERLESSNESS, SEPARATION, PHYSICAL VIOLENCE, MENTAL DISTRESS – AS WELL AS THE CALLOUS HYPOCRISY OF SLAVEHOLDERS."

named Julius tells stories to John and his wife, Annie, about slave times. These inner stories, told in a slave dialect, encode the deep horrors of slavery in folklorish tales of transformations and conjuring. People literally become products like grapes and lumber and ham; they lose their sanity after separations and traumas; they are sometimes cursed and sometimes saved by the power of conjuring. John and Annie occasionally understand the anguish of Julius's outlandish stories, but mostly they don't. In sympathy, Annie bestows gifts on Julius – gifts that are a kind of payment for his stories – but his character remains largely opaque to them.

One of the most disturbing scenes occurs in "Po' Sandy" when Julius tells John and Annie about Sandy, a slave so competent that all his masters' children, having established their own households, request his service. As a result of being sent away for months at a time, Sandy is often separated from his wife, Tenie, a conjure woman, until she turns him into a tree to keep him in one place. When the tree is cut down and chopped up into boards, Tenie is forced to watch the loud and horrifying mutilation; the experience drives her insane. After hearing the story, Annie grants Julius the use of a wood building haunted by Sandy's spirit, though John remains skeptical. Through its rich symbols of powerlessness and physical beatings, the story depicts the traumas of slave life that still "haunt" the plantation, but the full meaning of this legacy is lost on Annie and John.

Like Sandy, the main character in "Sis' Becky's Pickanninny" also suffers for her competence. Julius relates the tale of Becky, whose only beloved child is left behind when she is traded to another plantation because of her skill as a fieldhand. She and her baby both become physically ill and depressed. Through the help of a conjure woman, the baby is able to visit his mother (in the form of a bird) and they eventually reunite permanently and ultimately gain their freedom. Hearing this story lifts Annie out of her own depression, but John considers the story, and Annie's reaction to it, somewhat silly. The story is a poignant depiction of family reunion achieved by supernatural means, a reminder that such reunions were not actually available to real slaves.

These stories, like Chesnutt's other conjure tales, represent the traumas of slavery – powerlessness, separation, physical violence, mental distress – as well as the callous hypocrisy of slaveholders. The slaves' attempts to survive and endure through conjuring sometimes succeed and sometimes fail. Similarly, Julius's connection with his white listeners, John and Annie, sometimes succeeds, in part, but often fails. The result is a profound and disturbing empathy available to readers, but only if they read into the imaginative plots and symbols and transcend the models of "understanding" provided by Annie and John.

Enslavement is so different from the lifestyles we know, readers may initially feel like Annie and John. In twenty-first-century America, we have nothing that compares to being owned, body and soul,

by another person operating with the full backing of the government. If slaves truly hid beneath a house in Washington, Pennsylvania, how can we begin to understand the mix of fear, vulnerability, and hope that they felt? To recreate this past, we can turn to slave narratives, recordings of interviews conducted in the 1930s, public documents, and histories. We can also read Chesnutt carefully. In their complexity and creativity, the conjure stories give readers an imaginative connection to slaves.

Julius's tales, fantastical though they are (or even because of their symbolic richness), enable an empathy with slaves through an almost mythical transformation of their daily traumas. Reading into the symbols, I imagine how it must have felt to live every day with no rights or autonomy and constant threats. I try to imagine what it would have been like to discover, like Becky, that I'm going to another plantation and my baby is staying behind. Or to be informed, like Tenie, that my husband will have to leave home for most of the year. Or to be commanded by a master (the secret story encoded in the skin of all of Chesnutt's biracial characters), "come here, girl."

Chesnutt had to cross an experiential divide when depicting slave life. He was able to transport himself imaginatively into the lives of slaves with whom he had very little in common and to create literature from the brutal conditions in which they actually lived. When it came to the fierce realities of slavery, Chesnutt was an outsider, but his ironic and double-voiced stories reveal an understanding of slave life and a compassion for slaves.

Looking and Seeing

I looked for Chesnutt at his final resting place. It was pleasant. Unlike Zora Neale Hurston, he was easy to find. Lake View cemetery gave the illusion of a pleasant integrated world, one where I could easily discover my favorite author and spiritual great-grandfather. But when I looked for Chesnutt's house in his old neighborhood, I found his legacy and home gone. And when I looked for evidence of people escaping slavery in another old house, I could only imagine them.

"IN HIS DEPICTIONS OF SLAVES, SLAVE MASTERS, AND THEIR BIRACIAL DESCENDANTS, HE TOLD STORIES THAT WERE ONLY WHISPERED BY OTHERS, IF MENTIONED AT ALL: STORIES OF THE INHUMANE CONDITIONS OF SLAVERY, OF ILLEGITIMACY, OF 'GOOD' WHITE FATHERS AND 'BAD' WHITE FATHERS, OF CONFUSING AND CONFLICTED IDENTITIES, OF PASSING."

ABOVE TOP **Charles W. Chesnutt Library at Fayetteville State University, constructed in 1937, Fayetteville, NC**

ABOVE BOTTOM **The Chesnutt Library in Fayetteville, NC, today**

The best guide I have for seeking an understanding of the historic black experience is Chesnutt himself. In his depictions of slaves, slave masters, and their biracial descendants, he told stories that were only whispered by others, if mentioned at all: stories of the inhumane conditions of slavery, of illegitimacy, of "good" white fathers and "bad" white fathers, of confusing and conflicted identities, of passing. He stubbornly insisted that biracial people and their stories were interesting and distinct. But in his stories, he also mocks biracial characters who try to distance themselves from other black people, like an elitist "Blue Vein" society in his story "The Wife of His Youth." He saved his most biting satire for white men whose callous power could destroy black families. He depicted slaves with sympathy and humanity.

I am in the habit of looking into the past to find Charles Chesnutt. He was in the habit of looking to the future to imagine us. In 1905 Chesnutt wrote, "Looking down the vista of time I see an epoch in our nation's history, not in my time or yours, but in the not distant future, when there shall be in the United States but one people . . . when men will be esteemed and honored for their character and talents" (Ferguson 93). He noted that "Race prejudice will not perhaps entirely disappear until the difference of color shall have disappeared, or at least until all of us, white and Colored, shall have resolutely shut our eyes to those differences" (Ferguson 92).

How surprised Chesnutt would be to discover that we have not even come close to this goal. Yet how pleased he would be to learn that he is now labelled the first black author to write nationally-recognized novels and stories in a long and increasingly celebrated tradition of African American literature. He could not have foreseen that many people would one day recognize black art, music, and literature as the most original American tradition, or that he would appear in a series of stamps devoted to Black Heritage and in every major American literature anthology.

Chesnutt was a great black writer, and he was a great brown writer. Chesnutt had a complex understanding of his own racial identity as both African American and biracial. His unflinching stories depict the intersecting legacies of black, white, and mixed-race Americans, including people and topics that in his era were often treated as invisible. The best place to find Charles Chesnutt, I've concluded after my pilgrimage, is the place where he wanted to be found: in his literature. ■

> "THE BEST PLACE TO FIND CHARLES CHESNUTT, I'VE CONCLUDED AFTER MY PILGRIMAGE, IS THE PLACE WHERE HE WANTED TO BE FOUND: IN HIS LITERATURE."

"**WHETHER THE FRAMERS OF THE CONSTITUTION OR ANY OF THE PERSONS WHO HELD BLACK FOLKS IN BONDAGE PAUSED TO CONSIDER THE** *PECULIARITY*, **THE INCONSISTENCY, OR THE INHUMANITY OF THEIR ACTIONS, IT IS CLEAR THAT** *PECULIAR* **DID NOT MEAN STRANGE ENOUGH TO CALL AN END TO THE PRACTICE.**"

AUN' PEGGY: CHARLES CHESNUTT'S VAMPIRE SLAYER?

BY TRUDIER HARRIS

TRUDIER HARRIS is an American literary scholar whose work focuses on African American literature, especially women writers, African American culture, and Southern literature and culture. Her numerous honors include, most recently, the Richard Beale Davis Award for Lifetime Achievement in Southern Literary Studies. A native of Tuscaloosa, AL, Harris earned her BA in English from Stillman College and her MA and PhD from The Ohio State University. She is the author of ten books and the editor or co-editor of more than a dozen more. Formerly the J. Carlyle Sitterson Distinguished Professor of English at UNC Chapel Hill, she is now a University Distinguished Research Professor at the University of Alabama.

HISTORIANS AND SCHOLARS have routinely referred to slavery in the United States as "the peculiar institution."[1] While not exactly a misnomer, the phrase, nonetheless, gives one pause. If the institution were so *peculiar*, then why did it garner such popularity? Or does *peculiar* refer to the inexcusably inhumane ways in which people of African descent were treated, thus making it peculiar that human beings could paradoxically treat other human beings in such monstrous ways? Or, did *peculiar* mean that it was strange for Americans to hold human beings in bondage when they, themselves, had come across the ocean seeking various kinds of freedoms? Was the absence of freedom for people of African descent the basis for the *peculiarity*, especially since slavery is diametrically opposed to every tenet of American democracy? What did that nearly oxymoronic concept convey? Whether the framers of the Constitution or any of the persons who held black

Trudier Harris is grateful to Dr. Briana Whiteside of the University of Nevada at Las Vegas for reading this essay and offering helpful suggestions. Dr. Whiteside agrees that Aun' Peggy "uses small tranquilizing daggers that could subdue [slavery], if only for a short time" (correspondence with the author on 9 Aug. 2018).

[1] In fact, in 1956, Knopf published *The Peculiar Institution: Slavery in the Ante-Bellum South* by Kenneth M. Stampp, an eminent historian.

folks in bondage paused to consider the *peculiarity*, the inconsistency, or the inhumanity of their actions, it is clear that *peculiar* did not mean strange enough to call an end to the practice. As we know, the *peculiar institution*, with its various peculiarities, existed on United States soil for hundreds of years. And we know that it was only with great mental and physical force that the most egregious forms of the institution were eradicated.

As the phrase "the peculiar institution" lingers in historical and scholarly imagination, I want to suggest another possibility for its interpretation. I accept the labeling of slavery as the peculiar institution because slavery could be interpreted as a form of vampirism. And vampirism is nothing if not peculiar. I posit, therefore, that slavery, like the mythical vampirism, sucked the life blood out of the people of African descent who were unfortunate enough to be caught in its bloodthirsty clutches. No black human beings trapped in this system could remain fully whole as its practices drained them of energy (labor), drained them of expectations for escape, drained them of family members and family ties, and drained them, finally, of their very lives. For the most part, though, the vampiric system operated as Jewelle Gomez's vampires do in *The Gilda Stories*.[2] It took what it needed without destroying its victims completely – or at least not right away. Unlike Gomez's vampires, however, it gave little, if anything, positive in return. This greedy and destructive system experienced few effective challenges to its existence. Certainly, we hear of (mostly failed) slave rebellions, but, usually, blacks had little redress and little opportunity to escape from their oppression.

WITH ILLUSTRATIONS BY PAULA JORDAN-MAYO

Born and raised in Rocky Mount, NC, **PAULA JORDAN-MAYO** is an illustrator pursuing a career in graphic novels. She earned her BFA in Illustration from East Carolina University in 2018. While attending ECU, she interned for Pitt County's Emerge Gallery & Art Center, which featured her art in brochures for Emerge Gallery's annual Jolly Trolley Polar Express and commissioned her to illustrate a design for the annual PirateFest. She also worked as a graphic designer for ECU's Joyner Library. In the 2017 Undergraduate Exhibition, she received an Award of Excellence in Illustration for her work "Fish Hippie Labels: Chardonnay, Merlot, & Riesling." She currently resides in Asheboro, NC.

[2] Jewelle Gomez, *The Gilda Stories* (IFirebrand, 1991).

This is not, however, to say that all was lost. Through various means, enslaved persons sometimes found ways to thwart the system that was intent upon using them up and then destroying them. Lawrence Levine documents several of these resistive strategies in *Black Culture and Black Consciousness: Afro-American Folk Thought from Slavery to Freedom*, including instances in which blacks mutilated themselves in order to escape, however briefly, from the arduous demands of the work they were required to do.[3]

Before Gomez and Levine, however, there was Charles W. Chesnutt. A North Carolina native who lived for a while in Cleveland, Ohio, Chesnutt took his creative energies from the peculiar institution and used them in *The Conjure Woman*.[4] This volume of short stories features John and Annie, a Northern white couple who have relocated to the South following the Civil War; Uncle Julius, the faithful retainer coach driver and raconteur extraordinaire who befriends them and earns employment from them; and the stories that Uncle Julius tells of the days "befo' de wah" (14). Some of these stories feature Aun' Peggy, after whose profession the volume is titled, who has extraordinary abilities to manipulate natural and human phenomenon.[5] The enslaved seek her assistance for a variety of reasons, ranging from being worked too hard, to wanting to remain in place instead of being sold, to solving love relationships, to preventing the separation of families. As an outsider and a free black woman who resides near but not on the Dugal' McAdoo plantation where most of the action occurs, Aun' Peggy uses her powers to disrupt the system's impact upon those who are enslaved. Although she does not wield a wooden stake or a silver bullet, she nonetheless succeeds in various ways in reducing slavery to a manageable inconvenience from its status as an all-consuming, devouring monster.

Aun' Peggy operates within a set of givens that define slavery. It is a given that the vast majority of human beings enslaved would experience that condition from birth until death (the small numbers who managed to escape are the obvious exception). It is a given that whites who owned blacks did not take their physical, emotional, or spiritual welfare as their primary consideration. Thus their actions echo those of traditional vampires: any concern for physical well-being was directly tied to the individual's ability to provide the labor (sustaining blood) upon which the system of slavery rested. Remember as well that many iterations of slavery, including those on the rice plantations in Louisiana, adhered to the philosophy of treating enslaved persons as expendable commodities that could be replaced easily, so slaveholders simply worked the enslaved to death. As vampires did not place the comfort levels of their victims first, so too levels of

> "ALTHOUGH SHE DOES NOT WIELD A WOODEN STAKE OR A SILVER BULLET, SHE NONETHELESS SUCCEEDS IN VARIOUS WAYS IN REDUCING SLAVERY TO A MANAGEABLE INCONVENIENCE FROM ITS STATUS AS AN ALL-CONSUMING, DEVOURING MONSTER."

[3] Lawrence Levine, *Black Culture and Black Consciousness: Afro-American Folk Thought from Slavery to Freedom* (Oxford UP, 1977).

[4] Charles W. Chesnutt, *The Conjure Woman* (1899, U of Michigan P, 1969); subsequently cited parenthetically from this edition.

[5] While Aun' Peggy is a prominent character in Chesnutt's collection, including, in addition to the stories discussed here, "The Grey Wolf's Ha'nt" and "Hot Foot Hannibal," there are other magic practitioners in the book: Tenie, a former conjure woman who transforms her lover into a tree in "Po' Sandy," and an unnamed conjure man referenced in "The Conjurer's Revenge."

comfort or spiritual contentment were never a slaveholder's priority in dealing with those enslaved. In fact, many of the punishments and other physical violations that occurred were designed specifically to cause dis-ease and to induce acquiescence in those enslaved. The slaveholder's primary objective was financial gain and physical comfort in a world that was created to ensure that whites dominated blacks and that anything whites wanted took precedent over the wishes of blacks; indeed, blacks had no legitimate wishes as far as white slaveholders were concerned. Within these strictures of an oppressive system, therefore, where the end game was nearly always death, what any individual could do to affect this vampiristic structure was, in turn, limited. It would be stretching things, then, to assume that Aun' Peggy could bring about an end to the system of slavery or even that she could affect such a termination with a single enslaved person. Nonetheless, it is illuminating to consider the small impacts she does have and to read them in the context of curtailing some of the effects of the monster of slavery.

It is perhaps best to view Aun' Peggy as an intervener/intercessor, an outsider who understands the habits of the hunters and the hunted (like the traditional slayers of vampires and other monsters). As such an outsider, she might have motives that are at times altruistic and perhaps at other times self-serving. In *The Conjure Woman*, Aun' Peggy is paid for her services, just as vampire slayers in various literary and mythical towns received payment from the put-upon citizens who solicited their services. Equally as adept as her literary and folkloristic predecessors, Aun' Peggy possesses a particular set of skills that makes her services invaluable to those who solicit them. However, her skills do not mean that she is unwaveringly committed to one side, and ambiguity overlays at least one of the stories in the volume. Overall, though, it is safe to assert that Aun' Peggy mostly works – at times rather aggressively – against the system of slavery.

Aun' Peggy's assaults on the vampire of slavery take many forms in *The Conjure Woman*. While she does not kill the monster completely, she succeeds in various ways in neutralizing or toning down its destructively negative effects. She attacks slavery by transforming the enslaved as well as their so-called masters, by shapeshifting enslaved persons into creatures who escape – however briefly – their legally defined status as expendable human beings, and by generally offering hope for better conditions to those who find themselves in the grip of slavery. Perhaps the most memorable instance of transformation of the enslaved occurs in the first story, "The Goophered Grapevine." In that narrative, Aun' Peggy comes onto the McAdoo plantation at the request of the slaveholder himself. It is a rare instance in which a

> **"IT IS PERHAPS BEST TO VIEW AUN' PEGGY AS AN INTERVENER/INTERCESSOR, AN OUTSIDER WHO UNDERSTANDS THE HABITS OF THE HUNTERS AND THE HUNTED (LIKE THE TRADITIONAL SLAYERS OF VAMPIRES AND OTHER MONSTERS)."**

"THE BUYING AND SELLING OF HUMAN BEINGS OBVIOUSLY REINFORCE THE IDEA OF SLAVERY AS A VAMPIRE THAT SUCKS THE LIFE BLOOD OUT OF PERSONS OF AFRICAN DESCENT, FOR IT UNCONSCIONABLY SEPARATES PARENTS AND CHILDREN, WIVES AND HUSBANDS, AND THOSE WITH ANY OTHER RELATIONSHIP BONDS."

so-called master recognizes the ability of the conjure woman and solicits her help in what he hopes is a scheme to make his vineyard even more profitable. Suspecting that those enslaved on his plantation are eating too freely from his luscious scuppernongs, Mars Dugal' asks Aun' Peggy to conjure the vines so that any enslaved person who violates the injunction to stay away will suffer dire consequences. Having done her job and then having learned that a newly arrived and unsuspecting black man has eaten some of the conjured grapes, Aun' Peggy in turn conjures him to survive her initial spell. By so doing, she seems to go against what she has done for Mars Dugal' and seems to undermine somewhat his desired control over the grapes. Henry, whose fate is tied to the seasonal rising and declining of the grapevines, is young and supple in the spring and aged and rheumatic in the fall and winter. When Mars Dugal' realizes what is happening, he sells Henry for a high price when he is young and buys him back when he appears to his new owners to be at death's door.

The buying and selling of human beings obviously reinforce the idea of slavery as a vampire that sucks the life blood out of persons of African descent, for it unconscionably separates parents and children, wives and husbands, and those with any other relationship bonds. The life blood of the enslaved is all that matters, and it is the only thing of value to those who profess to own them. Indeed, the enslaved become hunted prey as Mars Dugal' and several neighbors pursue an enslaved person who has run away (this distraction causes Henry not to be warned about the conjured grapes): "ole Mars Dugal' en some er de yuther nabor w'ite folks had gone out wid dere guns en dere dogs fer ter he'p 'em hunt fer de nigger" (19). The valuable life blood of property must be retrieved at all costs and used up only at the master's discretion. Also, recognition that the life blood of the enslaved – given freely or otherwise – to sustain the system is apparent in steel traps that Mars Dugal' sets to prevent them from eating the grapes. With these vampiric practices in place, it hardly seems necessary for Aun' Peggy to enter as another force to control the enslaved. Yet, that is what happens, and that is what leads to the one conspicuous instance of ambiguity in the text.

We can certainly argue that Aun' Peggy appears to be helping instead of slaying or crippling the vampiric system of slavery, for Mars Dugal' earns a lot of money over several years as a result of buying and selling Henry. From Henry's point of view, however, I argue that she slays slavery sufficiently enough to enable Henry to enjoy the fruits of his master's favoritism over an extended period of time. Instead of Henry's being considered merely disposable labor, Mars Dugal' comes to value him as a very special human being. Although he perhaps does not understand what happens to Henry (and Chesnutt does not give us the privilege of his interiority), he understands that he has a very valuable commodity in this newly-acquired

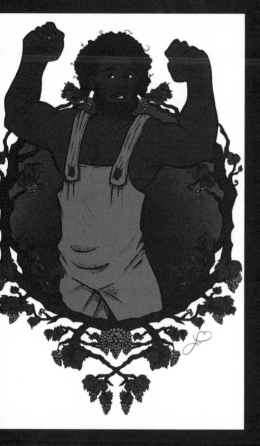

black man. Echoing some of the actions in Gomez's *The Gilda Stories*, where vampires often provide gifts in exchange for their bloodsucking, Julius asserts of Mars Dugal's treatment of Henry: "He tuk good keer uv 'im dyoin' er de winter, – give 'im whiskey ter rub his rheumatiz, en terbacker ter smoke, en all he want ter eat, – 'caze a nigger w'at he could make a thousan' dollars a year off'n did n' grow on eve'y huckleberry bush" (27). Through Henry, then, Aun' Peggy succeeds in transforming not only the physical appearance of the enslaved, but the mental responses of those who profess to own them. As a representative of the system of slavery, Mars Dugal' thus steps outside that system long enough to be transformed, however temporarily and financially inspired, by the transformation that Aun' Peggy has affected.

Additionally, we could argue that the fate of Mars Dugal's vineyard is also linked to Aun' Peggy and what she initially does to the vines. As a result of selling and buying Henry, Mars Dugal' earns enough money to buy another plantation. He then figures that he can make even more money off the grapes. So, he allows a Yankee to prune and fertilize his vineyard. By hiring this inexperienced entrepreneur, ostensibly to make a profitable situation even better, Mars Dugal' embraces the hell of greed, which leads not only to the demise of the vineyard, but to Henry's demise as well. Sadly, the Yankee gets Mars Dugal' to cut too close to the roots of the vines, applies too much fertilizer, and within a year, both the vines and Henry die. Having been the one to put the original goopher on the vine, the goopher that tied Henry's fate to that of the vine, Aun' Peggy, therefore, is the cause of a loss of profit to the McAdoo plantation and its falling upon hard times. Aun' Peggy's original intervention now disrupts the profit inherent in the system of slavery, and that disruption, even in this small and isolated instance, illustrates how Chesnutt's conjure woman has gone up against the vampiric system of slavery and won. Certainly, Henry dies; his death under the system of slavery, however, would have occurred with or without Aun' Peggy's intervention. The fact that she has enabled him to have several years of supple and flirtatious existence beyond what he might normally have had bolsters the argument for Aun' Peggy's attack upon slavery.

Still, the ambiguity remains. As mentioned, Aun' Peggy is consistently paid for her conjuring; while Mars Dugal' gives her the queenly sum of ten dollars to conjure his vineyard, those enslaved resort to paying her with scarves, hams, and garden vegetables. If Aun' Peggy is using her skills merely to sustain herself, then what difference does it make to her who pays her? Would she not act on the behalf of whoever hires her services and, in turn, work for whatever they request? Conjurers in New Orleans, which Zora Neale Hurston treats in *Mules and Men,* mostly fit this description; they will work for anyone who pays them well.[6] On the other hand, when we consider how Uncle Julius characterizes Aun' Peggy in the other stories, where her actions are always *unambiguously* applied to the aid of those enslaved, those latter actions tend to overshadow this initial presentation. This first story, therefore, may be an instance in which Uncle Julius creates ambiguity for his own purposes. After all, he tells John not to buy the vineyard

6 Zora Neale Hurston, *Mules and Men* (Lippincott, 1935).

because it is conjured. Readers learn – according to John, at least – that Uncle Julius has been earning money from the grapes on the abandoned plantation. He therefore conjures a story that potentially clutches both Mars Dugal' and Aun' Peggy in the arms of greed. The difference is that Aun' Peggy's rewards are so minimal in comparison to Mars Dugal's that she still garners sympathy from readers, and most of those, I would argue, would agree that she attacks slavery.

That attack is even more apparent in "Mars Jeems's Nightmare," in which Aun' Peggy transforms a vicious slaveholder into an enslaved person who is about to be sold "down the river" just before he is rescued from that potentially terminal fate. Mars Jeems McLean, like any vampire, has absolutely no concern for the bodies upon which his plantation feeds. He forces blacks on his plantation to work from daylight to dark, directs them not to sing, dance, or play the banjo, and does not allow courting or any other rec-

> "MARS JEEMS MCLEAN, LIKE ANY VAMPIRE, HAS ABSOLUTELY NO CONCERN FOR THE BODIES UPON WHICH HIS PLANTATION FEEDS. . . . THEIR LIFE BLOOD BELONGS TO HIM, AND THEY FIND THEMSELVES QUICKLY CORRECTED IF THEY DARE TO BELIEVE OTHERWISE."

reational activity that would detract from the enslaved devoting *all* of their attention to laboring for him. Their life blood belongs to him, and they find themselves quickly corrected if they dare to believe otherwise. If he learns that a couple wants to get married, he sends one off to his second plantation some distance away or sells him or her outright. Complaints lead to forty lashes or even harsher punishment. "Mars Jeems did n' make no 'lowance fer nachul bawn laz'ness, ner sickness, ner trouble in de min', ner nuffin; he wuz des gwine ter git so much wuk outer eve'y han', er know de reason w'y" (72). In other words, Mars Jeems is a strikingly cruel, relentlessly punishing, and insensitive slaveholder, the epitome of the vampiric system that he helps to keep in place. His personality and practices lead a disgruntled black man named Solomon, who is angry about his girlfriend being moved to another plantation, to approach Aun' Peggy about remedying the situation.

Aun' Peggy transforms Mars Jeems into a black man who is brought to his own plantation the next morning in payment for a debt. Unaccustomed to enslavement, thus unaware that his life blood is not supposed to belong to him, the "noo nigger" suffers mightily under Mars Johnson, the overseer. Work puzzles him, he has no idea as to how to use plantation tools, and he knows nothing about staying in his place. Brash and backtalking, the new hired hand receives lashes galore. Unbroken in spite of constant punishment, the new hand is sold and on his way to harsher conditions of slavery before Solomon reports to Aun' Peggy that he has disappeared. She sends Solomon on a mission to feed him a conjured sweet potato, which he eats, awakes from his nightmare, reverts to his white slaveholder self, and returns to his plantation, where

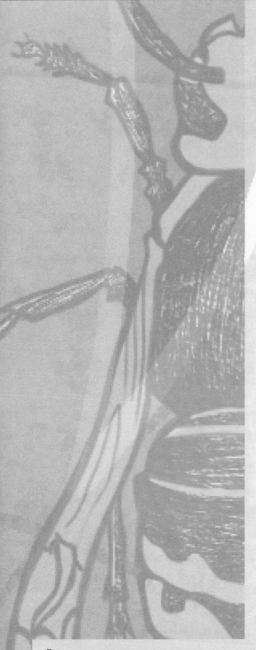

formed consciousness to go along with his previously transformed physical being. First, he fires Johnson, the harsh, whip-loving overseer. Then he shortens the work day for those enslaved, allows occasional Saturday night dances, permits Solomon's girlfriend to return, and does not complain about additional courting, so "eight er ten couples got married" (99). Indeed, when the young woman who rejected Mars Jeems during his mean days learns about the new occurrences on his plantation, she changes her mind about him, and they also get married.

This is perhaps Chesnutt's clearest example of Aun' Peggy's ability to hinder the vampire of slavery. As Uncle Julius remarks about Mars Jeems, "Aun' Peggy's

goopher had made a noo man un 'im enti'ely" (98). Through her pedagogical conjuration, Aun' Peggy ensures that Mars Jeems learns valuable lessons about how human beings should treat other human beings – even across racial lines, especially when they are in positions of power. By forcing Mars Jeems to experience the physical conditions of slavery, to know slavery viscerally, to understand the draining power of the vampire, and to balk at its inhumanity, Aun' Peggy again disrupts cruelty, negates profit that is measured solely in terms of finance, and inspires a little utopia in the midst of bloodsucking conditions. While Mars Jeems never knows the source of his transformation, he embraces the effects, and he acts upon what he has learned. By creating a little oasis of tolerance in the midst of an evil system, Mars Jeems weakens the power and effect of slavery. Chances are great that Solomon and his companions will be enslaved for life, but, even better than Henry, they will live those lives with less direct punishment than previously, and they will have the companionship of wives and husbands who can soothe the horrors of slavery. Again, Aun' Peggy might not put a stake through the heart of slavery, but she serves a significant purpose in mitigating its effects.

In the one instance in which Aun' Peggy transforms an enslaved person completely (unlike changes of features with Henry in "The Goophered Grapevine"), she also enables that person to have moments of freedom from a stultifying system. When we consider that transformation/shapeshifting is crucial to vampirism,

> "BY FORCING MARS JEEMS TO EXPERIENCE THE PHYSICAL CONDITIONS OF SLAVERY, TO KNOW SLAVERY VISCERALLY, TO UNDERSTAND THE DRAINING POWER OF THE VAMPIRE, AND TO BALK AT ITS INHUMANITY, AUN' PEGGY AGAIN DISRUPTS CRUELTY, NEGATES PROFIT THAT IS MEASURED SOLELY IN TERMS OF FINANCE, AND INSPIRES A LITTLE UTOPIA IN THE MIDST OF BLOODSUCKING CONDITIONS."

it is noteworthy that Aun' Peggy uses a tool associated with vampirism to affect her assault against slavery. In "Sis' Becky's Pickaninny," Chesnutt, through Aun' Peggy, addresses the issue of husbands and wives being sold away from each other as well as children being separated from their parents, especially from their mothers, during slavery. Sis' Becky's husband is sold away when his owner, who owns the plantation next to the one on which Sis' Becky lives in North Carolina, dies and all his assets are liquidated. Sis' Becky's husband is sold away into Virginia, and she never sees him again, which emphasizes again how the vampiric system has absolutely no concern for the wellbeing of those caught in its clutches. Only the comfort of her infant son, Mose, saves Sis' Becky from despair. Sis' Becky loves her child dearly, and her expressions of that love are another way in which Chesnutt debunks some of the myths surrounding slavery, in this case the one about enslaved parents not being particularly loving toward their children. Sis' Becky's love for little Mose, though, does not prevent her from being shunted away to another county when her owner trades her for a horse named Lightnin' Bug. The trader refuses to take Mose in the bargain; indeed, he, like any bloodsucker, is callous enough to assert, "Nemmine de baby. I'll keep dat 'oman so busy she'll fergit de baby; fer niggers is made ter wuk, en dey ain' got no time fer no sich foolis-ness ez babies" (142). Both mother and child are thus forced into positions in which they pine away until the child's sympathetic caregiver, Aun' Nancy, goes to Aun' Peggy to seek a remedy. That remedy involves a couple of instances of shapeshifting in the story.

Initially, "Aun' Peggy tuk 'n wukked her roots, en tu'nt little Mose ter a hummin'-bird, en sont 'im off fer ter fin' his mammy" (146–47). Mose quickly succeeds in doing so and sings prettily enough as Sis' Becky is working in the yard at the new plantation that she believes it is her baby Mose singing to her. Both Mose and his mother are satisfied for several days, and their spirits are uplifted. But despondency returns, which leads Aun' Peggy to turn Mose into a mockingbird for a return trip to see his mother. These temporary solutions, as Aun' Nancy recognizes, do not ultimately solve the issue, so she beseeches Aun' Peggy to come up with a more permanent solution, including one that will return Sis' Becky to her child. Aun' Peggy then devises an elaborate scheme in which she sends a hornet to sting Lightnin' Bug so that Colonel Pendleton will think that he has been cheated when he sees the horse's swollen knees. She sends a sparrow to watch the results and report to her, as well as to drop a conjure bag in front of Sis' Becky's door so that she will believe she is going to die. Sis'

> "AUN' PEGGY UNDERSTANDS THE GREED OF SLAVEHOLDERS AND USES THAT TO HER ADVANTAGE. HER KNOWLEDGE OF SLAVEHOLDER NATURE AND HER SKILLS AS A CONJURE WOMAN MAKE HER A POSITIVE FORCE OF ASSISTANCE TO THOSE ENSLAVED."

Becky's new owner, who has been resistant to Colonel Pendleton's accusation that the traded horse was damaged and who has refused to accept responsibility for its condition, relents when Sis' Becky takes to bed and seems determined to die. This leads to the exchange being reversed –

Sis' Becky's new owner asserts that "a lame hoss wuz better 'n a dead nigger" (156) – and to Sis' Becky's being reunited with Mose. As far as happy endings are ever possible under a system as oppressive as slavery, this would certainly qualify as one, and Aun' Peggy, the conjure woman, has been the moving force behind everything that happens. And what has happened?

Although Colonel Pendleton, Sis' Becky's original owner, is initially reluctant to separate Sis' Becky from her "pickaninny," he nonetheless does so when his love for horses supersedes that twinge of conscience he has. What may look like an enlightened – or even sympathetic – slaveholder turns out not to be so. Any suggestion that he might be benign or incipiently opposed to the horrible effects of slavery is quickly neutralized, and his participation in the vampiric system of slavery is highlighted. His love of animal flesh over human flesh, combined with his greed (he has wagered so much money on horses that he does not have enough money to buy Lightnin' Bug outright and must acquiesce to the trade), makes clear that any hint of an exception to his slaveholding personality is just that: a hint. Instead of focusing on transforming him, however, as she did Mars Jeems, Aun' Peggy instead targets doing whatever is necessary to effect the mother/child relationship. In the process, she undermines the greed and the exchange that has led to the separation of mother and child. Her abilities as a conjure woman enable her to bring nature into submission as her partner in righting this particular wrong. With the aid of birds and a hornet, she undermines what Colonel Pendleton and the horse trader have done. She changes circumstances instead of minds, and those changed circumstances enable the greedy natures of the two white slaveholders to work to the advantage of those enslaved (Sis' Becky, Mose, Aun' Nancy). By manipulating the greedy men to adhere to their true natures, Aun' Peggy succeeds in bettering the conditions of those on whose behalf she works.

> "AS FAR AS HAPPY ENDINGS ARE EVER POSSIBLE UNDER A SYSTEM AS OPPRESSIVE AS SLAVERY, THIS WOULD CERTAINLY QUALIFY AS ONE, AND AUN' PEGGY, THE CONJURE WOMAN, HAS BEEN THE MOVING FORCE BEHIND EVERYTHING THAT HAPPENS."

Adhering to his true, bloodthirsty, and vampiric nature is especially clear in the case of Sis' Becky's new owner. By putting a spell on Sis' Becky, which leads her to believe that she is going to die, Aun' Peggy indirectly affects the slaveholder's attitude. When the horse trader measures the possible financial loss involved in the death (Sis' Becky's death and no horse) versus the tradeoff (a sick enslaved woman returned to her master in exchange for the return of a horse that he believes can be cured of whatever is ailing it), he gives in to the disrupting sequence that Aun' Peggy has created. The horse trader is therefore a kind of pawn in a game of Aun' Peggy's devising. He believes he is in charge, when in fact she is the impetus to all the decisions he makes in this affair. His actions, though keeping in line with his beliefs as a slaveholder, are simultaneously in alignment with Aun' Peggy's wishes. Aun' Peggy understands the greed of slaveholders and uses that to her advantage. Her knowledge of slaveholder nature and her skills as a conjure woman make her a positive force of assistance to those enslaved.

Similar to the horse trader, Colonel Pendleton also adheres to his greedy, bloodthirsty nature as a slaveholder. When the horse's knees swell repeatedly, he is outraged that the horse trader would saddle him with a damaged horse. He is even more outraged when the horse trader refuses his initial request to reverse the trade. Everything that suggests whiteness and control slips from him in the face of the resistance the horse trader offers, especially when the horse trader insinuates that the Colonel does not know enough about horses to take care of a good racer. The "how dare he?" attitude almost drives the Colonel to distraction before Aun' Peggy enters to alleviate the situation for him – even as he recognizes how lengthy a lawsuit would be. As the Colonel is about to blow a gasket about a race horse with severely swollen knees, Aun' Peggy is on a mission to get the horse trader to change his mind about the trade by encouraging Sis' Becky to believe that she is going to die. The horse trader, skeptical at first, very quickly comes to realize how serious Sis' Becky is in believing that her death warrant has been signed. The greedy natures of the two white men thus meet in the black woman's plans. The horse trader gets what he wants, and the Colonel gets what he wants, without either one ever being aware that they have been the victims of an elaborate scheme put in place by a conjure woman, a trickster whose skills of indirection trump whiteness, control, and the implicit directives of slavery.

Although Aun' Peggy assaults the vampiric system of slavery, she does not end slavery for any of the characters in the narrative (Mose will achieve that later), but she reunites mother and child. As in "Mars Jeems's Nightmare," Aun' Peggy disrupts the immediate impact of slavery upon those enslaved. While Sis' Becky and Mose will undoubtedly serve quite an additional amount of their lives in bondage, *how* they do so is the significant consideration. Mother and child have each other. Sis' Becky's mind is at ease, which means that she can resume being a good field hand without worrying about her own demise or the whereabouts of her child. And Sis' Becky's and Mose's futures – within the system of slavery – are brighter than they would have been before Aun' Peggy intervened. Uncle Julius relates that Mose grows up to be a wonderful, smart young man who can imitate the sounds of birds so well that his master frequently invites him to the Big House to entertain. This favored status certainly increases his quality of life during slavery. Mose learns the blacksmithing trade, Colonel Pendleton allows him to hire out his time, "En bimeby he bought his mammy en sot her free, en den he bought hisse'f, en tuk keer er Sis' Becky ez long ez dey bofe libbed" (158). By restoring mother to child, Aun' Peggy creates the positive atmosphere that leads to a happy outcome for both mother and child.

As a conjure woman, Aun' Peggy has the power that accrues to all such figures. And she, like many other conjurers who are portrayed as operating during slavery, is primarily out of the limelight. She completes most of her actions in secret, and those who enlist her services acquiesce when she commands their silence about her activities. The one exception to this pattern is the case of Henry in "The Goophered

Grapevine." Even there, however, whites are not precisely aware of what Aun' Peggy does to the vineyard or to effect Henry's appearance. She remains in the shadowy realm of conjurer and trickster. Both roles enable her to serve as Chesnutt's effective mediator of slavery, one who understands the psychology of the slaveholders as well as that of the enslaved. Given her positioning in the text, she plays a role comparable to that Uncle Julius plays in relation to John and Annie, all of whom occupy the outer frame of the narrative. Just as Uncle Julius uses Aun' Peggy to effect outcomes with John and Annie and their neighbors – whether it is a matter of acquiring a meeting space, reconciling estranged lovers, or simply getting Annie to feel better – so too Aun' Peggy serves to influence the world that Chesnutt and Uncle Julius create for her. She may not slay the monster of slavery, but she pokes enough holes in it for those trapped in its grip to embrace small changes and perhaps to envision hopes for the ultimate large change, that is, the termination of the peculiar institution. ∎

"SHE REMAINS IN THE SHADOWY REALM OF CONJURER AND TRICKSTER. BOTH ROLES ENABLE HER TO SERVE AS CHESNUTT'S EFFECTIVE MEDIATOR OF SLAVERY, ONE WHO UNDERSTANDS THE PSYCHOLOGY OF THE SLAVEHOLDERS AS WELL AS THAT OF THE ENSLAVED."

DISEMBODIED INTIMACIES AND SHADOWS OF TRUE WOMANHOOD:

Reclaiming Agency in Harriet Jacobs's *Incidents in the Life of a Slave Girl*

BY ASHLEY BURGE

with art by
John Biggers

OPPOSITE *The Contribution of Negro Women in American Life and Education*, 1953 by John Biggers, located at the Blue Triangle Community Center in Houston, TX

The John Biggers mural is featured here with the permission of the BLUE TRIANGLE COMMUNITY CENTER of Houston, TX. The photograph of the mural is by Scott Haskins of Fine Art Conservation Laboratory in California.

One of the most effective tropes of the slave narrative genre in pre-Civil War America is the emphasis on violence and bodily trauma associated with chattel slavery. Many abolitionist texts, such as Frederick Douglass's *Narrative of the Life of an American Slave Written By Himself* (1845), emphasize the flesh, bone, blood, and tears that emanate from black bodies at the hands of white slaveholders. By revealing the physiological ruptures of the black body, black writers were able to reclaim their humanity through bodily vulnerability while also appealing to the pathos of Northern white abolitionists who were often ignorant of the impact of chattel slavery in the South. Though this trope promptly became the standard for abolitionist protest literature, its hyper-masculine focus on the black male body hardly fits the realities associated with black female bodies in turmoil during the nineteenth century in America. Further, the black female body was often deemed as invisible and the black female voice often silenced in the presence of her black male counterparts. Patricia D. Hopkins argues that both the violated black male body and the violated white female body have traditionally taken precedence over the degradation of the female black body: "The lynching of black men and rape (whether real or imagined) of white women thoroughly overshadow the violence black women endured within the discourse on violence and the body."[1]

Harriet Jacobs offers an alternative to black male and white female focused discourse in *Incidents in the Life of a Slave Girl* (1861), deemphasizing the physical ruptures of the enslaved black female body in order to expand the parameters of sexual exploitation and

"The lynching of black men and rape (whether real or imagined) of white women thoroughly overshadow the violence black women endured within the discourse on violence and the body."

—PATRICIA D. HOPKINS

[1] Patricia D. Hopkins, "Seduction or Rape: Deconstructing the Black Female Body in Harriet Jacobs' Incidents in the Life of a Slave Girl," *Making Connections: Interdisciplinary Approaches to Cultural Diversity* 13.1 (2011) 4; subsequently cited parenthetically.

JOHN BIGGERS (1924–2001) is originally from Gastonia, NC. He has a BS, MS, and PhD from Pennsylvania State University. In 1943, his mural *Dying Soldier* was included in an exhibition of Young Negro Art at the Museum of Modern Art. Biggers founded the art department at Texas State University for Negroes in 1949 (now Texas Southern University), and he taught there until his retirement in 1983. The artist is perhaps best known for the murals he painted in Texas.

Biggers's *The Contribution of Negro Women to American Life and Education*, which gives voice to African American women, is located in the Blue Triangle Community Center in Houston, TX. Flood waters from Hurricane Harvey damaged the mural. Scott M. Haskins of Fine Art Conservation Laboratories (Santa Barbara, CA), restored the mural. The restoration was completed in February 2019.

"In a society where values changed frequently, where fortunes rose and fell with frightening rapidity, where social and economic mobility provided instability as well as hope, one thing at least remained the same – a true woman was a true woman, wherever she was found."

—BARBARA WELTER
(151–52)

undermine the white gaze on the black female body. Jacobs creates a literary aesthetic that I call "disembodied intimacies," which liberates the black female body from the confines of sexist, white supremacist ideologies. The result allows readers to contextualize female sexual oppression from both historical and contemporary perspectives. Through Jacobs's harrowing tale, we can see the turmoil of antebellum women like her protagonist, Linda Brent, but we can also see how sexual exploitation has evolved and continues to haunt contemporary public figures, such as Anita Hill. Regardless of the time or era, Jacobs's narrative creates a space for resistance and empowerment because it aligns with the social, emotional, moral, and spiritual concerns of black women in the antebellum period and beyond. Through disembodied intimacies, Jacobs is able to regain black female subjectivity in the midst of various forms of gendered, racialized oppression.

Jacobs's narrative dramatizes the unique traumas that black women experienced as a result of racialized sexual exploitation while simultaneously critiquing the pre–Civil War obsession with the Cult of True Womanhood, which espoused "purity, piety, domesticity, and submissiveness in all women."[2] Jacobs's distinct perspective accounts for the gendered concerns of black women who were divested of control of their sexuality, their bodies, and their offspring. Further, Jacobs transposes the stereotypical sexualized black body from one of passive submission to one of empowered control. In *Incidents*, she presents Linda Brent as a character who denounces the racist, patriarchal systems of enslavement and the Cult of True Womanhood through a series of resistant acts. Through these disembodied intimacies, Linda gains the agency to disrupt the power structures and exert her control while subverting and transcending the ideologies linked to the gendered, racialized body. By resisting the tyrannical system of enslavement and renegotiating the standards associated with "True Womanhood," Jacobs creates a redemptive space that allows black women to reclaim their humanity while simultaneously reclaiming their body from the ravages of racist patriarchy.

Jacobs creates a redemptive space that allows black women to reclaim their humanity while simultaneously reclaiming their body from the ravages of racist patriarchy.

[2] Jennifer Larson, "Converting Passive Womanhood to Active Sisterhood: Agency, Power, and Subversion in Harriet Jacobs's *Incidents in the Life of a Slave Girl*," *Women's Studies* 35 (2006): 739; subsequently cited parenthetically. See too Barbara Welter, "The Cult of True Womanhood: 1820–1860," *American Quarterly* 18 (1966): 151–74.

Historically, the black female body has been used as a tool to differentiate racialized and gendered differences in order to justify the enslavement of African/African American men and women and to validate the superiority of the white race. Many scholars attest to the pervasiveness of early European discourses that used racialized female attributes such as skin color, hair texture, and body dimensions to link Africans and other "raced" peoples, to use Jennifer Morgan's term, to "monstrous," "bestial" beings that were inferior to white men. For instance, Morgan emphasizes these constructs when she argues, "As the tenacious and historically deep roots of racialist ideology

become more evident, it becomes clear also that, through the rubric of monstrously 'raced' Amerindian and African women, Europeans found a means to articulate shifting perceptions of themselves as religiously, culturally, and phenotypically superior to those Black or brown persons they sought to define."[3]

These sentiments become more nuanced and more profound once gender and sexuality intertwine with constructions of race, especially as it concerns the black female body. Trudier Harris argues, "The female body, as it has been written in the oral tradition and in sexist literature, is in part a source of fear, both an attraction and a repulsion, something that can please, but something that can destroy."[4] Though Harris focuses on the female gendered body generally, specifically the black female body has been portrayed as much more dangerous, much more sexualized, and much more deviant when compared to the "ideal" feminine body of the "chaste" white female. As Janell Hobson points out, the black female body has historically been associated "with heightened sexuality and deviance."[5] Further, the black female body has often been relegated to its physical characteristics apart from cognitive, emotional, or spiritual elements. Mary Vermillion asserts that many writers have historically "constructed the black woman as the sum total of her bodily labour . . . depicting her] as breeder, wet nurse, field laborer, and most significant, as sexually exploited victim."[6] These racist, patriarchal constructs had not diminished in the era in which Jacobs wrote *Incidents*. Indeed, they had become even more

---

ABOVE **Harriet Tubman leading slaves to freedom in Biggers's mural**

[3] Jennifer Morgan, "'Some Could Suckle over Their Shoulders': Male Travelers, Female Bodies, and the Gendering of Racial Ideology, 1500–1770," *Skin Deep, Spirit Strong: The Black Female Body in American Culture*, ed. Kimberly Wallace-Sanders (U of Michigan P, 2002) 38.

[4] Trudier Harris, *Fiction and Folklore: The Novels of Toni Morrison* (U of Tennessee P, 1991) 153.

[5] Janell Hobson, *Venus in the Dark: Blackness and Beauty in Popular Culture* (Routledge, 2005) 7.

[6] Mary Vermillion, "Reembodying the Self: Representations of Rape in *Incidents in the Life of a Slave Girl* and *I Know Why the Caged Bird Sings*," *Biography* 15.3 (1992): 244; subsequently cited parenthetically.

detrimental to enslaved black women as the Victorian-inspired Cult of True Womanhood flourished in Northern and Southern domestic spaces. The racist, gendered stereotypes disseminated by early European travelers and early American settlers about the black female body continued to plague constructions of black female identity well into the nineteenth century, hindering black women from inhabiting positive gendered spaces in America. Beverly Guy-Sheftall articulates these sentiments when she asserts,

> the Black woman was devalued not only because of her supposed racial traits but also because she departed from whites' conception of the True Woman – which is indicative of the degree to which prevailing notions about race and gender interacted in the minds of whites (male and female) and resulted in a particular set of attitudes about Black women. Whites felt that notions about the "ideal woman" did not apply to Black women because the circumstances of slavery had prevented them from developing qualities that other women possessed and from devoting their lives to wifehood and motherhood, the proper roles for women.[7]

Jacobs was, undoubtedly, cognizant of the precarious position of the black female body during this time of rigid moralism, as is apparent by the sentimentality of her text.

I argue that Jacobs remedies these incongruities by relying on disembodied intimacies to illuminate other modes of interaction that violate constructs of black female identity. I use the term disembodied intimacy to describe a pragmatic literary aesthetic that Jacobs uses to alert Northern white women to the rampant sexual and spiritual degradations that resulted from slavery as she emancipates the black body from racist, patriarchal constructions that pervaded American discourse. Intimacy designates these acts as private instead of public and occurring between individuals who are familiar or in close proximity to one another by way of forced engagement. Jacobs's use of disembodied intimacies has two purposes. The first is to illuminate intangible traumas that were too "delicate," as her editor, Lydia Maria Child, designates them, to describe in the sentimental genre used for *Incidents*.[8] The literary aesthetic acts as a form of resistance that subverts racist and sexist ideologies associated with the black body while also combating the system of enslavement. Further, it expands the parameters of sexual exploitation to illuminate the ways trauma can occur without physical threats to the body. These parameters include sexually oppressive communications executed in lieu of physical bodily exploitation. Jacobs's second purpose in employing disembodied intimacies in her narrative is to transcend the confines of ideologies associated with systems like the Cult of True Womanhood as a means to validate black female identities associated with traditionally

"The black woman was devalued not only because of her supposed racial traits but also because she departed from whites' conception of the True Woman."

—BEVERLY GUY-SHEFTALL

7 Beverly Guy-Sheftall, "The Body Politic: Black Female Sexuality and the Nineteenth-Century Euro-American Imagination," *Skin Deep, Spirit Strong: The Black Female Body in American Culture*, ed. Kimberly Wallace-Sanders (U of Michigan P, 2002) 23; subsequently cited parenthetically.

8 L. Maria Child, "Introduction by the Editor," in Harriet Jacobs, *Incidents in the Life of a Slave Girl, Written by Herself*, ed. Lydia Maria Child (1861, Documenting the American South, 1998, UNC Libraries) 8; Jacobs's narrative will subsequently be cited parenthetically from this edition.

> "Jacobs simultaneously emancipates the black female body from racist stereotypes while creating a space where black women can inhabit a transcendent form of womanhood and motherhood not dictated by American slavery or the Cult of True Womanhood."

gendered roles. In this form, the literary aesthetic renegotiates the confines of gender roles to account for the distinct status of black women in pre-Civil War society. Both modes allow Jacobs to appeal to the salient ideologies of Northern white women who have the power to help enslaved black women in the South. These ideologies include appeals to matriarchy, piety, virtue, chastity, liberty, and domesticity. By making these often-times abstract ideologies pronounced, Jacobs simultaneously emancipates the black female body from racist stereotypes while creating a space where black women can inhabit a transcendent form of womanhood and motherhood not dictated by American slavery or the Cult of True Womanhood.

Incidents in the Life of a Slave Girl is set in a close-knit community that evokes Edenton, North Carolina, the small town where Jacobs was raised. Although the narrative content is autobiographical in nature, Jacobs and Child chose to obscure Jacobs's identity as well as the identity of her family, probably to ensure that they would be safe during and after the Civil War. The protagonist, Linda Brent, is often positioned as more of a character device than a realistic representation of Jacobs herself. Stephanie Li argues that Linda is more of a "reflection of the political aims of her author."[9] For instance, at various points in her life, Jacobs acted as an abolitionist, writer, and reformer; however, Jacobs foregoes these roles and singularly focuses the narrative on Linda Brent's maternal roles as a nurturer, caregiver, and protector, all roles that would appeal to Northern white women who upheld the standards of domesticity in that time period. The narrative follows Linda's harrowing journey from naïve child to vulnerable teenager to tormented "fallen woman" to liberated, self-actualized mother.

COURTESY OF DURWOOD BARBOUR COLLECTION OF NORTH CAROLINA POSTCARDS

ABOVE **Main Street, Edenton, NC, circa 1900**

9 Stephanie Li, "Motherhood as Resistance in Harriet Jacobs's *Incidents in the Life of a Slave Girl*," *Legacy* 23.1 (2006): 20; subsequently cited parenthetically.

"I was born a slave; but I never knew it till six years of happy childhood had passed away."

—HARRIET JACOBS

Linda's early childhood is marked by naiveté as she lives a sheltered life ignorant of the realities of enslavement: "I was born a slave; but I never knew it till six years of happy childhood had passed away" (11). Jacobs explains this seeming impossibility by portraying the insulating security that her well-respected family offered her in the midst of their enslavement. In the care of her mother, father, and grandmother, she experiences a form of independence unusual for a slave child. Jacobs attributes this to Linda's strong family unit: "They lived together in a comfortable home; and, though we were all slaves, I was so fondly shielded that I never dreamed I was a piece of merchandise, trusted to them for safe keeping, and liable to be demanded of them at any moment" (11–12). Linda's idyllic environment changes, however, when her mistress dies and bequeaths her to the family of Dr. Flint, a well-respected physician who becomes a constant threat to her physical and spiritual well-being.

The crux of Jacobs's tale lies in exposing the ways that white slaveholders oppressed enslaved black women through degrading sexual exploitation. She uses her antagonist, Flint, to expose the various corrupt practices that white slaveholders employed to dehumanize black women and rob them of agency and subjectivity. Initially, Linda is powerless to protect herself from the degraded sexual demands of Flint, which are protected by laws under the institution of slavery. She rightly laments her helpless position when she describes Flint's motives: "When he told me that I was made for his use, made to obey his command in *every* thing; that I was nothing but a slave, whose will must and should surrender to his, never before had my puny arm felt half so strong" (29). Despite her diminished

agency under enslavement and under American laws such as the Fugitive Slave Act of 1850, Linda maneuvers a plan to thwart Flint's advances by having children for a well-respected white lawyer as a means to resist the patriarchal power dynamics of slavery. To save her children from enslavement, she escapes from Flint's household and hides in her grandmother's garret for seven years until her children are sold to their father and taken to the North where they are liberated. Later, Linda leaves her hiding place and escapes to the North to reunite with her children and reclaim the life that slavery has previously denied her. Jacobs successfully frames Linda's traumatic journey from enslavement to freedom by portraying a variety of disembodied intimacies that disrupt the power dynamics of slavery while also subverting and transcending the rigid race and gender dynamics projected onto black women in pre–Civil War America.

ABOVE TOP **The now empty lot in Edenton, NC, where Jacobs's grandmother's house once stood**

ABOVE BOTTOM **Rope used by tour guide to depict the amount of space in which Jacobs lived while in hiding for seven years, 7'x9'x3'**

OPPOSITE RIGHT **Edenton Bay coastline (Jacobs used the Maritime Underground Railroad to escape to the North.)**

Jacobs foregrounds her disembodied appeals by critiquing the ways that the Cult of True Womanhood is incongruous with the valuation of the black female body. She does this primarily through her portrayal of Linda's highly esteemed grandmother, Aunt Marthy. Aunt Marthy is an ideal character to demonstrate the need to emancipate the black female body from one-dimensional constructs because Jacobs portrays her as a woman who is defined by her bodily economies despite her "noble" status in the narrative. As a female character who is unique because she is uninvolved with any white slave holder in *Incidents*, Aunt Marthy symbolizes a canvas on which Jacobs can illustrate the long-standing ideologies associated with the female black body in the absence of illicit or predatory sexuality of any kind. Jacobs also uses Aunt Marthy's tragic incidents as a means to critique the Cult of True Womanhood, which was supposed to provide comfort and solace to all women but instead, as is the case for Aunt Marthy and other enslaved black women, further persecutes and exploits them. By illuminating the ways that Aunt Marthy is denigrated despite her elevated status, Jacobs creates tension that can only be remedied by the empowering effects of disembodied intimacies.

Jacobs emphasizes the ways that the Cult of True Womanhood exploits Aunt Marthy despite her devotion to cult ideologies. Marthy is fiercely devoted to submission and piety even in the direst of circumstances. Instead of protesting the sale of her grandchildren or openly mourning the death of her daughter, she often says in a dignified manner, "'Who knows the ways of God?'" (18) or "'God's will be done'" (35). As Georgia Krieger posits, "In every scene in which she appears, Aunt Marthy upholds the morals and values associated with true womanhood, giving voice to the ideals of Jacobs's white female readers."[10] Jacobs firmly situates her in the lauded domestic sphere in Linda's vivid descriptions of her early in the narrative:

> She was much praised for her cooking; and her nice crackers became so famous in the neighborhood that many people were desirous of obtaining them. In consequence of numerous requests of this kind, she asked permission of her mistress to bake crackers at night, after all the household work was done; and she obtained leave to do it, provided she would clothe herself and her children from the profits. (9)

Jacobs cleverly relays Aunt Marthy's domestic prowess in a move that simultaneously builds rapport with Northern white women and challenges the notions that enslaved black women could not possess the skills needed to be an "ideal" woman. Jacobs further links Aunt Marthy's industriousness and ambition to protecting the well-being of her children, solidifying the overarching theme of her narrative: the liberation of the enslaved black family.

"The attributes of True Womanhood, by which a woman judged herself and was judged by her husband, her neighbors and society could be divided into four cardinal virtues – piety, purity, submissiveness and domesticity."

—BARBARA WELTER (152)

Photographs of 2019 Edenton, NC, are by *NCLR* Assistant Editor Angela Love Kitchin

[10] Georgia Kreiger, "Playing Dead: Harriet Jacobs's Survival Strategy in *Incidents in the Life of a Slave Girl*," *African American Review* 42.3-4 (2008): 611.

"Though she upholds the values that would allow Northern white women to empathize with her plight, she also symbolizes the consequences of submitting to a system that subjugates and terrorizes black women and their families at the behest of 'proper' gender roles."

Aunt Marthy also represents the problematic moral ideologies that relied on religious dogma to force women to submit to patriarchal demands. For instance, though Linda and her brother William adamantly condemn enslavement throughout the narrative, Aunt Marthy consistently discourages their willful resistance through her Christian rhetoric. While Linda illustrates the despair that she and her brother and young uncle, Benjamin, experience under enslavement, she reveals the stark contrast of her grandmother's resolve: "Most earnestly did she strive to make us feel that it was the will of God: that He had seen fit to place us under such circumstances; and though it seemed hard, we ought to pray for contentment" (28). It would not have been uncommon for Jacobs to characterize Aunt Marthy as a submissive, all-suffering "ideal" woman in this time period; as Larson argues, "[t]he cult was a significant feature in women's writing at the same time as it worked socially to promote their continued subjugation" (740). However, even as Jacobs appeals to Northern white sentiments, she also challenges them by demonstrating how the idealized cult undermines black enslaved women in ways akin to slavery.

While Aunt Marthy is well respected for her industriousness in the kitchen and other domestic arenas, her value is relegated to the exploitation of her body for white consumption. Linda describes her in ways that only reflect her economic viability: "an indispensable personage in the household, officiating in all capacities, from cook and wet nurse to seamstress" (12). Later, Linda reveals that Aunt Marthy breastfed both Linda's mother and her mistress's daughter only to wean her mother early so "that the babe of the mistress might obtain sufficient food" (14). These roles point to how black female bodies were used to sate the needs of white slaveholders while black mothers and their families lived in a perpetual state of physical and emotional lack. As Guy-Sheftall argues, "it was the exploitation of the Black woman's body – her vagina, her uterus, her breasts, and also her muscle – that set her apart from white women and that was the mark of her vulnerability" (30). Aunt Marthy's vulnerability illustrates the incongruities between the Cult of True Womanhood and the valuation of the black female body. Though she upholds the values that would allow Northern white women to empathize with her plight, she also symbolizes the consequences of submitting to a system that subjugates and terrorizes black women and their families at the behest of "proper" gender roles.

Aunt Marthy's agency is greatly diminished because she cannot challenge the systems that allow her children and grandchildren to waste away in despair. She tries unsuccessfully to buy her children and liberate them from enslavement, but she cannot combat the system with the limited resources and diminished social status that represent her lived reality. By critiquing the Cult of True Womanhood,

ABOVE **St. Paul's Episcopal Church (Harriet Jacobs's grandmother, Molly Horniblow, was a member.)**

OPPOSITE **Chowan County jail in Edenton, NC, where Dr. Norcom held Jacobs's children, brother, and aunt in hopes of flushing Jacobs out of hiding**

"Notwithstanding my

grandmother's long

and faithful service

to her owners, not one

of her children escaped

the auction block."

—HARRIET JACOBS (16)

"For enslaved women, the auction block was a particularly traumatic experience within a life of slavery because it was used to scrutinize their bodies to assess their physical viability under

Jacobs undermines it as a pathway to salvation and redemption. In essence, the cult cannot validate the black female body and lead to empowered agency. This void creates tensions that are further compounded by the injustices of slavery.

Aunt Marthy's portrayal in the narrative also serves to indict American slavery's commodification and further oppression of the black female body. Jacobs ensures that the humiliating and despicable facets of American slavery are unveiled and critiqued throughout *Incidents*. This includes the act of selling black bodies on the auction block. Despite Aunt Marthy's virtuous persona, she is the only character in the narrative forced to endure the public indignities of being examined and commodified like chattel, which points again to Jacobs's literary appeals to the Northern sentiments. Once Aunt Marthy's mistress dies, her family is thrown into disarray as they are shuffled from one master to another. Though she loses her beloved grandchildren to the Flint household, Aunt Marthy finds comfort in knowing that her mistress intended "at her death, she should be free." However, Flint, the ever-cruel executer of injustice and deception, refuses to adhere to the will, instead telling Aunt Marthy that she must be sold, but in private so as not to "wound her feelings" (20). Jacobs portrays Aunt Marthy as a shrewd discerner of character who sees right through Flint's lies. Once she realizes that Flint is trying to protect himself from the public embarrassment of selling a high esteemed member of the community, Aunt Marthy quickly orchestrates a plan that shifts the humiliation from herself to him: "Her long and faithful service in the family was also well known, and the intention of her mistress to leave her free. When the day of sale came, she took her place among the chattels, and at the first call she sprang upon the auction-block. Many voices called out, 'Shame! Shame! Who is going to sell *you*, aunt Marthy? Don't stand there! That is no place for *you*'" (21). Here, Jacobs illuminates a rare irreverence in Aunt Marthy that acknowledges that she wields a certain amount of agency even as she submits to the confines of domestic ideologies.

Aunt Marthy's scheming reflects how enslaved black women in hopeless situations resisted the degrading practices of slavery. However, Jacobs's more poignant revelation points to the indignities associated with black female bodies that are commodified and exploited on the auction block. She emphasizes the crowd's repulsion from seeing a vulnerable Aunt Marthy on the platform as an allusion to the shameful practices of "negro sales" that dehumanized black people as they degraded their exposed bodies. For enslaved women, the auction block was a particularly traumatic experience within a life of slavery because it was used to scrutinize their bodies to assess their physical viability under enslavement. Their very being was diminished to their bodily capabilities as laborers, "breeders," and domestics. This was especially true of their reproductive capabilities as Guy-Sheftall asserts: "On the auction block, their bodies were exposed, handled, even poked to determine their strength and capacity for childbearing" (24). The auction block exposed black women to a variety of

"But I now entered on my fifteenth year – a sad epoch in the life of a slave girl. My master began to whisper foul words in my ear. Young as I was, I could not remain ignorant of their import."

—HARRIET JACOBS (44)

bodily vulnerabilities that humiliated, dehumanized, and objectified them. By poking, prodding, and handling the black female as chattel, white slaveholders designated them as less-than human, which provided further justification for enslaving and "civilizing" them.

These vulnerabilities were compounded as their private bodies became public fetishizations for white slaveholders and the community at large. Patricia Hill Collins astutely articulates these notions when she posits, "One key feature about the treatment of Black women in the nineteenth century was how their bodies were objects of display. In the antebellum American South white men did not have to look at pornographic pictures of women because they could become voyeurs of Black women on the auction block."[11] Jacobs makes these sentiments heartbreakingly vivid once she positions Aunt Marthy, the embodiment of virtue and piety, on the auction block to be soiled and tainted by the depraved mechanizations of enslavement. The shame of this incident arises from the fact that Aunt Marthy has been stripped of her control, self-respect, and humanity as she stands on a platform that represents a microcosm of pre-Civil War era America, a country that has built its wealth on the exploitation of black bodies. These attacks on fundamental tenets of humanity – like those of identity, esteem, and security – are fuel for Jacobs's literary maneuvers, which illuminate the trauma associated with slavery in ways that redeem the black female body and reclaim black female identities, creating a space for healing, wholeness, and fulfillment.

In order to divorce the black body from vilification and expose the sexual exploitation of young black women, Jacobs exposes the traumatic disembodied intimacies between Linda and Flint. In these interactions, Jacobs reveals how the institution of slavery allows white slaveholders to corrupt young black women morally, socially, and with impunity. Her chief concern is to relay how white slaveholders use their power to exploit black women and diminish their control over their bodies, labor, and offspring. However, instead of relying on physical vulnerabilities of the female black body, Jacobs relies on the mental, psychological, and emotional vulnerabilities that arise from disembodied sexual exploitation. These disembodied intimacies are especially evident when analyzing Linda's initial interactions with Flint. As a fifteen-year-old, Linda is rendered helpless in the presence of Flint. She describes him as a cruel and degraded man "whose restless, craving, vicious nature roved about day and night, seeking whom to devour" (29). Flint's domineering presence not only diminishes Linda's agency, but it also diminishes her voice, which greatly impairs her ability to seek solace. Though Flint's attacks weigh heavily on her, Linda laments, "I longed for some one to confide in. I would have given the world to have laid my head on my grandmother's faithful bosom, and told her all my troubles. But Dr. Flint swore he would kill me, if I was not as silent as the grave" (46). Jacobs most effectively demonstrates the weight of these attacks by portraying Linda's sexual

ABOVE **Inside Saint Paul's Episcopal Church (Jacobs's two children were baptized here.)**

[11] Patricia Hill Collins, *Black Feminist Thought: Knowledge Consciousness and the Politics of Empowerment* (Routledge, 1990) 168.

exploitation as disembodied intimacies without exposing the physical vulnerabilities of the black female body. Her major concern is to portray the pervasive rape and sexual exploitation of young black women without further indicting the body in terms that align with racist and sexist ideologies. Her literary maneuvers are apparent in her mentions of Flint's harassment in her fifteenth year:

> He tried his utmost to corrupt the pure principles my grandmother had instilled. He peopled my young mind with unclean images, such as only a vile monster could think of. I turned from him with disgust and hatred. But he was my master. I was compelled to live under the same roof with him – where I saw a man forty years my senior daily violating the most sacred commandments of nature. He told me I was his property; that I must be subject to his will in all things. (44-45)

Linda further describes his verbal assault when she states that Flint left her "with stinging, scorching words" (29). In both instances, Jacobs illustrates the ways that Flint weaponizes intimacy through words instead of bodily violations. Rather than focusing on the black female body as a sexually exploited vessel, Jacobs emphasizes Flint's degraded character and Linda's purity. When Linda states that "[h]e peopled [her] young mind with unclean images" (44), she directs her audience to the intellectual and spiritual capabilities of young black women, which subvert racist ideologies that deemed black women as intellectually and spiritually inferior. This strategy challenges the historical portrayal of black women as only bodies that are acted upon; instead, her cognitive abilities are attacked by the "unclean images" that this worldly man forces upon her. Flint's impure "whispers" threaten the virtue and purity of Linda's impressionable mind, which could inevitably result in degradation of her spiritual state.

What Jacobs orchestrates is a forced intimate engagement that deemphasizes the corporeal body in order to magnify the corruption of proper values. This assertion aligns with Hopkins's analysis of this incident when she asserts "that value is being placed on the sexual act and not the body being acted upon – the corruption of her mind and moral values, not her physical body" (14). However, there is not a blatant sexual act evident in this interchange, at least not in the traditional sense. Jacobs does not emphasize this exchange as a physical act. Here, Jacobs frames this forced disembodied intimacy as a metonym for the violated and persecuted female black body;

"[Jacobs] directs her audience to the intellectual and spiritual capabilities of young black women, which subvert racist ideologies that deemed black women as intellectually and spiritually inferior."

yet the emphasis in the text is still firmly situated on the vulnerabilities of the mental and spiritual state of the victim. What is profound about Jacobs's maneuver is its highly progressive stance about the sexual exploitation of women by men who hold power in American society. Though this is a nineteenth-century text, Jacobs effectively illuminates the ways that sexual trauma can have a detrimental effect on women even though the physical body may not be the central focus of attack in the exchange. These are violations that would not have been ignored by the primarily white female audience that Jacobs addresses, women who would subscribe to the rigid beliefs of the domestic cult.

In Jacobs's portrayal, violating spiritual and moral values is as detrimental as violating the physical body. Further, Jacobs validates the complexity of black female identity by showing how these attacks can hinder the moral character of young black women. She establishes Linda's complexity by resisting one-dimensional stereotypes that characterize black women as sexually deviant and intellectually and spiritually inferior. When Linda states that she had to endure Flint "daily violating the most sacred commandments of nature" (44-45), Jacobs lays claim to the fact that black women have a spiritual nature intact that is constantly threatened by white slaveholders. She challenges the construction of black women as sexually deviant, racialized bodies by portraying Linda as a mentally sound, spiritual individual who deserves empathy and protection in her precarious state. By focusing on Flint's disembodied violations and their effects on Linda's moral welfare, Jacobs frees the black female body from historically racist discourse that had been used to justify enslavement. As Vermillion asserts, Jacobs emphasizes Flint's threat as a "predominantly psychological/spiritual one and thus lessens her reader's tendency to associate her body with illicit sexuality" (246). Further, Jacobs uses the disembodied intimacies between Linda and Flint to attack the American institution of slavery.

Jacobs further attacks the repressive system of enslavement by showing how it undermines one of the most transformative elements of the slave narrative genre: literacy. Once again, Jacobs relies on Linda's toxic master/slave relationship with Flint to represent the injustices associated with the institution of slavery. Flint's disembodied threats extend beyond foul whispers and depraved suggestions as he begins to harass Linda through written notes and letters. This form of disembodied intimacy acts as the antithesis to most slave narratives that thematically portray literacy as an evolutionary act that delineates the "old" slave from the transformed liberated man or woman. In Frederick Douglass's seminal *Narrative*, literacy marks a distinct turning point that makes his journey to freedom possible. Douglass credits literacy with giving him the knowledge of his diminished state. Once he begins to read, he describes his discontent by saying, "As I writhed under it, I would at times feel that learning to read had been a curse rather than a blessing. It had given me a view of my wretched condition, without the remedy. It opened my eyes to the horrible pit, but to no ladder upon which to get out."[12] Though Douglass initially curses his newfound literacy, he realizes that it instills in him the profound desire to escape and reclaim his humanity and masculinity. He also realizes it gives him agency in a way that his illiteracy had not. Similarly, literacy is redemptive and transformative in *Incidents* because it makes true womanhood accessible to Linda. Linda's first mistress teaches her to read and sew at an early age and, as a result, provides Linda with a pathway to "ideal" womanhood that valued activities like reading and sewing, which could be done in the domestic sphere without disrupting family dynamics.

Linda's literacy coincides with a turning point in her life as an enslaved woman because it elevates her status under the Cult of True Womanhood while also giving her a form of agency that was not experienced by many other blacks and whites in pre-Civil War America. However, Flint's exploitative motives attempt to divest her of the little agency she has by harassing her through notes and letters in much the same way that he harasses her through vile whisperings. Jacobs exemplifies these violations when she writes, "One day he caught me teaching myself to write. He frowned, as if he was not well pleased, but I suppose he came to the conclusion that such an accomplishment might help to advance his favorite scheme. Before long, notes were often slipped into my hand. I would return them, saying, 'I can't read them, sir.' 'Can't you?' he replied; 'then I must read them to you'" (49–50). It is telling that Jacobs conflates Linda's mastery of reading and writing with Flint's pervasive sexual exploitation. This is but one instance that distinctly reveals the complexities associated with black women under the oppression of enslavement. A resounding theme in *Incidents* is how enslavement is distinctly detrimental to women in contrast to men. This reality is relayed in Linda's mournful realization that, "Slavery is terrible for men; but it is far more terrible for women" (119).

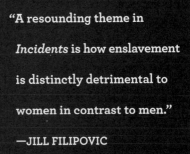

"A resounding theme in *Incidents* is how enslavement is distinctly detrimental to women in contrast to men."

—JILL FILIPOVIC

While male portrayals of literacy in slave narratives, like Douglass's *Narrative*, are often wholly transformative and result in some recognition of agency, Jacobs reveals that Linda's mastery of literacy is mired by her corrupt slave master as he attempts, once again, to divest her of control. Once he realizes that she can read, he transfers his harassment to insulting notes that will further people her "young mind with unclean images" (44). Linda does have some agency in choosing not to read the letters as some scholars, such as Larson,

---

[12] *Narrative of the Life of Frederick Douglass, an American Slave. Written by Himself* (1845, Documenting the American South, UNC Libraries, 1999) 40.

> "[B]lack women have been forced to endure sexist and racist language in American discourse, which fragments their identity and diminishes their ability to define themselves and find their voice."

persuasively argue (748). However, Flint divests her of this agency when he insists that he will read them to her, once again acting upon Linda's mind as a sexually exploited object in similar ways that slaveholders acted upon the bodies of enslaved women. And, once again, Jacobs deemphasizes attacks on the body and refocuses them on attacks of the mind through written notes and letters. Linda's interactions with Flint allude to the ways that racist and sexist stereotypes are metaphorically "written" on black female bodies in various racist, sexist American discourse such as historical documents, medical journals, and entertainment media. As Linda notes, she was forced "to stand and listen to such language as he saw fit to address me" (50). While Flint perceives this act as a form of fleeting verbal foreplay, Linda's reaction points to a lasting dismantling act that undermines her subjectivity. Linda's position in this incident is symbolic of the ways black women have been forced to endure sexist and racist language in American discourse, which fragments their identity and diminishes their ability to define themselves and find their voice. However, Jacobs illuminates the consequences of these disembodied intimacies as a means to justify unique forms of gendered resistance, which reclaims agency in the text while reclaiming the humanity of the black body.

These disembodied intimacies lead Linda to execute a sacrificial sexual act that transcends the Cult of True Womanhood and reclaims the agency that slavery has divested from her. Jacobs portrays these disembodied incidents as mentally, psychologically, and spiritually traumatic enough to force Linda into an act of desperation that would commonly label her as a "fallen woman" in sentimental texts. Linda's prospects for freedom are continually thwarted by Flint, and Linda is aware that his initial attacks, though more emotional and psychological than physical, will only lead to more brutal expressions of his power. Though Jacobs veils the "delicate" realities of enslavement through revelatory disembodied intimacies, she has not disregarded rape as an inevitable next step for Linda. In fact, Linda expects Flint's next violation with dread and preemptively engineers a plan to resist his power while reclaiming her own. Instead of further acquiescing to Flint's draconian rule, she gravely alludes to the sacrificial act:

> I was determined that the master, whom I so hated and loathed, who had blighted the prospects of my youth, and made my life a desert, should not, after my long struggle with him succeed at last in trampling his victim under feet. I would do anything, everything, for the sake of defeating him. What *could* I do? I thought and thought, till I became desperate, and made a plunge into the abyss. (82–83)

> "Linda's ability to choose her sexual partner and choose the father of her children gives her the ultimate power under enslavement."

> "Linda cannot be pure and virtuous under slavery because it is a corrupt system that cannot foster virtue."

Linda's "plunge into the abyss" is her consensual sexual relationship with Mr. Sands, the well-respected white lawyer, with whom she conceives two children. This act symbolizes Linda's reclamation of her sexual autonomy. Linda's ability to choose her sexual partner and choose the father of her children gives her the ultimate power under enslavement. In this instance, she is no longer a "breeder" who is relegated to the economies of her reproductive organs, but a willful, cognizant individual who makes a choice of her own volition. Some scholars challenge the notion that Linda's character aligns with any form of sexual agency. For instance, Li argues that Linda is an asexual character who is "never motivated by sexual desire" and only engages in a sexual relationship to "escape the advances of Dr. Flint" (21). However, Jacobs's later rhetorical strategies prove that she accepts and defends Linda's choice for sexual autonomy under a newly informed ideology of true womanhood. Jacobs's description of her intimate act as a "plunge into the abyss" is a rhetorical move relayed to appeal to her white female audience. In this instance, she cannot disregard the Cult of True Womanhood, which favors purity above all else; however, she can attempt to subvert the ideology to accommodate the precarious position of enslaved black women. By juxtaposing her traumatic life under slavery with her white counterparts, Linda reveals that the Cult of True Womanhood's narrow ideologies are incompatible with the repressive system of slavery that black women are forced to endure. Linda cannot be pure and virtuous under slavery because it is a corrupt system that cannot foster virtue. She exemplifies this when she asserts, "in looking back, calmly, on the events of my life, I feel the slave woman ought not to be judged by the same standard as others" (86). Further, even though she seems to undermine her decision by calling it a "plunge," it is obvious that she revels in the control that she gains by resisting Flint. This assumption is evident when she states, "It seems less degrading to give one's self, than to submit to compulsion. There is something akin to freedom in having a lover who has no control over you, except that which he gains by kindness and attachment" (84–85). By denouncing forced submission, she directly undermines slavery and subverts the Cult of True Womanhood. Linda gains agency and freedom by disrupting these patriarchal structures, and she gains this power by using her sexuality and her body as weapons of resistance.

Despite Linda's empowered decision to disrupt patriarchal power structures, many women in this era would still have derided her act as shameful and reckless when viewed through the lens of the Cult of True Womanhood. However, Linda presents this act as one that is necessary because it allows the character to disrupt oppressive systems, and it also gives her agency in ways that could not be accomplished through any other means. Further, this gendered act of resistance is one that is distinct to Linda's position as a woman bonded by the traumatic institution of slavery. This assumption aligns with Kristine Yohe's assertions about gendered resistance in slave and

ABOVE **Dr. James Norcom's headstone in the Saint Paul's Episcopal Church churchyard, Edenton, NC**

neo-slave narratives: "These women's responses to abuse have always been gendered: their resistance often had direct connections to their status as women, including their roles as cooks and house servants, as well as their status as mothers and objects of sexual predation."[13] Linda validates her particular form of gendered resistance by reminding her audience of the incongruities associated with enslavement and the concept of choice. As Linda reveals the detriments of slavery, many of her arguments rest on the inability of black women to choose because of their oppressed status. Early in the narrative she juxtaposes her fate to that of white women by saying, "O, ye happy women, whose purity has been sheltered from childhood, who have been free to choose the object of your affection. . . . If slavery had been abolished, I, also, could have married the man of my choice" (83). Here, Jacobs exposes the disparate realities for black women and white women in a way that simultaneously denounces slavery while critiquing the ideals associated with true womanhood. This statement is both empowering and disheartening because it alludes to the sacrificial physical, mental, and emotional journey that Linda had to traverse in order to reclaim agency in ways that were inherently more accessible for white women in that era.

By exposing the traumas of American slavery for black women, Jacobs expands the parameters of sexual violation in ways that would not be fully recognized by American society until much later. Her progressive strategies mirror the recent consciousness surrounding sexual harassment in contemporary American society. On the cusp of the twenty-first century, women flooded the corporate, entertainment, and education sectors, and the parameters of sexual harassment have just recently become more defined with the indictment of powerful men who have used their positions of authority to exploit female employees. As Jill Filipovic points out, as late as the 1960s and 1970s, guidelines for sexual harassment were vastly different from what has become standard: "It may not have been O.K. to ask your female subordinate to watch you shower, or offer her a naked massage, but tolerating inappropriate sexual behavior from men was a cost many women entering the workforce assumed they had to bear."[14] Filipovic, like many other observers of American culture, emphasizes bodily violations to define sexual harassment while subtly alluding to more indirect forms of exploitation such as verbal sexual harassment. These forms of harassment became more pronounced, however, through the activism of women such as Anita Hill who resisted the patriarchal trappings of the corporate field to expose the traumas associated with various forms of verbal sexual harassment. Hill's 1991 sexual harassment accusation against Supreme Court Justice nominee Clarence Thomas redefined language for sexual harassment to include inappropriate sexual communication. In her deposition,

"It may not have been O.K. to ask your female subordinate to watch you shower, or offer her a naked massage, but tolerating inappropriate sexual behavior from men was a cost many women entering the workforce assumed they had to bear."
—JILL FILIPOVIC

[13] Kristin Yohe, "Enslaved Women's Resistance and Survival Strategies in Frances Ellen Watkins Harper's 'The Slave Mother: A Tale of the Ohio' and Toni Morrison's *Beloved* and *Margaret Garner*," *Gendered Reistance: Women, Slavery, and the Legacy of Margaret Garner*, ed. Mary Frederickson (U of Illinois P, 2013) 99.

[14] Jill Filipovic, "What Weinstein's Downfall Means for Other Predators," *Time* 12 Oct. 2017: 29.

Hill vividly recounted ways that Thomas verbally assaulted her in the workplace and violated her civil rights, creating psychological trauma. Though Thomas was neither indicted nor denied the Supreme Court seat, Hill's subsequent case against him elicited a monumental shift in workforce ideologies about gender and power in American society. As Helen Lewis states, "Hill's case galvanized a whole generation of American feminists, because it wasn't just Thomas, or her, on trial in the court of public opinion: it was a high-profile airing of all the dirty linen of sexual harassment, its myths and misunderstandings."[15] Since the veil has been lifted on sexual harassment, powerful men in authoritative positions have been increasingly censured for sexually inappropriate behavior. Incidents such as (now President) Donald Trump's inappropriate comments about female genitalia in a 2005 taped interview and (now Supreme Court Justice) Brett Kavanaugh's alleged sexually inappropriate behavior toward Professor Christine Blasey Ford while both were teens in the 1980s have been met with disdain and criticism in American society. Though contemporary society has only recently acknowledged these behaviors as sexually oppressive, Jacobs had already revealed their traumatic consequences centuries earlier, and her literary aesthetic is a testament to her progressive activism against the violations of vulnerable Black women in oppressive patriarchal systems. ∎

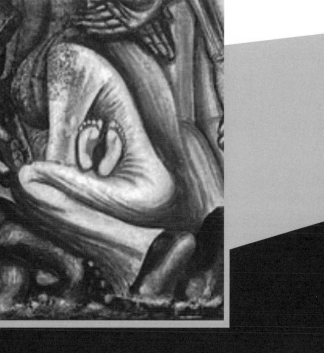

"Though contemporary society has only recently acknowledged these behaviors as sexually oppressive, Jacobs had already revealed their traumatic consequences centuries earlier, and her literary aesthetic is a testament to her progressive activism against the violations of vulnerable Black women in oppressive patriarchal systems."

[15] Helen Lewis, "Two Decades After Anita Hill, the Promise of #MeToo Is Women Can Stop Paying a 'Creep Tax,'" *New Statesman* 26 Sept. 2018: 27.

ASHLEY BURGE is a PhD candidate at the University of Alabama with concentrations in nineteenth- and twentieth-century African American literature. Her work emphasizes literary constructs of gender, race, and sexuality and their portrayal in oppressive American systems. She also focuses on theories associated with Black Feminism, pop culture, ecocriticism, ecofeminism, critical race theory, and black female identity.

2019 JOHN EHLE *Prize Winner*

THE LITERARY FRIENDSHIP OF GEORGE MOSES HORTON AND CAROLINE LEE HENTZ

BY PATRICK E. HORN

ART © THE CLAUDE HOWELL ESTATE/CAMERON ART MUSEUM, WILMINGTON, NC

selling love poems in Chapel Hill on Sunday

ABOVE **An illustration of George Moses Horton by renowned North Carolina artist Claude Howell (1915–1997), which appears in** *The Black Poet* **by Richard Walser (Philosophical Library, 1956)**

ONE OF VERY FEW American poets to have their work published while enslaved, George Moses Horton first gained recognition by composing love poems for students at UNC Chapel Hill. Born in or around 1797, Horton was only a few years younger than the university itself; and when he first began his Sunday visits to sell fruits and vegetables to UNC students in 1817, he would have been close in age to them as well. Horton recalled that "the collegians . . . were fond of pranking with the country servants who resorted there for the same purpose that I did. . . . But somehow or other they discovered a spark of genius in me, either by discourse or other means, which excited their curiosity, and they often eagerly insisted on me to spout, as they called it."[1]

"Spouting" was Horton's primary mode of sharing his poetry (and other forms of oratory) at the time, as he had not yet learned to write. When Augustus Alston, an undergraduate from Georgia, became the first customer to purchase a Horton poem for twenty-five cents in the early 1820s, he established a precedent that would forever change the young poet's life. Subsequent customers would sometimes pay fifty or seventy-five cents;[2] Horton also received payments and gifts of clothing and used books, including *Paradise Lost*, the *Iliad*, a collection of Shakespeare, and

---

[1] George Moses Horton, *The Poetical Works of George M. Horton, the Colored Bard of North Carolina. To Which is Prefixed the Life of the Author, Written by Himself* (1845, Documenting the American South, UNC Libraries, 1996) xii–xiv; subsequently cited parenthetically from this edition.

Jupiter Hammon is often credited with authoring the first published poem in the African American literary tradition, "An Evening Thought" (1760), while still enslaved in New York or Connecticut. Phillis Wheatley was emancipated in Boston soon after or just before her collection *Poems on Various Subjects* was published in September 1773 (Henry Louis Gates, Jr. and Nellie Y. McKay, eds., *The Norton*

Anthology of African American Literature, 2nd ed. [Norton, 2004] 163, 214). William H. Robinson, Jr. counts George Moses Horton fourth (chronologically, after Lucy Terry, Jupiter Hammon, and Olaudah Equiano) among what he calls the "orator poets" but considers Horton "America's first professional black poet" (*Early Black American Poets: Selections with Biographical and Critical Introductions* [Wm. C. Brown, 1969] 18).

[2] Richard Walser, *The Black Poet: Being the Remarkable Story (Partly Told by Himself) of George Moses Horton, A North Carolina Slave* (New York: Philosophical Library, 1956) 25; subsequently cited parenthetically. While twenty-five to seventy-five cents seems a small sum in contemporary exchange, we should recall that in 1825, UNC students were often allotted "only a dollar a month [or less] for pocket money"; therefore, some of Horton's customers were spending their "full allowance on such gems" (Walser 26).

a book that also inspired Frederick Douglass, *The Columbian Orator* (*Poetical* xvi). Horton would become one of the most important early American poets. Joan R. Sherman summarizes his signal achievements: "the first American slave to protest his bondage in verse; the first African American to publish a book in the South; the only slave to earn a significant income by selling his poems. . . . Horton also stands out among African American poets of the nineteenth century for his wide range of poetical subjects and unorthodox attitudes."[3]

A lesser-known aspect of Horton's legacy is his literary friendship with another influential nineteenth-century writer, Caroline Lee Hentz, whose fiction challenged traditional gender roles and called for greater interregional understanding during the decades leading up to the Civil War. Because of their respective positions as an enslaved black man in the antebellum South and a white Northern

> "HORTON WOULD BECOME ONE OF THE MOST IMPORTANT EARLY AMERICAN POETS."

PATRICK E. HORN serves as Associate Director for UNC Chapel Hill's Center for the Study of the American South. His scholarship has appeared in the *Journal of Southern History*, *Studies in the Novel*, *Southern Cultures*, and *a/b: Auto/Biography Studies*. Prior to attending graduate school at UNC Chapel Hill (where he earned his PhD), he served as an Air Force Intelligence Officer, completing tours in Iraq, Afghanistan, Turkey, Kuwait, and East Africa.

The John Ehle Prize was created by *NCLR* in collaboration with Winston-Salem publisher Press 53 to encourage scholarship on forgotten or neglected North Carolina writers. Terry Roberts called Horn's essay "the perfect essay to receive the inaugural John Ehle Prize," explaining his choice, "Not only does this essay shed light on two writers associated with North Carolina that deserve more attention – George Moses Horton and Caroline Lee Hentz – it also illuminates how Hentz championed Horton as a human being and supported his poetry. John Ehle was famous for helping others achieve their dreams, and so it's all the more appropriate that the author has given us the story of how one writer aided and abetted another in this prize-winning essay named for Ehle." Roberts picked this essay under blind review of all qualifying content in this issue. For more information about the John Ehle Prize, see the submissions section of the *NCLR* website.

ABOVE **A chromolithograph of the UNC Chapel Hill campus by E. Valois & Rau, circa 1861**

[3] Joan R. Sherman, ed., Introduction, *The Black Bard of North Carolina: George Moses Horton and His Poetry*, (U of North Carolina P, 1997) 1; subsequently cited parenthetically.

woman, Hentz and Horton's literary friendship was unavoidably asymmetrical. And although their relationship was influential for both writers, it would not prevent Hentz from becoming an apologist for the Southern social and economic system based on white supremacism and human bondage.

"HENTZ AND HORTON'S LITERARY FRIENDSHIP WAS UNAVOIDABLY ASYMMETRICAL."

Fortune seemed to smile on Horton in 1826, when Hentz moved to Chapel Hill. Born Caroline Lee Whiting in Lancaster, Massachusetts on June 1st, 1800, she was the youngest of eight children from a prominent New England family. Her father, a bookseller, died when she was ten, and she began working as a schoolteacher at the age of seventeen.

In 1824, she married Nicholas Hentz, a French immigrant who had studied medicine at Harvard, and two years later Nicholas received an appointment as a professor of modern languages at the University of North Carolina. In his spare time between classes, Nicholas conducted extensive field research on spiders, and his writings were posthumously published under the title *The Spiders of the United States* (1875).

The Hentzes had a tumultuous relationship, which biographer Miriam Shillingsburg attributes to Nicholas's "easily provoked jealousy," represented in Hentz's fiction by a variety of jealous husbands, prone to "melodramatic fits of rage."[4] The couple and their growing family moved frequently, living in Chapel Hill from 1826 to 1830; in Covington, Kentucky from 1830 to 1832; in Cincinnati, Ohio from 1832 to 1834; and in Florence, Alabama from 1834 to 1843. This erratic course would take Caroline Hentz away from George Horton after only four years, but during her sojourn in Chapel Hill, she would make an indelible mark on his life and work, and he on hers. She would go on to publish twelve novels and six story collections, beginning in the 1830s, and she supported her family single-handedly as a professional writer after Nicholas's nervous condition rendered him unfit to work.[5]

"SHE WOULD MAKE AN **INDELIBLE MARK** ON HIS LIFE AND WORK, AND HE ON HERS."

---

[4] Miriam Shillingsburg, "Caroline Lee (Whiting) Hentz," *Antebellum Writers in the South*, second series, ed. Kent P. Ljungquist, *Dictionary of Literary Biography*, vol. 248 (Gale, 2001) para 6; subsequently cited parenthetically. Much of the biographical information about Hentz referenced in this essay is from this source.

[5] The Hentzes' son Charles recalled, looking back on the summer of 1842, "I found my poor father more nervous & irritable than ever before – ; the forerunning condition to that general breaking down of the nervous system that in a year or two more overcame him, and gradually wore him out" (Charles A. Hentz, *A Southern Practice: The Diary and Autobiography of Charles A. Hentz*, M.D., ed. Steven M. Stowe [U of Virginia P, 2000] 483).

Horton's biographers have noted the importance of Hentz, not only as an inspirational teacher who flouted Southern conventions against educating slaves, but also for her active efforts to get his work published and to secure his freedom. Sherman notes that Caroline not only sent two of George's early poems to her hometown newspaper, the Lancaster *Gazette*, which became the first to publish them, but also likely transcribed the twenty-one poems included in his first collection, *The Hope of Liberty* (11). Over the next two years, Hentz and other sympathetic locals attempted two "subscription" campaigns to purchase Horton's freedom; both times they raised considerable sums of money, but his master rejected both offers.[6] In 1829, *The Hope of Liberty* was published in Raleigh, making Horton the first black poet to publish his work in the American South. The collection includes these powerful lines, composed "On hearing of the intention of a gentleman to purchase the Poet's freedom":

And sure of Providence this work begun –
He shod my feet this rugged race to run;
And in despite of all the swelling tide,
Along this dismal path will prove my guide.

Thus on the dusky verge of deep despair,
Eternal Providence was with me there;
When pleasure seemed to fade on life's gay dawn,
And the last beam of hope was almost gone.[7]

These lines reveal the "rugged race" of hopes raised and dashed that Horton had already experienced as a young man. The race would turn out to be longer than he may have anticipated, even when these lines were published.

In 1830, the Hentzes left Chapel Hill, to George's chagrin. Fifteen years later, he would conclude his autobiographical account by acknowledging the help of a "celebrated lady" who "discovered my little uncultivated talent, and was moved by pity to uncover to me the beauties of correctness" (*Poetical* xvii). He went on to liken Hentz to Thalia, classical Greek muse of comedy, good cheer, and bucolic poetry, as well as Thalia's sister Euphrosyne, the Greek goddess of gaiety and mirth.[8] Horton lamented that "This celebrated lady, however, did not continue long at Chapel Hill, and I had to regret the loss of her aid, which I shall never forget in life. As her departure from Chapel Hill, she left behind her the laurel of Thalia blooming on my mind, and went with all the spotless gaiety of Euphrosyne with regard to the signal services she had done me" (*Poetical* xviii).

COURTESY OF ALABAMA DEPARTMENT OF ARCHIVES AND HISTORY

"AS HER DEPARTURE FROM CHAPEL HILL, SHE LEFT BEHIND HER THE LAUREL OF THALIA BLOOMING ON MY MIND, AND WENT WITH ALL THE SPOTLESS GAIETY OF EUPHROSYNE WITH REGARD TO THE SIGNAL SERVICES SHE HAD DONE ME."
—GEORGE MOSES HORTON

ABOVE **Caroline Lee Hentz**

6 William Carroll, "George Moses Horton," *Afro-American Writers Before the Harlem Renaissance*, ed. Trudier Harris and Thadious M. Davis, *Dictionary of Literary Biography*, vol. 50 (Detroit: Gale, 1986): para 14.

7 George Moses Horton, *The Hope of Liberty, Containing a Number of Poetical Pieces* (Gales, 1829) 21; subsequently cited parenthetically.

8 For an explanation of Thalia's and Euphrosyne's roles and identities in Greek mythology, see Jenny March, *Dictionary of Classical Mythology* (Oxbow, 2014) 209, 322.

"HENTZ'S NOVEL ATTEMPTS TO WALK A MORAL TIGHTROPE, CLAIMING THAT IT DOES NOT DEFEND THE SYSTEM OF CHATTEL SLAVERY, WHILE CASTING WHITE SLAVEOWNERS AS GENTEEL ARISTOCRATS AND ENSLAVED AFRICAN AMERICANS AS BEING CONTENT WITH THEIR LOT."

According to George's account, Caroline Lee Hentz recognized his genius, assisted in his literary education, and elevated his work. He recalled her fondly as a joyful muse and mentor. But this narrative of the cheerful Northern giver of inspiration would be complicated by the proslavery novels she went on to publish. The woefully incomplete historical and biographical records of Horton's life leave open the question of whether he ever had the chance to read them.

The 1830s would see Hentz embark on her own career as a professional writer, beginning with the publication of her novel *Lovell's Folly* in 1833. Three of her plays were performed during this decade (in Philadelphia, New York, and New Orleans), but during the 1840s and '50s she would turn exclusively to fiction, publishing nine novels between 1850 and 1856 and selling over ninety thousand copies per year of her various works during the height of her popularity (Shillingsburg, para 7).

Lovell's Folly opens with the arrival of a fashionable Southern carriage in the fictional Northern town of Cloverdale, somewhere outside of Boston (like Hentz's hometown of Lancaster). Just as the "travelers of distinction" pull up to the Washington Hotel, a runaway stagecoach crashes into their carriage, causing the mother, Fanny Sutherland, to break her arm and fall into a "death-like swoon." Fanny and her daughter Lorelly are traveling with two slaves, November, a coachman, and Venus, a lady's maid. From their very first appearance, these black characters are described through blunt racial stereotypes. The "huge Negro" coachman swings his whip "lazily" and rolls his "ivory balls" (signifying his eyes) toward the setting sun.[9] Another character refers to Venus as "Blackey," and the narrator refers to her as "the dingy being" accompanying "the fair speaker" Lorelly. At one point the narrator editorializes, "There is not a more genuine model of true politeness, than the house-hold family-bred slave, the privileged nurse, or as the children of the South call them, the *mammy* of the establishment" (42).

Hentz's novel attempts to walk a moral tightrope, claiming that it does not defend the system of chattel slavery, while casting white slaveowners as genteel aristocrats and enslaved African Americans as being content with their lot. Venus and November appear to be more dismayed than their white mistresses at merely having to remain for a time in the North. After the stagecoach accident, Venus comments, "No good Yankee land. Me thought Misses only come to die. Venus die too" (22). On one occasion the narrator muses, in the royal tones of the first-person plural, "Far be it from us to advocate the cause of slavery, or to attempt to cover with too broad a mantle the blot which sullies our national purity; but it should be remembered in sorrow rather than indignation. . . . As well might we reproach the sable African for the color which severs him from our race, as the descendent of the southern planter for being *born* the hereditary owner of a race

---

[9] Caroline Lee Hentz, *Lovell's Folly* (Hubbard and Edmands, 1833): 19; subsequently cited parenthetically.

"I DETEST THEM ALL –
THE WHOLE RACE
OF COLD, SELFISH,
CALCULATING YANKEES."
—CAROLINE LEE HENTZ,
LOVELL'S FOLLY

learning alphabet while tending cows

"THE **LIPS** OF
GEORGE HAVE
BEEN BATHED
WITH PURE
CASTALIAN DEW.
HE IS A LEGITIMATE
CHILD OF THE
MUSES."
—CAROLINE LEE HENTZ,
LOVELL'S FOLLY

of slaves" (77). By depicting both race and slaveowning as qualities that are "natural" and conferred at birth, Hentz's novel effectively defends the very cause it claims to eschew.

The great theme of *Lovell's Folly* is that regional stereotypes and hostilities between Northerners and Southerners can be overcome through contact and exposure. Early in the text, numerous characters express their contempt and distrust for the other region and its residents. The Southern belle Lorelly announces, "I detest them all – the whole race of cold, selfish, calculating Yankees" (55). Similarly, the erudite character Mrs. Elmwood admits of her fellow Northerners, "*We are too apt to believe, that in the regions where slavery dwells, there is less of the 'milk of human kindness,'*– more of haughtiness and cruelty, than really exists" (139). But after Lorelly and Russel meet down by the river, "the prejudices of education melted away on both sides, like the icicle in the sunbeam, before the warm and kindred socialities of nature." Among these "prejudices," we learn, is the Northern belief that "all the kindliest charities of the heart [could not] flourish in a soil moistened by the sweat of the negro's brow"(76–77). By depicting the symmetrical melting away of these prejudices as a sign of progress and civility, the novel suggests a moral equivalency between Northern and Southern political positions and lifestyles.

Midway through the novel, as a seeming digression, we come across the story of George Moses Horton. Lorelly tells Mrs. Elwood, "I have never told you of the black poet, we have on our plantation – another Burns, – who sings the requiem of the wild violet, that he turns ruthlessly up with his ploughshare. . . . Poems, romances, dramas, mythological works he devoured as eagerly as the famished child the cakes and sweetmeats within his reach." With a "doubting smile," Mrs. Elmwood replies, "I suspect you are imposing on my credulity, Lorelly," but Lorelly insists otherwise:

No, indeed I am not. The lips of George have been bathed with pure Castalian dew. He is a legitimate child of the muses, as you would not hesitate to acknowledge. . . . *He has panted for liberty . . . and his prayers have been granted.* He found no companionship in feeling with his fellow slaves, and his spirits fluttered like the imprisoned eagle, to be released from bondage. Whatever argument you may find against our own cause, I cannot resist the temptation of quoting a few lines, *which proved his ransom.* As soon as my grandfather read them, he gave him his liberty, on condition that he should continue with him till he was of age, and then go to Liberia. (256–59; emphasis added)

In the page on which Lorelly first introduces "George," Hentz includes a lengthy footnote asserting that "the black poet mentioned here, is not an imaginary character. The author has only changed

ABOVE **Another of Howell's Horton illustrations**

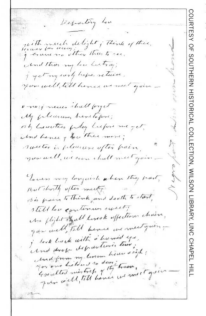

"**THE PSYCHOLOGICAL MACHINATIONS OF HENTZ-AS-AUTHOR EMPLOYING THIS ALMOST-TRUE STORY OF THE 'REAL HORTON' AS AN ARTIFICIAL LIMB IN HER DEFENSE OF SOUTHERN SLAVERY, WHILE FANCIFULLY WISHING HER HORTON CHARACTER AN UNLIKELY FREEDOM, SERVE AS A POWERFUL EXHIBIT OF THE CONVOLUTED LOGIC OF PROSLAVERY ARGUMENTS.**"

the place of his birth, and given him the reversion of a freedom he has little hope of enjoying" (256). Hentz/Lorelly goes on to quote from George's poem "On Liberty and Slavery." Here are his words, which Hentz found so compelling that she misrepresented them as George's "ransom":

> Oh, Liberty! thou golden prize,
> So often sought by blood,
> We crave thy sacred sun to rise,
> The gift of nature's God!
>
> Bid Slavery hide her haggard face,
> And barbarism fly –
> I scorn to see the sad disgrace,
> In which enslaved I lie.
>
> Dear Liberty! upon thy breast,
> I languish to respire;
> And like the Swan unto her nest,
> I'd to thy smiles retire. (Horton, *Hope* 8–9; Hentz, *Lovell's* 259)

In this passage, we enter into a fictional narrative in which a character alludes to an actual historical figure. Although the author notes that the person is "not imaginary," she nevertheless fictionalizes him. Hentz concedes that she has granted her almost-real character George "the reversion of a freedom he has little hope of enjoying" (256). The psychological machinations of Hentz-as-author employing this almost-true story of the "real Horton" as an artificial limb in her defense of Southern slavery, while fancifully wishing her Horton character an unlikely freedom, serve as a powerful exhibit of the convoluted logic of proslavery arguments.

If Hentz's early defenses of Southern slavery were equivocal and conflicted, by the 1850s her tone had grown more strident. She conceived of her 1854 novel *The Planter's Northern Bride* as an "anti-Tom novel," one of many such works written as Southern rebuttals to Harriet Beecher Stowe's *Uncle Tom's Cabin.* Hentz questions the veracity of the "dark and horrible pictures" that Stowe and others have "drawn of slavery and exhibited to a gazing world," offering her own personal observations and her fictional account as counter-narratives.[10]

Nina Baym has described *The Planter's Northern Bride* as "less a defense of slavery than a frantic plea to the North to curtail abolitionist meddling with southern life before it initiates a bloodbath."[11] But the book contains numerous defenses of slavery that were commonplace in nineteenth-century American literature. In a preface, Hentz informs readers that having been "born at the North," she can vouch that she has "never *witnessed* one scene of cruelty or oppression"

ABOVE **"Departing Love" by George Moses Horton, in his own hand, 1856**

[10] Caroline Lee Hentz, *The Planter's Northern Bride* (1854, Documenting the American South, 2003, UNC Libraries) 3; subsequently cited parenthetically from this edition.

[11] Nina Baym, *Woman's Fiction: A Guide to Novels by and about Women in America, 1820–70,* 2nd ed. (U of Illinois P, 1993) 136; subsequently cited parenthetically. Some biographical information about Hentz referenced in this essay is from Baym.

by Southern slaveholders. Rather, she notes the "cheerfulness and contentment of the slaves" and asserts that "the negroes of the South are the happiest *labouring class* on the face of the globe" (v–vi; author's italics). Indeed, the slaves love their masters, according to one (unnamed) "negro woman" whom Hentz quotes as stating, "I wouldn't have left my master and mistress for all the freedom in the world. . . . I loved their children too. . . . I loved 'em a heap better than I done my own" (vii–viii).

"HENTZ ASSERTS THAT 'THE NEGROES OF THE SOUTH ARE THE HAPPIEST *LABOURING CLASS* ON THE FACE OF THE GLOBE.'"

The Planter's Northern Bride tells the story of a New England girl named Eulalia, the daughter of a fiery abolitionist, who meets a Southern plantation owner, Richard Moreland, when he travels to her village, somewhere near Boston. Moreland agrees to a public debate with her father, Squire Hastings, and he speaks eloquently of Southerners's duty to save their slaves from "the misery, the degradation and hopelessness" of "their native Africa," to say nothing of "the horrors of cannibalism" (83–84). Eventually Richard wins Eulalia's heart, and after his initial refusal, Hastings changes his mind and allows his "delicate child" to become a missionary to "a benighted race," noting that her disposition requires "milder skies than ours" (148–49).

During their postnuptial journey south, Richard impresses upon Eulalia the "principle of homogeneousness" – a "great law of nature" that serves as a "dividing line" between the races, "as distinct as that which separates the beasts of the field, the birds of the air, and the fishes of the sea." She is initially unconvinced – isn't this the same logic that allows families to be separated "by the stroke of the auctioneer's hammer?" (204). But as time passes, the arguments against black freedom accumulate. At times the unnamed narrator interrupts the plot with lengthy bits of commentary, such as the following:

> Turn to the islands where the emancipated slave revels in unmolested freedom. Turn to St. Domingo, where, more than sixty years since, it placed upon its brow a sable crown, and took into its hands an ebon scepter, and abjured the domination of the white man. . . . What aspect does its government and society now present? Lawlessness, rapine, and murder . . . idleness, licentiousness, and blasphemy. (294–95)

If Haiti itself does not offer sufficient evidence for her readers, Hentz points to the British West Indies, where "the same dark scenes of violence and rapine destroy the brightness of these gems of the ocean" (295). Such depictions of postcolonial carnage were common among nineteenth-century proslavery advocates, and they were often deployed to stoke white fears about abolitionist futures. As Frederick

[12] Frederick Douglass, *Narrative of the Life of Frederick Douglass, an American Slave. Written by Himself* (1845, Documenting the American South, 1999, UNC Libraries) 744.

"EULALIA'S EXPERIENCE IN THE SOUTH SEEMS TO CONFIRM, FOR HER, THE WISDOM OF RICHARD'S WHITE SUPREMACIST IDEOLOGY."

Douglass observed in 1892, from the very inception of Haiti's independence, "the whole Christian world was against her. . . . She, by her bravery and her blood, was free. Her existence was therefore a menace to [slaveholding nations]."[12]

Eulalia's experience in the South seems to confirm, for her, the wisdom of Richard's white supremacist ideology. Viewing him surrounded by his admiring slaves, she muses that freedom and education "could never make them equal to him" (334). Eulalia and Richard are not the only characters through whom Hentz asserts white superiority or defends the slave system. An enslaved character named Dilsey gazes lovingly upon Moreland from her deathbed and says that when he sees "poor Dilsey" again in heaven, "she'll be beautiful, white angel den" (351). In a comical plot twist, a free black character named Judy, living in Cincinnati, begs Moreland's sister Ildegerte to take her back to the South as a slave: "Won't missus let poor Judy wait on her? I'd go down, crawling all de way on he hands and knees, if you only let me go back to de South when you go." Ildegerte promises to oblige her, and the narrator comments that "poor Judy had never known what real kindness and sympathy was, before" (292–93). Readers will be hard-pressed to find similar anecdotes in nineteenth-century narratives (whether fictional or autobiographical) published by African American writers. Like Joel Chandler Harris's fictional "happy slave" character Uncle Remus and Harriet Beecher Stowe's minstrel characters Sam and Andy, Hentz's Judy is rooted firmly in white fantasy.

The literary friendship of George Moses Horton and Caroline Lee Hentz was complicated, for it seems difficult to square Hentz's mentorship and advocacy for Horton with her most strident proslavery arguments. How could she transcribe *The Hope of Liberty* and grant Horton an imaginary freedom in her first novel while also claiming that black people were constitutionally unfit to rule themselves? Did the Hentz family's long residence in the South (and eventual migration from North Carolina to Alabama) gradually affect her thoughts on the matter? Were her proslavery statements and narratives influenced by the need to sell copies to a reading public eager to consume white supremacist characters and plots? Did she rationalize Horton's case as that of an "exceptional" slave whose story had little bearing on the larger questions confronting the nation? It is difficult to answer these questions authoritatively through the evidence we have available to us as twenty-first century readers. However, it is tempting to view Hentz's subject position as an analog of Eulalia's: a former Northern abolitionist whose residence in the South slowly persuaded her that slavery was a legitimate basis for social order.

Nina Baym has observed that Eulalia is one of Hentz's most "conservative and traditional" heroines, "fulfilled in the most traditional kinds of wifely behavior and happy to be ruled by Moreland" (136). Indeed, in her growing acceptance of the Southern way of life, Eulalia at times appears rather captive herself. In one scene, after she hugs

"HENTZ AND HORTON'S LITERARY STARS WOULD RISE AT DIFFERENT SPEEDS, BUT HIS WOULD EVENTUALLY OUTSHINE HERS."

her charming Southern husband, he "imprison[s]" her "timid arms . . . in his own, and retain[s] her in willing bondage" (344). In such passages it seems evident that "Hentz recognizes that patriarchy is an institution affecting women as well as slaves; but since she is defending it for the slave, she must defend it for women as well" (136).

Hentz and Horton's literary stars would rise at different speeds, but his would eventually outshine hers. Once a bestselling and influential author, Hentz is now forgotten to all but a few students of American literature, who remember her mostly for being on the wrong side of history. For his part, Horton would remain in bondage until Emancipation, some thirty-four years after *The Hope of Liberty* was published. He had what appears to have been an unhappy marriage, judging from the poems he wrote about it, but after gaining his freedom, he moved north to Philadelphia.[13] His later poetry appeared in the collection *Naked Genius* (1865), published first in Raleigh and then in Philadelphia. Horton would die in relative obscurity, but subsequent generations would take new interest in his poetry and his life story. A North Carolina Highway Historical Marker, erected in 1999, now identifies the Chatham County farm where he once lived. In 2002 a new dormitory at UNC Chapel Hill was named Horton Hall in his honor, and in 2015 a popular children's book was published under the title *Poet: The Remarkable Story of George Moses Horton*.[14]

The complicated friendship of Caroline Lee Hentz and George Moses Horton can remind us that it is possible to rise above political differences in our interpersonal dealings, that a love of beauty and knowledge can unite us despite our differences, and that the long arc of history often reflects our actions quite differently than the political winds of particular times and places. It seems fitting to leave the last words to Horton, who inscribed the following lines in 1845 to "the much-distinguished Mrs. Hentz":

COURTESY OF MARJORIE HUDSON

When nature's crown refuses to be gay,
And ceaseless streams have worn their rocks away;
When age's vail shall beauty's visage mask
And bid oblivion blot the poet's task,
Time's final shock shall elevate thy name,
And lift thee smiling to eternal fame. (*Poetical* xix) ∎

[13] See, for example, "Connubial Felicity," which observes that
The gaudy charms of May,
Are quickly past away,
The honey moon,
Will change as soon,
And love to ills betray
Other poems from *Naked Genius* that take a dim view of marriage include "Snaps for Dinner," "A Wife," and "The Treacherous Woman."

[14] Don Tate, *Poet: The Remarkable Story of George Moses Horton* (Peachtree, 2015).

"THE COMPLICATED FRIENDSHIP OF CAROLINE LEE HENTZ AND GEORGE MOSES HORTON CAN REMIND US THAT IT IS POSSIBLE TO RISE ABOVE POLITICAL DIFFERENCES IN OUR INTERPERSONAL DEALINGS, THAT A LOVE OF BEAUTY AND KNOWLEDGE CAN UNITE US DESPITE OUR DIFFERENCES."

ABOVE **Children's book author Don Tate with North Carolina writer Marjorie Hudson, who published an essay on Horton in** *NCLR* **1999**

WITH ILLUSTRATIONS BY CLAUDE HOWELL

"THE VERSES FROM OUR PEN TO HIM BELONG":

ON DECEMBER 29, 1849, the *Raleigh Register* published a letter written by George Moses Horton. Addressed "To the Public," Horton's editorial responds to a dispute around a toast that took place at a dinner party. Some of the guests believed that the "Regular Toasts" presented to the president-elect of Hungary (who was present for the commemoration of General Saunders) "contained sentiments not suited to all present." Horton relayed to his readers that, though the situation did not concern him personally since he would likely "never be before the People for any office," he would not have "assented" to the toast on the grounds that a foreign poem was read in the president-elect's honor:

> I am for developing our own resources and cherishing native genius. . . . As a North Carolina patriot, I ask, why leave our own to stand on foreign soil? Why go abroad for poetry when we have an infinitely superior article of domestic manufacture? I am too modest to speak of my own, but surely there is poetry of native growth . . . without straying off into foreign parts.[1]

In what would seem like an otherwise immaterial dispute, Horton's letter reflects both the sophisticated manner in which he thought about the world of American letters and his own sense of loyalty for the progress of American writers. As Joan R. Sherman suggests, one hears in Horton's letter a "defense that echoed the cultural nationalism of America's most prominent writers from Philip Freneau through Ralph Waldo Emerson."[2] Yet, what makes Horton's claims markedly more unusual than Emerson or Freneau's is when one considers the subject position Horton brings to this cultural nationalist position.

The first North Carolina artist to exhibit work at the Metropolitian Museum of Art in Wilmington, NC, native **CLAUDE HOWELL** (1915–1997) is best known for his paintings depicting life on the North Carolina coast. He helped create the Art Department at Wilmington College (Now UNC Wilmington), where he taught for many years. Howell's art is also in *NCLR* 1998, 1999, 2005, and *NCLR Online* 2012.

Regarding his George Moses Horton illustrations featured here and in the preceding essay on Horton. Claude Howell wrote in his journal: "Dick Walser's book The Black Poet [has] just been published. I have just received my copy. This is the book for which I did the four drawings for Dick and suprisingly enough they turned out rather well. They were among the first things I had done after I was sick and I was a little apprehensive as to how they would look" (26 Dec. 1966).

[1] George Moses Horton, "To The Public" *Raleigh Register* 29 Dec. 1849: 3.

[2] Joan R. Sherman, ed., Introduction, *The Black Bard of North Carolina: George Moses Horton and His Poetry* (U of North Carolina P, 1997) 22.

What, after all, does it mean for a black man, who has been enslaved for his entire life, to be a "North Carolina patriot" and a cultural critic of literary consumption? Horton's patriotism is, in one sense, a means of establishing common ground with his white readers. After demonstrating his loyalty to the cultural nationalist position, Horton reduces the threat of subversion and agitation that is constituted in his very ability to read and write by reassuring his reader that he is "too modest" to think that his own writing ought to be considered in this call for poetry of "native growth." Rhetorically, we see the complex gymnastics that Horton must undergo in order to speak on behalf of American letters. As in his letter "To the Public," Horton dons a cultural nationalist position in his homages to Andrew Jackson and Ulysses S. Grant, extolling the accomplishments

NATIONAL IDENTITY IN THE POLITICAL HOMAGES OF GEORGE MOSES HORTON

BY JUSTIN WILLIAMS

ART © THE CLAUDE HOWELL ESTATE; CAMERON ART MUSEUM, WILMINGTON, NC

dictating poems to a student

of domestic American martial figures. Presenting these figures as national heroes, in these poems, Horton, simultaneously reflects, perpetuates, and shapes popular narratives about them. In these poems, too, Horton makes tacit appeals for membership in a national consciousness that has, since birth, denied him the possibility of citizenship.

> "IN THESE POEMS, HORTON, PRESENTING THESE FIGURES AS NATIONAL HEROES, SIMULTANEOULY REFLECTS, PERPETUATES, AND SHAPES POPULAR NARRATIVES ABOUT THEM."

JUSTIN WILLIAMS was born and rasied in Jackson, TN. He received his BA in French and English at Tennessee Technical University and is currently a fourth year PhD student in literary and cultural studies at the University of Memphis, focusing on twentieth–century and contemporary African American poetry.

To understand the singularity of Horton's appeals, it is helpful to consider that only three years after the *Raleigh Register* published Horton's letter, Frederick Douglass asks the Ladies Anti-Slavery Society in Rochester, New York, "What to the Slave Is the Fourth of July?"[3] Douglass, troubled by the idea of celebrating American independence when there were still so many still enslaved, asks, can black people living in American – even those who have managed to obtain freedom – rightly call themselves patriots? Douglass's stance in his address illustrates the stark difference in the respective authors's sense of national belonging. When taken next to Douglass, Horton's qualm with domestic versus international poetry seems as if he were indulging in a sort of philosophical excess. Indeed, the African American literary canon has no shortage of writers who have stridently and unequivocally addressed the deeply problematic history of America's treatment of black people. Horton's writings, however, do not fit neatly into a framework of protest literature. Perhaps the most salient aspect of Horton's poetry is that his silences speak more loudly than his rare instances of protest. In his 1845 volume of poetry, *The Poetical Works of George Moses Horton: The Colored Bard of North Carolina, To Which is Prefixed the Life of the Author, Written by Himself*, Horton's "Life of the Author" section details the events that lead him to write poetry.[4] The autobiographical sketch is far from anything resembling what one might recognize today as a slave narrative. Rather than the narrative of a runaway or an account of the vicissitudes of a cruel master, the sketch is drawn more as the portrait of an artist, recounting the extraordinary circumstances under which Horton pursued his passion for writing poetry.

Living in Chapel Hill, just eight miles from the newly founded University of North Carolina, Horton describes frequenting the campus on the sabbath to sell fruit to the students. Before long, he becomes renowned for his poetic ability and he transitions from fruit peddler to a kind of unofficial poet-in-residence on the university's campus. Horton is quick to point out the factors that "stifle[d] the growth of [his] uncultivated genius." Reflecting on his old master, Horton writes, "One thing is to be lamented much . . . that ever I

COURTESY OF THE LOUIS ROUND WILSON SPECIAL COLLECTIONS LIBRARY

UNIVERSITY OF NORTH CAROLINA.
Chapel Hill.
Hon. David L. Swain L.L.D. President.

"BEFORE LONG, HE BECOMES RENOWNED FOR HIS POETIC ABILITY AND HE TRANSITIONS FROM FRUIT PEDDLER TO A KIND OF UNOFFICIAL POET-IN-RESIDENCE ON THE UNIVERSITY'S CAMPUS."

ABOVE **A line drawing of the UNC Chapel Hill campus, circa 1850**

3   His speech, delivered on 5 July 1852, is collected in Philip S. Foner, ed., *Frederick Douglass: Selected Speeches and Writings* (Lawrence Hill, 1999) 188–206.

4   George Moses Horton, *The Poetical Works of George M. Horton, the Colored Bard of North Carolina. To Which is Prefixed the Life of the Author, Written by Himself* (1845, Documenting the American South, UNC Libraries, 1996) xii–xiv; subsequently cited parenthetically.

was raised in a family or neighborhood inclined to dissipation" (xi). For Horton, the culture of drinking and riotous living that took place on the farm did far more to impinge his progress as an artist than his status as a slave. His genius is "uncultivated" because of the lack

> "FOR HORTON, THE CULTURE OF DRINKING AND RIOTOUS LIVING THAT TOOK PLACE ON THE FARM DID FAR MORE TO IMPINGE HIS PROGRESS AS AN ARTIST THAN HIS STATUS AS A SLAVE."

of positive role models, rather than a problem with human bondage. True, Horton points out the moral decadence of his previous master, who permitted and encouraged this behavior, but this complaint is more like wishing to have been born in a different family rather than wishing to have not been born under the yoke of slavery. To this effect, it was more important for Horton to be taken seriously as an artist than to convince people of the ills of slavery.

It is difficult then to imagine that Horton himself did not dream of the kind of recognition he claims poets of "native growth" deserved. As much as Horton's letter in *Raleigh Register* addresses American letters writ large, it is also about his own literary production, since garnering prestige and renown could mean the ability to purchase his freedom with the earnings from selling his poetry. Horton's letter illustrates the complex negotiations that permitted him the relative freedom to speak his mind on American literary culture, and it also gestures to the ways in which Horton used patriotism as a tool for artistic legitimization. In a similar fashion, "The Death of Gen. Jackson – An Eulogy," from his *Poetical Works,* and "Gen. Grant – The Hero of the War," from his book of Civil War poems *Naked Genius,* are attempts to immortalize these figures for their successes in combat, depicting them as flawless leaders and exemplars of patriotism. Although they were written some twenty years apart (and the latter after Horton was emancipated at the end of the Civil War), both poems rely on the same rhetorical formula to illustrate the cultural significance of these men. These models of patriotism are distinctly masculine portrayals, highlighting a kind of rugged individualism that Horton, given his own exceptionalism, must have admired. Having made their mark on their nation, Horton uses metaphors around stars and constellations to cast these men both literally and figuratively into a new American cosmology. That the same combination of rhetorical figures is used when Horton writes his homages to other renowned national figures – like Henry Clay, Abraham Lincoln, and General Sherman – suggests that Horton had a distinct vision of what constituted the nation's heroes. To this effect, Horton places himself in the roles of both inheritor and cultivator of an American mythos. Horton calls attention to his own American-ness, implying that America's narrative is *his* narrative to create and embody.

> ## "HORTON CALLS ATTENTION TO HIS OWN AMERICAN-NESS, IMPLYING THAT AMERICA'S NARRATIVE IS *HIS* NARRATIVE TO CREATE AND EMBODY."

The first lines of "Death of Gen. Jackson" establish this national audience by donning a kind of universal cry of a nation in mourning at the recent loss of Andrew Jackson. The effulgent tone of the poem depicts the narrator's initial emotional shock upon hearing of Jackson's death. However, the individualized experience of the narrator is presented as a kind of universal experience that everyone who remembers hearing of Jackson's death shares, including the black poet hiding behind the page:

> Hark! from the mighty Hero's tomb,
> I hear a voice proclaim!
> A sound which fills the world with gloom,
> But magnifies his name. (45, ll. 1–4)

The disembodied "voice" that emerges from "the Hero's tomb" beautifully mimics the slow yet assured dissemination of bad news, the source of which is completely overshadowed as the content of the message takes over. If one can say that the poem takes in any particular setting, its setting is the moment in which the narrator hears of Jackson's death. Implicitly, the poem asks the reader to relive the experience of learning that Jackson is dead, thereby cultivating a sense of universality. In leaving it up to the spectator to determine for himself the actual location when he heard about the death, he invites the reader to share in the shock and awe felt by the passing of a figure who was foundational to a nineteenth-century conception of the country's identity. The only consolation the narrator can provide for the nation is that Jackson's death is one that will only "magnify" his great name as he is written in to the pages of history. For Horton, the greatest honor is never to be forgotten.

> ## "FOR HORTON, THE GREATEST HONOR IS NEVER TO BE FORGOTTEN."

ABOVE **"Presidents North Carolina Gave the Nation,"** featuring Andrew Jackson (center), James K. Polk, and Andrew Johnson, located in front of the State Capitol in Raleigh, NC

L II

ANDREW JACKSON
——— ••• ———
Seventh president of
the United States,
was born a few miles
southwest of this
spot, March 15, 1767.

ARCHIVES, CONSERVATION AND HIGHWAY DEPARTMENT 1938

COURTESY OF NC DEPARTMENT OF NATURAL AND CULTURAL RESOURCES

ABOVE **North Carolina Historical Highway Marker,
placed in 1938 near Andrew Jackson's birthplace
on South Main St. in Waxhaw, NC**

The poem further elaborates on Jackson's heroism, suggesting that "He scorn'd to live a captured slave, / And fought his passage through; / He dies, the prince of all the braves" (l. 9–11). Horton, of course, uses "braves" to play on Jackson's bravery in battle, but he also suggests that all Americans live in the tradition of a Jacksonian patriotism. Jackson is, Horton seems to say, part of the DNA of America's genealogy. But as much as Horton writes a patriotic poem appealing to his reader's sense of nationalism and love for a well-known American figure, it is also a poem about Horton's own patriotism. It is a poem that says to his reader, "I, too, am a patriot," and it begs the question of the reader what it means to feel a sense of nationalism and pride in one's country and yet also be a slave in that country.

As a stand-in for the ideal American "brave," Horton's eulogy is also a celebration of America's revolutionary past and the refusal to remain British subjects. Jackson's victory at the Battle of New Orleans in 1815 is,

"I, TOO, AM A PATRIOT."

synecdochally speaking, America's victory over the British in the War of 1812. Just as Jackson "scorn'd to live a captured slave" and never became "enslaved" as a prisoner of war, the result of the War of 1812 was that Americans could finally be secure in their status as a sovereign nation, having escaped the danger of being "enslaved" to Great Britain. Horton here posits a curious definition of what it means to be American: if Jackson is the "prince of all the braves" because he was never enslaved, Horton who is literally a "captured slave" is himself incongruous with his own definition. Though this irony was likely not lost on Horton, he does not pursue this moment in the poem as an occasion to call attention to his own enslavement.

That Jackson's presidency is never mentioned is telling as to the version of Jackson that Horton wanted to depict. In the title, he is "Gen. Jackson" and not President Jackson, highlighting the relative importance of the military accomplishments over his legislative ones. Horton only touches on the aspects of Jackson that are the most accessible and well-known to his audience. Jacksonian heroism is indistinguishable from his accomplishments on the battlefield. In the poem, Jackson wields a "glittering sword" and can be seen "marching from his tomb" (46, ll. 17, 22). In his passing, "He goes down like a star" and "leaves his friends behind / To rein the steed of war" (ll. 25, 27–28), ever returning to the scene of the battle. Nineteenth-century Americans remembered Jackson more for his contribution to the War of 1812 than for his presidency. Some of Jackson's contemporary politicians even jeered that his ascent to the presidency was largely due to this military success rather than his aptitude for public office. In the poem, Horton does not even bother to mention the name of the battle for which Jackson is famous. He is a hero, and that is all one needs to know.

ART © THE CLAUDE HOWELL ESTATE/CAMERON ART MUSEUM, WILMINGTON, NC

reciting poems to Union Army

One could simply dismiss the eulogy for its sanitized view of Jackson, a presentation that is easily digestible and in line with the cultural mythology that characterized Jackson in the nineteenth century. Uninterested in offering a portrait of human foibles, Horton presents Jackson as a flawless American patriot. However, this narrative equating Jackson's military victory with American ideals is still prevalent today. Consider, for instance, the affinity of Horton's poem with the title of Brian Kilmead and Don Yaegar's 2017 history *Andrew Jackson and the Miracle of New Orleans: The Battle That Shaped America's Destiny*. Moreover, Horton's seemingly benign depiction plays into the problematic notion that the nation as a whole was still united in the noble pursuit of freedom over British tyranny rather than on the verge of sectional crisis. The second stanza of the poem depicts the nation as perfectly aligned in mourning the loss of Jackson, imagining it as touching not only the people of every state but also people living on foreign shores:

> His flight from time let braves deplore,
> And wail from state to state,
> And sound abroad from shore to shore,
> The death of one so great! (ll. 45, 5–8)

Here any differences between the nation and its states are collapsed into issues without nuance or disagreement. Of course, in 1845, the United States was far from unified, especially on the subject of slavery, as the Civil War would indicate with violent clarity. Matthew Dennis notes that popular beliefs around the War of 1812 "helped support the illusion of national unity as that unity was increasingly challenged."According to Dennis, the lack of acknowledgement further sowed the seeds of the looming conflict, by "allowing [Americans] to construct and embrace alternative models of Americanism without fully confronting growing sectional, social, or political riffs."[5] Horton's misattribution then falls into step with a wider cultural position around the war of 1812.

Horton's sense of Jackson as American paragon is not, as Dennis explains, the "evidence-based, critical, revisable" account of the historian but part of the public memory, a "collective mentality or popular historical consciousness – the past that ordinary people carry around with them in their heads, the big stories we share that explain our world and organize the shorter stories that we tell about our communities." Horton's poetry acts as carrier and disseminator of this "popular historical consciousness," and casts the poet in the role of fortifying the myth around these figures (Dennis 273). Beyond calling attention to his own patriotism, Horton introduces his own version of how American ought to remember these figures.

"IN 1845, THE UNITED STATES WAS FAR FROM UNIFIED, ESPECIALLY ON THE SUBJECT OF SLAVERY, AS THE CIVIL WAR WOULD INDICATE WITH VIOLENT CLARITY."

ABOVE **Another of Howell's Horton illustrations**

5   Matthew Dennis, "Reflections on a Bicentennial: The War of 1812 in American Public Memory," *Early American Studies* 12.2 (2014): 285, 271.

Just over twenty years after he wrote the eulogy for Jackson, Horton penned several homages to those who participated in the Civil War. Having traveled around with Union soldiers for several months following the war, Horton developed a sense of the widespread carnage and death wrought by the Civil War, and so, in the poems of *Naked Genius*, one notes a marked difference from his earlier poetry. *Naked Genius* includes many poems about anonymous soldiers and mothers who lost their children, but it also addresses the already ascendant figures like Ulysses S. Grant and William Sherman who were thought to have decided the course of the war.

Horton exercises more nuance and maturity in his depiction of Ulysses S. Grant in his poem "Gen. Grant – The Hero of the War" than in his eulogy to Jackson.[6] One notes several distinct departures in Horton's depiction of Grant and his relationship to the nation that help to index the shifting public perceptions in the wake of the Civil War. In his homage to Grant, "Brave Grant" is still, like Jackson, the "hero of the war," only this time Horton begins with an apostrophe, directly addressing General Grant, in place of the more omniscient third-person speaker in the eulogy.

"BRAVE GRANT, THOU HERO OF THE WAR."

"GRANT'S LIGHT SHINES BRIGHTER THAN ANYONE ELSE'S. FROM HIS VIEW FROM THE SKY, HE IS DEPICTED AS A KIND OF GUARDIAN OF THE NATION."

COURTESY OF NC DEPARTMENT OF NATURAL AND CULTURAL RESOURCES

The direct address implies a more familiar positioning on Horton's part, perhaps highlighting his indebtedness to the Union victories:

> Brave Grant, thou hero of the war,
> Thou art the emblem of the morning star,
> Transpiring from the East to banish fear,
> Revolving o'er a servile Hemisphere,
> At large thou hast sustained the chief command
> And at whose order all must rise and stand,
> To hold position in the field is thine,
> To sink in darkness or to rise and shine. (16, ll. 1–8)

Like Jackson's eulogy, Horton again employs the metaphor of the star, but here develops it into a conceit. The morning star, otherwise known as Venus, is the brightest "star" in the sky. Thus, Grant's light shines brighter than anyone else's. From his view from the sky, he is depicted as a kind of guardian of the nation, "revolving o'er a servile Hemisphere" and "banish[ing] fear." The language attempts to capture the reach and expansiveness of the sweeping changes to the political landscape of the United States after the Civil War. Unlike Jackson, Grant's accomplishment is not simply rooted in the fact that he was a good general. Signifying powerfully on the institution of slavery as something that demeaned the nation, Horton depicts Grant

LEFT **North Carolina Historical Highway Marker H-31, placed in 1940 on South St. in Raleigh**

6 "Gen. Grant – The Hero of the War" is cited from the Chapel Hill Historical Society's 1982 edition of *Naked Genius*.

as someone who refused to allow the nation "to sink in darkness." Grant's presence illuminates and lifts up the nation out of its sin into righteousness. The contours of Grant's profile then become rooted in his moral as well as his military accomplishments.

Grant is also instrumental in ensuring that "the love of Union burned in every heart" (17, l. 17). "Union" here is obviously opposed to the secession of the Confederates. The poem goes on to expand how Grant was also a great and admired leader: all "must rise and stand" at his "order," and, like Jackson, Grant is practically invulnerable as he never "fail[s] . . . to take the spoil" in his battles. In some respects, this appears strikingly similar to the unity that follows Jackson. Grant is seemingly universally beloved and respected like Jackson. A dramatic shift occurs in the fourth stanza when the narrator shifts from addressing Grant to addressing the South:

> "HORTON POSITIONS HIMSELF AS A KIND OF LIAISON OR ARBITER BETWEEN THE NORTH AND THE SOUTH. REFLECTING ON PAST TRIUMPHS AND DEFEATS, HE DEPICTS BOTH THE LOSERS AND THE WINNERS AS STANDING ON EQUAL GROUNDS."

Ye Southern gentlemen must grant him praise,
Nor on the flag of Union fail to gaze;
Ye ladies of the South forego the prize,
Our chief commander here to recognize,
From him the stream of general orders flow,
And every chief on him some praise bestow,
The well-known victor of the mighty cause
Demands from every voice a loud applause
(17, ll. 25–32).

No longer restricted from what he could say in his environment in the South, Horton uses his homage to Grant, as he does on many occasions in *Naked Genius*, to tell a few jokes at the South's expense. As someone who spent his entire life in the South, Horton's fourth stanza illustrates his complicated relationship with Southerners. In these lines, Horton is basically asking the South to be a good sport about losing the war. He begins his address with a pun on General Grant, urging the "Southern gentlemen [to] *grant* him praise." Perhaps naively, but sincerely, Horton urges the South to accept defeat with sportsmanlike conduct. Horton positions himself as a kind of liaison or arbiter between the North and the South. Reflecting on past triumphs and defeats, he depicts both the losers and the winners as standing on equal grounds.

In what seems like a rarity in nineteenth-century African American texts, Horton allows for quite a bit of humor to flow through his homage to Grant and several other poems in the collection. Horton makes light of the dreadful occurrence and the heavy grief felt by many families across the nation. But Horton is also making a grand statement about the war and the potential for reconciliation.

"YET, WHILE HORTON'S POETRY IS OFTEN CHARACTERIZED BY ITS DISENGAGEMENT WITH POLITICAL ISSUES LIKE SLAVERY, HIS WRITING NEVERTHELESS POSSESSES A KEEN SENSE OF HIS PLACE IN THE NATIONAL LANDSCAPE."

Perhaps Horton had the sense that the South might double down on its allegiance to the Confederacy and predicted the dangers of what became the Lost Cause. For this reason, he might have made it his mission to cast *Naked Genius* as a book of poems about the potential for national healing in the face of a violent war. Faith Barrett supports this notion, going as far as to say that *Naked Genius* is itself a meditation on the severed nation in which Horton attempts to act as healer to help the Northerners and Southerners move past these dark times.[7] It would make sense then that Horton imagines the North and South as being reunited. While "Gen. Grant – The Hero of the War" explicitly addresses a Union audience, it leaves room for the South to enter into the discussion about how to rebuild in the wake of the war. In these poems, there emerges a marked difference between the eulogy to Jackson, where the nation was depicted as being united to the more blatant acknowledgement in the poems of *Naked Genius* where national division is impossible to ignore.

In this regard, Horton's Civil War poems write both back to the South and forward to the future of the nation. Horton concludes his homage by urging other poets write their own commemorations of Grant: "the verses from our pen to him belong" (l. 38). As both participant and recruiter to the creation of an American mythology, Horton acknowledges the need to contour this memory in such a way that will allow America to heal.

It is likely that Horton recognized that being viewed as the precocious slave with a penchant for doggerel would get him nowhere, especially in the South, if the foremost theme of his writing was his enslavement. Ironically, the clearest path toward securing funds for his emancipation meant downplaying as much as possible the markers of his status as a slave. Yet, while Horton's poetry is often characterized by its disengagement with political issues like slavery, his writing nevertheless possesses a keen sense of his place in the national landscape. In his patriotic homages, one detects the seeds of his desire to construct an affinity between himself and his nation, regardless of its contradictions, for better or for worse. ∎

COURTESY OF NC DEPARTMENT OF NATURAL AND CULTURAL RESOURCES

H 108
GEORGE MOSES HORTON
ca. 1798–1883
Slave poet. His *The Hope of Liberty* (1829) was first book by a black author in South. Lived on farm 2 mi. SE.

NORTH CAROLINA OFFICE OF ARCHIVES AND HISTORY

ABOVE **North Carolina Highway Historical Marker, placed in 1999 on US 15/501 at Mount Gilead Church Road north of Pittsboro**

7 Faith Barrett, "*Naked Genius*: The Civil War Poems of George Moses Horton," *Literary Cultures of the Civil War*, ed. Timothy Sweet (U of Georgia P, 2016) 77–98.

On Timing, Friendship, Loss, and Gratitude
by Margaret D. Bauer, Editor

On occasion, we receive a submission just right for an issue's theme when it is too late to get it ready for inclusion in that issue. For example, journalist/poet Zoe Kincaid Brockman was a suitable subject for the 2018 issue's special feature section, "North Carolina on the Map and in the News," but in spite of deadlines, it really is never too late to submit. Such cases as Rebecca Duncan's essay and Lyn Triplett's remembrance of Brockman are exactly why we created a "Flashbacks" section for *NCLR*. So if you have something that suits an earlier issue's theme, don't hesitate to send it for our consideration.

Earlier in the week that I sat down to draft this introduction, I was exchanging emails with one of *NCLR*'s regular contributors, and I noted to him that one of the gifts *NCLR* continues to give me is friendship. Relationships that begin as I engage with writers to prepare their works for publication in our pages develop over the years into genuine friendships, though most of these people I see in person very rarely, if we've met face to face at all.

I assure you all, however, that submissions are screened anonymously – and creative writing submitted for our competitions is both screened and selected for publication without my input, since I can see behind the curtain. I am likely no longer objective, for I do appreciate so much when writers from our past pages show up again among our submissions. And when they win, I am happy for them and pleased to have the opportunity to work with them again. Though not part of the selection process, I do insist upon the privilege of sending the notices to the prize winners. I've noted before how much I like finding out it's someone's very first publication that has won the prize. I equally relish the times I am sharing the news with an *NCLR* "veteran." Congratulations again, Catherine Carter, on your Applewhite Prize. And thank you for continuing both to share your poetry with our readers and to take on book review assignments for our writers.

Congratulations also to repeat finalists J.S. (Stan) Absher and Nilla Larsen, whose poems are in this section too. To all of our finalists, I remind you to send us your books for review consideration as you publish them. Once you've been in our pages, we really do consider you one of our writers and thus find particular pleasure in supporting your work. You'll find a review of a collection of Stan's poetry, for example, in *NCLR Online* 2017.

One of *NCLR*'s most beloved writers has suffered a terrible loss since we published the 2019 online issue, which included one of his poems. In February, James Applewhite lost his dear wife Jan after over sixty years together. Those who never met Jan in person may know her from her husband's poems. At her memorial service David Cecelski reported that among her final instructions to her family members was telling Jim to continue to "write beautiful poems." She may have been biased, but we feel certain readers will agree with her characterization of his poetry. We have been so fortunate that he continues to send *NCLR* new work each year. And since we've always known him to follow Jan's advice, we believe we will have more for you next year. In the meantime, we send our deepest condolences to Jim and to their three children, as well as to others who mourn this beautiful soul who will, we know, continue to inspire all who knew her – and her husband's poetry.

I am grateful to have had the opportunity to know Jan, to know Jim, and for my many other *NCLR* friends. Grateful too for the wonderful people I work with on staff like longtime Assistant Editor Christy Hallberg, promoted this year to Senior Associate Editor in acknowledgement of her many years of excellent work on behalf of *NCLR* and its writers, as well as the sheer amount of her voluntary service. Besides screening submissions along with the other assistant editors and editorial board members, Christy continues reading

OPPOSITE RIGHT
James and Jan Applewhite with *NCLR* **Editor Margaret Bauer at the 2011 Eastern North Carolina Literary Homecoming, Greenville, NC**

COURTESY OF THE GASTON COUNTY PUBLIC LIBRARY

COURTESY OF THE GASTON COUNTY PUBLIC LIBRARY

and editing after acceptance, and her astute feedback is invaluable. Her western North Carolina location also helps us to attend more events, and I appreciate her service this spring as moderator of some of our bookstore events in celebration of our writers.

Congratulations and gratitude too to Meredith College Professor Dana Ezzell Lovelace, who, with this issue, begins a second decade serving as *NCLR* Art Director. We unveiled Dana's prize-winning redesign of *NCLR* with the 2009 issue. Her stunning designs set a high bar for our other graphic designers, Karen Baltimore and Stephanie Whitlock Dicken, who rise to the challenge. It is always, a pleasure to work with them. Read more about all three of these talented women with their designs within this issue.

Continuing on the subject of staff, two ECU colleagues new to the staff are Sean Morris, serving as Managing Editor thanks to the support of the ECU Provost, and Helen Stead, who volunteers her time and expertise as an Assistant Editor. Back in a new capacity is Max Herbert. Max was an *NCLR* intern for two semesters, the second one working with Art Editor Diane Rodman. So some time after Diane went on hiatus for six months after her retirement, I asked Max if she could step in to help the interns with some art-related tasks. Like the many people who volunteer their time for *NCLR*, Max accepted the moniker and duties of Assistant Art Editor, and Diane and I are both grateful. Max and I happily welcomed Diane back in March. You can enjoy Diane's selections with the poetry throughout this issue, and appreciate Max's guidance on art selections featured with other content in the previous section of the issue.

Read more about new staff members in the introduction to the last section of the issue. But first, enjoy the next several pages of "Flashbacks" to past themes and new work by *familiar* (with an emphasis on *family*) writers. ∎

PHOTOGRAPH BY PEAT BURNETT

A LITERARY SURROGATE
CONTEMPLATE THE LIFE AND

Lyrical Journalism, Investigative Poetry
BY REBECCA DUNCAN

In the days when Americans relied almost wholly on the local newspaper for world news, area happenings, and the price of eggs, a typical masthead might include a lone woman, listed as "society" or "women's" editor. This staff member would spin elaborate accounts of weddings, civic events, and even the birthday parties of the town's privileged children. Through her efforts, the community could discover who among their acquaintances had spent a Sunday afternoon receiving out-of-town guests and who had ventured to the next town to visit a special cousin.

This particular brand of social media nurtured readership and created bonds in the community, even as the content may have been buried among lost and found notices and grocery store ads. In North Carolina, Zoe Kincaid Brockman leveraged her position as society editor of the *Gastonia Gazette* to discover a writing voice that chronicled

twentieth-century life through insightful columns and nationally recognized poetry. Her reporting, commentary, and verse – developed concurrently – blend the linguistic and cultural conventions of journalism and imaginative literature. As she helped to develop the *Gazette*, Brockman pioneered many of the standards and practices of today's professional journalists. In her poetry she revived classic forms and rhythms to explore and express her inner life and topical themes. These two strands of her writing life are woven together throughout her career.

Brockman lived from 1889 until 1975; public records, memories of friends and family, and information shared in her "Unguarded Moments" column help to anchor a few key details of her life.[1] She was the youngest in a family of unknown size; her father referred to her simply as "the Child." Among her "distinguished forebears" were a state

REBECCA DUNCAN earned a BA in History and an MA in International Affairs from Ohio University and a PhD in English from Florida State University. She teaches British and global literatures and professional writing courses at Meredith College in Raleigh, NC. Her essays and fiction have appeared in *Mosaic, Journal of Commonwealth Literature, Pisgah Review, Southeast Review*, and *Bella Online Literary Review*.

[1] Several of these columns are collected in Brockman's *Unguarded Moments* (Heritage House, 1959); quotations from these columns cited parenthetically within this essay.

SCHOLAR AND A GRANDDAUGHTER

WORK OF ZOE KINCAID BROCKMAN

> **Zoe Kincaid Brockman** leveraged her position as society editor of the *Gastonia Gazette* to discover a writing voice that chronicled twentieth-century life through insightful columns and nationally recognized poetry.

senator and a ruling elder in a Presbyterian church and "leader in the whiskey fight when Gaston was over-run with distilleries."[2]

Brockman valued her Scottish heritage and wrote nostalgically about the Grandfather Mountain Highland Games and summers at her Kincaid grandparents' expansive farm. In 1909, at the age of twenty, she married Thomas M. Brockman of Spartanburg, South Carolina. She bore two children: Sarah Frances in 1910 and Thomas (Tommy) in 1912. Sarah Frances married in 1928 and died five years later after a lengthy but undisclosed illness. Tommy served in the United States Navy during World War II; he and his wife, Kitty, often shared Brockman's home. Family records and public documents gathered by Lyn Triplett indicate that Zoe and Thomas divorced in 1939.

Brockman's formal education most likely ended with a high school diploma, although there

The Gastonia (N. C.) Gazette — October 20, 1948

UNGUARDED MOMENTS

By Zoe Kincaid Brockman

Being horribly allergic both to cold and coal bills, I should be the last pale piper to hold forth on the mirabilia of autumn. I should see October as a gay deceiver, waving scarlet and gold and bronze' before our eyes in order to blind us to the fact that 'chill November's icy blast' is just around the corner. I should see the leaves as sere and yellow, as one of my favorite poets, Byron, described his life, instead of jewel-tones of unbearable beauty. I should see Autumn as a strip-tease dancer who bows off the boards just before Winter stages his Dance of the Skeletons. But do I? Oh, no, indeed.

To me, Autumn is the season of seasons, and October is the queen of all the months. I love its wild, free pageantry, its prodigality of color, the way uncut gems are heaped in the very gutters. I love the mist that veils the landscape, lest too much color, blind us for always. I love the way the mountains draw amethyst cloaks about them for a brief season. I love the way the valleys have their one mad day, flinging a riot of gypsy colors in the face of towering hills that have, for once, withdrawn a little. I love in a very special way the willow trees which suddenly discard their soft green chiffon for tissue robes

in my neighbor's yard turns slowly to pure gold, so that I call it my Midas tree. I shall hear the clanking of the furnace, feel the chill of clammy dawns, and begin fiercely to hate John L. Lewis, who has hoisted my coal bill to towering heights.

It may be, but that time has not yet come. When the first tree is lighted, the first vine becomes purple, the stripped cornstalks turn to burnished bronze, then a sense of overpowering beauty envelops me. I'm drinking 'a nectar never brewed in tankard scooped from pearl', and I'm feeling lighter and freer and I've felt since last Autumn.

Later, Winter will take his toll of me. But, for now — and who need think further than now in so blinding a season as this? — the magic of Autumn has me completely hypnotized.

Of course, with Autumn, comes the falling of the leaves, and the raking up and disposing of same. As to this latter, the citizenry falls into three schools of thought—the rakers who carelessly call the city wagons to haul away the rustling grandeur; the rakers who immediately touch a match to the gem-colored heaps, sometimes on the asphalt and in direct defiance of a city ordinance which forbids such

---

[2] Quoted from Mina B. Huffman, "Mrs. Brockman Nominated for North Carolina Poet Laureate," *Gastonia Gazette* 3 Dec. 1934. Other biographical information was found in this source.

ABOVE **Header of Brockman's "Unguarded Moments" column in *The Gastonia Gazette*, 20 Oct. 1948**

Unless otherwise indicated, all photographs and clippings are courtesy of the Gaston County Public Library.

SEPTEMBER 8, 1939

SHORT STORY WINNER Mrs. Zoe Kincaid Brockman of Gastonia was announced last night at a meeting of the Charlotte Writers' club as winner of the 1939 North Carolina short story contest. She was presented an award of $25 and the silver cup donated by Mrs. R. A. Dunn of Charlotte. Mrs. Brockman is shown seated. Standing left to right are President Harold A. Steadman of the Charlotte club and J. H. Boyce, who made the presentation in the absence from the city of Mrs. Dunn. (Observer staff photo.)

I can conjure up the lovesome sight of blackberry bushes in flower in the same manner that Wordsworth evoked his daffodils, but I can't give you the picture in tripping verse as he did. **"**
—**Brockman**

is mention of some correspondence courses undertaken at the University of North Carolina at Chapel Hill. She noted that her father and her early teachers encouraged her to write and submit her poetry for publication. She also acknowledged the friendship and mentoring of the Daniels family, longtime publishers of the Raleigh *News & Observer,* and she wrote a moving tribute to Josephus Daniels upon his death.

Brockman's work at the *Gazette* began in 1919, when the paper became a daily, and the first "Unguarded Moments" columns appeared around 1930. The initial society page, "In Social Circles: Latest Events in Woman's World," eventually expanded across several column widths under the heading "Of Interest to Women," and by the 1950s a banner headline, "The Woman's Page," covered her contribution to the paper. In the 1960s, book reviews listed her as Literary Editor. Although in failing health for several years, she was said to have remained involved with the paper until the time of her death.

In an interview, Brockman admits to having destroyed the poetry of her youth out of shyness and embarrassment.[3] From a young age, Brockman worked seriously at the craft of poetry and in 1920 won her first prize, awarded by the North Carolina General Federation of Women's Clubs. In 1932 she co-founded the North Carolina Poetry Society and served as the group's first president. Published in *The New York Times, Poetry World, Versecraft, Bozart, Kaleidograph, Blue Moon,* and *North Carolina Poetry Review,* Brockman's verse was also collected in the volume *Heart on My Sleeve* in 1951.[4] Various additional awards and recognitions, along with multiple reprintings of the book, ensued throughout her life.

Blending these complementary interests, Brockman approached her society column with an ear for the lyrical. She occasionally slipped in a short poem amid the personal announcements and event coverage, at times recognizing the accomplishments of a fellow North Carolina poet. For example, she writes in a 1935 column, "I've been ringing Barbara Bowen's telephone at intervals all morning. I wanted to ask her what she's going to do with the prize money she got for the lovely poem 'Notations of Spring' that appeared in the *Charlotte Observer*'s Charmed Circle on Sunday," and the poem follows.[5]

The "Unguarded Moments" column often draws upon a literary or cultural reference to contextualize a topic. Rudyard Kipling's song "Danny Deever" introduces a discussion of the death penalty, while stanzas of an Emily Dickinson poem ground a remembrance for a friend who has died. Shakespeare summons lilacs; Wordsworth, daffodils; Fitzgerald and Faulkner, ghosts. A discussion of prepared foods arises from a quoted passage of Pearl S. Buck. In "On Contemplating Blackberries," Brockman writes that "Buddha's attraction to and fascination with his navel has always baffled me," yet "When I read of the rural philosopher who loved to contemplate blackberry bushes, I could

[3] The interview by J.A. Yarbrough, "Interesting Carolina People," published in the *Gastonia Gazette,* was found in a clipping file at the Gaston County Public Library. The date is not quite legible, but appears to be August or perhaps April 1934. Citations that do not include page numbers are also columns found in this clipping file.

[4] Zoe Kincaid Brockman, *Heart on My Sleeve* (Banner Press, 1951); quotations from Brockman's poetry will be cited parenthetically from this collection.

[5] "Unguarded Moments," *Gastonia Gazette* 2 Apr. 1935: 4.

and did fall right in step with him" (*Unguarded* 1). While proposing an official "Spring Onion Week" in North Carolina, she even alludes to the Bataan Death March of World War II. With these allusions, she reveals the breadth and depth of her intellect and broadens the horizons of her small-town neighbors.

Rendered in precise language with an economy typical of both poetry and reporting, Brockman's advocacy journalism also explores a variety of perspectives. A Depression-era column narrates a visit to the home of a sick woman in "one of the tenement houses over which we shudder when we mention them at circle meetings" (*Unguarded* 81). With telling details and the voice of the narrative artist, she makes it difficult for her prosperous readers to turn away:

> There are no shades nor curtains at the smeared cobwebby windows, but faded, torn strips of green crepe paper afford a semblance of privacy. A meager fire sulks in the broken grate and over it a sooty iron kettle sends up a wisp of steam. Water heating, perhaps, for the washing of the sticky, greasy piles of dishes and pans heaped high on two goods boxes covered with newspapers. Or maybe for the bathing of the sick woman who lies in the disheveled bed, which is the only other article of furniture the room contains. To be sure, six people live, eat, and sleep in this room, but – at night – two mattresses are dragged from the closet and spread before the fire. A little boy wanders aimlessly around, and there are two puppies contributing to the general dirt and disorder in all the ways known to puppies. (*Unguarded* 81)

With her newspaper readers in mind, Brockman contextualizes the doctor's absurd order that the ailing woman drink orange and other fruit juices: "'[W]e ain't got sich as that'" the woman explains, and Brockman adds, "In much the same manner that you haven't caviar and champagne in the house at the moment" (*Unguarded* 82). The piece then deploys a literary second person in a rather unsettling and confrontational tone: "You make inane remarks, your face assuming a false brightness. . . . You pass hastily into the hall, retching slightly" at "the rancid smell of old grease, the penetrating, nauseating odor of decaying garbage." In this harsh yet compassionate piece, Brockman implicates her more fortunate readers by concluding, "Russia? China? New York? Chicago? Oh, no, indeed. Gastonia, in the year of our Lord 1937" (*Unguarded* 83).

Likewise, in "Martha Jones, Whom Nobody Knew," Brockman conveys harsh truths by imagining the final hours of a young woman jailed for drunkenness who dies in her cell after eating roach powder. She regrets that Jones died alone without medical care, one of the "lost and lonely people [who] grope in the darkness of our so-called

> **"She brought her characters to life with words so the reader could almost see them and hear her speak. "**
>
> —Myra Tidwell, *Gazette* Woman's Editor, 4 Aug. 1974

OPPOSITE **Brockman announced as the 1939 short story winner for the Charlotte Writers' Club, 8 Sept. 1939**

> **"[S]he was a crusader for that which she thought was right in government, politics, morals, and local issues and was a harsh critic of fallacies in the same issues."**
>
> —Myra Tidwell,
> *Gazette* Woman's Editor,
> 4 Aug. 1974

Students Publish Magazine

FIRST ISSUE of "The Rhetor," literary magazine published by students at Ashley High School has been dedicated to Mrs. Zoe K. Brockman, shown above receiving her copy and a scroll from the staff. Making the presentation is Mike Yelton. Looking on, at left, is Cary Osborn, advisor to the students. (Photo by Everett Walker)
At Ashley High School

civilization" (*Unguarded* 26). She expresses a wish that "in Gaston County, we had a hospital maintained by public funds to which the forgotten man might always be taken, a door of mercy through which a Martha Jones might pass." To conclude, she returns to the lyrical, quoting a poem by Thomas Hood that begins with the lines

> One more unfortunate,
> Weary of breath,
> Rashly importunate
> Gone to her death. (*Unguarded* 26)

A descriptive 1969 column revisits the topic of the "town drunk" to laud the town's plans for a mental health clinic and alcoholism center. Brockman shares frightening youthful memories of one such disruptive "drunk" and common views of mental illness: "Mental cases were treated like animals," she writes, but with the new center she hopes that "people are remembering that some are made of frailer dust than others, that for some very fine people the proper exercise of self-control is difficult and that a visitation of real trouble throws them off base. That they need tolerance, understanding, and care."[6] One can sense an intimate remembrance and an empathetic tone in these lines that will also emerge in the poetry.

In commentary on a national scale, Brockman muses lyrically on President John F. Kennedy's potential and his unfinished work, offering this simile: "a young man in a hurry and a young man totally unafraid. He was like a strong, brilliant, beautiful bird among barnyard fowl." A few weeks later she stretches her readers' imaginations with a fictional dialogue between the president and his assassin, Lee Harvey Oswald, in the afterlife. Kennedy, in this exchange, comments on the consequences of the act on individuals and the nation. Asked "why," Oswald can only assert that he hates members of the ruling class. Consistently the reporter, Brockman brings the topic back to town by publishing a letter of condolence sent to a Gastonian from Germans he met while in the service.[7]

Lighter, nostalgic columns evoke readers' memories and hone precision, figurative language, and the voice of the poet/storyteller. Changing weather patterns and passing of the seasons take Brockman back to her childhood, when "September wore grapevines in her hair, but she wasn't exactly a party girl. She busied herself with ripening the grains and sprinkling a bit of silver gilt on the willows, leaving the rest of the paint job for October." She remembers that in her younger days, "You didn't turn off the furnace with one hand and the air-conditioning on with the other. God had control of the weather and tempered it to human needs" (*Unguarded* 63). In an essay on children's school clothes, she compares the "loose, bright hair"

ABOVE *The Rhetor,* a literary magazine at Ashley High School in Gastonia, dedicating its first issue to Brockman, 1967

6 "We've Come a Long Way Since 'Town Drunk' Times," *Gastonia Gazette* 5 Jan. 1969: 3.

7 "Much Has Been Said: Here's A Little More," *Gastonia Gazette* 26 Nov. 1963; 6; "If the President and His Assassin Could Converse," *Gastonia Gazette* 8 Dec. 1963: 6-C.

The Gastonia (N. C.) Gazette
May 2, 1950.

North Carolina Press Women's Prize-Winning Column For '49

(Ed. Note: The following column by Mrs. Brockman was declared the best in a contest for members of the North Carolina Press Women during 1949. The Gazette is proud to reprint this column.)

Men hate the periodic upheavals that are spring and fall cleaning, since, for them, they are seasons of sketchy meals and confusion and the inability to locate one's ties and shoes and hats. But, in the women who inaugurate the seasonal chaos, they engender an ache that is deeper than any hate. And I don't mean an ache of the bones—reddened knees and grimy elbows, for instance. Not that kind of an ache at all. Something different and poignant and unutterably sad. For women are inveterate and incurable hoarders—and it is the hoarding that brings about the ache.

Women keep the most inconsequential things — snapshots and clippings and tags of ribbon and lace, club programs and tally cards; buckles and dried, scentless bouquets and baby shoes. And this business of putting baby shoes into bronze is all right, if the baby is still here to come stalking into the house as a big noisy man or rushing fragrantly in as a graceful lovely girl. But, if the person who wore the shoes as a baby is gone, better leave the soft, shapeless things in that box in the attic. For women do pack such odds and ends into boxes and park them in the attic—but then, the attic, too, has to be cleaned.

A desk is, perhaps, the most prolific purveyor of the sort of aches women have at house-cleaning time. A desk has so many pigeonholes, so many secret drawers. And, in most of them, every recess is full. And a desk, of all things, must be 'straightened up' at cleaning time. You find letters written six months ago, a year ago. The ink is arrogantly black; the script is clear and vital. But the hand that penned them is quite still ("But you are nowhere . . . you are gone . . . all roads into Oblivion")—you stood beside that terrifying oblong, that narrow [...] the red earth, and liste [...] 'dust to dust, ashes to ashes' intoned by a tired preacher who had yet another chore to do before his day was over. You heard the terrible finality of "Into Thy hands we commend her spirit." And yet, here is a letter. "Will see you Tuesday at about four. Will tea be from the Chinese pot?" she wrote in her funny slanty hand.

Tea, you forlornly recall, was from the Chinese pot. You remember how she praised the brown bread sandwiches with walnuts in them, she ridiculous red feather on her hat, her solicitude for the welfare of the Poetry Society, and how she hoped we'd be able to get a good banquet speaker.

You hold the note above the waste basket; no more of this 'dust to dust, ashes to ashes business', you think. But you don't drop it in—back it goes into the dusted pigeon-hole. You can't forget the rosebuds in her hand as she lay in the casket, the orchid scarf about her shoulders, the strange, aloof look of her. And yet, she had wanted, and had drunk, tea from the Chinese pot.

The bridge tally . . . and you remember how the peach pickle skidded off your plate and landed, fortunately enough, in the log basket by the fireplace, and how relieved you were that it didn't careen through the freshly washed windows and splatter the freshly washed curtains. It was, you recall, a pretty party—but why keep a bridge tally for a year at least?

Here's a road map. You unfold it gingerly. There are many markings penciled on it, arrows pointing this way and that. You had crept out of bed at 4 o'clock that morning, lighted the gas under the coffee pot, had a hurried breakfast and gone softly out of the house on a wonderful trip. Put the road map in the waste basket . . . . . people who know how to use road maps expertly sometimes quite hopelessly lose their way in the labyrinth of human living.

In a pigeon-hole there's a bulky envelope labeled in a sprawling, unformed hand 'Important Papers.' You've been taking that one out, dusting it and returning it for year. How fresh the ink looks, how youthful the sprawling writing! And yet, years ago, you composed the stiffening fingers that penned the words, had been grieved and astonished that the lips—a little aloof, just a little scornful—hadn't responded to your pleading for just one more word.

Not for all the gold at Fort Knox would you open that envelope. It never has been opened, and yet you can't throw it away . . . a bright brown head bending over the desk in the light of a copper lamp . . . slim fingers penning 'Important Papers' on a long envelope and tucking it into the desk. No, you couldn't throw that away, not if a hundred years had passed instead of what seems like a million. It was Edna Millay who said:

"Form in the shadow of the trees,—
Things that you could not spare
And live, or so you thought,
and these
All gone, and you still there."

One should, of course, dump them all into the trash basket—the letters, the silly bridge tallies, the envelope marked 'Important Papers.' One should instruct the maid to take them out and burn them. But one doesn't—and it happens, some degree, to house-cleaning women all over the land every spring and fall. They're dusted carefully and slipped back into pigeon-holes and chests—so many knives to turn and twist in one's heart.

Why? Do t ask me! I'm just one of you—a woman who turns her house upside down spring and fall, and walks toward cleanliness and order over sword blades and red hot coals and acres of broken glass. But don't ask me why.

"I think you will have need of tears;
I think they will not flow;
Supposing in ten thousand years
Men ache, as they do now."
—EDNA ST. VINCENT MILLAY.

> I'm not a kleptomaniac, really. It's only that, whenever or wherever I see a package of Camels, I think it's mine.
> —Zoe Kincaid Brockman

ABOVE *The Gastonia Gazette* announcing Brockman's prize-winning column for the 1949 North Carolina Press Women's contest, 2 May 1950

and "frocks and sweaters . . . designed to do the most for them" with the layers of clothing into which she and her schoolmates had been packed: union suits, drawers-body, Fay stockings, and at adolescence, a Ferris waist (*Unguarded* 38). Perusing models and designs for mid-century homes in Gastonia, she remarks on the lack of sleeping porches, which in her day "were all the rage and a householder who didn't have one could scarce hold up his head" (*Unguarded* 89). She could be writing about the twenty-first century when she observes, "Young mothers have for some time now worked hard at family life projects, arranging that a set night each week be reserved for family activities" (*Unguarded* 50). In contrast, Brockman recalls a simpler time: "looking far back over my shoulder, I can see a day when family life came about simply and naturally, without planning, club meetings, or fanfare. Family life just was, and that's all there was to it" (*Unguarded* 50). That life, dating back to the turn of the twentieth century, involved gathering wood to heat the house, grinding coffee beans, mending, calling out spelling words, snacking on apples and milk, reading scripture, and offering bedtime prayers.

While appealing to older readers through shared memories, Brockman courts a more contemporary audience through humor and irony, a practice echoing the work of columnists such as Irma Bombeck. She confesses that "The federal income tax man and I had it up one side and down the other. It wasn't that either of us was inclined to be argumentative or contentious – it was rather that we didn't seem to understand each other" (*Unguarded* 65). Apparently the man is trying to help her augment her deductions. When he asks if she owns an automobile, she responds, "At which query I giggled girlishly. I can't, I told him, even drive an automobile. . . . Why, with my hand on the steering wheel and my foot on the gas, nothing in the animal, vegetable or mineral kingdom would be safe – to say nothing of humans, either afoot or on horseback" (*Unguarded* 65–66). In this piece she also jokes about the smoking habit that will eventually end her life: "I'm not a kleptomaniac, really. It's only that, whenever or wherever I see a package of Camels, I think it's mine" (*Unguarded* 66).

Herself a chronicler of weddings, Brockman nevertheless takes a humorous jab at coverage that falls short. A reader would need to be well-versed in fabrics and lace to comprehend the fun Brockman makes of a wedding story from a "small out-of-town paper." After citing such details as "lover lace lined with silk organza and matching lace galoon followed the waterfall lines of the high fronted falling dress," she adds, "If you're still following me, you're good. Not even an

GASTONIA AUTHOR—The Gazette's Zoe Brockman looks over the display of books by local authors and the new Literary Map of North Carolina on which she is featured at the Gaston County Public Library.

Zoe is placed in limelight with spot on literary map

Gazette Sept. 1, 72

Gastonia's Zoe Brockman is among the authors spotlighted on the new Literary Map of North Carolina now on display at the Gaston County Public Library.

The decorative map lists 166 North Carolina writers — going back to Sir Walter Raleigh — but some 30 are represented with illustrations including Gastonia.

Asheville is on the map with Thomas Wolfe's cemetery angel for "Look Homeward, Angel," while Charlotte is represented by two pennies for Harry Golden's "For Two Cents Plain."

Gastonia and Shelby share an illustration including a heart backed by flames. They are for Mrs. Brockman's "Heart on My Sleeve" and Thomas Dixon's "The Flaming Sword."

The large map just published

Mrs. Brockman, a long-time newspaperwoman, has published not only a book of poems, "Heart on My Sleeve," but more recently a collection of essays which first appeared in her newspaper column. It has the same title "Unguarded Moments."

Mrs. Brockman has been with The Gastonia Gazette since it became a daily in 1919 when she became woman's editor and general news reporter. Her columns is still a feature of the newspaper.

Former editor of the Raleigh News and Observer, Jonathan Daniels, praises Mrs. Brockman for keeping up the grand tradition of the "old-time essay" with a "wise gaiety." This column published in 1950 includes columns on everything from "On Contemplating Black-

berries" to "This Do-It-Yourself Business Started in England."

The book of poems came out a little earlier in 1951 only after long urging by many friends. She had been instrumental in organization of the North Carolina Poetry Society in 1932. She was its first president and the associate editor of its successful monthly North Carolina Poetry Review.

The Shelby author, Thomas Dixon, was a controversial figure who grew up during The Reconstruction. He wrote a screenplay about those turbulent times in which he interested an unknown director. The result was D. W. Griffith's classic "Birth of a Nation."

Before his death in 1946, Dixon wrote not only "The Flaming Sword" but an even better-known novel called "The Klansman."

> "
>
> At the intersection of humor, empathy, and accuracy, Brockman anchors herself professionally as a journalist."

---

apprentice typesetter could garble descriptions as these are garbled."[8] Invoking her own and her paper's standards for wedding reporting, Brockman devotes another column to critiquing the Associated Press coverage of Lynda Byrd Johnson's 1967 White House wedding. In Brockman's perspective, the reporter "makes a few boners," even misquoting the ceremony to suggest that the minister and bride were marrying each other. Most hilarious to Brockman was the suggestion that the bride and her father "strode into the East Room":

> Who ever heard of a bride "striding"? I can see LBJ doing that, but not lovely Lynda Byrd. On second thought, maybe Texas brides do stride, but down here in the abysmally ignorant South, our brides don't. They walk daintily down the aisle with their fathers, and their fathers are too dashed over giving their daughters up that they wouldn't have the heart to stride.[9]

At the intersection of humor, empathy, and accuracy, Brockman anchors herself professionally as a journalist. Later in her career, however, she concedes to an interviewer that she has often embellished coverage of local weddings. One such piece finds the ceremony "of exceptional beauty and dignity." The bride is "an attractive and popular member of young society."[10] Brockman defends these subjective departures from the standards of reporting with a long-term perspective. These pieces, she suggests, live on in scrapbooks and help to preserve memories of special occasions and therefore deserve a unique voice and careful attention to the smallest detail. She is, in this manner, documenting with words the images that subsequent videographers and macro-photographers capture in their wedding visuals today.

Likewise, Brockman offers insights on life in a newsroom of a growing daily paper. It is difficult to trace her earliest reporting because 1920s issues of the *Gazette* did not typically include bylines. She does, however, offer a glimpse of the paper's growth from a staff of three – herself and two members of the Atkins family – to more than fifty. She teaches readers about deadlines and the challenge of tracking down busy housewives to clarify a date or a crucial detail. In contrast, the sports editor, she notes,

> thinks he has it tough but he doesn't know from nothin'. He can at least call men from their beds, and – if they cuss him out he can cuss back and no hard feelings. But a woman's page editor knows a darn sight better than to call a woman on the 'phone when she's cooking breakfast, warming the baby's bottle, and frantically jerking on something presentable so that she can chauffeur her husband to work and the children to school.[11]

ABOVE **Brockman honored on the Literary Map of North Carolina, displayed at the Gaston County Public Library, 1 Sept. 1972**

[8] "An Old, Annoying Phobia Has Found a Name for Itself," *Gastonia Gazette* 15 Sept. 1963: 3C.

[9] "Did they Really 'Stride'?" *Gastonia Gazette* 24 Dec. 1967.

[10] "Miss Beverley Moore Weds Grade Eugene Pearson," *Gastonia Gazette* 7 Apr. 1942: 3.

[11] "This is a Piece Concerning Deadlines," *Gastonia Gazette* 22 May 1966: 5.

At times self-deprecating and playful, at others melancholy, her columns provide glimpses of a woman alone in a world of tight families, a restless intellectual pacing the floors of "insomnia lodge," and a sufferer of family misfortune and personal loss. "

Mrs. Brockman honored by N.C. Press Women

Gazette march 13, 73

Zoe Kincaid Brockman. The Gazette's woman editor for many years, was named an honorary member of the N.C. Press Women at NCPW's weekend spring institute in Chapel Hill.

Mrs. Brockman, a former president of the organization, was one of the charter members instrumental in setting up the annual writing contest in which prize money and certificates are awarded at the institute. Through the years she has won many NCPW awards, which are displayed in The Gazette lobby.

Mrs. Brockman, writer of "Unguarded Moments" in the women's pages, is author of a book by the same name. A member of the N.C. Poetry Society, she has also published several books of poetry.

It is unlikely that the sports editor took offense at this quip; in time the staff would show their affection by referring to her as "unguarded mom." She conveys a sense of professional community in pursuit of excellence in a column on "wacky" journalists:

> People who are so wacky that they're interested not only in themselves and their personal affairs, but in every inhabitant of this dizzy planet . . . wacky enough to go to the trouble and expense of making the front page over if a story of tremendous import comes in at the last minute . . . wacky enough to miss their lunch if a fire breaks out or there's a car smash . . . wacky enough to slosh about in sloppy weather to get a story that could have been had over the telephone, except that those most concerned relish a little on-the-spot attention . . . people just screwy enough to move heaven and earth to find out for sure if the bride's gown was of marquisette or permanent-finish organdy.[12]

On another day, she explains the function of newspaper fillers, those random facts that cover typesetting gaps between bottom-up advertising and top-down editorial content. She delights in lampooning the soaps, perfumes, and lotions that manufacturers and publicists send with the hope of receiving a free promotion. Just as her playful remarks ride on serious undertones, Brockman reflects on the ethical responsibility of journalists to convey the truth, another vital issue in the media today. Her report on a panel of North Carolina writers held in 1963 raises the possibility that truth is varied and multiple, that it "is something that can't quite be captured but is always striven for."[13]

Beyond the newsroom, Brockman comes to belong to the town as a formidable yet beloved public figure. At times self-deprecating and playful, at others melancholy, her columns provide glimpses of a woman alone in a world of tight families, a restless intellectual pacing the floors of "insomnia lodge," and a sufferer of family misfortune and personal loss. Holiday columns, while focused on others and the community in general, reveal a closed cycle of grief over the death of her daughter, Sarah Frances, at the age of twenty-four. All of these dimensions contribute to her emerging poetic persona.

The most naked emotions, expressed contemporaneously with the lively columns and the upbeat society news, appear in Brockman's poetry. Two Gastonians, women interviewed while in their nineties who knew Brockman personally, recall the sadness that surrounded her and emerged in poems about Sarah Frances. One of these women, Mary Caldwell, remembers feeling Brockman's eyes upon her throughout a luncheon out. "I wondered if I was using my fork improperly," she says. Eventually Brockman approaches her and says, "Pardon my staring, but you remind me of my daughter."[14]

ABOVE **Brockman named honorary member of the NC Press Women, Chapel Hill, NC, 13 Mar. 1973**

[12] "Newspaper People: Just a Bunch of Wacky Folks," *Gastonia Gazette* 8 Feb. 1968.

[13] "Writers Find That 'Truth' Is Difficult to Define," *Gastonia Gazette* 3 Nov. 1963: 3-C.

[14] Margaret Caldwell, telephone interview, 4 Apr. 2018.

"I would say that the only way to classify Zoe Brockman is as one of the North Carolina greats."

—Leonard Eury, former Librarian for Appalachian State University

The poems, which include sonnets, odes, and lyrics in couplets and quatrains, capture Sarah Frances's blue eyes and her posture in a doorway. Spring evokes a particular sorrow: "No sun can ever warm me, since you were sun, moon, and tide" (*Heart* 35), as does autumn, season of the young woman's death:

Empurple the landscape,
Make crimson the leaf,
Artist of Autumn,
Camouflage grief. (*Heart* 32)

Contrasting her plight with that of a dog barking in the night, she summons the restraint that defines her public image:

While I, who battle grief that rends and shakes,
Am schooled to swallow every bitter pill;
To make no outcry, and to show a face
That bears no markings of the storm within;
To tread swordblades at firm and even pace;
Endure the prickings of the constant pin. (*Heart* 67)

Brockman seems to have favored the Shakespearean sonnet, and neither its fixed rhythms nor its rhyme scheme seem to force her phrasing into an unnatural syntax. The gentle, contemplative voice is inward-facing, more like that of Keats than the radiant, roving energy of Wordsworth:

So short a time June spreads her scented mirth,
So brief a space are April's bugles heard,
Yet beauty is recurrent to the earth,
Year after year her lagging pulse is stirred. (*Heart* 17)

The full range of Brockman's voice – both public and private – culminates in her writings on war. Her first journalistic involvement with war begins in the 1940s, when the society pages nearly burst with marriage announcements as women married their enlisted sweethearts in support of the cause. Society news reaches beyond civilian life and acknowledges such topics as deployments and Victory Gardens. One "Unguarded Moments" column features a reader's proposal to start a candy wrapper collection at the schools to support the war effort; a story on shortening men's shirt tails illustrates one of numerous strategies undertaken to conserve vital resources. This 1942 column on a war-time blackout poetically recalls the beauty of moonlight in Brockman's rural past; that moonlight "sifted through pink and yellow powder puffs" of the mimosa trees, "slanted across the cherry trees in the orchard,"

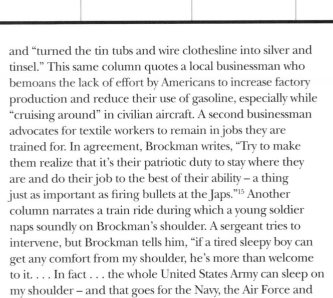

and "turned the tin tubs and wire clothesline into silver and tinsel." This same column quotes a local businessman who bemoans the lack of effort by Americans to increase factory production and reduce their use of gasoline, especially while "cruising around" in civilian aircraft. A second businessman advocates for textile workers to remain in jobs they are trained for. In agreement, Brockman writes, "Try to make them realize that it's their patriotic duty to stay where they are and do their job to the best of their ability – a thing just as important as firing bullets at the Japs."[15] Another column narrates a train ride during which a young soldier naps soundly on Brockman's shoulder. A sergeant tries to intervene, but Brockman tells him, "if a tired sleepy boy can get any comfort from my shoulder, he's more than welcome to it. . . . In fact . . . the whole United States Army can sleep on my shoulder – and that goes for the Navy, the Air Force and the Marines. Maybe the Coast Guard."[16]

Contrasting this civic-minded endorsement of the overall war effort, Brockman experiences the war quite differently through her son's deployment to the South Pacific. A moving column describes his first thirty-day leave in that gripping second person voice that holds the reader captive. We feel the young man's exhaustion; we watch his hands shake. We cringe at the mindless chatter the mother has tried not to indulge in, especially when the sailor says, at parting, "'We ask that ship's company remain calm at all times'" (*Unguarded* 59). And we must agree with Brockman that a person in her position is "always going to ache, even when this thing is over. . . . You'll ache always for the lifeless young bodies – limp in the tropics, frozen and stiff in the snowdrifts – that are being piled into an awful and awesome sacrifice before the altar of the inexorable, insatiable god of war" (*Unguarded* 60). The sonnet "For the One I Love" conveys the anxiety of hoping for her son's survival:

Tonight I miss you achingly, my dear,
Tonight my pulses far outrun my mind;
The news the radio sends forth, I hear;
My love and yours are pledged and sealed and signed.
Only the morning sun can still my fear:
Another day – and you are alive, my dear. (*Heart* 11)

The World War II writings blend community news, personal involvement, poetic sensibility, and broader perspectives on the war effort; Brockman moves among genre and purpose to fulfill multiple aims. By the 1960s, however, she has done with being civic-minded; her

" There are no outward and visible scars of battle but you know the scars are there in the memory of sights he should never have seen, sounds he should never have heard, experiences he should never have had. "
—**Zoe Kincaid Brockman**

ABOVE **Brockman with her son, Thomas, during his active service in World War II**

15 "Unguarded Moments," *Gastonia Gazette* 23 June 1942: 4.

16 "Mom Tangles with an M.P.," *Gastonia Gazette Weekender* 3 July 1966: 3.

66

Embracing antiwar sentiments must certainly have raised eyebrows among her conservative readers. 99

son having never fully recovered from the "jangled nerves and tensions" brought on by the war experience, and she has devoted time and considerable resources to holding his life together. She writes angrily that the VA hospital will not treat World War II veterans whose afflictions emerged after discharge. And the Vietnam War enrages her: "This is the fourth [war] I've lived through – two World Wars, what was known as the Korean Conflict, and now this. When it was World War I, I was very young and high-hearted. I believed President Wilson when he uttered the 'making safe' bit. I was sure we'd never have another war; we were through with wars." In another column, Brockman adds, "and now this terrible thing in Vietnam. Terrible because our boys are being killed, as they always have in all wars."[17]

Brockman is angered that Americans are involved in a war against communism in Southeast Asia, and she deploys her sharpest pen to arouse emotion in her readers. Visiting a hospital nursery, she writes:

I was particularly interested in the bassinets to which blue cards were attached. Boy babies, with little helpless, curled-up hands. Was a gun already being designed for such hands as those? And how can the young women bear to go through with all it takes to bring a baby into the world when they must know, if that boy baby lives to be 18, there'll be a war somewhere for him to fight? ("Does")

The *Gazette*'s news and editorial attention to the Vietnam War is otherwise spotty; a lone syndicated column by Paul Harvey in 1968, for instance, takes a hawkish stand against the Paris Peace Talks. Major milestones, such as the Tet Offensive and the invasion of Cambodia, receive cursory coverage and no local commentary. Embracing antiwar sentiments must certainly have raised eyebrows among her conservative readers.

By then Brockman would surely have understood the price of her freedom to write unguardedly about any topic that inflamed her formidable heart or mind. Although sure of her voice and encouraged by some of the most accomplished poets, writers, and journalists of the state, she also cultivates a certain aloneness, as celebrated in her poem "In Praise of Loneliness":

The lonely hold enchantment in their hands,
Theirs is the breadth of sky, the sweep of sea,
They know white moonlight's searching, cool demands,
The urgency of bloom-embroidered tree.
The lonely lie awake while others sleep, –
Companioned people, happy and at rest, –
They watch the sky as night grows still and deep,
And strange, dark music beats against the breast.
The lonely have a sixpence, bright and new,

ABOVE **Zoe Kincaid Brockman, circa 1974**

[17] "A Vet with No Hospital," *Gastonia Gazette* 9 Nov. 1969: 3-C; "Where Have All the Young Men Gone?," *Gastonia Gazette* 24 Sept. 1967; "Does Anyone Really Enjoy His Dinner?," *Gastonia Gazette* 18 June 1967: 5; subsequently cited parenthetically.

Brockman ultimately savors – and owns – a world of words that ask us not to look at her but rather at life with clarity and compassion. "

They spend it daily, yet it reappears
In dawn, in sunlight, in the argent dew,
For sustenance through solitary years.
The lonely live apart, yet worlds they own,
Since they were fated thus to walk alone. (*Heart* 53)

Reeling through Brockman's prolific writings, retracing her steps along Gastonia's sidewalks, and mining details and memories of her life, one is tempted to seek an essence or at best some coherence to define her. This poem perhaps captures her best, but only if the notion of loneliness is, as she suggests, to be praised. While living among and writing to and for "companioned people," Brockman ultimately savors – and owns – a world of words that ask us not to look at her but rather at life with clarity and compassion. ∎

Remembering Grandmother Zoe

by Lyn Triplett

Some people look into their DNA to find lost connections and perhaps a deeper significance in their lives. This urge can intensify as time passes or when we realize it's up to us to nourish and preserve our family's legacy. For me, this sense led me back to Gastonia and eventually to microfilm reels of the town's newspaper, in which the columns of my surrogate grandmother, Zoe Kincaid Brockman, annotated daily life in our town and reflectively linked us to events and issues in the wider world. Her writings stirred memories of that quiet but impressive presence in my young life.

To my brother, David, and me, she was "Grandmother Zoe." My aunt Kitty, my father's sister, was married to Tommy, Zoe's son. Tommy and Kitty were childless and rather wild and thus eager to shower their affection upon us. In the absence of grandchildren, Zoe Brockman seemed willing to step in for us, but on her own terms. From a young age David and I knew she was different from most Gastonia ladies. She held a job at the *Gazette*, and she lived in a home filled with books and cut glass that cast rainbows in the sunlight. Most of my early memories of her are dim, yet when the family got together, she seemed always to be there, dressed in church clothes and smoking Camel cigarettes.

Occasionally we would spend a weekend afternoon at Grandmother Zoe's home. It was Mother's way of keeping the extended family together, although it could be torment for a couple of kids on a pleasant summer day. I remember one such day in detail. David was around nine years, and I was five or six. The day began with Mother's order to "Get dressed!" This meant baths, on a Saturday! Then a suit coat, tie, long pants and polished Sunday shoes for David. Crinolines, patent leather shoes shining with a film of Vaseline, hat and gloves for me. And then came the reminders of "visitation etiquette" of the South:
"No arguing."
"No loud talking."
"No roughhousing."

ABOVE **Left to right, Leola Kincaid, mother of Zoe; Kitty Hovis Brockman, Zoe's daughter-in-law; and Zoe Kincaid Brockman, Gastonia, circa 1943-44**

LYN TRIPLETT was born and raised in Gastonia, NC. She earned a bachelor's degree in Music Education at Mars Hill College (now University). In 2007, after teaching elementary music in the Wake County Public School System for numerous years, she attended a week-long writer's workshop at Meredith College called "Focus on Form." This essay is an outgrowth of a project she began while at Meredith College.

> "[T]he columns of my surrogate grandmother, Zoe Kincaid Brockman, annotated daily life in our town and reflectively linked us to events and issues in the wider world. Her writings stirred memories of 'Grandmother Zoe,' that quiet but impressive presence in my young life."

"Say yes ma'am and no ma'am. Speak only if directly spoken to."

"Do not ask for a snack or a drink. And if one is offered, refuse at least two times, saying we are not hungry." To our painful howling, Mother responded, "Good heavens, children! Do you want her to think we can't afford to feed you?"

We could sense an anxious tone in Mother's voice; she interrupted the orders only to apply the typical feminine layers to herself: girdle, long-line bra, stockings, heels, and shirtwaist dress with starched cuffs, collar and pleats, probably ironed before dawn.

On the hot, thirty-minute walk, Mother and I carried our hats and gloves. David had to wear his coat and tie, and he was not happy about that. "You are a Southern gentleman," Mother told him. "You cannot walk in public with just your shirt sleeves and no coat. Have you not heard a thing I have tried to teach you?"

Grandmother Zoe met us at the front door in her Sunday best, probably a dark skirt and a silken light blouse. I remember the matching bracelet, broach, and ear bobs. Yes, ear bobs, those huge, heavy, beaded clip-on monsters that were so very popular then. On that day I noticed Mother had chosen ear bobs as well, matching them to her best pearl necklace and a pearl pin on the collar of her dress.

Time passed slowly, as always. David and I waited for the moment when we might be released from the smoke-filled receiving room to sit on the porch while the adults finished their conversations.

On this particular day, I spent some of that dull afternoon staring at Zoe's wall of books. Somehow having gotten her attention and permission to speak, I asked, "Where did all of those books come from?"

"Well," she said, "I know most of the people who wrote them."

I then asked, "Why do you still have them?"

And she said, "I will read them again and again."

In a moment that remains etched in my mind, I said, "Well, if you don't have a husband, I guess you have time to read a lot."

Grandmother Zoe laughed, and although I don't remember any particular consequences, I can still picture Mother's face sinking down and her mouth dropping open, her look of mortification.

Our contact with Grandmother Zoe, reinforced by Mother's deference as well as things whispered or assumed, led David and me to understand how different the woman was. We saw her as famous, connected to books and people far beyond our little town. Another encounter, a few years after the "husband" comment, exposed me to the controversy that she occasionally sparked through her writings.

This time we were grocery shopping at the A&P, a two-mile walk. Once there, Mother became Queen of Stretching the Budget, a true product of the Depression and World War II. Grocery shopping was a challenge to her very soul; the more she could save, the happier she was. Foods were weighed, measured, calculated to the best price per ounce; she could do math in her head like a modern calculator. The rewards were a balanced budget and a long trail of gold stamps, to be pasted into books and redeemed for things we could not otherwise afford.

Suddenly two women approached us. I remember phrases flying back and forth like, "How could she even think that way?" or "She *is* your relative; you should do something about it." And "I will never be able to show my face at the Garden Club again."

The women had Mother cornered, and I watched her shoulders tense. She gripped the bar of the overflowing buggy so tightly that her hands turned red and then white. Now, as her child, I knew the signs of when Mother had "had enough of it." She had a way of tilting her head to the right and pursing her lips together that meant you were toeing the line and better not cross it. But these women were not so well informed. They kept pushing and pointing and complaining until Mother's right ear was almost completely touching her right shoulder. David and I knew she was on the verge of a complete and true hissy fit. Time to duck and cover.

Like any well-bred Southern lady, my mother would go to extremes to avoid a public display of temper. But this was going to be close. David and I were in awe. David swears that buggy was actually shaking with her grip and anger. We had enough sense and experience to be afraid but were fascinated that these two women could provoke her to this point. Had we angered her to that degree, she would have put the brakes (and a switch) on us much sooner.

Finally, Mother found her tongue and blasted out something like, "Good Lord – she's a relative by marriage – do you think I can tell her what to think or what to write? Nobody tells Zoe Brockman anything – ever."

She wheeled around and glared at David and me and said, "We are leaving. Now. Leave the buggy."

The walk home that day was more like a march in double time. Those fists were clenched, that head was tilted and those lips pursed together until we got to South Street, where my Grandmother Kimbrell lived. Mother ordered us to play outside. "I need to talk to Mother," she said. We had just enough sense to say "yes ma'am" and run to the safety of the giant magnolia tree in Grandmother Kimbrell's front yard. Several cups of strong black coffee and many cigarettes later, Mother walked us home. Dinner that evening came from Black's BBQ, and I don't remember how we next got any food into the house.

Looking back on the controversial Vietnam era, I can reconstruct and imagine the stance Grandmother Zoe took on the war and its effect on the community and our extended family. Gastonia was like most American towns as this conflict escalated under Kennedy, Johnson, and Nixon: those who remembered past world wars valued patriotism and respect for authority, while a younger generation expressed doubt and resistance to a distant war that might pull them away from their studies or professions and a prosperous, peaceful life at home. Having survived the violent Loray Mill strike in 1929,

which was said to involve some communist infiltration, Gastonians may even have embraced an attack on this faraway threat to democracy and the free market.

Zoe, as noted, came to oppose not only this war, but the idea of war and the damage it imposes on everyone touched by obligation or attachment. Vaguely, I remember sensing that Zoe's position caused some friction between my mother and her brothers. My father and most of Gastonia would have been of the "unconditional respect for authority" persuasion; for many, military service provided a viable career option (and escape from labor in the mills). At our kitchen table, talk centered on David's prospects as he graduated from college in 1972 and contemplated his low draft number. He recalls intense discussions in which Mother resisted the thought of sending her only son to war.

The extent to which Grandmother Zoe influenced her family or her readers on this issue is unclear. She would have been in her mid-seventies by this time; she was not an impressionable young hippie, and her credibility in the town was secure. We lost Aunt Kitty in 1966, and so Uncle Tommy's grief and lifelong struggles must surely have weighed upon Zoe as she contemplated yet another war on behalf of her community. The warm celebration of her life on Zoe Brockman Day in 1974 suggests she must have been forgiven any indiscretions, as the focus shifted to her achievements as a poet, journalist, and local treasure.

I was a sophomore in college when Zoe Brockman died, and over time and with this research my sense of Grandmother Zoe has sharpened and magnified. I only wish we had enjoyed more conversations, and that I could have spoken to her more and drawn inspiration from her uniquely gifted mind while we both lived. ∎

COURTESY OF LYN TRIPLETT

ABOVE **Lyn Triplett with a bust of Zoe Kincaid Brockman at the Gaston County Public Library, 2018** (The bronze bust was created by Dr. B. Graham Weathers, Jr., and unveiled at the Gaston County Public Library on Zoe Kincaid Brockman Day, 4 Aug. 1974.)

"Our contact with Grandmother Zoe, reinforced by Mother's deference as well as things whispered or assumed, led David and me to understand how different the woman was. We saw her as famous, connected to books and people far beyond our little town."

COURTESY OF THE ARTIST

The Morning Tree (watercolor on paper, 16x20) by Michael Dorsey

BY JAMES APPLEWHITE

A Calling

Cascading whitewater tongues thrum
through the stone harp, here spread by
this ruined ford. Up river on the other
shore the Titan stones of an early mill
bulk out into the winter air. This scene
I share with the past sent wagons on
across this river, behind the sexless mules.
Then in summer, water lower, they
forded these shallows, iron-rimmed wooden
wheels bumping over the stones, women in
calico bonnets perched among the bags of corn.
Water arcing around in the hidden turbine
spun the granite rounds, the tooth-like
grooves then gnashing the kernels, smashing
the hard brittle corn into edible meal.
I seem to see the driver of the wagon,
his meaty forearms rising, lashing down –
urging his mules onto the other shore.
These still-living lives of the dead arise,
inflaming the chill, inhabiting the wind
now rushing again down river. A red-
shouldered hawk takes flight from a tree
across from these rapids, crying sharply into
this cold flame of air that floods down
past with the current. I feel generations
living on with me, unknown, lusting
for more life, I myself a physical harp
that their unheard cries thrill through –
and I shudder in tune with them, my solitary
manhood buffeted beside turbulent waters.

MICHAEL DORSEY received his MA and MFA in Painting from Bowling Green State University. Before retiring from East Carolina University, he served as Dean of the School of Art and Design and then Interim Dean of the College of Fine Arts and Communication. He is a Signature Member of the Watercolor Society of North Carolina, and he has served as an exhibition juror for professional competitions in North Carolina, South Carolina, Alabama, Mississippi, and Illinois. His work is shown nationally and is included in permanent collections at the Muscarelle Museum of Art, the College of New Jersey, the Library Collection of the School of the Art Institute of Chicago, and the University of Perugia in Italy. He has participated in the annual *James Applewhite Art Invitational* exhibit at City Art Gallery in Greenville. One of his paintings inspired by Applewhite's poetry is published in *NCLR Online* 2013, and the painting featured here was part of the 2016 Applewhite exhibit.

JAMES APPLEWHITE is the author of thirteen poetry collections and is the recipient of four Roanoke-Chowan Awards for Poetry. He has also received the North Carolina Award for Literature, and he has been inducted into the North Carolina Literary Hall of Fame and the Fellowship of Southern Writers. His poetry appears regularly in *NCLR* and has been the inspiration for several years of annual exhibits featuring City Art Gallery artists. The works of art with his poems in this issue are from some of these exhibits.

BY JAMES APPLEWHITE

Travelers

He walks by the autumnal forest
in a glory of sunshine. Prismatically,
the hickory and maple leaves refract
these rays of light, that bear coloration
to our eyes – incandescently returning these
goldens and maroons in an exhilarating chill.
So trees in mute glory testify to the air
to the swallow already arcing the high sky
as it darkens toward evening. The walker's
head is bowed toward an instrument that
he holds in the hollow of his hand – blind
to the beauty about him. He is ignorant
of the climbing liner, of the silver light
on its angle-winged arrowing, sublime as
so seen from afar, in the coming sunset.
Inside, there is bother and impatience among
the canned travelers – those so lifted by
mathematical marvels of aluminum and glass
and steel, and now mastering the high air –
this arrogant glory not felt inside,
where one of the already bored passengers
may be communicating with the one below,
asking him to check, when he gets back,
whether she has left the outside basement
door securely locked. He'll find it so –
their love not now expanded by the quick
light, this sublime coloration of a nature
we have so mastered, so miniaturized, against
this expansion of being in autumnal sunset.

Sunset (oil on canvas, 20x30) by Richard Fennell

RICHARD FENNELL earned his BFA from East Carolina University and his MFA from UNC Greensboro. His work can be found in the permanent collection at the North Carolina Museum of Art, as well as numerous private and corporate collections nationwide and in City Art Gallery in Greenville. His numerous honors include a purchase award in the North Carolina Arts Competition in 1977, the Best-in-Show Award at the Atlanta Arts Festival in 1978, and two purchase awards at the Third Annual Exhibit of North Carolina Sculpture in 1984. The painting featured here was part of City Art Gallery's Applewhite exhibit in 2017. See another of his Applewhite-inspired works in *NCLR* 2014 and more of his work on his website at richardfennell.com.

BY JAMES APPLEWHITE

April in October

Afternoon's late sun-slant now *suspends* –
glancing upon the enameled magnolias in its
declining shine. The sequacious recessional
intimates vistas of *beyond* – auguring with
moodier transparencies against those maroons
and mauves, that more usually denote
October's evanescence – those edging-and-spotting browns,
all too readily signing the eye with a sigh of conclusion.
Now one spider's strand is signaling to me
in white singularity – a brightness of immaculate
essence here crossing my glance – pure line of light
caught still in its transiency, from a permanent
source, as if remaining from Beginning.
An immanence, an ever-livingness,
stretches from a leaf-edge to my sight
in incarnating its far origin. And now
I see how all distance is also a nearness,
that this leaving of us by the seasons beams
a legacy of Beginning: an immaculate start
encoding all meaning. I feel how this
drift of cloud is a gift, this motion
of light toward evening holding an
ever-returning morning, wherein our
breathing is born again as praises –
here, in their momentary stasis of *always*.

COURTESY OF THE ARTIST

Spider Web Vase (ceramic, 10x10x13)
by Colleen Black Semelka

Canada native **COLLEEN BLACK SEMELKA** received
her BA from the University of Manitoba. She currently
creates her ceramic art in her Chapel Hill and rural
Chatham County studios. Semelka was the recipient
of the 2012 Joyce Wilkins Pope Grand Prize for First
Place Sculpture. Her work has been displayed in the
Duke Eye Center Connector Gallery at Duke University
Hospital in Durham, NC; 123 Art Studios in Pittsboro,
NC; and City Art Gallery in Greenville, NC. See more of
her work at www.colleenblacksemelka.com.

Sacred Feminine (graphite and oil on clayboard, 18.5x48.5) by Kiki Farish

WINNER, 2018 JAMES APPLEWHITE POETRY PRIZE
BY CATHERINE CARTER

Womb-Room

You always pictured it black in there, if less black
like a windowless underground cell than black
as an iris, a silky queen-of-night tulip, why not?
what the speculum saw, stabbing its annual spear
of light, you never did, that room had neither sun
nor sea nor even the blood-tide moon.
Only now there's the screen, its mystic
mirror promising terrible truths. Now,
now, here's all you never thought to see –
and it's not black. No tulip-cup, no sealed cell,
but a witch-cathedral of rose quartz, peony petals, arched,
vaulted, glimmering with moisture like the geode
walls of hidden caverns at the first candlelight
in that deep underground. Made to hold a life
it couldn't hold, still this could be a secret chamber
of Luray, Fingal, Lascaux, this room
inside yourself into which you could almost step,
whose curved walls you could almost inscribe
with ochre does, cows, mares, wild
cats, new countries, charts of unnamed stars.

CATHERINE CARTER is Professor of English at Western Carolina University. Her poetry collections include three from Louisiana State University Press: *The Memory of Gills* (2006; reviewed in *NCLR* 2007 and recipient of the Roanoke-Chowan Award), *The Swamp Monster at Home* (2012; reviewed in *NCLR Online* 2013), and *Larvae of the Newest Stars* (2019). Her poems have appeared in *Ploughshares, Orion,* and *Best American Poetry 2009,* and she was the recipient of the 2009 Randall Jarrell Poetry Prize.

Final judge Amber Flora Thomas said of Carter's winning poem, "I was very moved by 'Womb-Room,' which takes us inside the human body as the speaker considers her inability to bear a child. In the cavernous beauty of the human interior, the speaker finds a connection with nature; how we see and experience the earth is rooted within our bodies. I care deeply about poems that recognize our connection with our environment and nature."

KIKI FARISH is Professor of Art at Meredith College in Raleigh, NC. She earned a BA from Meredith and an MFA from ECU. Farish received a 2014-15 North Carolina Fellowship Award and was among twelve artists included in the North Carolina Museum of Art's exhibition *Line, Touch, Trace.* She has been the Jentel Artist in Residence at Banner, WY, and the New York Mills Artist in Residence in New York Mills, NM. Her art is in the collection of the Ackland Art Museum in Chapel Hill. See more of her art at www.kikifarish.com.

FINALIST, 2018 JAMES APPLEWHITE POETRY PRIZE

BY J.S. ABSHER

How Rhodon the Tutor Prepared Cleopatra's Son

*Caesarion has a belt he loves – Cavafy
will describe its rows of amethysts and sapphires –
and obeys his tutor while traipsing dominions
of waste and sea to exceed Octavian's grasp.*

Form: hexameters. *Theme:* a king's power. *Governing
image:* snow. *Questions for thought:* in the delta's heat,
did your mother while still a child ever conceive
snow's possibility? When history cold-shouldered

her to Ephesus, where it chilled her spicy wine
with last year's ice; when it unrolled her from a rug
in a little avalanche, and then dispatched her
into the beds of Roman studs, her melting point

lowered by ambition; when it brought her to Rome
blazing, mistress of Caesar in his last winter,
to melt her sweetness into the boiling Tiber
and to raise you, dear boy, to lead *Res Publica*,

did she ever see it fall, or hold out her hand
palm up like a child to catch and see it vanish,
or watch its slow white liquefaction on the down
of bare arms, setting goose-bump legions on parade,

or roll it into a man that, like Anthony
when the nations were burning, could not hold his shape
but flowed unmanned away? *Process*: Collect your thoughts
and images, arrange them neatly, end on this

moral: snow that lingers on field and forest kills,
but dissolved in spring heat gives life. *Application:*
like a fistful of snow in summer's hot dry mouth,
little Caesars must melt to give Augustus life.

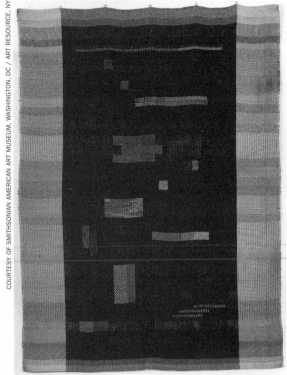

COURTESY OF SMITHSONIAN AMERICAN ART MUSEUM, WASHINGTON, DC / ART RESOURCE, NY

Ancient Writing (woven fabric, 59.25x44) by Anni Albers

Printmaker and textile artist **ANNI ALBERS** (1899–1994) was born to Jewish parents in Berlin, Germany. In 1933, Albers and her husband fled to North Carolina, and she began teaching art at Black Mountain College. In 1949, she became the first textile artist to have a solo exhibition at the Museum of Modern Art in New York City. She received half a dozen honorary doctorates and won many awards for her art, including the Craftmanship Medal by the American Institute of Architects and the American Craft Council Gold Medal for "uncompromising excellence."

FINALIST, 2018 JAMES APPLEWHITE POETRY PRIZE

BY J.S. ABSHER

In my yard are henbit

henbit but not henbane
chickweed and henbit but not hens-and-chicks
and here wild mustard and muscadine
fat hen and chick wittles and henbit again
(edible and everywhere and unobtrusive)
and bee-beloved abelia (not yet in bloom) and black cherry

sorrow for ingratitude (a small red bloom)
azalea showily in front of the house
mayapple and pawpaw modestly in back
a few more chances to do things right
(they bear large white blossoms)
begonia and rock foil and stonecrop

and debts incurred to dirt and rain and sun
one rose, wild blackberries its cousin
evening fears and morning's graces (also cousins)
phlox and foxglove
unpayable debts to the lord
of hellebore and dogwood and bleeding-heart

two weeks after Easter, 2018

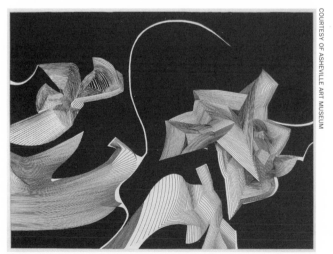

COURTESY OF ASHEVILLE ART MUSEUM

untitled (ink drawing on paper, strathmore, 18¹/₈x24¹/₄) by Lorna Blaine Halper, Asheville Art Museum, Black Mountain College Collection, gift of the Artist, 2009.27.10.41, © Estate of Lorna Blaine Halper/Asheville Art Museum

J.S. ABSHER's first full-length book, *Mouth Work* (St. Andrew's University Press, 2016; reviewed in *NCLR Online* 2017), won the 2015 Lena M. Shull Book Competition sponsored by the North Carolina Poetry Society. He previously published two chapbooks, *Night Weather* (Cynosura Press, 2010) and *The Burial of Anyce Shepherd* (Main Street Rag, 2006). His poems have appeared in approximately forty journals and anthologies, including *Visions International, Tar River Poetry*, and *Southern Poetry Anthology, VII: North Carolina*. He has twice been nominated for the Pushcart Prize, and he has twice before been a James Applewhite Poetry Prize finalist, his poems appearing in *NCLR Online* 2016 and *NCLR* 2018. He is a native of both northwestern North Carolina and southwestern Virginia. He currently lives in Raleigh with his wife, Patti.

LORNA BLAINE HALPER (1924–2012) was born in New York City and studied at Black Mountain College in Black Mountain, NC. Her work is most prominently displayed at the Black Mountain College Museum and Art Center in Asheville, NC. Prior to her death, Asheville Art Museum curated an exhibition titled *Lorna Blaine Halper: The Space*, which featured a sizable portion of her art and art by other Black Mountain College artists, which she donated.

**HONORABLE MENTION,
2018 JAMES APPLEWHITE POETRY PRIZE**
BY NILLA LARSEN

Girl Praxis

Before blood loss turned banal,
you bound your own aster crowns.

You brushed fire across cheekbones,
smeared crow wings beyond edges of lids.

At 14, first acrylic nails & hardcore crush.
You felt glossy. Two broke off in a hot hatch

backseat. Rumor oozed. Come recess, you pressed
a used panty liner inside his uncracked *American Pageant*.

With girlfriends, you ached for the movie makeover
montage: powder clouds, Motown & heels worth the hurt.

The girl-woman-us in red satin mist. A slow tilt-up reveal
when the boy-man-them drinks her in, this misfit finally femme.

Cue Destiny Outlet: cookie auguries, plum balms & $5 jars of stars.
You paused the gospel of softer, softest. Axed pixel-ninjas & talked smack.

No matter how spent, together, you braided & undid doubts. Your bodies
morphing & being morphed, inheritors of half-stifled laughs & loopy whistles.

You gambled on extensions of your selves. Prayed the double tape stuck to roots.
Wished for the filters to forgive less & your friends to hug you longer. *Please, please,*

not today, you chanted before looming graduations & second dates, when half a lash
drooped caterpillar-style & you rummaged the bag for glue. You cursed what you were

missing & what came too soon. You took comfort in metallic palettes & doing the math.
Composed curves of ≈, lilac & bold as you chose. Margins of twisters & wide-open hover-eyes.

Did you ever get it right? Was it like that never-again newness of a fresh dollar? Bittersweet like
tomorrow? Do you hide & apply your extra, gush & cuss on dream girls, go damn & bask in your trappings?

COURTESY OF THE ARTIST

Origin Story (48x24, oil on canvas)
by Gordon C. James

A Denmark native, **NILLA LARSEN** earned an MFA in poetry from UNC Wilmington and then moved back to Copenhagen. She received a 2016 poetry fellowship to attend Martha's Vineyard Institute of Creative Writing and was a finalist in the 2016 Applewhite Prize competition, her poem then published in *NCLR Online* 2017. In 2018, she also placed honorable mention with a second poem, which was accepted for publication elsewhere before *NCLR*'s results were announced, and a third poem was a finalist and published in *NCLR Online* 2019. Her poems have also been published in or forthcoming from *Quarter After Eight, The Boiler, Nimrod, Crab Creek Review, Waccamaw, Asheville Poetry Review,* and elsewhere.

GORDON C. JAMES is an award-winning fine artist and illustrator. He attended high school at Suitland Center of the Visual and Performing Arts in Forestville, MD, and earned a BFA in illustration from the School of Visual Arts in New York City. His paintings have been featured in *International Artist Magazine* and are part of the Paul R. Jones Collection at the University of Alabama. In addition to illustrating children's books by Patricia McKissack, he recently received accolades for illustrating *Crown: An Ode to the Fresh Cut*, by Derrick Barnes. Barnes and James received honors from the Newbery, the Caldecott, the Ezra Jack Keats, the Coretta Scott King, and they won the Kirkus Prize. James also won a Gold Medal in 2018 from the Society of Illustrators. He resides in Charlotte, NC, with his wife and children. See more of his work on his website at www.gordoncjames.com.

On New *NCLR* Friends
by Margaret D. Bauer, Editor

I noted introducing the Flashbacks section how I have developed friendships with some of *NCLR*'s regular writers over the years. And sometimes I become "fast friends" with new writers I meet – like Nancy Werking Poling, whom I met in person at the fall North Carolina Writers' Network conference. We sat down over a cup of coffee and talked about our writing to such an extent that by the time we rose, I had a new friend. It was fun too to introduce her to Randall Kenan, who had selected her story "Leander's Lies" for our 2018 Albright Prize. Congratulations again to Nancy, and thank you again to Randall for serving as judge.

At that same Network conference, the 2018 Linda Flowers Literary Award was presented to Jennifer Brown, who read her winning essay for us. Quite moved by it, I asked her if the story was being published and, if not, if we could publish it in *NCLR*. The North Carolina Humanities Council, which sponsors the award, welcomed this offer and funded the design and art. Now I am going to confess something to *NCLR* readers, which I admitted to the author and to Melanie Moore at the North Carolina Humanities Council when I spoke to each about publishing the essay: I submitted an essay to that competition myself, and while of course I would have been thrilled to win, I am also pleased to find the judges' selection for the award in a competition I've entered to be so deserving of the prize. I commend the judges and thank the North Carolina Humanities Council for their support of the prize and of our publication of it in these pages.

Finally, find here three more of the Applewhite Prize finalists, including Sally Thomas's, which was selected by final judge Amber Flora Thomas for second place. Thanks to the 2018 finalists and Amber for participating in readings this past year, and thanks to *NCLR* Assistant Editor Angela Love Kitchin for organizing most of these events. Angela gets a congratulations, too, for her promotion between the online and print issues, in recognition of her contributions as a staff member, which so exceeded the already high expectations for student staff that some formal recognition seemed appropriate.

I will take this last bit of space then to express my gratitude to all of the student staff members for their hard work and to the ECU English Department and Graduate School for providing graduate assistantships. In addition, a record nine undergraduates enrolled in *NCLR*'s internship class last fall, three of whom took on a second semester internship in the spring. As I watch for new works by writers after they've appeared in our pages, so too do I enjoy following the careers of our former student staff members. So please, to all of you, stay in touch. ∎

NORTH CAROLINA
Miscellany

NORTH CAROLINA
HUMANITIES
C O U N C I L

MANY STORIES, ONE PEOPLE

ALSO IN THIS ISSUE

2018
AlexAlbright
Creative Nonfiction Prize Winner

BY NANCY WERKING POLING

LEANDER'S LIES

photographs courtesy of the author

HE CLAIMED to have represented North Carolina in the US Congress from 1897 to 1903. A lie.

That he grew up on a plantation. A lie.

That he was with Teddy Roosevelt in the Dismal Swamp when Roosevelt shot his first bear. A lie.

That he visited the Holy Land in 1907 while circling the globe by ship. A lie.

Of course, when Elias Leander Smith told his daughter Virginia all these fabrications, as she wrote down every detail, he had no way of anticipating the internet and Ancestry.com. Nor that a hundred years later, persistent descendants would uncover his past.

In June 1910 Elias Leander Smith arrived by train in Nevada, Missouri. When he was young, he'd gone by Elias; now, as the new pastor of the local Church of the Brethren, he chose to be called Elder Leander Smith. He claimed his wife and children back in North Carolina had died.

A LIE.

Two months earlier, the news section of the *Gospel Messenger*, periodical of the Church of the Brethren, had printed, "While [Brother Leander Smith was] stopping at a private home in Friendship, S.C., the house was destroyed by fire, and his trunk, containing his books and clothing, was also burned."

Was this true? Or might Leander have deliberately burned all evidence of his previous life and reported a disaster? In either case the misfortune allowed the forty-four-year-old minister to erase all that lay behind him. He set out to start a new life and revise the narrative of the former one.

Elias Leander, in fact, had two wives and five children still living in North Carolina. (Note: Don't worry about keeping the wives straight. I identify them as evidence of his duplicity.)

In 1883, at age seventeen, he married Sarah Emma Wright (who went by Emma). This marriage must have ended in divorce, as records show her remarrying in 1897. However, by the time Leander

After years of living in many parts of the country, **NANCY WERKING POLING** reports that she is "now happily settled in Black Mountain, NC, an area where nature and history are honored." Poling is the author of the nonfiction book *Before It Was Legal: A Black-White Marriage (1945–1987)*, which she self-published in 2017, as well as a short story collection, *Had Eve Come First and Jonah Been a Woman* (Wipf and Stock, 2010), and the novel *Out of the Pumpkin Shell* (Spinsters Ink, 2009). Randall Kenan, the final judge for the 2018 Alex Albright Creative Nonfiction Prize competition, said of Poling's essay, "It was love at first read to me, and stands out in originality and in tone."

arrived in Missouri, she and their three sons lived in Cleveland County and had taken back the Smith surname. Why, we may never know.

In 1902, Leander married a second time: Mary Jane Alexander. The December after he deserted her and their two daughters, she gave birth to a son, naming him Leander.

And there was a third wife: Mary Susan Wine of Nevada, Missouri. My husband's mother, Virginia, was a product of that marriage. She wrote of her father's "fascinating" life for a college paper. As long as she lived she believed his lies.

So, Elias Leander Smith, "a man of God," left two families back in North Carolina. He had to have anticipated the challenges they would face. Censuses show that Emma could neither read nor write. In 1910 she lived in a rented home with their middle son, who worked in a monazite mine. Ten years later she lived with their youngest son, a carder in a Gastonia cotton mill. Hers had to have been a life of struggle.

> BUT FACTS ARE NOT THE SAME AS TRUTH. THE TRUTH OF WHY HE ABANDONED HIS CHRISTIAN PRINCIPLES AND FAMILIES. WAS HIS DECISION SELFISH AND ARROGANT? PERHAPS NOT.

It's nearly impossible to trace a woman named Mary Jane Smith. However, censuses after 1910 show her two daughters growing up in the homes of relatives. She isn't listed with them. She had to bear the death of their little boy at age two.

The internet and Ancestry.com have uncovered the facts. Who married whom. When. Names and birthdates of children and grandchildren. When individuals died and where they're buried. The fact that Leander left two families leaves me outraged over the hardship and heartbreak he surely caused.

But facts are not the same as Truth. The Truth of *why* he abandoned his Christian principles and families. Was his decision selfish and arrogant? Perhaps not.

Maybe he wanted to escape the financial and physical hardships of farming.

1866. Not the best time to be born. The Civil War had ended only a year before, leaving North Carolina reeling from the deaths of thirty-three thousand men (Leander's oldest brother among them) and a shattered economy. Over much of the state, homes and businesses had been destroyed, the region's major work force emancipated or stolen, depending on which side of the conflict you supported.

The four-year war had brought Leander's father, Joseph, few material losses, as he had little to begin with. The devaluation and eventual failure of Confederate script mattered little to him or to his Burke County neighbors who relied on a barter system. Subsistence farming put food on the table.

ABOVE **Leander and Mary Smith with their two children, Virginia and Esther, circa 1918**

There's no evidence that Leander ever owned land. The only census information found about him as an adult, before he headed for Missouri, is from 1910. He, Mary Jane, and their two daughters lived in Pineville, Mecklenburg County. He was a farmer, renting the land.

After the Civil War, plantation owners, unable to make a profit without slaves, divided their land into plots cultivated by sharecroppers and tenant farmers. Toward the end of the nineteenth century, more than one-third of Mecklenburg County farmland was rented to tenant farmers, Leander most likely one of them.

Given his bent toward reading and scholarship later in life, it's not inconceivable that he hated farming. Hated the strain on his back, sun-scorched days spent navigating a plow behind a mule. Hated the fickleness of weather – too wet, too dry, too hot, too cold. Most of all hated the financial insecurity. A failed crop would put him in debt, for he had to pay rent to land owners and repay merchants who had extended credit for the purchase of seeds and tools.

> **"HE NEVER LEAVES A DEBT UNPAID, NO MATTER WHAT THE SACRIFICE MAY BE ON HIS PART."**

During the economic depression of the 1880s, small farmers were hit especially hard. Might Leander have despaired over being unable to provide for his family?

In her written account of her father's life, Virginia shared an observation: "He never leaves a debt unpaid, no matter what the sacrifice may be on his part." Did earlier struggles against indebtedness inspire later diligence?

Maybe he felt conflicted by a love of learning and a call to ministry.

At age fourteen Leander no longer attended school. Neither did his ten-year-old sister. Yet in his post-North Carolina life he was a strong advocate for education. Articles he wrote for the periodical of the Church of the Brethren were articulate and well informed. A thirst for knowledge must have inspired him to educate himself.

Between the Old and New Testaments of a family Bible the following was written: "Elias L. Smith . . . joined the Baptists at St. John's Aug 11/81 . . . was ordained to the office of Deacon at Corinth Feb 9th/84 . . . and was liberated by the church at Corinth to preach January 12th 188[smudge]."

Leander felt called to preach the Gospel, but heeding that call in Burke or Cleveland County, or just outside the small town of Pineville, may have offered a dismal future. Rural Baptist churches depended on farmer-preachers, so ministry was paired with hard physical labor and limited intellectual encouragement.

During the 1880s Charles Spurgeon, a "Particular Baptist" from England, had an international reputation as an outstanding preacher. He was known to be an avid reader and a prolific writer whose works were translated into many languages. Spurgeon Brantley, Leander's third son by his first wife, was likely named after the famous preacher.

ABOVE **Leander Smith, circa 1915**

Charles Spurgeon represented an alternative to the farmer-preacher. His was a model that relied on reading and writing and that offered recognition for oratory skills.

Still, Leander's call, whether as a farmer-preacher or as professional clergy, would surely have been invalidated. If his marriage to Emma ended in divorce – worse yet, if he then remarried – the Southern Baptists would have revoked his ordination.

God had called him to preach the Gospel. "Here, Lord, am I," Leander had responded. What was a man who felt such a strong call to do?

Join another denomination. Divorce would have been a barrier in the Church of the Brethren too. But the Brethren were a small, scattered denomination with no centralized structure and little presence in North Carolina. Knowing nothing about his history, Brethren would have welcomed a man who presented himself as a dedicated minister.

Could it be that leaving his family and the state in which he'd spent his whole life was a sacrifice that ripped his heart in two? Yet God's call took precedence over everything.

Maybe North Carolina politics influenced his decision.

At the end of the nineteenth century, North Carolina farmers, black and white, united in political action and for four years met with success. But by 1910 any hopes Leander (a Republican, according to Virginia) may have had about the future would have been dashed. The Democrats were back in firm control of government. The progressive agenda of the Republican-Populist movement – banking and transportation reforms, and other issues of importance to farmers – had been defeated. Coalitions with black farmers had been sabotaged by the Democrats' white-supremacy stance. The welfare of the small farmer was of no concern to men in power.

Two decades earlier, in 1886, North Carolinian Leonidas L. Polk had begun publishing *The Progressive Farmer*. What started as an effort to educate farmers had transitioned into a political movement: The Farmers' Alliance. Polk went on to serve as its president. United, farmers could impact governmental policies dealing with railroad transportation and the availability of money. By 1891 more than one hundred thousand white North Carolina farmers were members. Convinced that neither major political party was looking out for them, the Alliance became instrumental in forming the Populist Party.

An entry in Leander's expenses ledger years later (1945) hints at his ongoing support of farmers and his identification with them: "subscription to Progressive Farmer, 25 cents."

At the turn of the century North Carolina Democrats codified Jim Crow laws. In 1900, to

> COULD IT BE THAT LEAVING HIS FAMILY AND THE STATE IN WHICH HE'D SPENT HIS WHOLE LIFE WAS A SACRIFICE THAT RIPPED HIS HEART IN TWO?

disenfranchise black voters, they enacted legislation requiring voters to pay a poll tax and demonstrate literacy skills.

Leander was a son of the South. He likely had a heavy drawl. He certainly had the Southern gift of telling a good yarn. We can assume that, like his neighbors, he held racist attitudes. But Virginia's account – largely based on lies, don't forget – offers clues that he may have had personal contact across racial lines and not shared his neighbors' strong animosity against blacks. We know that he taught his daughters by his third marriage to respect children of other races and ethnic groups.

In 1910, as he looked to the future, surely despair hung over Leander. Though native born, he may have felt alienated from a state that pitted black against white, business against the farmer, the wealthy against the poor. Maybe he felt he had no choice but to leave.

Elias Leander Smith went on to serve the Church of the Brethren for more than thirty years. He devoted most of that time to "home missions," newly formed congregations scattered across the western United States: North Dakota, Missouri, Iowa, Arkansas, Arizona, and Oregon. He died in 1947 without ever returning to North Carolina.

A man's death doesn't end his story. His life's choices can impact generations. As I've uncovered Elias Leander's past, I've shed tears on behalf of his first two families. I've stood by the grave of Emma, his first wife, who died in 1927 and is buried on the grounds of the old Broughton State Hospital in Morganton. I've visited the Gastonia church cemetery where Mary Jane, his second wife, lies alongside her parents, sisters, and daughters Othella and Ruth.

Leander's sons and grandsons by his first marriage worked in the cotton mills near the South Carolina border. Census data and death certificates say spinner, carder, stitcher, spooler, warper, winder. In 1930 two sons' families, ten people, lived together in a small mill house in Kings Mountain. Only one son could read and write.

Leander's third family had opportunities the other two didn't have. Mary Susan was an accomplished church musician and likely attended college for a year. Virginia and her sister received college educations and married professional men. Nearly all of Elias Leander's and Mary Susan's grandchildren earned college diplomas; some have advanced degrees.

Recently, a scene in the movie *Mr. Holmes* reminded me of the mystery of Elias Leander Smith. Sherlock Holmes recalled a case in which a Japanese man went to England and stayed, abandoning his wife and son. The man wrote a letter to his son explaining that Holmes had urged him to remain in England. A lie. Holmes told the son bluntly, "A man abandoned his family and wrote his son a story. He wouldn't be the first to cloak his cowardice in the flag of sacrifice."

We'll never know whether it was cowardice or courage that inspired Elias Leander Smith to leave North Carolina forever. Maybe a bit of both. ■

> **A MAN'S DEATH DOESN'T END HIS STORY. HIS LIFE'S CHOICES CAN IMPACT GENERATIONS. AS I'VE UNCOVERED ELIAS LEANDER'S PAST, I'VE SHED TEARS ON BEHALF OF HIS FIRST TWO FAMILIES.**

ABOVE **Leander Smith, circa 1930**

SECOND PLACE, 2018 JAMES APPLEWHITE POETRY PRIZE

BY SALLY THOMAS

Daybreak

The trees shrug off the faded dark as you'd
Flick rusty tap water from your fingers in
Some gas-station john so filthy you avoid
Touching the paper towels. Across town,
On a wedge of land between two highways' knees,
A rented single-wide's burned to its metal bones.
Nothing to see but a glum woman eating Cheez-
Its. In the pallid light of her salvaged cell phone's
Screen she thumbs some message. *Wear r u?*
What's the answer? Where, now, is he or she,
Husband, lover, mama? What's gone wrong?
A lighter flares. She breathes bitter blue.
Hidden in the one shining dogwood tree,
A mockingbird unravels a stray end of song.

Walstonburg, Greene County, NC, (gelatin silver print, 10x10)
by David Simonton

SALLY THOMAS is the author of two poetry chapbooks, *Fallen Water* (2015) and *Richeldis of Walsingham* (2016), both from Finishing Line Press. Her poetry and fiction have appeared most recently in *Dappled Things, Wild Goose Poetry Review, and Windhover*. In 2017, she received the Editor's Choice Award in Fiction from *Relief: A Journal of Art and Faith* and Honorable Mention in *Ruminate*'s Janet McCabe Poetry Prize competition. A native of Memphis, TN, she lives with her family in Lincolnton, NC. Read another of her finalist poems in *NCLR Online* 2019.

Final Judge Amber Flora Thomas says of her second-place selection, "The poet moves our eye with care in this poem, presenting a vision of our particular American moment. Our attention moves quickly from the personal, hands flicking tap water, to the farther scene, a desolate landscape of a burned home between two highways, to the figure of the woman at the center of the poem whose face is lit in a cell phone's glare, and finally to the mockingbird whose song captures the near and far. We need more poems that aren't afraid to look at the world honestly."

DAVID SIMONTON moved to North Carolina in 1989. His work has been widely exhibited and has appeared in *Photography Quarterly, The Photo Review*, and *Southern Quarterly*. He is the recipient of numerous grants and commissions, including a commission from the North Carolina Museum of Art to photograph the abandoned Polk Prison on land adjacent to the museum, and two Visual Artist Fellowships from the North Carolina Arts Council. His art is included in the collections of the North Carolina Museum of Art; the Asheville Art Museum; and the George Eastman Museum in Rochester, NY. His work is currently (through 2021) featured in the traveling exhibition *SOUTHBOUND: Photographs of and about the New South*.

2018 LINDA FLOWERS LITERARY AWARD WINNER

BY JENNIFER BROWN

Landscape *with* Death *and* Birth

"EVEN THE CORPSE HAS ITS OWN BEAUTY."
—RALPH WALDO EMERSON, "NATURE"

A deer died in the woods by my house last month. When it stank, someone shoveled a grave-mound of red clay over the rotting flesh. Now, tufts of fur and bones protrude where other animals have burrowed in. A furled ear stands up from the pile, as if alert to my approach. The world has ended for the deer, but around and on its carcass, the world thrives. What harm might we do a child by not permitting her to witness such a thing?

When I visit my parents' house, out in what we used to think of as "the country," it is easy to imagine the new houses gone: their newness glares from unsmudged windows with efficiency-rating-labels still stuck smartly in the corners. My parents' house rises in red mud flowing like lava around fresh concrete foundations in the rain; it rests in the pile of boulders extracted and laid aside when the earth-movers began working a metamorphosis on this unnamed, small-time cattle farm. I remember when, looking out my bedroom window to the south and west, it seemed that there was no such thing as time. Every year, I thought, the same cows ate their way slowly toward the fence, accepted the apples we tossed them with what my brother and I as small children believed was happiness. The cedar, despite its mean habit of rusting the apple trees, stood sentinel over our games and forays beyond the barbed wire. Down the easy slope, the creek was the prized destination, shaded and smelling of damp mystery and clay. We did not own the cows or the pasture, but they might as well have belonged to us. Or, more precisely, they seemed to belong to a

JENNIFER BROWN is a native of Greensboro, NC. Until recently, she taught English literature and writing and was a dorm-parent at a college-preparatory boarding school; before that, she taught literature and writing in various colleges and universities. She has studied and written poetry and nonfiction for many years, and her writing has appeared in *Southern Poetry Review, Ellipsis, Colorado Review,* and *American Literary Review,* among other venues.

The Linda Flowers Literary Award is sponsored by the North Carolina Humanities Council. The 2018 contest judges described Brown's "Landscape with Birth and Death" as a "very well-written, thoughtful essay," noting that her "narrative felt attentive and deliberate" and showed "maturity on the page."

The Guest House (archival inkjet print, 5x5) by Linda Fox

> **IF EMERSON IS CORRECT, WE, THEN AND NOW, MIGHT AS WELL BE BURNING BOOKS AND ALLOWING ELEMENTARY SCHOOLS TO FALL TO RUIN EVERY TIME WE RAZE MORE FOREST AND PAVE A PASTURE FOR PARKING.**

world to which we also belonged, a summer-realm without clocks or cars, with dogs and rabbits, ticks and mosquitoes, and red dirt that turned white tube socks orange. It was a kind of live-action *Peanuts*, a small place populated by children in which adults were large, shadowy, unintelligible figures on the periphery, brandishing school books and dinner plates and trash cans that needed emptying before dark.

Emerson, whose voice, if we have ears to hear, still rings clearly through the muddle of one hundred-seventy years, knew that the scholar – "Man Thinking" – received his first lessons in the fields and barns and forests that were, much more then than now, the child's domain: "Thus to him, to this school-boy under the bending dome of day, is suggested, that he and it proceed from one root; one is leaf and one is flower; relation, sympathy, stirring in every vein. And what is that Root? Is not that the soul of his soul?"[1] Nature, Emerson argued – even as his countrymen were heading west in greater and greater numbers, even as the Cherokee Indians were being rounded up and forced to march out of their ancestral land so that Georgians could lay sole claim to the gold in the ground – is much more than "natural resources," that nomenclature dear to the profiteer, one who seeks raw materials to transform into goods to be bought and sold – base-metal into gold, gold into power. If Emerson is correct, we, then and now, might as well be burning books and allowing elementary schools to fall to ruin every time we raze more forest and pave a pasture for parking. She can adequately begin to ponder her place in the world who has spent an

Born in California, **LINDA FOX** received an MFA and BFA in Photography at East Carolina University School of Design. She currently lives in Raleigh and works for the Market Department of the North Carolina Department of Natural and Cultural Resources as the staff Photographer/Photo Editor. Find another sample of her art in *NCLR Online* 2014.

[1] Ralph Waldo Emerson, "The American Scholar," 1837.

afternoon testing the patience of the single bull in the herd and dodging manure piles in retreat, who has watched a fallen fledgling as its parents abandon it, who has smelled the decomposing deer, dead in the woods for no apparent reason, its eyes still shiny enough that it seems almost ready to struggle upright and bound away. True, there are indoor activities that confront us with consequences, bring us up close to animal fact, but even what we read, even what we eat, the sounds our music makes, and our aging bodies are ultimately inseparable from Nature. The old concept might have wisdom for us yet: we read in "Nature" what we are, what the world is, the necessary relation of living beings to one another. Emerson thought that our ignorance of nature is in proportion to our ignorance of our own minds; most signs suggest that although we may still like the way his words sound a warning, we still do not believe them.

> **EMERSON THOUGHT THAT OUR IGNORANCE OF NATURE IS IN PROPORTION TO OUR IGNORANCE OF OUR OWN MINDS . . .**

More weeks of digging and natural erosion have exposed enough deer-carcass that it again reeks of decay if one is downwind. My dog, who leads me on an almost daily pilgrimage to the site, would like to chew on a particular patch of bone and tendon where the skin is black and curls away from the inner layers. She eases close, almost casually sniffing at the edges of the mound, seeming to savor the tickle of loose deer fur in her nostrils. The tension grows; she knows that an attempt to eat dead things will provoke a reprimand, but she can't resist a furtive lick. I pull her away gently, trying to understand how this travesty of a body can be appetizing. This is the power of instinct. Although I do not want to eat raw, decaying meat, I almost wish I knew what the pure drive of instinct

felt like; for me, desire is bound up with thought, with internal narrative – mediated. For the dog, protein, in whatever revolting form, smells like life.

I was not an adventurous child, but along with the neighborhood kids – all, like me, now grown and gone away – I grew up with red dirt ground into my clothes and shoes and scalp. Everything turned orange, despite bleach and warnings. The garden produced, more or less dependably, tomatoes, corn, beans, okra, potatoes, squash, even asparagus and raspberries some years. We learned how difficult it is to take care of living things, and we learned that the plants and animals around us were indifferent to our emotional attachments to them, our small-time fears and depressions. They grew and died regardless, and the Earth went on revolving and rotating; rain fell, wind blew, everything survived or not, according to its endurance and subject to chance or fate or God, all of which seemed inadequate words for the same unknown. What seemed true was continuance pitted against disruption, eternity against time, and what was true, finally, for us in our limitations, was the constant, gradual inevitability of change and the constant, inevitable longing for the world to be as it seemed it would be forever: unchanging. How can we learn, finally, that it is all right to die if we swaddle ourselves utterly from the world?

The low ridge over which I looked to the pasture from my bedroom window – on which a cedar still grows – is no longer crested by a barbed-wire fence. The deer can walk from trees to clipped lawn at a meandering pace without gathering to leap or thrashing their momentum

into the underbrush. There are no cows to keep in, no predators to keep out, no neighborhood kids to test their emerging toughness by touching the live wires and pretending to laugh off the shock. Now, four houses rise from the rolling former pasture. Compared to the houses that have flanked that field for thirty-odd years, these are elaborate, glistening shells, as if abandoned by their now extinct, gigantic, original owners to new tenants, fossil shells to hermit crabs. The old ranch style holdouts are like an architect's model, small and neatly fastened to their much larger rectangles of well-tended land. From the perspective of the new houses, out a window, perhaps, the older houses are doll-sized, a Neighborhood of Make-Believe attained without a transformative trolley ride.

The pasture has taken on a glow in the warm bath of memory, especially now that it's gone. I have made it, in my nostalgia, sound like a paradise, a type of the familiar, bygone, rural American childhood, the *Andy Griffith Show*. It was and it wasn't. That the pasture seemed untouched and untouchable by time is true. Any stretch of undeveloped land must seem this way in the short term. After all, what changes? A tree falls, grass grows up, animals burrow and feed and breed, but each of these rising and falling actions is balanced by its opposite, and the larger regularity of the seasons offsets the constantly changing particularities of life. But those particularities, the intersection of our human lives with those acres of pasture and woods, were dirty and awkward and sometimes painful. The small dramas of friendship unfolded against the scenery of midsummer. My brother knocked out a tooth, there were countless wounds and sprains and bruises, and in all honesty, I spent more time riding my bike in the street than I did braving the electric fence and wading in the creek. I was a big chicken when it came to the threat of physical pain, and the sequence of things that could go wrong with a trip into the pasture generally sent me towards safer pastimes – turning cartwheels, badminton, croquet.

That pasture, well-traveled by me or not, nonetheless is a permanence, a place in my mind of experience, emotion, imagination – a touchstone. When I think of home, it is part of the image. When I think of the state of North Carolina, which I know to comprise widely various terrains, I think of the places like that pasture that used to define the central swath, the Piedmont. They still exist, of course, but in smaller and smaller patches, and now it is not unusual to see a herd of Brobdingnagian mansions shepherded by a tin-roofed, formerly bright red barn that gravity is slowly calling back to Earth. These tombstones of the rural – they are kept standing by these new estates for the upper middle-class to lend, I'm told, a touch of "authenticity" – are so out-of-place in the new world of single-family fortresses. They are, to me, clearly an elegy to what grows on this Earth and to our knowing how much we need it.

Mortality, despite its ever-presence, is our most difficult belief to master. Everything inside us at every moment resists acknowledging that it will die. It is easier to accept the idea that something immortal within us, an animating and indestructible spirit, lives on beyond our biological duration than to believe, utterly and without any doubt, that the body disintegrating beneath the mound of crumbled clay – or under the evenly replaced blanket of turf – is our only and terminal container. Even the word "container" subscribes, subtly, to the notion that there's something the body holds that is not a part of it. For a person, it is difficult not to impose this idea. The dog, on the other hand, directed by instinct, plays her part in the grand cycle by consuming the dead in her own way: she and all the other scavengers – from microorganisms to rats, raccoons, and crows – sustain their own lives and better the odds for their offspring. For those creatures, it is a matter of urge. For me, this verbal consumption – of the deer's

> THE PASTURE HAS TAKEN ON A GLOW IN THE WARM BATH OF MEMORY, ESPECIALLY NOW THAT IT'S GONE. I HAVE MADE IT, IN MY NOSTALGIA, SOUND LIKE A PARADISE, A TYPE OF THE FAMILIAR, BYGONE, RURAL AMERICAN CHILDHOOD, THE *ANDY GRIFFITH SHOW*.

body, the dog's compulsion, even of the ghost of my childhood landscape – is an act of belief, not instinct, a deliberate conversion of experience to a form that fixes what is ephemeral, gives it an immortal body. Thus, we use death to resist death because we know change and cannot escape it, we wish for a return to that which seems timeless and permanent, and we build it thus, in the most lasting material we have at hand. I deplore the loss of trees, of wild meadows and of cultivated fields, of creeks and the intricate ecosystems they support, and I can give plenty of reasons that are not derived from a sentimental or nostalgic attachment to a past that was not nearly as gentle as I remember it. I can speak, in moral and ethical terms, about human greed and wastefulness and disregard for life. I might mention how much good our money could do if spent not on the energy required to build and sustain these outsized mansions, but on the needs of humans who can't even afford a modest roof over their heads and minimal health care. But I wish that we could turn back to a world we have learned to ignore, simply because we recognize our need for beauty. Just that. Although I know that beauty is not necessarily the antidote to violence and greed and that some will argue, on the evidence of the Nazis' love of beautiful music among other things, that the aesthetic sense is amoral and does not cultivate compassion in its possessor, I cannot believe that we humans are not immeasurably better off when we seek to find and create beauty in our lives. Emerson, preaching the value of an active soul, writes in "Nature" that "The beauty of nature reforms itself in the mind, and not for barren contemplation, but for new creation."[2] Restoring our natural world alone won't do it. Caring to avert environmental cataclysms can only go so far. What matters is whether and how we think about the world and about ourselves, naturally, in it.

At least four months since its death, the deer in the woods is still recognizable, protruding from its burial mound as if to remind me, each time the dog pulls me back, of Whitman. I say with him as defiantly as I can, "And as to you Death, and you bitter hug of mortality, it is idle to try to alarm me."[3] With timing it is impossible to understand or predict one's preoccupations – those subjects obsessively considered until one feels a degree of

> **SOMETIMES I FEEL GRIEF SEND ITS SHOOTS OUTWARD UNTIL THE SHELL OF ME CRACKS AND WITHERS . . .**

certainty about them, a certainty that might be called confidence or, more dangerously, wisdom – are tested. Am I so sure that the bloodied bottom half of a rabbit in a patch of weeds or the inexplicably dead deer in the woods have shown me something crucial about mortality? I am. Yet I cannot say that, in writing of death, I have abolished grief. There is that rising and falling in me like the seasons' changing. Sometimes I feel grief send its shoots outward until the shell of me cracks and withers, as if the grief would take root in the world and, to feed its leafing-out, consume me. It is always unexpected, even if there is, like the seasons, a regularity to its return: October 14th for my grandmother; January 16th for my aunt; the first day of summer for a boy I barely knew when I was sixteen. Sometimes there is a welter of images that nonetheless seems inadequate in proportion to the sadness that clenches my throat: a funny bearded man arriving in the night and waking up on the sofa-bed as two children pelt him with questions; a trip to the grocery store in his red BMW for ice cream and artichokes; the same bearded man teaching the same children to pull weeds with their toes. He was my parents' friend, a traveler by nature, a kind of trickster figure, if the stories and my sparse memory can be believed. Although I can't separate in my mind what I remember of him and what I've been told, my parents recorded in my baby album that his nickname was one of the first three words I learned. Of my world, he was a founding father. Just over a week ago, in Maine on March 25th, as the spring thaw filled the rivers and warmed the air, he had a heart attack and died while kayaking a river he loved.

I did not know when I wrote my way toward the deer in the woods that I was preparing a place for Jim's body in my mind, which is for each of us the

---

2   Ralph Waldo Emerson, "Nature," 1836, Chapter 2, "Beauty."

3   Walt Whitman, "Song of Myself," 1855, section 49.

final resting place of everyone beloved. It changes nothing and everything to recall Whitman's "Song of Myself":

> They are alive and well somewhere,
> The smallest sprout shows there is really no death,
> And if ever there was it led forward life, and
>   does not wait at the end to arrest it,
> And ceas'd the moment life appear'd.
>
> All goes onward and outward, nothing collapses,
> And to die is different from what any one
>   supposed, and luckier.[4]

The rule of life is change, and we tend to think of death as cessation. Stasis. But this is certainly untrue. Each death is a still-frame in an unending documentary of change. The death of the pasture that stood for home to me is the birth of something: to be kind, call it civilization, which, despite its grand destruction of life, is by no means all bad. The dead deer is a necessary part of the ecology of my limited local wilderness. All these deaths, with their different species of grief at hand, are "good fertilizer," as Whitman says, for the field of memory, the burial ground of the mind. We must tend attentively and with tenderness both the inner and the outer landscapes, their range and borders remapped daily, their populations swelling slowly, a fact which we must mourn and embrace in time. ■

EACH DEATH IS A STILL-FRAME IN AN UNENDING DOCUMENTARY OF CHANGE.

HONORABLE MENTION, 2018 JAMES APPLEWHITE POETRY PRIZE
BY GWEN HOLT

Smoke and Oreos

When I got home from ditching
school, Mom sat in the kitchen.

"Hey," I said. "Sit down," she said.
A package of Oreos waited on the table

between us, one side torn open,
the sleeve of cookies peering out

of its blue plastic blanket,
next to the diabetes medication.

"Is there any milk?" I said. "I'll get it,"
she said. Her chair creaking

with relief. "What's going on tonight?" I asked,
her body, loose and reaching for a green plastic mug,

stretch marks etched under her open sleeves, one foot
swaying to the other as she grips the mug and empties the carton

into it, breathing heavy. "Just you and me," she said.
"No Roger?" I asked. "He's working out of town. Leave

Roger alone. He's good to us."
Last time she passed out, he stayed awake.

He might be good to her –
not me.

She pulled out her cigarettes, lit one, careful
to blow the smoke from the corner of her mouth.

"You want to watch a movie?" I said. "We can order
Chinese too. I got paid today," she said,

dabbing her cigarette in the red casino ashtray,
stray ash dusting the blue cookie package.

GWEN HOLT is the author of several Young Adult novels, in addition to
poetry and short stories, and she is the winner of the 2016 *Southeast
Review* Narrative Nonfiction prize. She lives in Raleigh, NC, and has an
MFA in YA fiction from Converse College.

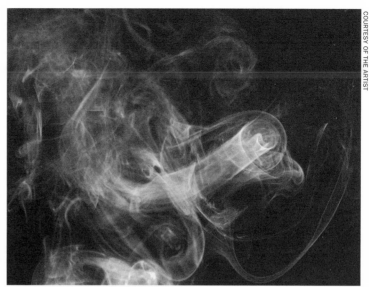

Sacred Smoke: SI 19 (photography 10x13) by Ron Greenberg

I told her, "You don't have to blow it away
from me. I don't mind."

"I mind," she said. I swallowed my bite.
Her face puckered as she watched me

take another cookie, sit back and cross my legs.
She shifted, chair creaking, relaxed a bit.

"I guess you're growing up faster than I'm ready for,"
she said. "It's a train with no breaks," I said.

She took another drag and tapped off the ashes,
then handed the cigarette across the table

and nodded her head. When my fingers pinched
next to hers, she let go,

right there over Oreos and milk –
Camel Menthol Lights.

I took her offering and pressed it to my lips,
careful not to cough,

to blow the smoke out
of the corner of my mouth.

RON GREENBERG lives in Asheville, NC. He received a degree in commercial photography from the Antonelli School of Photography in Philadelphia. He has shown in and juried dozens of shows along the East Coast. His *Sacred Smoke* series explores universal themes of life, nature, and spirituality. Examples of his work can be seen on his website at www.rongreenbergphoto.com.

FINALIST, 2018 JAMES APPLEWHITE POETRY PRIZE
BY MELINDA THOMSEN

Echeveria

You grow so slowly
while your wild hair

roots speed forth
like a lion from its lair.

I stare at you searching.
Look, your neck's lengthened

and a floret's emerged
in a pinhead bouquet.

Oh, why do you beg us
to quietude? Last night,

the moon shone through trees
like a cyclopean headlamp

with a Jupiter antenna, and drove
moonshine across the carpet in white

brilliance. Sleepless planets,
stars, and succulents twirl along

their way, and so do I. Tiny
Hens and Chicks burst forth

from a leaf, lying on its back
in your loam, water bereft,

happy to burgeon toward
our nearest star. Why not

the moon, too? My jade plant
turns up and out, beyond

and farther, with a new nub
pushing away from its stalk.

Why can't I do more than fret?
Share your chlorophyll

secrets with me, so I can drink
of the stars with you.

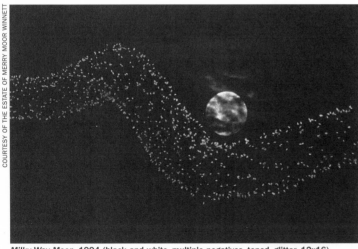

COURTESY OF THE ESTATE OF MERRY MOOR WINNETT

Milky Way Moon, 1994 (black and white, multiple negatives, toned, glitter, 12x16)
by Merry Moor Winnett

MERRY MOOR WINNETT (1951–1994) was a native of Virginia. She studied at Michigan State University and the University of South Florida. In 1978, she moved to North Carolina. Her work is the permanent collection of the Smithsonian Museum of American Art and is also represented at Guilford College, University of South Florida, Reynolds Collection, Greenhill Center for North Carolina Art, and New York's Floating Foundation of Photography. See more of her art at www.merrymoorwinnett.com.

Greenville, NC, resident **MELINDA THOMSEN** has published two chapbooks with Finishing Line Press: *Naming Rights* (2008) and *Field Rations* (2011). Her poems have also appeared in such literary magazines as *Tar River Poetry, Comstock Review, Poetry East, and New York Quarterly*.